Sons of War

A Civil War Saga

by
Carl J. Barger

Strategic Book Publishing and Rights Co.

Strategic Book Publishing and Rights Co., LLC
USA | Singapore
www.sbpra.com

For information about special discounts for bulk purchases, please contact Strategic Book Publishing and Rights Co. Special Sales, at bookorder@sbpra.net.

ISBN: 978-1-949483-28-4

Book Design: Suzanne Kelly

ACKNOWLEDGEMENT

*I would like to thank my wife, Lena Barger,
and our good friend, Jenny Nail,
for their help in bringing
"Sons of War, A Civil War Saga,"
to print. Thanks, Ladies!*

James Anderson Barger. Union Soldier, Civil War. Born September 5, 1843, Reynolds County, Missouri. Died February 19, 1912, Worth County, Allendale, Missouri. Missouri 26th Infantry Regiment, Company G.

Jesse Allen Barger. Union Soldier, Civil War. Born June 17, 1844, Reynolds County, Missouri. Died April 2, 1918, Marion Community, Cole County, Missouri. Missouri 26th Infantry Regiment, Company G.

CHAPTER 1

The air was cool, smelling of loam and pine needles as Henry Barger and his son Allen completed another exhausting day in the fields. Henry Barger wiped his brow, watching the sun sink behind the Crab Orchard Mountains in Morgan County, Tennessee, in the year of 1825. "Five acres plowed today. Only twenty-five more to go," Allen said standing by his father dripping with sweat.

"If the weather holds, we should be done with plowing the middle of next week," Henry said.

As Allen began unhitching the mules, he looked at his father and said, "It can't be over fast enough for me."

"You just don't like working with those stubborn mules," Henry said as he slapped his son on the shoulder.

"You're right about that," Allen said as he grabbed the bridled reins and led the mules to the barn. After he unharnessed the mules, he heard his mother holler from the back porch, "Allen, you hurry. The food is getting cold."

Sarah, his mother, a small thin lady with red hair and fair complexion, stood on the back porch wiping her wet hands on her apron. She again hollered, "Allen, John is joining us for dinner. He's really hungry, so you hurry up!"

Allen wondered how John, his older brother, could find time to go visiting in plowing season when he had one hundred acres joining them to take care of and only one son old enough to help. After washing, Allen entered the kitchen and bumped into his sisters, Anna and Rebecca, who were heading to the well with a bucket. Anna was eighteen and Rebecca was sixteen, but they still carried the bucket together the same way they had done since they were eight and six. As they passed Allen,

Rebecca poured the last drops of water on Allen's back. Allen, still hot and sweaty, jumped as the cold water hit his back.

Allen turned to Rebecca and said, "I'll get you for that, Rebecca!"

"Come sit down, Allen. The food is getting cold," Sarah said.

The biscuits were being passed by the time Allen reached his seat. He had missed the prayer, too. His father, a dedicated Christian, had never sat down to a meal without a prayer beforehand. As Allen received the biscuits from his father, he noticed a large scratch on his father's hand. The wrinkles in Henry's hands and face were visual proof of the hard work of a farmer.

Allen had also missed something his mother was talking about when he first reached the table.

"I sure hated to miss that celebration, but by the time I got the letter, it was too late to even think about going anyways," his mother said.

Allen wondered who she was talking about as he forked two pieces of fried squirrel and put it onto his plate. He knew a lot of young folks in Roane County where his family had lived before coming to Morgan County. He mentally ran through a list of likely marriage prospects.

"So, little brother, when are you getting married?" John asked.

John loved to tease Allen about not being married.

"I don't know," Allen stammered shyly. He felt an obligation to stay home and help his father provide for the family, especially now that John was married and away. His younger brother, Pointer, age fifteen, had not yet developed the skill of plowing and was delegated other farm shores such as feeding, watering the farm animals, and milking cows.

"Now, John, don't you go teasing your brother," scolded Sarah. "He's going to make someone a fine husband one of these days."

The delicious meal consisting of squirrel, potatoes, beans, and cornbread had been prepared by using a large fireplace in the Bargers' cabin. The fireplace doubled as a cooking unit as well as for heating the cabin. Sarah had cooked potatoes and beans in two large black iron kettles which hung from a crane over the fire. The crane could be swung in and out of the fireplace. The squirrel was fried in a frying pan with spider-like-legs which was placed over hot coals which had been pulled onto the hearth in front of the fireplace. The bread was baked in a Dutch oven. Again, coals were raked onto the hearth and the cast-iron Dutch oven placed on top of the coals. Hot coals were heaped on top of the lid giving a heat source from top and bottom.

The squirrel came from Allen's early morning hunting trip. Allen loved to hunt and fish. He was good at both, so the family always had wild game or fish to eat.

As John continued to tell how he planned to clear more of the rugged, mountainous land on his farm, his mother was busy refilling each person's bowl with beans and potatoes from the large black iron kettles.

Henry, Allen, and Pointer had been able to clear only forty acres of their land for plowing, and that was only after more than a year of backbreaking work. Most of that would now be planted in corn, the main crop, with a little held back for pasture. Allen doubted that John and his oldest son, Robert, could clear more than an acre a month maybe less in summer, a farmer's busy season, but still he had to admit that John had made a pretty good beginning already on his own farm.

"Tomorrow, Allen, would you be up to hunting again?" John asked.

He glanced at his father wondering if he would tolerate his being late to the field two mornings in a row. His father said nothing but nodded his approval.

"Hunting squirrel is fine but you two boys had better save up your money for more traps. When winter comes we can do without the squirrel if we must, but I don't know how we would get by without the money you two bring in from pelts," Henry said.

In the Barger family little money was available, and supplies had to be obtained through bartering. Furs, grain, and livestock were the more popular bartering items which were traded in the little town of Wartburg, Tennessee. Even the county tax collector accepted furs as payment for taxes. With the corn they were now planting, Henry and Allen would have grain to barter, along with the furs from trapping.

Maybe next year, thought Allen to himself, we can clear enough land to have a few head of cattle.

The conversation droned on into the evening, interspersed with frequent laughter.

"Y'all, I'm bone tired! I think I'm going to bed," Allen said getting up from the porch and stretching.

"I'll be here about 5:30," John said.

"Good night, Ma," Allen said as he gave her a kiss on the cheek.

"Good night, Son. I'll have breakfast ready about 5:15."

As Allen entered the house, he noticed Rebecca reading near the fireplace. This is a good time to get back at her, Allen thought. He went to the kitchen and took a dipper of water from the bucket and slipped up behind her. Without any warning he poured the water on her head. Rebecca let out a scream that could be heard on the front porch.

"Ma, Allen poured water all over me, just look at me. My clothes are all wet. Allen you'll pay for this," Rebecca yelled.

"I told you, I was getting back at you," Allen said as he climbed up the ladder to the loft. The rope mattress groaned as he lay down in his bed.

Pointer shared the loft area with Allen and had turned in earlier. He loved to read and used reading as a method of going to sleep. Pointer's favorite book was the King James Version of the Bible. He said on several occasions that he wanted to be a preacher someday. Below, Allen could hear Rebecca griping to his mother. To his satisfaction, Rebecca got little sympathy from her mother.

He heard John say goodnight to everyone and a few minutes later heard the creak of the other ladder which led to the loft that Rebecca and Anna shared. A few minutes later footsteps were heard as Henry and Sarah closed their door to the only bedroom in the cabin.

Allen and Pointer didn't mind sleeping in the loft. They had slept in a loft since they were children. The loft had a big window that opened outward for ventilation. Allen enjoyed watching the clouds move across the sky. He also enjoyed trying to map out the many twinkling stars that covered the sky on a clear night. Some nights he could count to a thousand stars without blinking an eye, but for the past several nights he had lain awake thinking about his future. When he thought he had worked his future out in his mind, several new things kept creeping into his thoughts.

Over the years he had listen to his father's history of coming from Baden Wurttemberg, Germany, as a young man and boarding a ship that landed at the Port of Philadelphia, Pennsylvania, with his wife Sarah and his son, John. He remembered the stories his father told about how hard it was for them to survive after getting to Philadelphia.

Allen remembered his father saying, "I owe my life and my family's livelihood to my older brother, George. If it hadn't been for George, I'm not certain what would have happened to Sarah, John, and me."

Henry was a good historian and a good story teller. It was never boring to hear him tell about his family's earlier lives in the Black Forest area of Germany. His close-knit family enjoyed worshipping together and performing their skills as clock and furniture makers as well as farming, their main source of making a living.

George had come from Baden Wurttemberg two years prior to Henry's arrival and had settled in Berks County, Pennsylvania. George had been able to purchase some good farming land which was close to other Barger relatives in Berks County who had also come out of Baden Wurttemberg's Black Forest.

Henry believed strongly in sharing Barger history with his family. He didn't want any of his family not knowing where they came from and how hard it was surviving in a new country called America. Henry shared with his family that they were Dutch Pennsylvanians. They spoke a little different German than some other Germans who came over from Baden Wurttemberg.

Allen's favorite memory of his father's teachings was his recollection of the war of 1812. This three-year war was fought between the United States and Great Britain. His father and brother, John, were enlisted in the 2nd Regiment Volunteer Militia under Col. William Lillard. All these memories in the last two weeks kept creeping into Allen's mind.

Allen recalled the story of how his father and other Barger relatives followed the trail of migration from Pennsylvania to Culpepper, Virginia, and ending up in Morgan County, Tennessee. Some of the Bargers migrated to Rowan County, North Carolina, and some went to Georgia. It was after the War of 1812, that Henry and John received land grants for properties in and around Wartburg, Tennessee. This had been their home since 1820.

Allen had watched his father change from a strong, young man to an old man. He worried about whether his father, who was now sixty-three years old, could continue to run the farm without him. His decision to leave his family behind would be the hardest thing he would ever do.

Allen's night had been very short after staying awake most of the night remembering stories of the past and worrying about leaving his family behind once he left to make a life for himself.

At 5:00 A.M. he jumped out of bed and quietly climbed down the ladder to see his mother, John, and Henry sitting at the table. Sarah had already made biscuits and white gravy, a favorite breakfast of both John and Allen. They quickly ate breakfast, grabbed their hunting guns, and headed off to the Little Emory Creek to hunt squirrels.

In no time, they had killed several squirrels, and John suggested that they find a spot and rest awhile before starting back to the house. Allen said, "That's a great idea. I'm worn out from lack of sleep."

"Why didn't you sleep well," John asked.

Allen hesitated, but finally decided that the best thing to do was to just blurt it out.

"John, I think it's time I leave Morgan County and start a new life. My only concern is whether Pa can run the farm with only Pointer here to help him."

"Little brother, I knew this was coming. I've been expecting it for some time."

"What do you think I should do?" Allen asked.

"Allen, you should do it! You owe it to yourself. Don't worry about Pa. I'll check on the family from time to time. Pointer is old enough now he can take on more of the work load. He's turned out to be a strong and healthy brother. You do what you have to do," John said.

"Thanks, John, I was hoping you would give me good advice!"

"When do you plan to announce to the family your decision to head out on your own?"

"I'm going to wait until the harvesting of the crops is completed, then I'll go," Allen replied.

"So, it will be awhile yet? Maybe we can work in several more fishing and hunting trips before you go."

"I would like that, John. In the meantime, I want our discussion to remain between the two of us. Will you do that, John?"

"You have my word, Allen."

Allen and John returned home with several squirrels to clean. Their father was sitting on the front porch in his old rocking chair.

"How many squirrels did you kill?" Henry asked.

"Oh, maybe a dozen!" John said.

"John and I found some really good squirrel territory today, Pa," Allen replied.

"Allen, you know where all the good squirrel areas are," Henry said, laughing.

"Pa, since you're so good cleaning squirrel how about you lend us a hand?" Allen asked.

"My Margaret will be pleased to have this fresh squirrel to cook for supper tonight," John said.

"I know she will be pleased not to have to clean them," Allen said.

"You're so right about that, little brother," John replied.

Morgan County was one of the most beautiful counties in East Tennessee. The Little Emory River floated through the county and supplied several nice fishing and camping places. There was an abundance of wild game to be had and the fishing was great. The county was a paradise to all who chose to live there.

John, Allen, and Pointer along with John's two sons, Robert and Tollett, got in several good hunting and fishing trips during the summer months. Sometimes on cooler days, Henry joined them.

The squirrel and fish were a big part of their daily diets, along with fresh vegetables they raised in their gardens.

Harvest time finally arrived, and during harvesting time, John and his sons, Robert and Tollett, helped Henry and Allen get their corn and hay crops in the barn. After that was completed, Henry, Pointer, and Allen went to John's place and helped harvest John's crops. This was a common practice for family members. It was a time of sharing as well as a time of rejoicing, especially when the harvest was over.

Allen noticed that Pointer, now fifteen, had grown a great deal during the summer and seemed to be a good hand for work. He felt more at ease knowing that Pointer could take on a bigger role in helping his father after he left home.

After the harvest, Allen decided the time was right for him to start a life of his own. He had heard talk in Wartburg that Jake Carson, a big land holder in Overton County, Tennessee, was looking for farm hands. He decided now was the time to visit with his father about his intentions. He wanted his father's blessing more than anything. After Allen finished feeding the mules, he saw his father coming from the house to the barn to get corn to feed the chickens which ran wild in the yard.

"Pa, do you have a few minutes, so I could visit with you?"

"You certainly can, Allen, let's grab some worms and go down to our favorite fishing hole on the Little Emory Creek and catch us a mess of fish for supper."

"That sounds like a good idea," Allen said.

After fishing awhile, Henry glanced over at Allen and asked, "What's this you need to talk to me about, Son?"

"Pa, I've been doing a lot of thinking lately."

"Thinking about what?" Henry asked.

"I was talking with Bill Tucker in Wartburg yesterday. He said Jake Carson who lives up in Overton County needed some more farm hands. I was thinking since we've got the corn and hay crops in the barn, plenty of wood for the winter, I might take off up there and get me a job. What do you think, Pa?"

His father looked at him for a long minute before he spoke. "Son, I've always trusted you to make the right decisions. If this is what you want, you have my blessing."

"Are you sure, Pa?"

"Don't worry one little bit about your old pa and ma. We'll do just fine. It's time for you to go. You have done more than is expected of any son. I've known for a long time this day was coming. You do it, Son, and don't worry about us. We'll make it."

"Pa, if something happens while I'm away, promise me you'll send for me. I'll get right back here as soon as I can."

"You have my blessing," Henry said as he placed his hand on Allen's shoulder.

"Thanks, Pa!"

"When do you plan to leave?"

"Since Mr. Carson is hiring, I figure I must go soon. I'm hoping he will have a job left for me. I was planning on leaving early in the morning."

"That soon, Allen," Henry said dropping his head.

"I know, Pa, but I figure it will take me four to five days to reach Livingston. Since it will take me that long, there may not be a job left for me if I don't go soon."

"I think you're right. I will break the news to the family at supper tonight. If I know your mother, she will want to make sure you have food to carry with you. She will need a little time to get that ready."

During supper time, Rebecca and Anna took their places on one of the two wooden benches which were placed on each side of the long dining table. Allen and Pointer took their places on the bench across from Rebecca and Anna. Henry and Sarah sat in straight back chairs made of white oak with seats made from woven bark strips at opposite ends of the table.

"After we finish supper, I have an announcement to make. I want everyone to stay seated until I finish," Henry said.

The remark brought about a puzzling look on everyone's face. It was certainly a change in procedure since the common thing was for each family member to leave the table upon finishing his meal. As soon as everyone had finished eating, Henry said, "I know you are all wondering why I've asked you to stay longer tonight. Allen's decided it's time for him to start a life of his own. He's now twenty-five years old, and most men of his age would already have a family. I've given Allen my blessings and I hope you will, too," Henry said with a soft, yet convincing tone.

It was a sad occasion, but everyone seemed to respect Allen's decision. Allen had watched his mother's expression as his father had spoken. He could see the hurt in her eyes and face, but not once did she cry.

It was later that night when he heard his mother crying in bed. He was very close to his mother, and it hurt him to hear her cry. She was a good Christian mother with a great faith in God. Allen was grateful for his mother and for what she had taught him over the years. Although his mother's education was limited, she had taught him to read and write, to be polite, to treat others with respect, and always be a gentleman. He owed his mother more than he could ever repay.

Allen already felt the sadness of the next day. Saying goodbye to his family would be one of the most difficult things he'd ever done.

Allen slept very little. He woke early in the morning to the fresh aroma of cooked bacon.

His mother had gotten up early and mixed a batch of flapjacks. She knew Allen's favorite breakfast was flapjacks, sorghum molasses, and bacon.

Sarah also baked a batch of sorghum molasses cookies because they were Allen's favorite.

As Allen climbed down the ladder he asked, "Whatcha cooking, Ma?"

"Your favorite breakfast."

Thanks Ma, you're the best ma in the entire world!" Allen said as he hugged Sarah from behind.

"Now go on, Allen. I'm not letting my son leave this house without his favorite breakfast. I've also baked your favorite cookies. You will need something to eat as you travel."

"Ma, you will always be my number one gal."

"Stop that now! You're going to make me cry!" Sarah said with tears welling up in her eyes.

After Henry called everyone to breakfast, he offered the morning prayer. This time he offered a special prayer for Allen.

"O, Lord, we ask your blessings upon our beloved son, Allen, as he leaves our home today. Lord, he's a good man and a good son. He's labored hard to help our family through hard times, and now, Lord, I pray your richest blessings upon him as he finds a place for himself in this great land you've made. Take care of him, Lord, and be close to him as he travels up to Overton County to find a job. Bless him, O Lord, with a good job, with happiness, and with good health. All these things I pray in your name, Lord. Amen."

Tears were rolling down Sarah's face at the end of Henry's prayer. Allen tried not to look toward her. It was all he could do to hold back his own tears.

Allen loved to hear his father pray. He admired his father's and his mother's faith in God. He knew God had blessed them because of their goodness and faith. Allen, too, knew God as his savior, and wherever he went, he too would keep the faith. All the Bargers knew God as their savior. Allen admired his little brother, Pointer, for his knowledge of the Bible. He knew in his heart that someday he would serve God as an ordained preacher of the word. He had seen his brother read the Bible for hours on end. He and Pointer stayed awake time and time again talking about God's word and their faith.

After breakfast, Allen fetched his bag from the loft. His mother packed a sack of cookies and other food for Allen's five-day walk to Livingston, Tennessee. Allen took the sack of food and placed it in his bag. He also packed the only two shirts and one pair of overalls he owned. He made sure he had the gun his father had given him when he was sixteen. He was now ready to make his journey. He hoped to be able to leave without anyone crying, but as it turned out, it was too much to expect. As he hugged Anna, she began to cry. He looked toward Rebecca, and she too was crying. Allen tried to hold back his tears but couldn't. As he turned toward his mother, he observed tears running down her cheeks. He took her in his arms and drew her close to his chest. "Ma, you take good care of yourself."

"You don't worry yourself about us. We'll be fine. You just take care of yourself. Write us often. We want to know you're safe," Sarah said as her tears mixed with Allen's.

John and his family had come to say goodbye.

Allen turned to John and said, "Please take care of them."

"Little brother, don't you worry. I promise you I'll look after them," John said.

His father was the last to say goodbye to him. As he hugged his father, he heard him say, "Remember one thing, Son. Do your very best at everything you do, and God will bless you. Please don't worry about us. You take care of yourself and write us a letter as soon as you get to Livingston," as tears began to run down his cheeks.

"I love you, Pa. Promise me you'll take care of yourself."

"I promise!" Henry said as he hugged Allen goodbye.

As Allen walked down the dusty road, he once again turned to wave goodbye.

His family was still standing and waving back to him as he topped the hill and continued his journey to Livingston, the county seat for Overton County, Tennessee.

CHAPTER 2

It took Allen five days walking dusty and narrow roads to reach Livingston, Tennessee, a town much larger than Wartburg. After arriving in Livingston, Allen went straight to the local hardware store. He asked the owner, Mr. Sam Butler, for directions to Jake Carson's plantation.

As Allen approached the big plantation house he was amazed by its size. He had never seen a house so big. The house was surrounded by big oak trees and flower gardens filled with beautiful roses and many wild flowers. As he climbed the steps leading to the porch, he felt fear growing inside him. What if Mr. Carson has already hired all the men he needs? What will I do? He told himself regardless of the outcome, it wouldn't hurt to ask.

The front door opened and a big, black lady with big, dark eyes stood looking straight at him.

"I'm looking for Jake Carson," Allen said.

"Who's you?" She asked.

"My name is Allen Barger. I need to see Mr. Carson about a job."

"Comes on in here, Mr. Barger. My name is Mamie. I's Mr. Carson's maid. You have a seat and I goes fetch Mr. Carson. You are some handsome man, Mr. Barger," she said as she smiled and left the room.

"Thanks, Miss Mamie," Allen said with a chuckle.

Allen had never been in a house this big. The parlor alone was as big as his father's house back in Morgan County. There were carpets on the floor, and curtains on the windows. The furniture was so fine that Allen decided he had better not sit since a week's worth of travel dust and grime now covered his clothes.

A tall man entered the room and said, "I'm Jake Carson. What can I do for you?"

"Mr. Carson, my name is Allen Barger. I'm from Morgan County. I heard you were needing some farm hands."

"Have you ever worked on a farm?" Mr. Carson asked while extending a hand of welcome to Allen.

"Yes, Sir, I've been working on my pa's farm down in Morgan County."

"Young man, how old are you?"

"I'm twenty-five years old."

"You've come all the way from Morgan County seeking a job on my plantation?" Carson asked amazed.

"That's right, Sir. I'm a hard worker. If you'll give me a job, I'll work real hard for you."

"Allen, I like your attitude. I'm pretty good at sizing up people. I believe you are sincere. I'll tell you what, I'm going to give you a try. If you want to work for me, I expect only the best," Carson said.

"Yes, Sir, I understand. I'll work hard for you."

"The pay is two dollars a week, plus room and board. Come with me, Allen," Mr. Carson said.

Allen followed Mr. Carson to another large, but much cruder, house. This was the bunkhouse where the farm hands lived. As they entered the house, Allen noticed a big, cast iron heating stove in the middle of the room. The walls were lined with beds. Off the big room was a hallway that led to a large kitchen. In the kitchen was a big cook stove, sink, and a long table with benches on each side.

After showing Allen around, Carson said, "You can put your things on that bed over there. It's not in use. The chalk board on the wall over there has the names of all the hands. The foremen will write everyone's assignment daily. You can read, can't you?"

"Yes, Sir," said Allen.

"Well, good, that makes things a whole lot easier. I'll feed you good, but I expect you to work hard too. My men work from sunup to sundown every day except for Saturdays and Sundays. We quit at noon on Saturday. This gives the men a chance to go to Livingston and enjoy the festivities there. Are you a church going man, Allen?"

"Yes, Sir, I'm a Baptist. I'm a member of the Union Community Baptist Church back home in Morgan County."

"Well, that's good too. There is a Baptist church in Livingston, and you're welcome to go on Sunday. In fact, you have the whole day free, but you must be back by dark. Other than that, the rules are simple: no swearing, no drinking, no carding, and no fighting. Keep those rules in mind and we will get along just fine.

"My foreman, Mr. John Birch, is out in the field now, but when he gets in this evening you can meet him."

"Thanks for the job, Mr. Carson," Allen said as he shook his hand.

"You're welcome, Allen. I look forward to a long acquaintance," Carson said as he left the bunkhouse.

Allen looked around the large room and found the bed which Carson had indicated was not in use and stretched out. He was bone tired from the long trip. It was not long before he fell asleep. The next thing he knew someone was shaking him and saying, "Wake up, Barger." He looked up to see a big man standing over him, who must have been at least six-foot-three and weighed at least two-hundred fifty pounds.

Allen guessed this must be the foreman, and quickly sat up in his bed and said, "Sorry, Sir, I must have dozed off."

"So, you are Allen Barger, huh?" the newcomer asked.

"Yes, Sir!"

"Well, I am John Birch. Mr. Birch to you. I'm the foreman here." Without even a pause for Allen to answer, he continued, "Where are you from?"

"I'm from Morgan County, Sir."

"Morgan County, huh? I've been through your parts a few times," Birch said. "Did Mr. Carson explain the rules to you?"

"Yes, Sir," Allen said.

"Good, then I don't need to go through them again. You just don't need to ever forget them, understand? If you don't obey, you'll be going back to Morgan County quicker than you can spit. If you want to work for me, Allen Barger, you must obey my rules. Do you understand?" Mr. Birch asked with a strong voice.

"I understand, Sir," Allen said, politely.

The field hands were now coming into the bunkhouse. Most seemed to have washed up before entering. They filed quickly through the bunkhouse to the kitchen. Allen became aware of the aroma of stew coming from that direction. The sack of food his mother had fixed for his journey had been good, but to have a hot meal after a week's traveling would be nice. Birch motioned for Allen to follow him, and Allen needed no second offer.

The kitchen was a bustle of activity. "Men, this is our new farm hand from Morgan County, Tennessee. His name is Allen Barger. Y'all be nice to him," Birch said with a smile.

At supper, Allen discovered that most of the men were there for the same reason he was, to save money to purchase a farm. Several of them were foreigners which attracted Allen's curiosity greatly. He had never met a foreigner before. A couple of them were older hands, down on their luck, but most were younger than Allen, in their twenties or their teens and were out on their own for the first time, trying to get enough money to get a start in the world. The first thing Allen did after supper was to write his family a letter. He wanted them to know he had reached Carson's farm safely and that Carson had given him a job. He decided not to mention the gruff Mr. Birch. No reason to worry his mother.

Despite his initial meeting, Allen found working for Birch was a pleasant experience. Although he had a curt way with words and seldom smiled, Birch was always a fair man, who would go out of his way to help his hands. The farm work was not bad, except for the long days, but Allen had been working long days on a farm since he was a boy.

After Allen's third week at work, he received a letter from his mother. Everything was going well back home. She told Allen of Anna's courtship with Jim Thompson and made it a point to inform him that everything was going well with his pa and the other members of the family. This was comforting news for Allen had worried about his pa's health.

On weekends, Allen frequently joined some of the men for a trip into Livingston. Most of them enjoyed the Saturday night street dance. While most of the men danced and had a good time, Allen normally just set and watched. He could square dance but really didn't care that much about dancing. Some of the men kidded Allen about not having anything to do with the girls. Allen always answered by saying, "The right one hasn't come along yet."

On Sunday, Allen faithfully attended the Faith Baptist Church in Livingston. He had promised his mother he would continue to worship in the Lord's house. Sunday afternoons he went fishing near the Carson farm and occasionally hunted. The men threw horseshoes in the yard by the bunkhouse, or just sat around in the shade talking or whittling.

Allen was a handsome man. He was about six feet tall and weighed about one hundred and eighty pounds. He had dark black hair and blue eyes. He was strong and could beat everyone in his bunkhouse at arm wrestling.

A year passed in this way. Allen heard from his parents regularly and made it a point to write each week. Anna had gotten married to Jim Thompson from Wartburg. Allen wanted to go to the wedding, but there was so much work that Birch could not spare him. His mother wrote that Anna had a fine wedding.

Since he had not been able to go home for the wedding, Allen decided not to miss the first opportunity for a trip to Morgan County. When the harvest was in and the work slowed down, Allen asked Birch for a leave of absence. Birch checked with Carson and got permission for Allen to go. Allen had almost one hundred dollars coming to him for his work on the farm and went to see Carson to collect his pay.

Carson was sitting on his porch when Allen arrived.

"Going home now, are you, Son?" Carson said.

"I miss my family a great deal, Sir. I've been pretty homesick of late."

"Well, I certainly can understand that. I do hope you will be returning. Birch tells me you are a fine worker, and I would really hate to lose you."

"Yes, Sir, I plan to come back. It's a good job and you pay good money."

"I will have your pay figured and it will be here for you when you leave in the morning."

"Yes, Sir. There is one thing. I figure it would be a lot easier to ride back to Morgan County than to walk. Would any of your horses be for sale? I would like to take a horse, a bridle, and a saddle as part of my pay."

"I tell you what, young man, you go pick yourself a horse and have one of the stable hands get you a bridle and a saddle. Come back up here with it, and we will shake on a price.

For the first time in his life, Allen owned something. It gave him a feeling of worthiness. He was excited to know that all the hard work for Mr. Carson paid off with handsome dividends. He had never had this much money. Now he had a good-looking healthy horse to ride back home in style.

CHAPTER 3

Allen set out for Morgan County the next day riding a fine, red horse with a white blaze in his forehead. Allen's horse had been trained to work cattle and was very obedient. He seemed to understand everything that Allen wanted him to do.

Allen looked forward to spending time with his folks and getting in some serious fishing and hunting with his dad and brothers. He looked forward to riding up to the house in style and not walking up like the Prodigal Son.

Getting home by horseback was faster than walking. After one-night sleeping under the stars Allen reached his father's house around noon on the second day. As he approached the house, he saw his mother drawing water from the well. Allen reined up and dismounted and started walking toward his mother. He had not written his folks about his coming home, and his mother had not yet noticed Allen. He was within fifteen feet of his mother when she turned and saw him.

"Lord, Allen, it's you!" She put down the water bucket and reached out her arms and began to cry.

Allen put his arms around her and held her for what seemed to be an eternity.

Sarah turned to fetch the bucket of water she left by the well.

"Let me get that bucket, Ma," Allen said. "Where's Pa, Pointer, and Rebecca?"

"They went into Wartburg to get supplies. I'm expecting them back in an hour or so. Your pa will be overjoyed to see you. I bet you're starving, aren't you?"

"I'm a bit hungry, especially for your cooking."

That was an understatement. Allen had been thinking about his mother's biscuits, flap jacks, and her sorghum malaises cookies for the past thirty miles. After washing his face and hands, he sat on one of the benches at the dinner table. "Ma, tell me. How's everyone doing."

"Well, let's see. John and Margaret are doing well. Your nieces and nephews are doing well. Pointer is growing into a fine-looking young man. He's sixteen now and has been such a big help to your father. Elizabeth, John's oldest girl, is getting married to Tom Henderson over in Roane County. John isn't too happy about that. Oh, and I almost forgot the most important news. Anna and Jim are expecting a baby in about six months."

"A baby!" Allen exclaimed.

"Anna and Jim are excited about the baby. They go to church regularly, and Jim is a good provider. They appear to love each other, and Jim is really good to Anna."

"What about Rebecca, Ma?"

"Rebecca thinks she's in love with Matthew Parson's son, John. Your pa's not too happy about that courtship."

"What about Pa?"

Sarah hesitated. "Your Pa isn't well," Sarah said sadly.

"What's wrong with him?"

"I don't rightly know. He won't go see Doc Jones. I know something is wrong. I've been watching him when he draws water from the well and feeds the hogs. He doesn't know I'm watching him. It may be just old age. You know what happens to us old people," Sarah said with a chuckle.

"Ma, you're not old," Allen teased.

"Yes, I'm getting old," she said laughing.

It was about 3:30 P.M. when Henry, Rebecca, and Pointer returned from Wartburg. Allen had put his horse away in the barn so neither Henry nor Rebecca knew he was home. Rebecca was the first one through the front door. Allen was hiding behind the door. "Hello, Ma," Rebecca said.

"Rebecca, we have a visitor," as she pointed to Allen standing behind the door.

Rebecca turned around quickly. "Allen, what are you doing here?" she screamed with excitement as she ran to him and hugged and kissed him.

Allen picked her up and swung her around a few times and said, "Gosh, it's so good to see you, little sister. You are a beauty!" Allen said as he stood gazing lovingly at his baby sister who had really blossomed since he saw her last.

"Well, thank you, Allen. John Parsons thinks I'm beautiful, too," she said smiling and looking at her mother.

"Has Ma told you that John wants me to marry him?" Rebecca asked with excitement and joy.

"Yes, she mentioned that, but what do you want, Rebecca?"

"I love John, but Pa thinks I'm too young to get married. Do you think I'm too young?"

"Little sister, I really don't want to get involved in this matter. You just be patient. I have a feeling Pa will come around," Allen said as he hoped the conversation would end.

After visiting a few minutes with Rebecca, Allen looked at his mother and said, "Excuse me, you two. I'm going to the barn and surprise Pointer and Pa."

Pointer had unharnessed the mules while Henry mixed a bucket of feed and was about to poor the feed into the trough when Allen entered the barn.

"Can I lend you a hand, Pa?" Allen asked.

"Allen, my Lord, it's you! What are you doing here?" Henry asked with joy in his voice.

After a long hug, Allen said, "Carson gave me a two-week break."

"God bless Mr. Carson!" Henry said with excitement. "It's so good to see you, Son! By this time Pointer came out of the crib and came running over to greet Allen.

"Allen, welcome home, brother! How long have you been here? I saw that beautiful red horse in the back stall and wondered who the owner could be."

"I bought him from Mr. Carson to ride home. That five-day trip by foot was a long way to Carson's plantation in Overton County, one I didn't want to experience again."

"Pa, you and Allen go on to the house. I'll finish up here and I'll be there in no time. I want to hear all about what's been going on in your life."

As Allen and Henry approached the front porch, they were greeted by Sarah handing them a cold glass of freshly made lemonade. While Henry, Rebecca, and Pointer were in Wartburg they had purchased some fresh lemons.

"It was like God impressed on Henry to get those lemons. It's like God knew that lemonade was a good way of celebrating our son's return home after a year's absence," Sarah said.

By the time Allen took his first sip of lemonade, Pointer had made his way to the house. Rebecca handed him a glass of lemonade. He immediately said, "A toast is in order, welcome home Allen!" Everyone got a laugh out of Pointer's toast.

Everyone grabbed a chair and sat back sipping lemonade as they enjoyed the sun setting in the west.

There is so much we want to ask you," Henry said.

"Tell us what's been going on in Overton County," Pointer said.

"On Mr. Jake Carson's plantation it is working from sun-up to sun-down. It is mostly working with cattle, but at times, it's bailing hay, harvesting corn, cutting firewood, and some cotton picking. Cotton picking is my least favorite thing. I'm telling you the first two weeks were awful. My fingers got infected from the cotton boll stickers. After about two weeks they become callused and the soreness went away.

I've been going to church at the First Baptist Church in Livingston. It's a nice church and the preacher, Brother Bob Fincher, is very good. Pointer, you would enjoy his messages."

"Have you seen any good-looking women up there in Overton County?" Sarah asked grinning.

"I've seen some, but not anyone I would want to court. Most of the good-looking girls are daughters to some of the big plantation owners in Overton County. I wouldn't think they'd be interested in just a farm hand."

"Allen, you always sell yourself short. You're a handsome man. A lot of girls would want you to court them, I'm sure of that," Sarah said.

"I've just not met the right one yet," Allen said.

"Pointer, I want you to take one of the mules and ride over to John's and tell him that I want him and his family to come for supper. There will be more than enough food for all of us. Tell John his brother Allen is home," Sarah said.

Pointer looked at Allen and asked, "Does your horse buck?"

"I don't think so," Allen answered.

"I was wondering if I might ride your horse instead of one of our old mules?"

"You certainly can! I call him Red. He is a speedy one so if you race him be careful. He's been trained well and obeys well. He knows what whoa means."

"I'll not run him much," Pointer said as he turned and headed toward the barn.

"Rebecca, you and I need to go inside and get supper ready. You guys stay out here and talk. I'll send Rebecca back with some more fresh lemonade," Sarah said.

"Pa, is everything all right with you?" Allen asked.

"What makes you ask that, Son?"

"You appeared to be struggling with that bucket of corn when I came in the barn."

"I've had a little soreness in my chest lately. I think I've pulled a muscle."

"Maybe you should see Doc Jones."

"Don't fret about me. I'm just getting old. Pointer has been so helpful to me after you left. It's like he thinks he must be with me every minute of the day. He makes sure I don't lift something heavy. He's a lot like you. He's a worker! I don't know if you know this, but he's planning on being a preacher someday."

"Yes, I know about him wanting to be a preacher. He knows his Bible well. He and I talked about God's word at night when he was studying his Bible. He's helped me on several occasions with his interpretations of certain scriptures. He's a pretty smart brother, if you ask me."

After dinner, Henry, John, and Allen sat on the front porch and visited while Sarah and Margaret finished cleaning the dishes. John's two boys, Robert and Tollett, joined Pointer for games of horse shoes.

Angeline, John's older daughter, and Rebecca compared notes on young men who had showed an interest in them.

"Your boys are really growing, John," Allen said.

"Yes, they're big helpers to me. I don't know what I'd do without them," John said.

"Allen, have you spotted you a woman in Overton County yet?" John asked.

"Not yet!" Allen answered quickly.

"I'm getting pretty worried about you, Allen. Looks like Pointer and me might be the only sons Pa will have to carry on his name," John said while looking at his father and winking.

"John, let me ask you a question," Allen said.

"Fire away!"

"When you courted Margaret how did you know she was the woman you wanted to marry?"

"Believe me, when you meet the right woman you will know."

"But how did you know?" Allen asked again.

"When I first saw my Margaret, I just knew. After spending the first ten minutes with her, I was double sure!" John said with excitement in his voice.

"You did good when you married Margaret. If I could find someone like Margaret, I would gladly marry her," Allen said.

"If you meet someone like my Margaret, you'd better marry her," John said.

There had been in times pass that Allen thought he might be abnormal not to be attracted to girls. All his friends were married and had children, yet he was still single. How was he supposed to feel inside when he was around a woman?

Margaret was the only woman he had feelings for and she was married to John. At times he felt a strong attraction toward her. He liked the way she touched him and smiled at him. He told himself that this feeling was wrong since she was John's wife. Would he feel the same way as he felt with Margaret when he met the right woman? If so, it would be a good feeling, he thought.

Allen spent the two weeks fishing and hunting with Henry, Pointer, John, and John's sons. He helped his father mend some fences and do some repairs to the barn. The two weeks passed much too fast. It was now time for him to return to Livingston. Again, it was hard for him to leave. His father's failing health made it even harder for him to go. He wondered as he left if he would ever see his father alive again.

CHAPTER 4

Allen was chopping firewood at the Carson plantation when Birch came up behind him. He was so intent chopping firewood that he was startled when Birch said, "Barger, Mr. Carson wants you to come to the big house right now!"

It took Allen a few seconds to regain his composure and finally said, "He wants to see me?"

"You are Allen Barger are you not?"

Allen had grown accustomed to Birch's smart remarks and dropped his axe.

"Now go on before he gets impatient!" Birch said.

The tone of Birch's voice sent Allen scurrying toward the big house. As he ran, he thought of everything he had done since returning from his trip home. Finding no cause to have aroused the ire of Mr. Carson, Allen wondered why he was being summoned to the big house. He had not neglected his duties, or at least, he didn't think he had. He imagined the worst as he slowed to a walk, and with a deep breath, mounted the steps to the front porch. It had been over a year since he started working for Carson, and although he had occasionally had conversations with his employer, he had never been summoned to come to the big house. Mamie was on the porch sweeping.

"Mamie, how's things going with you today?" Allen asked.

"I's doing just fine, Mr. Allen," Mamie replied with a big smile that revealed her shining white teeth.

"I received word that Mr. Carson wanted to see me."

"That's right, Mr. Allen. He's done told me to put you in the parlor when you get here. I's go and fetch Mr. Carson for you."

"Thanks, Mamie," Allen said, with more confidence than he felt. Still nothing in Mamie's expression, nor in her tone of voice, suggested trouble. Allen and Mamie had gotten to be good friends over the past year. On different occasions she would bring fresh baked cookies to the men at the bunkhouse. Allen would tease her about her big dark eyes and her beautiful white teeth. She loved every minute of his flirtation. Surely, he thought, if there was anything seriously wrong she would tell me. That is, of course, if she knew. The longer Allen waited, the more nervous he became, and his knees started knocking. He decided he couldn't stand any longer and took a seat in the parlor.

Mr. and Mrs. Carson entered the parlor where Allen was seated. Allen immediately stood up when Mrs. Carson entered the room.

"Hello, Allen, I want you to meet my wife, Mrs. Mary Carson."

Mrs. Carson walked over and shook Allen's hand. "I'm pleased to meet you Allen, I've heard some really nice things about you."

The pleasant tone of Mr. Carson's voice immediately set Allen at ease. The worries melted, leaving him with a flushed, mildly nauseous after-effect. He croaked out the words "Please to meet you, Ma'am," like a boy whose voice was changing, and then was immediately embarrassed by his own flustered state.

"Are you ill, Allen?" asked Mrs. Carson. Allen not wanting to speak again until he could show he had fully regained his composure, shook his head. "Well," Mrs. Carson continued, "my husband tells me you are one of his best hands."

"I do my best, Ma'am," Allen said.

Allen had seen Mrs. Carson before as she rode by in her carriage. He imagined her to be in her fifties. She was an attractive lady with a warm smile and a gentle Southern voice.

"I lost my coachman, Old Henry, last week. He died of pneumonia. I'm looking for someone to replace him. Mr. Birch tells me you are a man of character and one he can trust. I would like you to become my driver if you are interested. We will pay you more than you're making in the fields," Mrs. Carson said in her charming Southern accent.

Mr. Carson added, "The pay is three dollars a week. Since I always insist that my drivers are suitably attired, you will receive a new suit of clothes when you start. When they wear out, I expect you to replace them, understood?"

"Yes, Sir," responded Allen. Then, to Mrs. Carson he added, "I would be honored to be your coachman."

"Good! You can start tomorrow. I volunteer my time to our ladies' auxiliary at First Baptist in Livingston. I will also need to pick up some supplies. Bring my carriage around at eight o'clock," she said.

"Yes, Ma'am," Allen said with a look of gratitude in his eyes.

"We will see you in the morning, Allen," Mrs. Carson said as she left the room.

"I'll be here at eight," Allen said.

Mr. Carson followed Allen outside on the porch. "Allen, Old Henry, who was Mrs. Carson's driver, had been with us for several years. Mrs. Carson was very fond of him. I trusted Old Henry, and I'm putting a lot of trust in you."

"I'm honored, Mr. Carson, that you trust me. I won't let you or Mrs. Carson down."

"I believe you'll do just fine. By the way, you just got back from a trip home, recently didn't you? How did you find your family?"

"Everyone except for my father was doing fine," Allen said.

"What's wrong with your father?" Mr. Carson asked out of concern.

"I don't rightly know. Ma says he's not doing well, and he told me he had pulled a muscle in his chest. I'm not sure that a pulled muscle is what's ailing my pa," Allen said with concern showing in his voice.

"Allen, if you need to go see your folks again, let me know. I'll make arrangements for you to have time off."

"That's very nice of you, Sir," Allen said with genuine appreciation.

"It's very apparent you love your father," Mr. Carson said, putting his hand on Allen's shoulder.

"Yes, Sir, I truly do!" he said.

"Allen, I know what it's like to lose someone you love. Mrs. Carson and I lost our son, Matthew, six years ago in a hunting accident. He would have been twenty-six next week, about the same age as you. We loved and worshiped that boy," Carson said with tears welling in his eyes.

"I'm sorry, Mr. Carson," Allen said.

"Mrs. Carson had a rough time dealing with Matthew's death. For several years now, she's blamed herself for not being able to have another child. We lost two children prior to Matthew. They were both still born. She had complications giving birth to Matthew and couldn't have any more children. After losing Matthew, she blamed herself even more. I've assured her many times I didn't blame her, that it was God's will. Next week will be Matthew's birthday. I'm afraid, Allen, you will see a vast difference in her moods."

"How should I react to her moods?" Allen asked.

"Just be gentle and kind," Carson said.

"I'll do just that," Allen said as he shook Mr. Carson's hand.

As Allen left Mr. Carson on the porch, he wondered why Mr. Carson picked him for the job. How had he won the trust of Mr. Carson? He was thrilled about the job, and it paid more than the field hand job. The extra money would help in realizing his dream of owning a farm.

Allen's new job was not physically demanding in comparison to the field work. It consisted of driving the Carsons to social events, church, and working in Mrs. Carson's garden. In addition, Allen was responsible for the care of the carriage and grooming the horses. Allen got to know Mrs. Carson well as he worked and traveled with her. She was a fine Southern lady. He grew to admire, love, and respect her for her gentleness, kindness, and consideration for others.

As they had promised, the Carsons bought Allen a suit of new clothes which fit him perfectly.

Allen was quickly accepted by the Carsons and during long, lonely trips, he engaged in extensive conversations with both Mr. and Mrs. Carson. Up to this point, he had previously spoken with Mr. Carson only as an employee, but that changed somewhat after he became their driver.

While traveling with the Carsons he got to know them well. They were good people and were not pretentious like some big plantation owners in Overton County. They were Christians who tried to live a Godly life. They wanted Allen to feel a part of their lives. They treated him like a son.

After returning from a shopping trip in Livingston, Mrs. Carson said to Allen, "I will need you to help Mamie at our social event on Saturday night."

"Ma'am, I don't know if I'm cut out for that," Allen said with reluctance in his voice.

"You'll do just fine. I'll get Mamie to teach you what to do," Mrs. Carson said as she pulled her dress and petticoat up above her shoes and walked up the steps to the porch.

As Allen was getting back in the carriage, Mamie came out on the porch. "Mr. Allen, hold your horses!"

"What's up, Mamie?" Allen asked.

"Mrs. Carson told me to teach you some social graces. Tie them horses up to that hitching post and come up here now!" Mamie said as she motioned to Allen.

Allen thought to himself, what does Mamie mean by social graces?

"Mr. Allen, if you're going to learn social graces you got to do as I say."

Allen found Mamie quite interesting as she modeled the mannerisms. At times he found himself bent over with laughter. As Allen practiced what Mamie showed him, she also bent over laughing. "Mr. Allen, you going to do just fine."

"Do you think so, Mamie?" Allen asked in a flirtatious way.

"Mr. Allen, you got to learn the two-steps. You might have to dance with one of them purity Southern girls," Mamie said as she put on her big wide smile.

"I believe we can forget about dancing, Mamie. I'm my worst enemy when it comes to dancing. I just can't get the hang of it."

"You let me show you. I'll be you and you be me. Let me lead."

Mamie with her big hands wrapped around Allen's started leading him around the floor. "Look at me, Mr. Allen, quits looking at your feets."

Every time Allen looked at Mamie, he would break out laughing. "Mr. Allen, how's you expect me to teach you anything if you going to laugh at me?"

"I'm sorry, Mamie, but I don't think it's working," Allen said wanting to quit.

"If you be serious, Mr. Allen, it'll work. Now, get serious!" Mamie said as she continued to teach him the two-step.

"Count with me, Mr. Allen, count!" Mamie said as she began to count.

Allen was so embarrassed when he spotted Mr. and Mrs. Carson laughing hysterically from the living room window.

"Now, Mr. Allen, you try leading me," Mamie said with persuasion.

This is going to be a disaster, Allen thought. But since Mamie was trying so hard, he decided to do his best, which in his opinion, wouldn't be much.

Allen was relieved when Mamie said, "That's enough today, Mr. Allen. I'm plumb give out!" She lifted her apron and wiped the sweat from her brow.

Seeing that Mamie was bone tired, Allen asked, "Mamie, when can we do this again?"

Huffing and puffing, Mamie responded, "You go on and tend to them horses, Mr. Allen. I believe yours ready for the social." She got up from her chair and slowly walked inside.

At first, Allen was uncomfortable in his role, having never learned how to behave in "high society." However, with Mamie's coaching he soon was the picture of a discreet and unobtrusive, yet attentive and conscientious servant, whenever the Carson's hosted a party.

The Carsons noted his efforts and rewarded him with increasing duties. Like Joseph in Pharaoh's court thought Allen, he was now second to Pharaoh at least inside the house. Mr. Birch was still the boss outside the house.

CHAPTER 5

Allen first set eyes on Nancy Bullock when serving refreshments at one of the Carson's social events. She was beautiful. She was wearing a full-length white dress, and as she walked across the room, her long black hair bounced. Allen couldn't help noticing that several of the men guest turned their eyes in Nancy's direction. He had never in his life been attracted to any lady like this. Allen looked around the room and found Mrs. Carson visiting with several of her lady guests.

"Excuse me, ladies! I need to have a minute with Mrs. Carson," Allen said with the politeness and formality that Mamie had taught him.

"What is it, Allen?" Mrs. Carson asked, stepping aside from her guests.

"Tell me who that beautiful young lady is talking to the Gentry sisters."

Mrs. Carson glanced across the room, then smiled. "Allen, that's Nancy Bullock. She's the daughter of Joseph Bullock who owns a farm east of Livingston."

"Mrs. Carson, she's beautiful!" Allen said with excitement.

"It's about time you noticed a beautiful young lady. I was beginning to worry about you. Come on, I'll introduce you to her," Mrs. Carson said as she reached and took Allen by the arm.

Allen had only a moment to stammer. As Mrs. Carson led him across the room Allen was asking, "What if she doesn't like me?"

"Any woman would like you, Allen Barger."

He had never been this scared of anything and wondered what he would say to Miss Bullock. Fortunately, there was no more time to worry himself into a state. Mrs. Carson had already reached Nancy Bullock's side, and nervous or not, the moment of truth had arrived.

"Ladies, I want you to meet the most handsome man in this room tonight. Allen, this is Eliza and Mary Gentry and Nancy Bullock. Ladies, this is Allen Barger," Mrs. Carson said with a smile.

"Ladies, it's my pleasure," Allen said with a slight bow.

Mrs. Carson turned to Allen and said, Miss. Bullock is regrettably without an escort would you please be kind enough to join her for this dance?"

Allen was about to protest that he did not know how to waltz but a single glance from Mrs. Carson told him he had better fake it. The young ladies, Miss Bullock included, seemed to sense Allen's nervousness and probably guessed that he had never danced before in his life. Their amusement was evident as he led Miss Bullock out onto the dance floor.

Allen thought, I have seen it done fifty times and it does not look too difficult. I'll try to remember what Mamie taught me. At least if I stay in the heart of the crowd, no one can see.

"Miss Bullock, would you like to dance?" Allen asked, copying the manners that he had seen from the gentlemen at the Carson's party.

"Mr. Barger, I would be honored," she said.

Mrs. Carson who had been watching closely from the edge of the room motioned to the musicians. They struck up a waltz. In that moment twenty couples swirled in the center of the ballroom. It's dance or be trampled, thought Allen to himself as they began to dance.

The only dancing Allen had done was what Mamie taught him. But he could tell from the look on Mrs. Carson's face that he was a natural. Miss Bullock--did he dare call her Nancy seemed to positively enjoy the dance. Too soon it was over. But it had happened. Allen had finally found a lady he was interested in. This girl had to be the one. Surely God had sent her to this party just for him to see and dance with. After spending the rest of the evening with Miss Bullock he asked her if he could come calling.

"Mr. Barger, I would love that, but you must get my father's permission," Nancy said. The etiquette of courtship was a new experience for Allen. He would do whatever it took to court Nancy. Allen had little time to think about etiquette, however, because for the second time that evening a female grabbed him by the arm and dragged him across the room.

"Excuse me, gentlemen, I need to steal my father away for a minute," Nancy said.

"Father, I want you to meet Allen Barger."

"It's a pleasure to meet you, Allen," Mr. Bullock replied as he shook Allen's hand.

"It's a pleasure to meet you too, Sir," Allen said with confidence.

"Forget that sir stuff," Mr. Bullock said as he shook Allen's hand.

"Why don't I leave you two along to get acquainted?" Nancy said as she looked at Allen with a smile before walking away. Allen gulped. This was Allen's opportunity. His courtship of Nancy could be over before it began if he didn't say the right thing in the next two minutes. Out the corner of his eye he saw Mrs. Carson engaged in conversation on the far side of the room, but he noted that she seemed to be watching him, even as she talked. Mrs. Carson must have alerted her husband to what was going on, too, because he was gazing intently at Allen even as he expounded on his views on taxation with Judge Sinclair. Alone with Mr. Bullock there was nothing to do but try to make polite conversation and hope for a favorable first impression.

"Mr. Barger, what do you do?" Mr. Bullock asked. Bullock's easy-going attitude and engaging personality is going to make this a lot easier, thought Allen.

"I work for the Carsons," Allen answered.

"Where are you from?"

"I'm from Wartburg down in Morgan County."

"Morgan County? That's a beautiful county. I've gone through there on my way to Knoxville. I love those Crab Orchard Mountains."

"It's a nice place to live. Although, due to the mountains it's not a good place for farming. "My father, Henry Barger, has one hundred acres in Morgan County and only about half is suitable for farming. I'm working for Mr. Carson to save money to buy myself a farm. I'm really a farmer at heart," Allen said.

"Farming has been my life too. I've been farming for over thirty years now. I guess I'll die being a farmer," Mr. Bullock said.

Allen and Mr. Bullock visited for several minutes. As they visited, Allen would glance at Nancy now engaged in conversation with several other young ladies, and she would coyly glance back at him and smile. Mr. Bullock could not have failed to notice the flirtation.

Finally, after several minutes of polite but somewhat nervous small-talk, Allen realized he had to get to the point. "Mr. Bullock, I would like your permission to come calling on your daughter."

"So, you would like to court my daughter?" Mr. Bullock asked.

"Yes, I would," Allen replied.

"Allen, may I ask how old you are?"

"I'm twenty-nine years old."

"My Nancy is only eighteen years old. She has never courted a man before. Have you been married before, Allen?"

"No, Sir. I've never wanted to court any girl until now."

"Well, while you were dancing with Nancy, Mrs. Carson told me all about you. If half of what she says is true, you are a fine young man. If Nancy wants to see you again, you have my permission," Mr. Bullock said.

"Thank you, Mr. Bullock. I promise you, I will respect your daughter."

Allen made his way back across the room where he engaged Nancy in further dancing.

Three months after Allen and Nancy met, Allen received a letter from his mother in Morgan County. This letter was not the usual letter Allen received from his mother every few weeks. He opened the letter with the same anticipation as he always had.

My Dear Allen,

I have some bad news. Your pa passed on to be with our good Lord on August 17. Doc Jones said his heart just gave out. Allen, before he died, he asked me to tell you he was leaving you the farm. We buried your pa near the big oak tree in the Union Community Cemetery. I believe you will remember the big oak tree in the middle of the graveyard. Your pa always said he wanted to be buried there. John and I carved out a stone for his headstone. The neighbors have been so good to us. Your pa was liked by lots of people. I find comfort in knowing he has gone to be with our Lord and Savior.

Rebecca and I are both well. John is taking good care of us. I don't want you to worry about us. Please don't feel obligated to return to Morgan County. Your pa and me had many good years together. Those years produced many precious memories which I will cherish as long as I shall live. Those memories will encourage me to go on with my life. Don't you worry about me. Please stay in Morgan County and get to know Nancy."

Your Ma, with all my love,
Sarah Jane Barger

Allen couldn't hold back his tears. He was confident that his father was with the Lord, but the thought of never seeing him again on this earth was too emotional for him to handle. The pain he was experiencing was the worse he had ever endured. He wasn't a man who cried often, but today he would cry.

Allen took great pain in deciding what was best for him. He finally decided he would stay in Overton County and continue to work for the Carsons. His mother was right. He needed to get to know Nancy better, and in time he would return to Morgan County.

During the next three months the internal conflict which had been tearing away at Allen regarding his manhood quickly dissipated. He had fallen in love with the most beautiful girl in the world. John was right. His feelings for Nancy were strong and it had to be a sign from God.

The Carsons let Allen use their carriage for social events and to visit Nancy on Sunday afternoons. Allen would drop the Carsons off after church and then go to the Bullocks for dinner. He enjoyed Mrs. Daisy Bullock's cooking. Her cooking reminded him of his mother's. Allen also enjoyed Nancy's apple pie. He always made a point to say, "This is the best apple pie I've ever ate."

Everyone would laugh, and Daisy Bullock would say, "Allen, I do believe Nancy's apple pie gets better each time you eat it, doesn't it?"

Everyone laughed again as Allen grinned and blushed.

"My mother always told me the way to a man's heart was through his stomach," Daisy Bullock said as she looked at Allen and smiled.

Allen knew not only had Nancy touched his stomach with her apple pie, but she had also stolen his heart.

After one Sunday dinner, Allen and Nancy took a walk down at Caney Creek near the Bullocks' home.

This day would be different from other walks they had shared along Caney Creek. On this day, Allen asked Nancy to marry him. For weeks he had been trying to build up courage to ask Nancy to be his wife. He felt she loved him but feared she might say no. No was not what he wanted to hear.

"Allen, I love this place, don't you?" Nancy asked by grabbing Allen by his arm.

"Yes, it's a nice place, but would you want to live here the rest of your life?" Allen asked.

"If I could live with you, Allen, it wouldn't matter where I lived," Nancy replied.

After a few minutes of silence, Allen said, "Nancy, I have something very important to ask you."

"What is it, Allen?"

"Nancy, I love you and I want you to be my wife. I don't think I can go on much longer not having you as my wife."

"Allen, I thought you would never ask me. Why have you waited so long?" she asked.

"I wanted to be sure you would say yes. I don't think I could stand it if you were to say no," Allen said as he reached out and took both of Nancy's hands.

"Oh, my darling Allen. I will gladly be your wife. I love you more than life itself," she said.

"Nancy, you've made me the happiest man on earth today!" Allen said as he pulled her near and kissed her.

"Nancy, there is one other thing I must know before we marry," Allen said.

"What is it, Allen?"

"I want to go back to Morgan County and take over my pa's farm. He left me the farm, and I feel obligated to go. This will mean you'll have to leave your family and go with me. How do you feel about that?"

"Allen, I will go wherever you go. I love you, and I know you love me. I'll be happy as long as we're together."

That was what Allen wanted to hear. He knew it would be hard for Nancy to leave her folks, but he needed to return to Morgan County.

They decided it was time to ask Mr. Bullock for his permission to marry. Allen had just completed his third year with the Carsons. He had saved everything he made except for what he paid Carson for his red horse.

Nancy invited Allen to supper to help celebrate her father's birthday. They wanted to catch Mr. Bullock in a good mood and felt that his birthday would be the right occasion.

After supper, Allen and Mr. Bullock went to the front porch. As they sat in rocking chairs, Mr. Bullock lit his smoking pipe and began to puff.

"What's been on your mind tonight, Allen?" Mr. Bullock asked as he continued to smoke and rock in his chair. "You have been unusually quiet."

"Mr. Bullock, I'm in love with Nancy. I have been ever since I set eyes on her. I promised you, I would respect your daughter, and I have kept my word. I'm asking your permission to marry your daughter. I love her and want more than anything else in this world for her to be my wife."

"Allen, you are a good man. I've watched you closely during your courtship of my daughter. It's apparent that Nancy loves you. My question is how you hope to provide for her?"

"For the past three years, I've been saving my money to buy my own farm back in Morgan County. I enjoy farming and know I can make a good living farming. With the farm that Pa left me and with my savings, I should be able to make a good living for me and Nancy. I need your blessings to marry your daughter. I love her with all of my heart."

"If Nancy wants to marry you, I won't stand in her way. Let's call her out here and see what she has to say," Mr. Bullock said.

Mr. Bullock got up from his rocking chair and went to the front door. He called out for Nancy to join him and Allen on the front porch.

"Nancy, Allen has asked my permission to marry you. How do you feel about marrying Allen, and how do you feel about moving off from us to Morgan County?"

"Father, I love Allen. He's treated me like a lady, and I want very much to be his wife. I would go anywhere with Allen. You know I love you, Mother, and all the rest, but I also know the Bible teaches that wherever my husband goes, I should go. You've always taught me I should obey the Bible. I want to marry Allen and follow him wherever he goes," Nancy said convincingly.

Mr. Bullock embraced Nancy and then led her across the porch where Allen had been waiting anxiously for Joseph Bullock's decision. "You both have my blessings," Bullock said as he placed his daughter's hands in Allen's.

CHAPTER 6

Allen and Nancy were married on November 10, 1833, at the Primitive Baptist Church in Livingston, Tennessee, where they had worshiped together since they met. Nancy chose a long white gown with lace on the sleeves and hem. Her long black hair flowed freely down her back. As she made her walk down the aisle, Allen thanked God for this moment in time. He had waited so long for the right woman. I'm the luckiest man on earth today, he thought. How can I thank you enough, God? Allen chose a black suit, a gift from the Carsons for the wedding.

Mr. Birch was the best man. Despite his gruff exterior, Birch had a heart of gold and seemed truly touched when Allen asked him to be his best man. After the wedding, the guests returned to the Carson's plantation for a party in honor of the bride and groom.

The wedding reception was not the only honor the Carsons gave Allen. At the party, Mr. Carson presented Allen with a gift of two mules and a wagon. A wonderful gift that would be helpful in transporting personal items back to Morgan County.

Allen was amazed by the Carsons' generosity. They had treated him like a son, and their kindness couldn't be measurable. Before leaving, Allen promised the Carsons he would always keep in touch and thanked them once again for all they had done for him. "I will never forget you," Allen said as he left the front porch and helped Nancy into the wagon. As Allen glanced back over his shoulder, he saw both Mrs. Carson and Mamie wiping tears out of their eyes. This made him sad.

Nancy's father and mother had given Nancy several furniture items they wanted her to have plus a large trunk that was full of her very best clothing.

Upon arriving back at the Bullocks, Nancy's brothers helped Allen load the wagon.

It was getting late when Allen and Nancy said their final goodbyes. It was a sad time for Nancy. As Allen pulled away with Big Red tied to the wagon, Nancy turned one last time and waved goodbye to her family. She had never been away from her family and wondered what it would be like not to see them daily.

Allen figured it would take a good two days and two nights to return to his home in Morgan County.

Allen had previously written his mother to let her know the approximate date of his and Nancy's arrival at the family's home in Morgan County. It was too bad that his mother, John, and the rest of the family weren't able to make the long trip to Livingston for the wedding, but it was out of the question. He could hardly wait for his family to meet Nancy, especially his brother John. Never again would John be able to ask him the same old question, "Allen when are you getting married?"

On the way to Wartburg, Allen and Nancy spent their first night camped under the stars in a beautiful grove of oak trees. After eating, Allen helped Nancy clean and put away the dishes. Allen prepared their bed near the camp fire. The night was cool, but the fire crackled with warmth by their feet. The sky was full of bright twinkling stars.

"Allen, the sky is beautiful tonight," Nancy said as she lay next to Allen with her eyes fixed on the sky above.

"I was thinking the same thing. It reminds me of the times I lay awake counting stars from my bed at my father's house. At times, I could count to a thousand stars without blinking," Allen said.

Allen turned to Nancy and said, "You're so beautiful!"

"Thank you, Allen," Nancy replied, smiling.

"Nancy, I've never made love to a woman before."

"My darling this will be my first time, also," Nancy said with a warm smile and laying her head on his chest.

"Are you scared?" Asked Allen.

"A little bit," Nancy replied.

"I'll be gentle," Allen whispered.

"Hold me, Allen."

Allen made sure he was gentle with Nancy knowing she had never been with another man. He wanted their first love making to be special. He was now twenty-nine years old and had waited a long time for the privilege of making love to the woman he would spend the rest of his life with. He considered Nancy a gift from God. He would honor her and cherish her until death did them part.

Their first night as husband and wife was one they would never forget.

At mid-afternoon on November 14, 1833, Allen and Nancy arrived at his mother's home. They were greeted by all his family except for his oldest nephew, Robert, who had married and moved to Bledsoe County.

Everyone was excited to have Allen home and were very pleased with his new bride. Nancy soon became the hit of the party. She met people well, and it wasn't long until she felt right at home with her new family.

"Allen, your Nancy is a beautiful woman," John said.

"Thanks! I knew the first time I laid eyes on her, that I must have her for my wife," Allen said with a sense of pride.

"During all the years you spent in Roane and Morgan County, I couldn't understand why you didn't take a fancy to some of our local girls. I now see why. Nancy beats anything we have here in Morgan County!" John said with a chuckle, knowing he had impishly spoken loudly enough for half the unmarried women present to hear.

"She is beautiful, isn't she?" Allen said as he looked at John with a big smile.

"What are you planning on doing with the farm, Allen?" John asked.

"I don't rightly know. Since winter's coming on, I thought I'd give it a little time before making any decision about the farm."

"I hear there's good farming land down in Bledsoe County. The land is supposed to be better suited for farming than what we have here in Morgan County. I was hoping we could go down there and check things out. What do you think?" John asked.

Allen did not relish the idea of leaving his new bride, even for a few days, for a land hunt in Bledsoe County. "Gosh, I hadn't even thought about leaving Morgan County. Pa wanted me to keep this farm."

"I've struggled in Morgan County for several years and have barely made ends meet. We don't have enough rich farm land here to make a good living. I'm tired of just barely getting by. Think about it and we can talk about it another day."

"I will think about it, John," Allen said as he got up.

Allen's and Nancy's belongings were unloaded into the house. Sarah had moved her belongings from the master bedroom to Rebecca's room which became vacant after John and Rebecca married and moved to Wartburg. The master bedroom was now Allen and Nancy's.

Allen, John, Pointer, and Tollett spent the next few weeks cutting wood, fishing, hunting and trapping for fur. They were now prepared for the winter months.

The winters in Morgan County weren't extremely cold. The average yearly temperature was around seventy-two degrees during the day and in the mid-thirties at night. Allen loved Morgan County, but he wanted good farm land. He knew John was right about Morgan County. Because of the mountains and a large part of the land being in timber, it left very little fertile cleared land for farming. He had worked hard to save money for a good farm, and he wanted a farm which would permit him to make a good living for him and his family. Now that he had a wife to care for and soon might have a family, Allen realized that his duty to provide might take him away from Morgan County.

In early March, Allen and John set out for Bledsoe County. It took them two days by horse to get to Pikeville, the county seat of Bledsoe County.

After arriving in Pikeville, Allen and John visited the local surveyor's office. John, being the older of the two, did the talking. He explained to the surveyor that they were interested in buying land in the county, and the surveyor showed them sections of land that had been plotted in fifty and one hundred acres plots. He showed them a county map that showed land that was still available for purchasing.

The surveyor pointed out several good tracts of land close to Tollet's Mill. Tollet's Mill lay between Walden's Ridge and the Sequatchie River. The Sequatchie River area had the richest soil for growing corn in Bledsoe County and would provide transportation to get the corn to market. Like the settlers in Morgan County, the folks in Bledsoe County relied heavily on their corn crop.

With a hand drawn map from the surveyor to guide them, Allen and John rode to Tollet's Mill. From there a few questions to a boy with a fishing pole took them to the land the surveyor had shown. As soon as Allen and John laid eyes on the property around Tollet's Mill, they agreed they had to have some of this land. This land was not as rocky and hilly as they were accustomed to in Morgan County. They needed about one hundred acres each to make a good living at farming. The land was available for purchase, but there were two obstacles standing in their way. First, they needed money, and secondly, they needed to sell their farms back in Morgan County.

John and Allen were afraid if they waited until their farms sold in Morgan County that the land around Tollet's Mill would not be available when they returned. They were aware that settlers from the surrounding counties of Roane and Rhea were moving in weekly to purchase land.

Allen came up with an idea. He would take his savings he earned working for the Carsons and make a down payment on two hundred acres. The two hundred acres could be broken up into two equal hundred-acre plots. The two farms would join each other, and the land not used for farming could be used by both families for pastures.

John and Allen wanted very much to be together. They wanted the same thing, a good farm and a good life for their families. Allen's idea of financing the two hundred acres sounded like the best solution.

John was grateful to Allen for being unselfish with his savings. He realized Allen had worked hard to save the money for him a farm. He admired his brother for his willingness to step out on a limb to help him and his family. He would always be indebted to Allen for his generosity.

"Let's do it, little brother," John said as he reached out and shook Allen's hand.

"Pikeville, here we come!" Allen shouted as they marched toward their horses arm in arm.

They both agreed the gamble was worth taking to assure them good farms. They had no assurance their farms in Morgan County would sell but decided to step out on faith and let God help them sell their farms.

Allen and John returned to Morgan County and put their farms up for sale.

The land sold quicker than either John or Allen could have dared to hope. Sam Clayton's property joined John's farm on the south. Mr. Clayton had been looking to expand his one hundred acres. He needed pasture land and could make use of the rockier soil of John's and Allen's farms for pasture even if it was too rocky to plow. He purchased both John's and Allen's one hundred acres. He paid fair market price for both farms.

God had answered their prayers. They now had the money to build their new homes in Bledsoe County and to prepare their new farms for planting.

CHAPTER 7

April is not a good time to travel in Tennessee. The rain fell in sheets turning the roads into quagmires. A journey that should have taken a few days stretched out to infinity. The journey was particularly hard on Sarah, but she maintained a cheerful attitude throughout. John and Allen, having to pause every mile or so to dig a wagon out of the mud, found it much more difficult to be lighthearted.

"Push harder, Pointer, push!" John said as he tried to free the left back wheel from a pothole.

Allen who was standing by John trying to help him lift the wheel from the pothole said, "Maybe this wasn't such a good idea after all."

"We can't turn back now, Allen. Everyone, push! Lift, Allen! Lift!" John said mustering every ounce of strength and muscle he had.

This time the wagon moved forward. Allen, John, Pointer, and Tollett shouted with joy as the wagon moved forward.

"I pray to God, we won't hit another pothole," Allen said to John as he put his muddy hand on John's shoulder.

"Me too!" Pointer said as he joined in the celebration.

Finally, after an eternity, the wagons rolled into Tollet's Mill. The rain, however, had an advantage: warmer, spring-like weather followed, so the two families could camp out without discomfort. John and Allen selected a beautiful valley with a sparkling brook lined with oaks and elms on both sides to be their new home. Allen would build his home on the west side of the creek and John would build his on the east side.

"It will be like old times," said Allen. "We will be neighbors again!"

"It will be better than old times since we will be able to see each other's cabin," replied John. "We ought to be able to build a footbridge across the creek as soon as the cabins are built. First thing, we have to build is your cabin, Allen."

"Why mine?" Allen asked.

"Well, I am mainly thinking about Ma. At her age she doesn't need to be sleeping on the ground any longer than she must," John said.

Allen had no choice but to agree since there was no way to refute his brother's logic.

Building a cabin requires a lot of skill. The availability of ample oak trees nearby made it a lot easier. Chopping down one tree could take all morning. The branches then had to be removed and the trunk shaped to fit. It would be dragged by the team to the cabin and then notched to fit into the cross timbers. Raising a single log high on the wall required both John and Allen and both their teams. A ramp of inclined logs was built leaning against the wall and then the horses skidded the logs up the ramp as John and Allen guided them into position.

Sarah, Margaret, and Nancy helped with the chinking which was smearing mud into the spaces between the logs. Pointer and his nephews, Robert and Tollett, were good workers as well. They did good work by splitting slabs of wood and making shingles for the roofs. Robert who lived nearby came over daily and helped with building the two cabins. The women joined the men in gathering stones to build the chimneys.

John's wife, Margaret, and Nancy were relegated to the status of "housekeepers," a nickname both pretended offense to. While everyone else worked on the new house, Nancy and Margaret took care of the stock, cooked, sewed, gathered firewood and, in short, did one hundred chores including chinking.

The new neighbors were a friendly lot and dropped in to help on several occasions. But since it was planting season they could not afford to take too much time helping the newcomers. Still, Nancy, Margaret, Sarah, and John's girls were always ready to serve up a heaping plate of stew, some cider cooled in the stream, and fried fish courtesy of Robert, Pointer, and Tollett. Fish from the stream became a daily part of their diet.

As Allen and John divided their time between building a home and preparing their land for planting they caught themselves wondering whether they had made the right decision in moving to Bledsoe County when they did.

Allen and John had money left over from the sale of their farms. This money came in handy when supplies were needed from Pikeville, the county seat of Bledsoe County. Several large sacks of corn, beans, and seed potatoes were purchased for farming purposes.

Both John and Allen were strong men and didn't mind working hard to achieve their goals. They had taught each of their children good working ethics as well. Everything was going well for both families. A daily diet for the Barger crew consisted of cornbread, biscuits, eggs, bacon, fish, wild game, beans, potatoes, and wild fruits.

One day Tollett was given the responsibility to take the ladies and younger children to seek out wild strawberries. Wild strawberries were plentiful in the Tollett community. Each person was given a bucket for their berries. At the end of the day everyone brought their buckets together to see if they had enough berries for pies. It was discovered that Tollett had fewer berries than anyone else. He had no will power to resist eating most of the berries he picked. Consequently, he was relieved of his duties of picking wild strawberries. From that day forward Sarah assumed that responsibility while Tollett returned to his farming duties.

Allen and John were accustomed to knowing what items best to plant to supply food for the winter months. Lots of potatoes, beans, and corn were planted. What they didn't eat fresh was canned for use during the winter.

By late fall, both Allen's and John's cabins were completed.

When cold weather arrived, Allen and John and their family members joined others in the community for hog killing days. It was a time of celebration and tradition among the early settlers to come together once a year to slaughter their hogs to provide meat for the winter months.

Everyone who raised hogs participated in the event. The men would do the slaughtering. The hogs were killed by either shooting them between the eyes or cutting their throat. The hogs were then dipped in scolding water for removing all the hair. After the hog was scraped clean, the men used hand saws to cut the hog up into hams, tenderloin, ribs and bacon. No parts of the hog were wasted. Every part was eaten, including the feet and the head. Several people loved the brains of the hog. There was a belief that eating the hog brains made people healthy and protected them from getting certain diseases. Allen confessed he never ate any hog brains.

After the hogs was prepared for cooking, the ladies fried tenderloin in big black kettles over an open fire. They cooked biscuits and white gravy to go with the tenderloin. The women also cooked pies and cakes for dessert. It was a time of jubilee and everyone rejoiced and praised the Lord for His love and gifts that provided a good life in the little community of Tollet's Mill.

Allen's cabin consisted of a living room and a kitchen combination, a fireplace that acted as both heating and cooking, a master bedroom, and two rooms across from a breeze way called a "dog trot." The two bedrooms across from the dog trot were for Sarah and Pointer. Those rooms were heated by a large iron cast wood stove.

CHAPTER 8

The first winter in the community of Tollett's Mill went by without any hitches. In the spring, John and Allen decided to build a fence around their two-hundred acres so they could purchase more cows and horses.

Building the fence took several weeks since several hundred postholes had to be dug. Both John and Allen could each dig about twenty postholes a day --- they made a joking contest out of it-- while Pointer did about eight a day. Once, when Pointer hit a stretch of soft ground, he did twenty-one, beating his two older brothers. Neither John nor Allen heard the end of that for a week.

Robert and Tollett contributed several hours toward digging postholes as well. Together they could do about fifteen a day, with time out for a mid-afternoon swim in the creek with the boys from the neighboring farms.

Every few days they stopped digging holes and planted the posts in the holes they had dug. They used saplings cut from the river bank as the fence posts set in the holes. Wire was stretched from post to post to form the fence. Section by section, and foot by foot, the pasture was fenced.

Harvesting the corn crop was a family affair. All in all, they got about twenty acres planted that first season which surprised both Allen and John. The brothers had figured they would not be able to plant more than seven to ten acres.

Every member of John's family as well as Allen, Nancy, and Pointer worked gathering the corn. It was Sarah's job to stay at home and prepare dinner.

John was fortunate to have both of his sons, Robert and Tollett, helping with the harvesting. After the wagon was full,

Robert drove the load of corn to Allen's house where a crude lean-to had been built to use as a storage shed. The wagon was emptied and returned to the corn field for another load.

On the second day of harvesting, Nancy and Allen were working on opposite sides of the wagon. Allen heard Tollett cry out, "Uncle Allen, come quickly something has happened to Nancy."

As Allen ran around the back of the wagon he saw Nancy lying on the ground. She was not moving. Her face was flushed. As he bent down over her, he saw she was still breathing. "Thank God," gasped Allen with relief that was more of a prayer than an exclamation. He picked her up and gently placed her on a burlap sack in the back of the wagon. Grabbing the reins from Tollett, he galloped the team back to the house.

Sarah, hearing the commotion, opened the door as they approached. "What's happened, Allen?" Sarah asked.

"I don't rightly know, Ma. She may have gotten too hot."

Sarah immediately went for cold water and a towel. While she was out of the room Allen brushed back Nancy's long black hair which had fallen across her face. "God, let Nancy be okay! Please, God!" Allen said.

"Allen, let me put this cold towel on her forehead," Sarah said.

By this time John and all the others, panting from running all the way from the field, had entered the house to check on Nancy.

"What happened to Nancy?" John asked. "Tollett said she collapsed!"

"I think she fainted," Allen said.

Nancy began to groan and opened her eyes. "What happened to me?"

"Don't worry, child, it is nothing. You just fainted," Sarah said.

"I don't remember anything. How did I get here?"

"You're going to be fine, Nancy," Allen said as he lifted her hand to his cheek.

"I'm so sorry, Allen," Nancy cried.

"She needs rest, Allen. Ya'll go back to the field. I'll take good care of her," Sarah said.

"You rest, Nancy. Ma will take good care of you," Allen said as he got up from the bed.

Sarah followed Allen to the front porch. "Allen, Nancy may be with child."

"When will we know, Ma?" Allen asked with excitement.

"If she's expecting we will begin to see symptoms like dizziness and sickness of stomach. You go on back to work now and don't worry about a thing," Sarah said.

Sarah was right. Nancy was indeed expecting a child.

Allen was more excited about the impending birth of his child than he had ever been about anything in his life. After the harvest was in, he worked hard to clear more fields for the next year's crops, but all he could think of was Nancy and the baby. At night the couple lay awake discussing names for their child. Allen made a cradle, and John made a rocker which they gave to Nancy for Christmas.

On the bitterly cold morning of February 15, 1834, Allen was awakened by Nancy shaking his shoulder. "Allen, I think the baby's coming," she said.

"The baby's coming!" Allen screamed.

He jumped out of bed, put on his overalls, and ran across the breeze way to Sarah's room. "Ma, wake up! Nancy thinks the baby's coming."

Sarah went in and examined Nancy. She turned to Allen and said, "I do believe it's getting pretty close."

"What do we do?" Allen gasped. He suddenly realized that with all the thinking and planning for the child, the actual birth of the baby was something that he had given little thought to.

"Don't worry," said Sarah. "I have delivered plenty of babies in my time, including you. I know what to do. But you make yourself useful. Go across the creek and get Margaret."

Allen splashed across the stream at the shallow spot realizing, as the cold water took his breath away, that he should have remembered to bring the horse. Well, he would have to remember that for the next baby!

John and Margaret were awakened with loud knocking on their door. When John opened the door a blast of cold air filled the living room as Allen entered like a charging bull.

"It's the baby! It's the baby!" shouted Allen. John and Margaret looked at each other and burst out laughing. "What is wrong with you?" said Allen. "Don't you understand Nancy is having the baby?"

"It's all right, Allen," said Margaret. John and I talked just last night, and we predicted you would come running in here like a madman when Nancy went into labor. We just didn't know it would be so soon. Now, calm down and sit. I need to get myself together to go over and help Sarah. Don't stammer so. We have plenty of time. These things take a while."

By this time the commotion had awakened their children. Three heads peaked down from the loft. Seeing them, John said, "Children, Nancy is about to have her baby. You boys go get the wagon hitched up. Your mother is going to help with the delivery, and I don't want her to get to Allen's house looking like a drowned rat."

The boys glanced at Allen's water-soaked britches, and Tollett giggled.

"Allen, you come with me and I'll loan you a pair of my dry britches."

The boys hitched up the wagon, and John drove Allen and Margaret over to Allen's house.

The rest of the night and morning was something of a mystery to Allen. He waited outside in the dooryard for what seemed like an eternity. But, in later years, he could not remember for the life of him what he had done, what he had thought, or what had been said. John sat with him, and Pointer came over after his chores were done, but Allen's mind was a complete blank about what they talked about.

Finally, the door to the cabin opened and Sarah called out, "Allen! It's a boy!"

"A boy! Did you hear that? It's a boy!" Allen shouted as he looked at John and Pointer.

"Congratulations, Allen," John said as he shook his brother's hand.

"Nancy and I have decided that if it's a boy we will call him Henry. I want him to be named after Pa."

Sarah came back to the door and motioned for Allen to come to the bedroom. Margaret brought the baby over to Allen and said, "Allen, you have a handsome baby boy!"

Allen looked down at his son. His heart was beating with excitement. His smile said it all. You could see the happiness on his face as he stood gazing down at his son. Allen saw that his son was perfectly formed. He had all his toes and fingers. He had big feet and long, skinny legs. He had a lot of black hair that stood out all over his head. He was the most beautiful baby Allen had ever seen. The baby yawned and struggled unsuccessfully to open his eyes.

"Do you want to hold him?" Margaret asked.

"Sure do!" Allen replied with a big smile on his face.

Allen carried his son over to the bed where Nancy was sitting up. She had begun smiling as soon as Allen was given the baby to hold. As Allen sat down on the bed, he put his arm around Nancy and gave her a kiss.

"Nancy, we have a fine-looking son," Allen said with pride.

"Yes, we do, Allen Barger!" Nancy replied with a big smile.

"Henry Barger," Allen said.

"Your pa would be proud to have your first son carry his name."

CHAPTER 9

The two years following the birth of Henry were filled with both happy times and sad times and with much hard work. Between them, with the boys' help, John and Allen had cleared enough land to make a decent size corn crop. Both the houses had several improvements made to them. Barns had been built behind each house. The brothers now had more than forty acres enclosed in fence which meant they had more pasture than they needed for the stock, at least for now.

The high point of the year 1834, besides the birth of little Henry, was Anna giving birth to her first daughter, and Rebecca given birth to her first son. Like Allen and Nancy, Rebecca and John Parsons were very proud parents. On January 10, 1835, after several days of fever and difficulty in breathing, Sarah died of pneumonia. Her soul was quietly taken away by God in the early morning hours. She had been a pillar of support for both her sons and their families. She would be badly missed by all members of the family. John, Pointer, and Allen carried her back to Morgan County and buried her in the Union Cemetery next to her beloved husband, Henry Barger.

On May 5, 1836, Nancy gave birth to a beautiful baby girl. Margaret handled the chores of a midwife all by herself. Allen was surprised how much calmer he was the second time around, but anyway the water in the creek was warmer as he splashed across. Allen couldn't resist laughing to himself as he swam, and half waded the creek. "Next time, I resolve to remember to ride the horse."

Nancy and Allen named their new baby girl, Martha Jane Barger. Sarah's middle name had been Jane. Allen wanted his daughter to have part of his mother's name just as his son was named after his father, Henry.

On the last day of May 1836, Pointer returned to Morgan County to visit his sisters, Anna and Rebecca in Wartburg. While there, he met up with Mary Byrd a childhood acquaintance. Mary had grown into a beautiful woman. Pointer immediately took a liking to Mary, and they had a short courtship before Pointer asked Mary to be his wife.

Mary quickly said, "Yes, I will marry you, Pointer Barger!"

Mary's father, John Byrd had died and left her with over three hundred acres of land. She had already made a name for herself in Wartburg as being a lady with a good business head. She was making a good living off the land and was good at trading cattle and horses.

Mary was a Christian who right away admired Pointer for his ability to quote the scriptures of the Bible. It wasn't long that they were head-over-heels in love with each other.

On May 28, 1834, Pointer and Mary were married in the Bethany Baptist Church in the Union Hill community not far from Wartburg.

John and Allen Barger were both present for Pointer's wedding. They wouldn't have missed it for anything in the world. While in Wartburg, Allen and John stayed a couple of days with their sisters, Anna and Rebecca.

CHAPTER 10

For the next few years John and Allen had good years of crops and raised and sold several head of cattle and horses. Things were going well for both. They loved Bledsoe County and the little community of Tollet Mills.

In the spring of 1838 in Bledsoe County, several thousand Cherokee Indians were marched across Bledsoe County, five miles south of Pikeville. The Cherokees were being transferred from Georgia to their new home in Oklahoma. The whole county population of Pikeville came out to watch the Cherokees pass through their county.

Allen and Nancy felt compassion and pain for the Indians. As they passed by Allen turned to Nancy and said, "This is so shameful! Look, Nancy, how they herd them like sheep." Nancy shook her head in disbelief. "I don't think God meant this to happen. Lord, I hope you will forgive them for what they do."

Many of the older Indians were poor and appeared to suffer from hunger. The older women cried. Some of the older and weaker Indians were left to die in Bledsoe County. People from the church cared for those who were left behind. This disregard for human life was the cruelest thing Allen had ever experienced.

Up to 1804, the Cherokees had possessed the land in Bledsoe County. A treaty signed by the Cherokees and the government allowed the first settlers to move into the Sequatchie Valley in 1805. The early settlers found the Sequatchie Valley a farmer's paradise.

The trail the Cherokees passed over to get to their new home in Oklahoma was called The Trail of Tears, which got its name from the many tears that were shed by the Indians and from starvation and sickness suffered along the trail.

On May 10, 1839, while Allen was in Pikeville buying supplies he met Thomas Riley, a land speculator. Riley was in town recruiting settlers to join a wagon train he was guiding to a new settlement in Ripley County, Missouri. Mr. Riley was offering land for ten cents an acre for anyone who would agree to join his wagon train.

Mr. Riley described Ripley County as a place where wild game was plentiful and the soil fertile and easy to plow. He told Allen his wagon train would leave Bradley County, Tennessee, pass through Pikeville, and then head into Ripley County, following the same route the Cherokees had taken. As soon as he could reach his goal of signing up one hundred settlers he would be leaving. Mr. Riley was also recruiting people from McMinn, Rhea, White, Van Buren, Sequatchie, Grundy, Warren, and White counties in Tennessee.

Meeting up with Thomas Riley was the beginning of the first real conflict between John, Allen, and Nancy.

On the way home from Pikeville, Allen couldn't get Ripley County off his mind. When he was bothered about something, he always talked to John. Allen reached John's place just before sunset. As he climbed down from his wagon he saw Margaret drawing water from the well.

"Let me help you with those buckets," Allen said.

"Thank you, Allen," she said as she smiled. Margaret was a fine lady, whom everyone liked. Above all she was a fine Christian mother and wife. Allen had always admired her as a sister-in-law. Margaret had become Nancy's best friend, more like a sister. Allen was most appreciative to Margaret for filling a void in Nancy's life due to not having an immediate member of her family near.

"Where's that brother of mine?" Allen asked.

"He's at the barn feeding the stock."

After Allen carried the two buckets of water into the kitchen, he excused himself and went to the barn. As Allen reached the barn, John turned and said, "Hello, Allen! What are you up to?"

"I've just returned from getting supplies in Pikeville."

"Anything new going on in Pikeville?" John asked, concerned at the serious look on Allen's face.

"It's funny you asked that question. That's why I stopped by to see you," Allen said with a tone of excitement.

"What is it, Allen?" John asked being seriously concerned.

"I met a man named Thomas Riley from Bradley County in Pikeville today. He was recruiting settlers for a new settlement in Ripley County, Missouri."

"Ripley County, Missouri. Where on earth is that?"

"According to Riley, it's not far from Memphis, Tennessee. Riley is saying that the land is wonderful and for ten cents an acre, I can have all I want."

"Surely, you're not thinking about leaving Bledsoe County," John said.

"I can't get this off my mind. Something tells me I should seriously consider going to Missouri," Allen said.

"But, Allen, you have got a good farm right here in Bledsoe County. You've worked hard to get this place in top notch shape. Why would you want to start over?"

"I know it sounds crazy, but a new challenge excites me. When we came to Bledsoe County four years ago, Bledsoe County had already been established. Settlers had been here since 1805. Those earlier settlers were pioneers. I like the thought of being a pioneer," Allen said with excitement.

"Allen, what do you want me to say?" John asked with a sense of anger in his voice.

"I guess I wanted you to be as excited as I am and perhaps go to Missouri with us."

"Well, I don't share your excitement about being a pioneer. Maybe if I were as young as you it might be different, but I'm not, and I'm satisfied right here in Bledsoe County. I have my family to think about, and I am just getting a decent farm built up.

"Allen, think. It takes four or five years to get a good house and enough land cleared to make a good farm. You are just getting there now. Why give it all up?"

"John, I wish you would give it some consideration. We've been together a long time."

"Allen, I think you should go home and discuss this matter with Nancy. You may think differently about this tomorrow," John said with a tone of disappointment.

"You're right, John. I'll talk to you later," Allen said as he turned and walked away.

"Little brother, I'll visit with you tomorrow," John yelled as Allen was leaving.

As Allen pulled up in front of the house to unload the supplies, Nancy came to the door and announced that supper would be ready in twenty minutes. Little Henry ran out to hug his father while Martha Jane insisted on being picked up and hugged. After swapping kisses with the children, Allen sent Martha Jane back inside while he and Henry put the team away and handled the chores. Henry loved to help his father with the horses. After feeding the mules and giving the hogs corn, Allen and Henry returned to the house as Nancy was putting plates on the table.

"Go wash up. We're going to be ready to eat right shortly," Nancy said.

As Allen started across the room to wash his hands, Martha Jane and Henry both stood on chairs next to the washbasin to watch him. Martha Jane handed him a towel which made the three-year-old feel very important. Allen thanked her with exaggerated politeness, and Martha Jane curtsied as she always did, then giggled. Allen bowed back, with all the formality that he could muster. "What have you been doing today, young lady?" Allen asked Martha Jane.

"Just helping Ma," Martha Jane said as she smiled.

After washing his hands, Allen sat down at the table. Henry and Martha Jane seated themselves on opposite sides of the table on benches that ran the length of the table. Allen and Nancy sat at each end of the table in straight back chairs.

Nancy had prepared a good meal consisting of pork, fried potatoes, beans and corn bread. Allen loved Nancy's cooking. He commented several times during the meal how good things tasted. Somehow Allen's compliments tonight were a little different from usual Nancy thought but pretended she didn't suspect a thing.

It was at supper time when the family had time to share things together. Allen felt it was important for his kids to learn how to talk with adults. He also wanted to get to know his children and make them feel free to express themselves. Many children in Bledsoe County were not given the same privilege. Several parents who lived in the Tollet's Mill community disagreed with Allen and Nancy's viewpoint on raising children. Several of the parents felt children should be seen and not heard.

After the children shared, it was Nancy's time. "I've had a fine day. I finished sewing Martha Jane's dress. She will have a new dress to wear on Sunday." Martha Jane had a big smile on her face as her mother told of her new dress. She loved her new dress. Allen was always telling her how pretty she was.

"Allen, how was your day in Pikeville?" Nancy asked

"I met a Thomas Riley in Pikeville today who was recruiting settlers to move to Ripley County, Missouri. Land is ten cents an acre, and you can have all the bottom land you want. He is taking about a hundred families in a wagon train to settle the area."

"Where is Ripley County, Missouri?" Nancy asked.

"Mr. Riley says it's not far from Memphis, Tennessee."

"But, you have not even seen the land."

"Nancy, if it is half what Riley described, it will be wonderful."

"Did anyone in Pikeville seem to be interested in going with Mr. Riley?" Nancy asked.

"Riley says there are several who have signed up."

After a moment of silence, Allen said, "Nancy, I've been thinking a lot about Riley's offer. How would you feel about joining Riley's wagon train and joining other farmers in starting a new settlement in Ripley County, Missouri?"

"I like Bledsoe County, and I love our house and farm. Are you really serious about this?" she asked as she gathered everyone's plates from the table.

"Children, go outside and play while I help your mother with the dishes," Allen said knowing he had upset Nancy. He gathered up the remaining dishes that were left on the table and took them over to Nancy.

"Nancy, I really want you to give moving to Missouri some strong consideration."

"Allen, you've worked so hard here on this farm. It's a good farm. I don't understand how you could just leave everything behind," Nancy said with a trembling voice.

"I was hoping you'd be more understanding," Allen said with a little anger in his voice. He turned and went out on the front porch and sat down in his favorite rocking chair. In a few minutes Nancy joined Allen on the front porch. She sat beside him in another rocking chair. A few minutes of silence passed before Nancy reached across and took Allen by the hand.

"Allen, my love, when I married you, I made you a promise. I would go anywhere with you. I would stay with you during the good times and the bad times. Richer or poorer, we would always be together. My promise is still good tonight. I will follow you wherever you want to go. I know you love me and the kids, and I trust you will provide for our needs. Have you talked to John about this?" Nancy asked.

"Yes, I have. I stopped by his house on the way home. He, too, was surprised that I would want to leave our farm and go to a place that no one has ever heard of."

"When would we need to leave?"

"Riley said when he recruited one hundred settlers he would be leaving Bradley County. He was hoping to have his recruiting finished in a month."

"What about the farm, Allen?"

"Pointer may be interested in buying it from me. He has told me before that he would like to move back to Bledsoe County. I would be pleased if Pointer and Mary were to buy our property.

"What about their farm in Morgan County? He and Mary have over three hundred acres."

"Pointer has told me that only about seventy-five acres of the land in Morgan County was good for farming. The other acres are too rocky to get anything to grow. He would like our farm, I'm sure of that.

"The Byrds gave Mary a generous dowry, and she and Pointer still have some of that money left. Pointer should be able to purchase our farm without going heavy in debt. The corn crops he makes here on our farm will greatly help him pay off any debt he might incur by buying our farm. He will be taking over a farm with cleared fields, fenced pastures and a good solid barn. He will be able to do well here. For us to get started in Ripley County, the sale of our property here is important if we are to get a fresh start in Ripley County. Just think, we can purchase a lot of land for ten cents an acre."

"Didn't you say the land in Ripley County was new land? Isn't that going to take a lot of hard work to prepare for farming?"

"I realize it will be hard work, but I'm not afraid of hard work, Nancy," Allen replied with a sense of pride.

"I was just thinking. When we came here it took you, Pointer, John, and his boys a long time to get this land ready for farming. You won't have John and the boys to help in Ripley County."

"Nancy, please trust me. Things will be fine in Ripley County. The land is almost free. The money we get from this farm and the money we've got saved will give us a good start in Ripley County."

Nancy could see Allen had his mind made up about going to Ripley County. She would trust God to go with them every mile they traveled and to bless them upon their arrival in Ripley County. She couldn't get excited about being a pioneer, but she would support Allen in his decision.

In the next few days, Allen visited with Pointer about buying his property. Pointer was very interested. Over dinner that night, Pointer, John and Allen agreed on the sale of Allen's farm. It was arranged in less than forty-eight hours from the time that Allen had first heard of Ripley County. Allen was now irrevocably committed to starting his family on a new path.

Now that the farm was sold, Allen wrote Mr. Riley that he and his family would join his wagon train to Ripley County.

The move to Ripley County, Missouri, meant Allen and John might never see each other again. It was a long way from Bledsoe County, Tennessee. Two brothers who had spent most of their lives together would soon be parting ways.

CHAPTER 11

"Good-bye!" shouted Nancy as she waved farewell to Margaret, John, and their family. "Good-bye!" The clouds of June dust kicked up by the wagon immediately obscured John and his family. Nancy who maintained her composure up to this point broke down in sobs on Allen's shoulder. Allen slipped a comforting arm around her.

"I did not realize until now how close I have gotten to Margaret. She has become like a sister to me," Nancy said.

Allen nodded with understanding. He, too, was choking back emotion, knowing that he might never see his beloved brothers again.

Nancy stifling a sob continued, "You know when we got married I left my whole family behind. I haven't seen them but three times since we got married. But having John and Margaret just next door helped fill an empty spot in my heart. I don't know what I will do without them!"

Allen, watching his wife's tears, pondered for just a moment if maybe this whole idea was a mistake. No, he told himself, we have gone too far to turn back now. The farm is sold, and Tom Riley and his wagon train are going to meet us in Pikeville. Setting his jaw, he slapped the reins on the backs of the team and felt the wagon lurch forward with new purpose. Nancy perhaps reading his mind realized in that instant that they were committed to going to Missouri. She murmured something under her breath. Allen could not be sure, but he thought she said, "Whither thou goest, I will go," and then after drying her tears, sat up straight beside him.

As Allen entered Pikeville, he noticed several other wagons getting in line to make the long journey. He pulled his wagon up next to them and was pleasantly surprised to see Jacob Brooks waving a greeting. Nancy and Allen had gotten acquainted with the Brookes through social events in Bledsoe County. At least they knew another family who would be making the trip. There were forty families leaving Pikeville on June 12, 1839. Other families would join the wagon train as they traveled through central Tennessee.

Mr. Riley had chosen to take the northern route to Ripley County. It would start in Bradley County, Tennessee, cross central Tennessee and into southwestern Kentucky and southern Illinois. They would cross the Mississippi River north of Cape Girardeau, Missouri.

The wagon train grew as it traveled. At McMinnville, Tennessee, a dozen more families from Warren, Van Buren, Grundy and White counties were waiting to join up. As the wagon train pulled out of McMinnville, Allen felt a sudden lurch and pulled hard on the reins to stop the horses. A glance down showed him that the wheel was broken. He groaned with expectation of hours of backbreaking work followed by more hours of traveling into the night to overtake the train. Allen turned to Nancy and said, "We're going to be here a spell. You might as well let the children get down and play. But mind them so they don't wander off."

At that moment, Jacob Brooks wagon pulled alongside. He called out, "Allen, I'll lend you a hand." Allen tried to shout "thanks" over the rumble of the passing wagons, but figured it was useless to try. Jacob pulled his wagon to a stop and walked over to help.

Allen stepped down from the wagon, turned toward Jacob, and suddenly felt his hand being grabbed by a big, strong grip. A bearded man with a pipe protruding from a toothy grin shook Allen's hand with a firmness of a powerfully build man. "I'm Johnny Brawley, and this is my partner, Jim Hampton. It looks like you folks are having some problems."

Allen squinted through the dust being kicked up by the passing wagons. "Since it's a broken wheel, I figure if the two of us work quickly, we can get it fixed and catch up with the wagon train by midnight."

"Well," said Johnny with that same toothy grin, "I figure if the four of us work quick, we can catch up with the wagon train by dark." So, began a long friendship between the Bargers, the Brookses, Hamptons, and the Brawleys.

The four of them pitched in with gusto to raise the wagon and repair the wheel. Big Johnny Brawley was about the same age as Allen and Jacob. He and Jim Hampton were old hunting buddies from back in White County and were moving to Missouri largely on the strength of reports of bountiful game. Allen had not been able to do much hunting in the past couple of years. He enjoyed listening to their second-hand tales of woods swarming with deer, rabbits as big as dogs, and of streams full of fish.

By the time the wagon train reached Hopkinsville, Kentucky, the Brawleys, Hamptons, Brookses, and Bargers had become like family. They had aligned their wagons together and shared food and other items as they traveled. All had agreed when reaching Ripley County, they would settle in the same neighborhood.

As the wagon train traveled on to Golconda, Illinois, it began to experience some troubles. Some of the wheel spokes on several of the wagons began to break. The roads that the wagons had been traveling over were rough and full of holes. Some of the wagon wheels were not made to carry the weight of the wagons and to withstand the punishment of the rough roads. The wagon train was fortunate to have two blacksmiths traveling with it. Several of the men helped the blacksmiths repair the wagon wheels and reset the wheels to the wagons.

The wagon train averaged about ten miles a day. The humans could have stood a faster pace, but the livestock slowed them. Besides the horses, mules, and oxen pulling the wagons, there were a large herd of cattle being driven along behind the train. The wagons, loaded as they were, could not carry forage for so many animals, so it was necessary to stop each afternoon and let the animals graze and water. Several men from the train rode ahead each day to scout out the route-- not so much out of fear of getting lost, but out of the need to identify areas with good watering holes and good grass for the cattle.

The wagon train gained and lost travelers. Carissa Hampton, Jim's wife, gave birth to Joshua Hampton on the trail. She began having labor pains early in the morning and by the time the train stopped for camp the baby was on its way. Jim came running up to Allen's wagon all flustered and asked, "Nancy, have you ever helped deliver a baby?"

Nancy answered, "No, but if you will look at these youngsters in the back of my wagon, I have a little experience! Go check with Johnny Brawley. I think his mother, Matilda, said she had some experience as a midwife. I'll be along to help as soon as I get my youngsters fed."

Allen could not help thinking that he had probably been just as panicked the first time Nancy had given birth. He chuckled under his breath at the memory of charging into John's cabin to awaken him and Margaret that cold morning. Nancy stood looking at Allen sideways wondered what he thought was so funny, but she had no time to ask. She hurried as she fixed the children some corn cakes and beans then hurried over to the Hampton wagon to help. A few other ladies had already gathered around the wagon, so little help was needed. Still, Nancy remained to learn from an experienced midwife what to do in case she ever was needed to help deliver a baby. She returned to the Barger wagon after dark beaming, but exhausted. She only had time to murmur, "It's a boy!" to Allen before her head hit the pillow, and she was asleep.

Only a few days later, however, tragedy struck the train. Johnny Brawley was sitting by the Barger campfire sharing a pot of coffee with Allen, Jacob, and Jim when Mr. Riley arrived on horseback. Allen sensed something was wrong as he paused, dismounted, and walked over to where the group was sitting.

"Johnny, you had best come with me quickly," Riley said.

"What's happened, Riley?

"Your brother, Matthew, has been hurt."

"How bad is he?" Johnny asked.

"He was out hunting squirrels. I don't know all the details, but he's been shot. They are bringing him in on a farmer's cart now." Just then a shriek from the Brawley wagon revealed that Matthew's wife had also received the news. Allen, at a loss for words, watched the normally exuberant Johnny Brawley crumble before his eyes.

"Come on, Johnny, I will go with you to meet the cart. Jim, you ride into town and see if they have a doctor."

They didn't have a doctor in the little town, but it didn't matter. By the time the farm cart carrying Matthew reached the train, he had died. They buried him in a lonely grave just outside of Golconda, Illinois. Allen was heartbroken to watch Matthew's widow and orphans standing tearlessly beside the grave. Allen called Johnny off to the side and said, "You remember, Johnny, how you and I talked about buying adjoining land and being neighbors? Well, why don't we ask your brother's family to take up land next to both of us. I will pitch in to help them."

"That's awfully nice of you," Johnny said.

"Johnny," I believe we could make that happened. There must be a way to help Matthew's wife and children. She is now alone," Allen said.

"If you are worried don't be. I'm willing to help. If we all pitch in, I believe we could get a small house built for her and the children before winter sets in. I'm sure we can have our houses and Matthew's widow a house by October," Jim Hampton said.

Again, Jim Hampton had made his presence known. It wasn't long before the three of them were joined by Jacob Brooks. "I heard a little of the conversation. You can count me in on helping Matthew's widow and her family. I want to do what I can," he said.

The four could not help but burst out laughing which brought several disapproving glances from the bystanders at the funeral.

The wagon train reached Cape Girardeau on August 5. It took two days for the settlers to get their wagons across by ferry boat. Allen groaned at having to pay a whole dollar to get his wagon across and discussed with some of the others the possibility of building their own raft and saving the dollar, but eventually he had to give in and shell out the dollar.

On the fifth day after crossing the river at Cape Girardeau, they reached Van Buren, Missouri, the county seat for Ripley County. The town was filled with settlers purchasing materials and supplies. There were several buildings under construction. The little town of Van Buren had been founded only four years earlier. The bustle of activity boded well for this region. Where there is much happening, prosperity is bound to follow, Allen thought.

Still, it was not a very large town. Douglas Kelley ran the general store and a grist meal in town. James Murdock was the postmaster. Lee Ponder operated a hardware store, and Elijah Mason was the town's only blacksmith. There were only a few dozen other families living in the little town of Van Buren. Most of the earlier settlers had settled on their homesteads outside of town.

The arrival of Riley's wagon train had been expected and the people of Van Buren welcomed the new settlers with open arms. Some of the people who came with the wagon train were related to some of the earlier settlers. It was a time of celebration for them. There was a picnic on the town square, not actually a town square, just a cleared spot, but the people of Van Buren had big plans. After a feast on fried chicken and apple pie, the newcomers and their new neighbors square danced to the tune of a fiddle until late in the night.

Douglas Kelley had arranged a place just outside of Van Buren for the wagon train to camp. This would be a temporary camp for the new settlers until they could pick themselves a good spot. Within days of arriving families begin to buy up bottom lands around the county. Individual families left the main train camp saying goodbye to friends who had become very close during the journey.

Allen, Jim Hampton, Johnny Brawley, Jacob Brooks, and Stephen Lloyd scouted several likely areas before deciding on some prime land in Black River township, the southern part of Ripley County. This township would later become part of Reynolds County, Missouri, in 1845. They recorded their deeds and moved down there in mid-August, leaving the temporary camp at Van Buren. Allen was pleased that several of his friends would be living near. Not only could they share in the work, but his new neighbors had several young children who could be playmates to Henry and Martha Jane.

Everyone pitched in and helped build homes for each family. This job was completed before the first serious cold spell that winter. The logs for the homes were plentiful in Ripley County. It didn't take long with everyone working together to construct a cabin. John Brawley's father, William Brawley, a gifted carpenter, aided all five families in building their homes. The homes were like those left behind in Tennessee. Most were one room log buildings in which the entire family lived. Allen and Nancy's home was a large cabin with lofts similar to what Allen grew up in back in Morgan County.

Lighting for Allen and Nancy's cabin was accomplished from the flame of the fireplace, grease lamps, and candles. The fireplace, as usual, doubled for cooking meals as well as heating. Allen promised Nancy that he would continue building rooms on the house until it was finished.

By the time the new settlers finished their new homes it was too late for any kind of row crops to be planted. The settlers used their savings and other provisions they brought with them to get through the winter months.

In addition, Pointer's first payment for the sale of Allen's old farm was received in February which was a welcome addition to the Bargers' income. Pointer sent word that all was well, and that Allen and Nancy were sorely missed.

As advertised, Ripley County had an abundance of wild game. Allen and his friends spent several hours each day trapping and collecting animal furs. The furs were used to sell or barter for other needed household goods. The Bargers, Brawleys, Brookses, Hamptons, and Lloyds worked together in clearing and preparing land for the spring tobacco and corn crops. They also found time to build barns and a church for worshiping. They all shared the same religious beliefs, and all had been associated with Baptist churches back in Tennessee. James Hampton was very knowledgeable in the Bible and became the first preacher of the Black River Community Baptist Church.

Since the land was cheap, Allen bought two hundred acres of property in the Black River Community. Some of his land bordered a small creek that ran along the side of his property. The property along the creek was rich soil making it the best place to plant spring crops. The other portion of Allen's property was woods. He again faced many long hours of hard, back-breaking work to clear a lot of his land. This very thing was what Nancy reminded him of before leaving their beautiful home in Bledsoe County.

The life for the new settlers was very simple but carried with it long hours of arduous work and many hardships. When the federal census was taking in 1840, there were five hundred and sixty families living in Ripley County. Those families living near Allen and Nancy in the Black River Township were Richard Piles, Thomas Piles, Elijah Wardlow, Polly Jordan, Isaiah Hill, Jacob Hefley, William Brooks, William J. Davis, Griffith Steagall, John Brawley, Stephen Lloyd, James Hampton, Jacob Brooks, and William John Brawley, father to John Brawley.

The spring of 1840 was good for planting. Corn and tobacco were the principal row crops. Allen and his friends planted large gardens. They dried fruit and vegetables and stored them for the winter. Some were stored in fruit cellars and some stored in holes below the frost line. They salted, dried, and smoked their meat and hung the meats in a smoke house. Pigeons were killed in great numbers, fried, placed in jars or crocks and covered with hot grease. When fixed correctly the meat would keep for several weeks. The farmers relied heavy on wild meats and fish for their family diet. The one scarce ingredient that everyone used was salt. Salt had to be hauled long distance or made locally. To obtain salt locally, Nancy used huge kettles to boil water. As the water gradually disappeared into steam, the salt was left in the bottom of the kettle.

Nancy used wild honey as a sweetener and red pepper for seasoning. She would use wood ashes, lye, and meat scraps to make soap.

The farmers relied on milk cows for their milk, butter, and cheese. Chickens were raised for eggs, and geese for feather beds and pillows. Hogs for hams and bacon, and sheep to provide wool which was used in making clothing.

All feed for the animals had to be grown on the homesteads. The native blue stem grass of Ripley County was used for hay.

Nancy and her friends would get together to make quilts. After the quilt strips were pieced together the cloth was stretched on a wooden frame which hung from the ceiling of the cabin. The wooden frame was lowered and raised by ropes which were lapped over the rafters. It was an art to complete a quilt. Many friendships were made around a quilt frame. Quilts were very important during the winter to keep people warm because the log cabins were poorly heated. The only source of heat was the fireplace, and it couldn't keep the whole cabin warm.

The women worked as hard as the men during the day. If they were not working in the fields, they were at home chopping wood for the fireplace and preparing meals. Nancy chopped wood and little Henry carried the wood into the house and placed it in a large wood box near the fireplace.

One day when Nancy was chopping wood the axe came off the handle and struck Henry in the head. Henry collapsed, blood everywhere. Nancy thought she had killed him. She screamed, "Allen!" and fell to her knees beside Henry. He was still breathing. Her tears fell on his little chest as she immediately removed her apron and tied it around his head. She struggled to pick him up and carry him to the cabin. It was not an easy task since Nancy was now seven months pregnant with her third child.

Sobbing, "I didn't mean to hurt you, baby," she carried her son through the door and put him on the bed. She removed her apron from his head and immediately applied hog lard and packed the wound with cotton. Allen had not heard her scream and must have been out of an earshot from the cabin. After wrapping the wound with a piece of quilting cloth, she ran outside and frantically rang the big bell near the dug well. The bell was used to let Allen know when dinner and supper were about ready and was used to summons him should she need his help. This time she desperately needed his help. After ringing the bell, she rushed back into the house to attend Henry.

Allen was chopping away at the underbrush three hundred yards from the cabin when he heard the bell. At first, he was curious, as he laid his axe down and turned toward home. His first few steps were at a walk, but the urgency of the ringing caused him to break into a run.

A moment later Allen burst through the door panting and breathless. Martha Jane, his three-year-old, was the first thing he saw. Martha Jane was crying in the corner and was staring at the bed. Allen glanced at the bed and immediately saw his son motionless. Nancy was standing bent over holding his hand. Allen ran to the bed where he sank to his knees as he saw Henry laying there with bloodstained linens covering his forehead.

"Is he dead?" gasped Allen, his voice choking.

"He's not dead, Allen, but he's hurt badly!"

By this time Martha Jane had joined both Nancy and Allen at the bed. Nancy pulled Martha to her side and embraced her with one arm as she continued to wipe the blood from Henry's face. It was then that Henry, thankfully, stirred slightly. With that, a relief rushed over Allen and Nancy.

"Nancy, what's happened?" Allen asked with fear in his voice.

"It was an accident, Allen. Henry's hurt bad!"

"Nancy, can you tell me what happened?"

"I was chopping wood and the axe came off the handle and struck Henry in the head. I'm afraid he's going to die!" she said as she began to cry louder.

Allen tried to calm her. He pulled her near and embraced her as she continued to sob on his shoulder. At that moment both heard a groan coming from Henry. He was regaining consciousness. He opened his eyes and closed them again. He did this for several minutes as Nancy and Allen took turns wiping his face with cold clothes. Finally, he kept his eyes open. He looked up at his mother and said, "Why are you crying, Ma?"

Nancy bent down and kissed him on the forehead and said, "Son, there was an accident. The axe came off the handle and struck you in the head. You have been unconscious, and we've been very worried about you. How do you feel?" Nancy asked as she wiped the tears from her eyes.

"I'm a little dizzy, Ma," Henry answered as he closed his eyes.

"Nancy, I'm going to get Doc Steely. I'll be back as soon as I can," Allen said as he rushed out the front door.

"Please hurry, Allen," Nancy hollered.

It took Allen about an hour to return with Doc Steely. Doc Steely examined Henry and gave Nancy some ointment to use for the wound and told her to keep the wound clean.

"Doc, is he going to live?" Allen asked.

"He's a tough little boy. Yes, I believe he will live. He was lucky, one inch closer to the center of his head and it would been bad news," Doc Steely said as he closed his black medicine kit.

"Nancy, I'm going to walk Doc Steely back to his wagon. I'll be right back," Allen said.

Nancy went back to Henry and kissed him on the forehead. Henry looked up at her and smiled. Nancy felt relief for the first time. She knew God had given her back her son, and she would always be grateful.

Doc Steely was right. Henry quickly recovered from his head wound and soon returned to playing with his friends and doing his daily chores around the house.

Nancy continued her household responsibilities of preparing the family meals and drawing water and feeding the farm animals. She also milked the cow in the morning and afternoon. Everything had just gotten back to normal when Nancy started having labor pains. It was midmorning on August 17 when her contractions started. By dinner time, the contractions were about ten minutes apart. She could hardly wait for Allen to come in for dinner.

Allen entered the room as Nancy was setting the table. He went over to the kitchen and washed his hands. Nancy had not yet said anything about her contractions. As they sat eating, Allen noticed that Nancy wasn't smiling as she normally did. As Nancy got up from the table to get more bread from the oven, she grabbed her stomach. "What's wrong, Nancy?" Allen asked as he jumped up from his chair and crossed the room where Nancy was standing.

"Allen, I think you better go get Doc Steely," Nancy said, with her voice weak and her face twisted in pain.

"Is it the baby?" Allen asked.

"Yes, I believe it's getting close. My contractions are about five minutes apart," Nancy answered.

Allen took Nancy by the arm and helped her to the bedroom.

"I want you to lay down and don't be getting up. I'll go to William Brawley's place and ask Mrs. Matilda to come right over. I'll be back as soon as I can," Allen said as he rushed out.

Allen turned to Henry and said, "Henry, your ma is going to have a baby. I've got to go get some help. You and Martha Jane clear the table and you stay by your Ma's side. If she needs anything, you get it for her."

"I will, Pa," Henry replied.

Allen mounted his horse which was still saddled in front of his house. For the past two weeks he had taken his horse to the field with him. He knew the baby could come any day, and he wanted a quick way to return to the house should Nancy need him.

It was about 5:00 P.M. on August 17, 1840, that Nancy gave birth to her third child. Nancy had blessed Allen with another son. He had lots of black hair. They named him William Thomas Barger. William Thomas would later be called William T. by his family and friends.

CHAPTER 12

Allen and Nancy's family was steadily growing. They now had three children to feed and clothe. After getting married they decided they wanted a large family, and with the birth of William Thomas, they were well on their way.

Allen was a hard worker. He farmed from early spring to late fall. After his crops were harvested, he cut timber to sell. This was a way of life for most of the settlers in Ripley County.

The land in Ripley County was rocky and the soil was hard. Timber was plentiful and many of the settlers supplemented their income by cutting timber and trapping for furs.

Allen regretted several times leaving his good farm in Bledsoe County. He, along with other settlers from Tennessee, felt they had been misled by Thomas Riley, the wagon train trail boss, who recruited them to Ripley County. Mr. Riley had painted a false picture of what it would be like in Ripley County. Despite Allen's disappointment in his farm, he and Nancy were happy married and made the best of what God had given them.

On September 4, 1842, Nancy gave birth to her fourth child, a boy. She and Allen named him James Anderson Barger. James had strong lungs and made everyone aware he had entered the world.

While holding James, Allen looked at Nancy and said, "Someday this boy will make a great contribution to our country. I've always wanted a son who would preach the word of God. This boy may just be that person," Allen said as he laid James in Nancy's arms.

"I have a feeling James will have a mind of his own," Nancy said as she kissed his forehead.

Allen didn't know it at the time, but in later years, James Anderson would make a great contribution to his country.

Allen and Nancy continued to be active in community affairs. On Saturday nights, they joined their friends in the little town of Centerville, Missouri. Centerville was an active little town that came alive on Saturday nights with square dancing and pie suppers. Centerville would later become the county seat to Reynolds County, Missouri.

On Sunday mornings, Allen harnessed the mules, hitch them to the wagon, and off they went to attend the Black River Community Baptist Church. Allen wanted his children to know the importance of worshiping God in His house. He wanted to raise his children as his father raised him. Going to church was just another requirement in one's life as far as Allen was concerned.

Allen received letters from his brothers Pointer and John from time to time. Pointer wrote more often than John. The letters were all positive. No one had died, and the farms were producing money, and everyone was happy.

Pointer was now a preacher, just as Allen always thought he would be. He knew in his heart when he and Pointer shared the loft together back home in Morgan county, that Pointer would someday become a preacher. Pointer was always studying the Bible. He had become very knowledgeable of God's word. At this point in time, Pointer was a circuit preacher and was known throughout Morgan, Overton, Bledsoe, Rhea, and White counties in Tennessee. He preached wherever he was called on to preach and had a good reputation among those who previously heard him preach. He hoped someday to settle in as the head preacher of a local church, one where he could spend more time with his family.

He and Mary Byrd had started their family as well. When Pointer was away preaching, Mary managed the farm. Their children were not yet old enough to contribute much to farm chores. Mary was physically strong and anything she couldn't do, she hired someone to do it. The farm Allen sold to Pointer in Bledsoe County appeared to be doing well in providing a good living for Pointer and his family. The extra money Pointer received from his preaching helped the family income as well. Pointer was known throughout the counties he preached in as the preacher who rode the beautiful black horse with the white blaze down his forehead.

John and Margaret and their family were doing well on their farm in the community of Tollet's Mill.

Tollett was the only son John had living at home. He was a big help to John. In John's last letter he made mention that Tollett had met a nice girl, Tabitha Norris, whom he had become very fond of. He didn't know how much longer he would have Tollett around to help him.

On June 17, 1844, Nancy gave birth to her fifth child, another boy. She and Allen named him Jesse Allen Barger. Nancy wanted Jesse to carry Allen's name. This son, too, would someday make a great contribution to his country.

In 1845 the southern portion of what once was Ripley County and Shannon County became Reynolds County. On September 5, 1845, Centerville was named the county seat of Reynolds County.

It was at this time Allen entered politics. On August 1, 1845, He and his friend, John Brawley, were elected as two of the fourteen Justices of the Peace for Reynolds County.

On August 10, 1845, Nancy received a letter from her mother in Livingston, Tennessee. Nancy took the letter to the front porch where she sat in her favorite rocking chair. As she read the letter she began to cry.

Allen came to the front porch and saw Nancy crying, "Nancy, what's wrong?" Allen asked.

"It's a letter from Mother. She says Papa is in poor health. She's afraid he won't live much longer," Nancy said as she buried her face in her hands.

Allen knelt in front of Nancy and pulled her into his arms to comfort her. He held her close as she continued to cry. Allen hated to see Nancy cry. He hated to see the pain in her face. He knew what he must do.

"How would you like to take a trip back to Livingston to see your folks?"

Nancy looked at Allen with tears running down her cheeks and said, "Allen, could we? I've only seen my parents three times since we got married."

"The corn and tobacco crops are not yet ready for harvest. This would be a good time to go," Allen said.

"Do you really mean it?" Nancy said as she quickly threw herself forward, knocking Allen backward.

Allen sat up and Nancy flopped herself on his lap. "Yes, I really mean it."

"Allen Barger, you have made me the happiest woman in Reynolds County," she said, as she gave Allen a big kiss and a hug. "You are such a good man."

"When can we go?" Nancy asked.

"We should be able to leave in two days."

"I can be ready in one day," Nancy said.

"Let's don't get in too big a hurry. I've got to see if the Brawleys or the Lloyds can attend the stock while we are gone. If they can we will leave as soon as we can get packed."

"How are we going to get to Livingston?" Nancy asked.

"We will travel to Memphis, Tennessee, and from there we will make the rest of the trip by train.

"I'm so excited. I can't stand it!" Nancy said bouncing up and down on Allen's lap.

"You're really hurting my legs, Nancy," Allen said with a big smile.

"Sorry, my dear! I'm so happy! My parents will be so excited to see our children. They've never seen William T., James, and Jesse. Oh, I can't wait!" Nancy said as she finally quit bouncing on Allen's lap and ran into the house.

The Brawleys were happy to look after the stock while Allen and Nancy made their trip to Tennessee.

After dinner, Allen and Nancy prepared letters to the Bullocks and John and Pointer Barger in Bledsoe County. Allen wanted to see if John and Pointer could join them in Livingston for a few days' visit. He knew there would be no time to go to Morgan and Bledsoe counties.

Allen knew the letters would reach the Bullocks and John and Pointer before their arrival in Livingston. He asked Pointer to contact their sisters, Anna and Rebecca, who were living in Morgan County to come as well. He knew there would be plenty of camping room on the Bullock farm to accommodate lots of people. The family members would have to rough it a little, but it would be fun camping together.

On August 12, 1845, Allen and his family left for Livingston. After three days of tedious travel, they arrived in Livingston. Samuel Bullock, Nancy's brother, met them at the railroad station and carried them to the Bullock farm. The Bullocks had been waiting anxiously for the past three days. As soon as the wagon pulled up in front of the house, Daisy Bullock, Nancy's mother, and several of Nancy's family greeted them with hugs and kisses.

"Mother, you look well," Nancy said as she hugged her mother.

"You are as pretty as you ever were," Daisy Bullock said to her daughter.

"Children, come here and meet your grandmother," Nancy said to the children as she waved them to join her and her mother.

"Mother, this is Henry, our oldest. It's been awhile since you've seen him."

"My goodness Henry, I've not seen you in six years. You are certainly a nice-looking boy," his grandmother said as she hugged Henry.

"This is Martha Jane. She was a baby the last time you saw her."

"My goodness, child, you are the spitting image of your mother. You are beautiful," she said as she hugged Martha Jane and kissed her on the cheek.

"Mother, I want you to meet our latest three: William Thomas, James Anderson and Jesse Allen. Say hello to your grandma."

James stepped forward and gave his grandma a hug. He was not in the least bashful. He was followed by William T. and Jesse Allen.

"My lands! What a good-looking family you have!" Mrs. Bullock said as she was so excited to see everyone.

"Mother, where is Papa?" Nancy asked.

"Your father is in bed, Nancy. He is very ill."

"What's wrong with Papa?"

"He has dropsy. The doctor says he doesn't have long to live."

"May I see him?"

"You sure may. He made me promise that as soon as you arrived he wanted to see you," Daisy said as she took Nancy by the hand.

Daisy stopped and looked back at the children who were following them. "I think it would be best for the children to wait until you and Allen visit your papa. He's very weak. He may need to rest a spell before visiting with the children."

"Kids, let me have your attention. You heard what your grandmother said. Stay here with Uncle Samuel and play until we return. We shouldn't be long," Allen said.

As they entered the room, Daisy went over to Joseph and sat on the side of the bed. "Joseph, wake up, we've got company," Daisy said.

Joseph opened his eyes and looked immediately at Nancy. "My darling Nancy," he said as he reached out his hands.

Nancy walked over to Joseph as he put his arms around her and drew her near to him. Tears began to stream down both Joseph's and Nancy's faces. "You are so beautiful!"

"Thanks, Papa," Nancy said as she wiped back her tears with her hand.

"I've missed my beautiful Nancy."

"I've missed you too, Papa," Nancy replied as she wiped the tears from her father's cheek.

"I'm so glad you've come home. I didn't think I would ever see you again," Joseph said as he began to cry again.

At this time Allen stepped forward. "Papa, Allen is here too," Nancy said.

"Allen, it's so good to see you. Thanks for bringing my Nancy home," Joseph said as he reached out his hand to shake Allen's hand.

"Did you have a good trip?" Joseph asked.

"Yes, we did. We made it here in three days," Allen replied.

"Three days, that's really good, Allen," Joseph said as he began to cough.

Daisy handed Joseph a spit can, so he could spit the yellow mucous into the can. "Ya'll will have to excuse me. I know that doesn't look very good," Joseph said as he struggled to regain his breath. "When can I see the children?"

"Don't you think you had better rest a spell before the children come in?" Daisy asked.

"No, I want to see my grandchildren," Joseph said as he struggled to sit up in bed. "Very well, Joseph." Daisy said.

"I'll go get the children," Allen said.

As the children entered the room, Nancy looked at her father's face. He was smiling from ear to ear. "My Lord, Nancy, are these my beautiful grandchildren?" Joseph asked as he motioned the children to come closer. The children had never been around someone who was as sick as Joseph. They were a little scared.

"Come over here, kids, and meet your grandfather," Nancy said. Henry was the first to come close. "Papa, this is Henry. He's ten years old. Isn't he a big boy?" Nancy asked.

"Indeed, he is and handsome at that," Joseph replied.

"This is Martha Jane. She's seven years old."

"Come closer, young lady," Joseph said. Martha Jane made her way to the side of Joseph's bed. "My goodness, Nancy! She reminds me of you when you were her age. She's beautiful!" Joseph said as he picked up her small hand and held it close to his chest.

Martha seemed to sense his gentleness. She looked at Nancy and smiled.

"Papa, this is William Thomas. He's five years old, and James is three and Jesse is two."

"Come over here, boys, and let me get a better look at you," Joseph said.

"I'm really proud of my family, Papa," Nancy said.

"I can see why. You and Allen have done well. They are all beautiful children," Joseph said as he began to cough again. Daisy handed Joseph his spit can. "Maybe you had better take the children to the living room," Joseph said.

"I think that's a good idea," Daisy said as she led the children out of the room.

"Papa, is there anything I can do for you?" Nancy asked.

"You can get me some water. I'm really thirsty," Joseph said.

Nancy crossed to the other side of the bed where a pitcher of water was sitting on an end table. She poured a glass of water and handed it to her father. He drank about half of the water and said, "Come here and sit down by me, Nancy." Nancy returned to the other side of the bed and sat down by her father on the bed. "I'm dying, Nancy," Joseph said.

"Don't say that, Papa."

"It's true, my darling. I don't have long. I've been praying to God that he would find some way to let you come home. I needed to see my daughter before I die," Joseph said as tears began to roll down his cheeks.

"Papa, I prayed also that God would allow me to see you again, and He has. I wanted you to see my family." Nancy said as she too began to cry.

"I want to know, Nancy. Are you happy?"

"I'm very happy, Papa."

"I believe you are, Nancy. I can see it in your eyes. When I gave you permission to marry Allen Barger, I felt he would make you a good husband and provider. It appears he has done that."

"Yes, Papa, Allen is a good husband and provider. He's also a good father. He loves our children, and we are a happy family."

"I can now die in peace. You were the one that I've worried about. Your brothers and sisters have been close by. I knew what was going on in their lives, but I didn't know what was happening in your life. I've thought about you often. I'm so thankful that God has blessed you and Allen with such a nice family," Joseph said as he began to cough again.

"Papa, can I get you something for that cough?"

"Daisy will be coming in soon with my medicine. She's been a good wife and nurse. She's taking good care of me. I've been blessed by having Daisy," Joseph said as he closed his eyes.

"I'm going to leave now and let you get some rest," Nancy said.

Joseph opened his eyes and reached out his hand. Nancy took his hand in hers and bent down and kissed him on the forehead. "You get some rest, Papa."

"Nancy, I want to tell you one more thing before you go."

"What is it, Papa?"

"I'm leaving you some money. I'm going to divide the farm up and give Daisy her equal share of the farm, and the remaining part of the farm will go to your brothers. I'm giving you girls money which will equal the value of the land that I'm giving the boys. I know you won't be living here nor will your sisters. I felt you could find use for the money," Joseph said as he squeezed Nancy's hand.

"Papa, you don't have to give me anything. You know that."

"Yes, I do, Nancy. You're entitled to your share of this family's wealth. I'm not a rich person, but we're not poor. God has been good to me and Daisy. We want you children to share in our blessings," Joseph said as he began to cough again.

Nancy handed him the spit can and again up came a lot of yellow mucous. This was the hardest thing Nancy had ever had to stomach. She didn't want to get sick in front of her father, but she felt nauseated. "Papa, you get some rest now. I'll check on you in a while," Nancy said as she left the room.

When Nancy entered the living room, she found Allen, Daisy, and her brothers, and sisters visiting with each other in the living area. The youngsters had joined their new-found relatives outside in a game of Red Rover.

Nancy got her mother off to the side and said, "Mother, I kissed Papa on the forehead, I believe he has fever."

"He's been running fever off and on for two days now. It seems to get worse at night," Daisy said.

"Do you think infection is setting in?"

"Doc Baker came by yesterday to check on your father. He gave me medicine for his cough. He cautioned me about pneumonia and said pneumonia might get your father before the dropsy does.

"Isn't there anything we can do?"

"Everything is in God's hands, my dear."

On the third day after Allen and Nancy arrived at the Bullocks, Joseph took a turn for the worse. What they feared most had occurred. Joseph had pneumonia. He died on August 25, 1845. They buried him in the First Baptist Church Cemetery in Livingston.

On August 26, John and Margaret Barger and family, along with Pointer and his family, and Anna's and Rebecca's families arrived in Livingston from Bledsoe and Morgan Counties in Tennessee. Allen's relatives seem to help relieve some of the grief the family was experiencing from Joseph's death.

Nancy was so glad to see Margaret, who was like a sister. It was so good to be reunited with family.

For three days Allen, Nancy, and the children enjoyed sweet fellowship with their loved ones as they camped out on the Bullock farm. It was a time of joy, fun, and happiness.

On August 30th Allen's brothers and sisters with their family headed back to Morgan and Bledsoe counties. It had been a wonderful time which gave everyone an opportunity to reconnect as a family. There was never a quiet time other than when everyone was asleep. There were no complaints from anyone about having to sleep out under the stars. The weather was nice and warm, and it didn't rain.

On September 1, Allen's family said goodbye to Daisy Bullock and Nancy's family and started their long journey back to Reynolds County, Missouri.

Back in Reynolds County, Allen resumed his life as a farmer, timber worker, and a politician. He enjoyed being a justice of the peace. He enjoyed seeing the county grow and making government decisions necessary to govern the county.

On June 10, 1846, Nancy gave birth to their sixth child. This time it was a girl. They named her Mary Ann Barger. This made Allen four sons and two daughters.

After the birth of Mary Ann, Allen increased the size of his house. He built an additional room for the girls. The boys continued to use the loft.

In 1848, the first courthouse in Centerville was built. The county now had a permanent place to have their county meetings. Allen and John Brawley were instrumental in getting the courthouse built.

For the next several years Allen and his family kept adding additional members to their family, and more rooms to their house. Allen's farm was productive, and he and his family were enjoying a comfortable life style.

On September 12, 1848, Nancy gave birth to their fifth son, and seventh child. They named him George Washington Barger. George was spunky from the very minute he came into the world. He made his presence known. Nancy said many times, "This boy will need to be watched."

Two years later, on August 19, 1850, Nancy gave birth to a baby girl. This was Allen and Nancy's third daughter. They named her Delilah Elizabeth Barger. Delilah was a beautiful baby. She favored her mother.

It was a sight to be seen when Allen drove up in his wagon at The Community Baptist Church of Black River. The family wagon barely held Allen and Nancy's large family.

James Hampton, pastor and friend to Allen, stood at the front door on Sundays and greeted every church member as they entered the building. He got confused in trying to figure out who was who when it came to James and Jesse. They looked very much alike, and both had white hair.

It took an entire pew to seat the Barger family. To keep order in church, Allen assigned each member a place to sit on the pew. Henry the oldest sat at the end of the pew. He was followed by William T. and James who would sat next to William T. Martha Jane sat between James and Jesse to keep them from misbehaving. Everyone except James and Jesse was well behaved. James and Jesse were not bad, but wiggled a lot. Mary Ann sat by Jesse and Allen and Nancy held George Washington and Delilah in their laps. With these seating arrangements, Allen and Nancy had few problems with their children in church.

Allen and Nancy's children learned to sing at an early age. They enjoyed the singing part of church service but didn't care much about the preaching hour. During the song service their voices rang out as the sound mingled with others. The family's favorite hymn was "The Old Rugged Cross."

CHAPTER 13

Allen and Nancy wanted their children to read, write, and do arithmetic. In 1850, a meeting was held in Centerville to organize and build a school. The community turned out and, amid much eating and partying, raised the school in a single day. Allen joked that his children would go to school in a barn because the one room school house was shaped like a barn. The rafters were exposed and had a high-pitched roof. The school house could accommodate about forty children.

Ellen Brawley was chosen as the teacher. On the first day of school, Allen and Nancy enrolled five children: Henry, Martha Jane, William T., James, and Jesse.

After a few months, Henry decided school wasn't for him. He came home one day and said, "Pa, I need to talk with you. Since I can already read, write, and do arithmetic, I want to quit school."

Henry's request was immediately denied by both Nancy and Allen. They wanted all their children to have a good education and letting one of them quit was out of the question.

Despite Henry's dislike for school he continued. The school was a subscription school, which meant that Allen had to pay each week for each child who attended. With a whole tribe of children, it became expensive to send them to school, but Allen worked hard to earn enough money for his kids to attend.

The school was a "blab school," which was common on the frontier. The teacher, Mrs. Brawley recited the lessons aloud while Henry and other children repeated. This was necessary because of a shortage of books and paper. Sitting on long benches the children copied their lessons with chalk on slates saving the precious paper for when it was most needed. The children studied math by studying multiplication, division and fractions. Mrs. Brawley had no understanding of higher math and did not even try to teach it.

Math was not a problem for the Barger children. Nancy was well educated and knew math very well. Her early education back in Tennessee gave her a good understanding of math. She was able to teach her kids these math skills at home.

Much of the lessons involved reading, writing, spelling, and punctuation. The school had a few dog-eared McGuffey's Readers which were shared among the students. There was also a daily reading exercise from the Bible and a Bible study session. The children were mostly from Baptist and Methodist families with a few Presbyterians and Lutherans. There were no problems between the different denominations studying the Bible together.

History, a little science, and some geography rounded out the curriculum. The school met for two terms each year, in the spring from January to the end of April, and from early October until Christmas in the fall. The schedule was dictated by the need for the boys to help with the planting and the harvesting.

All forty students met in a one room school with a single teacher teaching children from age five to fifteen. In the cold weather they huddled together around the stove, scratching out their lessons with bits of chalk clutched in numb fingers. In warmer weather they swatted at flies which buzzed through the open windows to annoy the sweating students.

James loved reading books and read all he could get his hands on. His teacher, Mrs. Ellen Brawley, always enjoyed listening to James give his book reports. James had a vivid imagination, one that he used every time he gave a book report. He made his reports very interesting. During his presentations it was like he had been right there and participated in the events that took place in the book. He was both descriptive and dynamic in his delivery.

While Mrs. Brawley enjoyed James' vivid imagination and his knack for storytelling, he also caused her a few classroom problems. James loved to daydream. He fantasized a lot during class time. It was hard for Mrs. Brawley to keep James focused on the subject at hand. Although this occurred from time to time, he still made excellent grades.

Mrs. Brawley was a good teacher and a strong disciplinarian as well. One day during the lunch break, James and some of his friends decided to play a joke on Sally Hampton. They watched her enter the girls' outhouse and then tied a rope around the outhouse which prevented the door from being opened. The idea was to trap Sally Hampton inside. It worked. Just as Sally realized her predicament, Mrs. Brawley rang the bell to summon the students back from their lunch break for the afternoon class. Sally was left sobbing in the outhouse as four giggling boys trotted back to the school. After about half an hour of class Sally's absence was noted. James and the boys got a good whipping from Mrs. Brawley. This whipping was James' first and last received in school. He regretted the joke on Sally, not so much for the whipping, but because of the look on her tearful face as she was released from the outhouse. James was sorry he caused Sally to be upset.

In the days to come, Sally became James' first puppy love. Although the incident was over, the boys took turns standing guard outside the boys' outhouse for several weeks when each boy used the outhouse, just to make sure there was no retaliation.

A common practice in the Barger family was that if you got a whipping at school, you would get another one when you arrived home. James was really dreading sharing his whipping with the family at supper time.

Nancy always had a big pan of corn bread and buttermilk waiting for them when they arrived home from school. They loved hot corn bread and buttermilk which was needed before starting their afternoon farm chores. The boys' responsibilities were to milk the cows, feed the stock, and chop wood for heating and cooking. Sometimes the older boys would help Allen in the field.

At supper time everyone got to share what went on at school. On this night, James would get to share his experience about trapping Sally in the girls' outhouse. As he told his story the other children laughed. It was all that Allen and Nancy could do to refrain from laughing, but they felt compelled to act as parents on this occasion. Allen knew he would later have to punish James for his misbehavior.

James always felt he received double punishment for tying up the outhouse at school. Although he didn't like the custom at the time, he would later use the same practice in dealing with his own children.

On another occasion, James was again at the forefront of mischief in school. Mrs. Brawley came over to the Bargers' house one evening for dinner. James who figured that his recent mischief would be brought up at the dinner table was relieved when the meal passed amicably with Mrs. Brawley apparently ignoring James' recent misdeeds. It was only after the children had been sent to the loft while the adults enjoyed the warm spring evening on the porch that Mrs. Brawley mentioned the problem.

"Allen, I have a problem at the school, and I don't know what to do about it. Since you are on the board, I figured you might have some advice. And, since I think your son James is a ringleader in this problem, I figured you should know about it."

Allen, recalling the outhouse incident of a few months before figured another whipping was in store for James. But Mrs. Brawley continued, "It's been mighty warm the last two weeks, unseasonably so."

Allen nodded in agreement.

"About five or six days ago, after lunch, I called the children in as I usually do. About twenty of them came in."

"You have about forty enrolled, don't you?" Allen asked.

"Forty-two, to be exact. And twenty-one of them did not come in from lunch. They were gone. To be more exact, except for your younger son George, and a couple of the other five and six-year-old boys, every boy in the school had run off."

"Jesse, too?" asked Allen, figuring that wherever James went his little brother was bound to follow.

"Yes, him too. But the way I heard it from George and the girls, James is one of three ringleaders, along with Caleb

Hampton and Josiah Copeland. Well, anyway, as soon as the girls came in, I asked them where the boys had gone. Sally Hampton, who always delights in tattling on the boys ever since James tied her up in that outhouse, told me that they had headed for the swimming hole. There is a good spot in the creek only about two hundred yards from the school."

Allen laughed and said, "Well, I can't really blame them on a hot day. Did they come back after a while?"

"No," replied Ellen, "none of them came back that day or any day since."

Allen was no longer laughing. He now decided this was a serious matter since he was paying a lot of good money for a full day's schooling and James, Henry, and Jesse were getting only a half-day.

"And William T, too" added Ellen.

"The way I hear it, Jesse, William T., and Henry are all going along with this because James and a few other boys are the instigators."

"It's hard for me to believe that Henry and William T., would go along with James being that they are older than him, but since Henry doesn't like school I'm not surprised by his actions."

"But, Allen, what am I to do? If I went to the swimming hole and chased twenty naked boys back to school can you imagine the scandal? It would cost me my job. Half the school board would want me fired by nightfall. I can't very well send a girl down there to get them. That would create a big scandal as well."

"Ellen, if it was me, I would punish them. You have a paddle use it," Allen said.

"I can't do that very well either. I cannot punish one without punishing all, but there's no law that says those boys must be in school, and if I start to punish the whole lot of them, I am afraid about ten of the older ones will simply drop out of school. Some of the families are not as enthusiastic about education as you and Nancy are."

"I know," groaned Allen, reflecting on how much trouble it was to get some families to pay their subscriptions. Allen leaned back in his chair and looked up into the many stars in the sky. Finally, he leaned forward in his chair and grinned at Ellen. "I think I know what to do."

Ellen and Johnny Brawley leaned forward as Allen outlined his idea. Laughter from the front porch reached all the way to the loft where a drowsy James lay on his rope-mattress bed, wondering what the adults were laughing about.

The next day was blistering hot and the cool waters of the swimming hole would be inviting. Ellen was not surprised when exactly twenty-two students, all girls except for a couple of younger boys, returned to her classroom after lunch.

Her roll calls that morning had revealed two absences so that meant that eighteen of her students were swimming. She looked across the room and asked the students present to give her their attention.

"Students, I have a wonderful idea. Since it is such a pretty day why don't we find some shady spot to study outdoors? Bring your slates and your spellers!"

Ellen led the students out the door, across the road, and into the woods beyond. Before they had gone fifty feet, the girls began to giggle nervously, knowing that their route led directly to the swimming hole. Ahead, Ellen could hear shouts and splashing. Realizing that it would not do to surprise anyone who might be caught out of the water, Ellen announced to her students that they were going to sing as they walked and led them in a loud rendition of two verses of "Get Out the Way Old Dan Tucker." The singing served its desired purpose. By the time the girls reached the swimming hole all the boys were modestly cowering in the murky water with their clothes spread out on the grass beyond.

"This looks like a good place," Mrs. Brawley, said. Giggling, the girls followed her example, and sat upon the grass just a few feet from the water's edge. "Now, open your spellers to chapter seven. We are going to read it aloud. And read loudly, so that the boys can hear!"

Ellen knew that Allen's trick was working. From her vantage point she could see the boys' initial embarrassment give way to discomfort. Although the day was hot, the water was very cool. Kneeling in the shallow water, unable to move about and generate body warmth, the boys soon began to fall victim to the cold. In twenty minutes, they were fidgeting. In forty minutes, they were visibly shivering. And in fifty minutes they were whispering among themselves about what to do. After an hour of spelling lessons, Ellen figured the boys had had enough and led the girls back to the school house for their arithmetic lessons. Fifteen minutes later the door opened, and eighteen thoroughly chastised boys entered and took their seats. Ellen could not help but laugh at the drowned-rat looks on their faces which matched the drowned-rat look of their damp hair.

"I have decided," she announced, "that from now on, any of you boys who want to go swimming after lunch may do so. You have my permission. But next time it happens, the girls will have a spelling lesson and a math lesson outdoors"

CHAPTER 14

Most days after lunch the children played town ball in the schoolyard. Town ball was somewhat like modern baseball except there was only one out per side per inning, and the number of bases varied depending on how many children played.

Henry and William T. were usually picked first on opposite teams because they were older, and both were good at batting.

James particularly liked to be on Caleb Hampton's team since Caleb was his best friend. One day while Mrs. Brawley was inside, the children passed the lunch hour with an enthusiastic game of town ball.

After about half an hour of play, Mrs. Brawley, as usual rang the bell to summon the children back in for their afternoon classes. On this day, William T. swung a mighty swing and sent the crude leather ball sailing over the heads of the younger children and girls who played infield. Caleb, in the outfield, caught the ball as William T. scrambled around first base and headed for second. In modern baseball a catch would be an out, but in town ball the runners had to be tagged for an out. Caleb hurled the ball back over the heads of the younger children to his older brother, Robert, who was playing second base. William T. slid into second as Robert caught the ball.

"I'm safe!" shouted William T.

"Nope, I tagged you fair and square!" said Robert.

"Safe! That ball was nowhere close!"

"You're blind! I had you by a mile!"

James started to speak that he had seen it and that William T. had been out, but a little loyalty to his brother plus a fear of retaliation after school kept him quiet. Suddenly, William

T. tackled Robert and the two boys began rolling in the dust, flailing away at each other. William T. was bigger than Robert and soon started to get the upper hand. Blood ran from Robert's nose. Robert had a secret weapon. He had two brothers, Caleb and David, who charged into the fray knocking William T. off Robert and sending him sprawling in the dirt.

Jesse was down at the outhouse at that point, and George was too young to do anything but stand by helplessly. James hated to get involved in a fight against his friend Caleb and swore under his breath several words that Allen had ordered him never to say. The worst of it was that William T. had started it and that the Hamptons were in the right. Still there was nothing to do but uphold family honor and dive into the fray.

James caught David from behind and spun him around with one hand while landing a punch on his jaw that sent him sprawling. Before James could recover his balance, he was spun around by a mule-kick of a punch from Robert who had now regained his feet. Then, adding insult to injury, Caleb jabbed James hard in the jaw, and blood from James' lip now mixed with blood from his nose. James had the fleeting thought that his brother had started this and now was sitting back and letting James get the worst of it.

Just then, Mrs. Brawley arrived and separated the combatants. Sally Hampton had seen Robert getting the worst of it and had scampered for the schoolhouse to summon Mrs. Brawley. If she had just waited a moment until her three brothers had the upper hand over the two Bargers, she could have saved herself the trouble of getting the teacher.

Mrs. Brawley marched the boys into the classroom and seated them in opposite corners. Spelling lesson began as usual. James was aware that three pairs of eyes glared at him and William T. from the other corner and could not help glancing over at the Hampton brothers. Caleb, seeing the glance through an eye that was already beginning to blacken, mouthed the words, "I'm going to get you for that."

As the day went on, James was still angry with William T. for starting the fight and not coming to his aid. As far as James was concerned, school could have ended at noon. He could not concentrate on his studies. All he could think about is how he was going to get even with William T. He wanted William T. to feel physical pain as he had felt. After much deliberation he came up with a plan.

Earlier in the week, James had discovered, by accident, a big wasp nest which was in one of the wild plum bushes near the path which led across the Brawley's' farm. This path was used daily for the boys to take on the way back home. It was always the rule for William T. to be out front both ways. On that day, James was happy the rule was in place. As the boys started down the path, James began to collect a hand full of rocks as they approached the wild plum patch, James stopped. He made sure that Jesse and George were trailing behind him. As they approached the plum patch James stopped. He pretended to be lacing up his shoe. When James stopped Jesse and George stopped behind him. They were unaware of what James was going to do. James kept an eye on William T. as he approached the wasp nest. When William T. got within six feet of the wasps' nest, James let loose with his rocks, firing as fast as he could into the plum bush in which the nest was hung. His plan worked. The rocks disturbed the wasps enough that they began to swarm William T., stinging him as he started fighting them off and running as fast as his feet could carry him. James' plan had worked. As William T. continued to run down the path toward home, James bent over with laughter.

He had never seen William T. run so fast.

James turned to Jesse and George and said, "If Pa asked you about what happened here today, you are to say you don't know anything. I mean it. If you tell on me, I'll beat you up. No one is to know what went on here today. You got to promise me. Do you promise?"

"I promise," George said.

"I promise, too," Jesse said.

"This is our secret!" James said as he turned and started down the path.

When the boys reached home, Nancy and William T. we're sitting on the front porch. Nancy was attending to William T.'s stings. The wasps had stung him several times.

"What's going on, Ma?" James asked.

"William T. has been stung several times by wasps," Nancy replied.

"Is that the reason you were running so fast, William T.?" James asked.

William T. didn't answer. He was still moaning and groaning as Nancy applied a mixture of vinegar and snuff on the stings.

"You boys go inside and have your milk and cornbread. You've got some additional chores to do this afternoon," Nancy said.

As James entered the house he wondered if his mother suspected him being responsible for what had happened to William T. If she did, he would certainly not admit anything.

When everyone came in for supper, William T. was missing. "Where is William T?" Allen asked.

"I don't know," Nancy said.

"James, run out to the barn and see if William T. is still doing his chores. If he's there tell him to come on to supper. He can finish what he's doing after supper," Allen said.

James got up from the table and went immediately to the barn. As he approached the barn he heard William T. groaning. He went into the barn and found William T. lying on the ground near the hay stack. "William T., what's wrong with you?" James asked as he bent down over him.

"James, I'm so sick. Go get Pa. I think I'm dying!" At that time William T. began to vomit.

"Oh, dear God. What have I done?" James said to himself as he ran out of the barn. He was now realizing that William T. had gotten sick from the wasp stings.

James ran through the front door at full speed. "Pa, you've got to come quick. Something has happened to William T." James said with tears running down his face.

Allen sprung up from his chair and everyone followed him out the door down to the barn. "William, what's wrong, Son?" Allen asked.

"I hurt something awful, Pa." William was so pale. His skin had turned to a pale yellow. He was having a strong reaction to the wasp stings. It was at this time that Nancy informed Allen about the wasps' stings.

"I think the wasp stings are making him sick," Nancy explained.

"Let's get him in the house," Allen said.

As soon as William was in the house, Allen said, "Nancy, I'm going to run and get Doc Benson. I think William is going to need medical attention. I'll be back as soon as I can. Do whatever you can to make him comfortable."

James was now feeling terrible. If William T. died, he would be responsible for his death. He never dreamed something like this would happen. As he sat in one of the rocking chairs on the front porch he began to cry and pray. "O' God, please don't let my brother die. I beg you, please don't let William T. die. I'm to blame, God. Punish me, but please don't let William T. die. I'm so sorry for what I've done. Please, I beg of you. If you will let William T. live, I'll never do a foolish trick like that again."

As he finished his prayer, Jesse appeared on the front porch. "Do you think William T. is going to die?" Jesse asked.

"Lord, I pray not," James replied.

"Are you still happy about disturbing those wasps, James?" Jesse asked.

"No, Jesse, I didn't mean for William to get sick. You should know better," James said as he began to cry.

"I know you didn't mean to hurt him."

Allen returned with Doc Benson and hurried into the house. After Doc Benson examined William, he took Allen and Nancy to the side and said, "William is taking a bad turn for the worse from the wasp stings. I've seen several people who have been highly affected by wasp stings. I'm going to be perfectly honest with you. The next six hours is going to be crucial. William T. may not make it. I've seen several people die from wasp and hornets sting," Doc Benson said.

"You mean it's that bad?" Allen asked.

"I'm afraid so," Doc Benson answered.

"Is there anything we can do?" Nancy asked with tears running down her cheeks.

"We can get some whiskey into his system. This might help. Do you have any?" "Yes, I've got some in the kitchen cabinet," Allen replied.

Doc Benson, Allen, and Nancy stayed up all night administering cold towels to keep down the fever. William T. had fallen into a semi-coma state. Six hours came and went. There was no response from William T.

Allen and Nancy took turns praying for William T.

James was still on the front porch praying. Jesse had fallen asleep on the front porch in one of the other rocking chairs.

At 6:00 A.M. Allen heard the rooster crow. He looked at his son who still had not made a move nor sound. Another hour and half passed and still no response.

Suddenly at 7:45 A.M., William let out a groan. Nancy, Allen, and Doc Benson rushed to his side. As they looked down on him, William looked up and with a weak voice asked, "What happened to me?"

"Welcome back, Son," Allen said.

"You've given us all a big scare. You had a bad reaction to wasp stings, but I believe you are over the worst part," Allen said.

"Make sure he gets plenty of fluids and rest for the next few days. I do believe he's out of danger of dying," Doc Benson said.

"Praise the Lord! Praise the Lord!" Nancy said as she hugged Allen.

"Thanks for staying overnight, Doc," Allen said.

"That's my job, and I didn't want to lose William T. He's going to grow up to be a fine man," Doc Benson said as he turned, packed his medicine bag, and left the house.

Several days passed and William T. regained his strength and went back to school. James was still very much bothered about what he had done to his brother. He decided to confess to Allen and Nancy. After supper James asked to speak to Allen and Nancy alone on the front porch.

Allen and Nancy took their seats in the two rocking chairs on the front porch while James slid down the porch post and used it as a back rest as he sat facing his parents.

"What do you want to talk to us about, James?" Allen asked.

"This is really hard for me to do. Please try to understand that I didn't mean any harm to William T," James said as he dropped his head.

"James, what are you trying to say?" Nancy asked.

"It's all my fault that William T. almost died from wasp stings," James said as tears began to roll down his cheeks.

"What are you trying to tell us, Son?" Allen asked.

"I was mad at William T. because he started a fight with Robert Hampton at school. After he started the fight Robert, Caleb, and David all pounced on William T. and were getting the best of him until I jumped in to help him. After I did, William T. stood back and let me get the worst end of everything. That really made me mad. Anyway, I had discovered the wasp nest earlier in the week when I was picking some wild plums. One of them wasps stung me, but it didn't hurt me enough to tell you, Ma. I decided I would use the wasps to get back at William T. I wanted him to feel pain as I felt when my lip and nose got busted. As William T. passed the wild plum bush, I fired several rocks into the bush, hitting the wasp nest. The wasps swarmed William T. I thought it was so funny. I didn't have any idea the wasps would endanger his life. I promise you, I didn't!" James said as he made his plea for understanding.

Nancy looked at Allen with tears in her eyes. She knew James wouldn't do anything intentionally that would endanger someone's life. His confession took a lot of courage, and she respected him for being honest.

Allen looked at Nancy and shook his head. He then looked back at James and said, "Son, we've all done things we regret later. This appears to be one of those foolish things which you can learn from. I'm disappointed in you, but at the same time, I'm proud of you. I've always taught you boys that confession is good for the soul."

"I'm truly sorry. I'm asking for your forgiveness," James said.

"We will certainly forgive you, James, but there is something that you must do first."

"What is it, Pa?"

"You must ask William T's. forgiveness."

"I'm ready, Pa," James said.

"Come on. Let's go talk to William T.," Allen said.

"William T., James has something he wants to say to you."

"I'm responsible for you being stung by those wasps. I was mad at you for letting me get the worst end of the fight with the Hamptons. A fight that you started in the first place. I wanted to get back at you in a bad way. I see now that Satan led me to do what I did. I want to apologize to you and ask you to forgive me. I didn't realize you would be endangered by them wasp stings. I never dreamed that would happen. I'm truly sorry!" James said as tears begin to run down his cheeks.

William T. set up in bed. "It's going to be all right, James. I was wrong in starting the fight. I was also wrong in standing by and letting you take the punches you took. I might have done the same mean trick to you. I don't know, but I accept your apology," William T. said as he reached out his hand to shake James hand.

"Thanks, William T.," James said.

"Let's forget this incident ever happened," William T. said.

Allen and Nancy were proud of both their boys. They had handled the situation like grown men. Letting the boys settle this problem kept them from taking further action toward James. They agreed that the pain and anguish James had experienced through the ordeal was enough punishment. He had learned a valuable lesson!

CHAPTER 15

When the 1850 Reynolds County federal census was taken, there were 293 log cabins sparsely placed across Reynolds County's rugged terrain. These households averaged just over six people per household. The county had a population of about eighteen hundred people and covered about 817 square miles.

The next decade would find the county moving slowly but steadily forward with only one pending monumental event consuming every man's thoughts and concerns. This concern was what to do about the slavery question.

This uncertainty, as early as 1850, was starting to slow the county's progress as the government could not focus on the needs of its people because they were too preoccupied with the slavery issue.

Allen and Nancy believed ownership of slaves was wrong. They didn't own any slaves and never once thought of the possibility. Several of their neighbors in the community of Redford owned slaves. The issue of slavery had sprung up all over the United States. The slavery issue put the Northern states against the Southern states. Those families who owned slaves in Reynolds County were strong in their convictions of having the right to own slaves. They looked to slavery for free labor and prosperity at the same time. One might say, it was a status measurement among those who believed in slavery and ownership.

There was much discussion about slavery around the Bargers' dinner table. Allen and Nancy believed in teaching their children their convictions. They wanted their children to know they opposed ownership of slaves. They considered it a cruel act of humanity. They believed no one should own another person.

James shared his parents' views on slavery. He would never forget an incident that occurred at Black Creek swimming hole. He and Jesse had made friends with two of Mr. James Steagall's slave boys, Joe and Sam. On one afternoon, Joe removed his shirt to go swimming. James and Jesse both noticed the whelps on Joe's back with blood oozing from them.

James asked, "Where did you get those whelps on your back?"

"Oh, them come from Master Steagall's bull whip."

"You mean Mr. Steagall whipped you with his bull whip?" James asked.

"Yesim, he whupped me good," Joe said.

"Why would he do such a horrible thing?" James asked in disbelief, shaking his head from side to side.

"Master Steagall says I mess around and I doesn't do my work. He tied my hands together and strung me up to the big oak tree in his front yard. He says, 'Boy, let this be a lesson to you and all who's watching.' I's thinking he's going to beat me to death. I's crying as loud as I can. I's thinking he would stop but the louder I cry, the more he whips me. I finally pass out and he stopped. I'll tell you, he's a mean man. I hate him!" Joe said.

James could hardly believe what he was seeing and hearing. How could Mr. Steagall, a deacon at Black River Baptist Church be so cruel to his slaves? How could he do this and still be a Christian?

From that day forward James considered Mr. Steagall to be a hypocrite and avoided him like the plague. He had no use for any man who was a hypocrite.

James was the sharpshooter in the family. He could hit anything within his sights. He had already become one of the best hunters in Reynolds County.

Because of James love for hunting and trapping, he could always be depended upon to supply meat for the table. His love for hunting and fishing was shared by his brother Jesse. The two were inseparable. Where one was found, the other could be found also.

Each year after selling the winter furs, Allen would make a trip to St. Louis for supplies. These trips would take about two weeks during the winter months. The sale of the furs coincided with purchasing food and clothing for Allen and Nancy's large family.

While Allen was in St. Louis, he used a portion of the money from the furs to purchase a hunting rifle. He would keep this rifle hidden until James' fourteenth birthday.

On September 12, 1854, James turned fourteen. He arose early in the morning and crawled down the ladder into the kitchen where Nancy was preparing breakfast. "What are you cooking, Ma?" James asked.

"Just the same old thing I cook every morning," Nancy replied.

"It sure smells good this morning," James said.

"I tell you what, James, you go get some fresh water from the well, and I'll let you sneak a piece of bacon while it's hot."

"I'll be right back," James said as he picked up the water bucket and ran out of the house.

"What's James doing up so early?" Allen asked as he came through the bedroom door.

"It's his birthday, you know. I think he's just excited about turning fourteen. He may be wondering if we remember it's his birthday," Nancy said.

"Remember, I'm going to John Brawley's this afternoon and pick up the pup. I'll give James plenty of chores to do to keep him occupied while I'm gone. Tonight, when he comes in for supper, we will surprise him with the new rifle and the pup," Allen said.

James re-entered the room with the fresh bucket of water. "You are up mighty early this morning, James," Allen said.

"I couldn't sleep, Pa."

Nancy motioned for James to come over to the stove where she handed him a piece of hot bacon.

"Thanks, Ma."

"James, today I want you and your brothers to finish those jobs you've been working on. I'll be gone most of the day, and the barn chores must be finished before supper. You boys make sure they are all done."

"Yes, Pa," James replied.

"Call me when breakfast is ready," James said as he left to sit on the front porch.

"Breakfast will be ready in about thirty minutes," Nancy said.

"I think he's a little disappointed we've not said anything about his birthday," Nancy said as she stirred the gravy in the frying pan.

"He won't be disappointed after supper. By the way, I hope you've reminded the kids not to give this surprise birthday party away."

"They know not to say a word."

James couldn't believe the day was passing so slow. Why hadn't someone mentioned his birthday? It was almost time for supper. He finished his chores and headed for the house. As he entered the front door, he was greeted with, "Happy Birthday, James! Happy Fourteenth Birthday!" Everyone had shouted. James's face lit up like a lantern. He was completely caught off guard. His family had successfully pulled this surprise party off.

"Come on in here, James," Allen said as he motioned James into the house. "Did you think we forgot your birthday?" Allen asked.

"I really did, Pa."

"Well, we didn't. Let's all sit and enjoy this good birthday meal your mother has prepared for you."

After seeing that most everyone had finished with supper Allen rose from his chair and said, "Nancy, Henry and I will be right back for some of that birthday cake. Ya'll excuse us."

Jesse and George Washington began to giggle. Nancy cut her eyes around at them and they immediately stopped giggling. James wondered what was so funny.

Allen came through the back door and said, "James, I want you to close your eyes. Do you have your eyes closed?"

"Yes, Pa," James replied.

"Now you can open your eyes." When James opened his eyes, Henry was standing by James' holding a pup. The pup was a black hound. He began to lick James in the face.

"Is he mine, Pa?" James asked as Henry handed the pup to James.

"He's all yours, Son," Allen replied.

"I love him, Pa," James said with excitement.

"He came from John Brawley's prized coon dog. She's the best full-blood coon dog in Reynolds County. Your pup has some fine blood in him. If he turns out like his mother, he will be the best coon dog in Reynolds County," Allen said.

"Thanks, Pa, I love him."

"We have something else for you," Allen said as he handed James a long slender box wrapped in brown paper.

"What is it, Pa?"

"Open it, Son," Allen replied.

Before trying to open the box, James passed his puppy to Jesse to hold. The puppy had become overly aggressive in wanting to help James open his present.

James quickly pulled the hunting rifle from the box. His eyes became bigger and bigger as he eyed the beautiful rifle. "I can't believe it. I just can't believe it. This must cost you a pretty penny, Pa," James said with excitement.

"We all decided since you bring in the meat for the family table you deserved your own gun," Allen said.

"Thanks, Pa. This is the best birthday I've ever had," James said as he kept eye-balling his beautiful rifle.

What started out to be a bad day for James had turned into one of the best days of his life. He named his new rifle Old Faithful, and his puppy he called King. King would become his best companion and friend. Old Faithful would make him famous.

CHAPTER 16

James had built a reputation in Reynolds County. He had become known as being the best shooter, best trapper, the best student in the Redford Community School. His skills in writing, math, and reading earned him the privilege of becoming Mrs. Ellen Brawley's assistant teacher. His writing skills, in the opinion of Mrs. Brawley, were equal to some famous authors. Mrs. Brawley was amazed with James' ability to communicate with the other students.

James was not a paid assistant but counted it a blessing to help Mrs. Brawley teach. He soon found he became more knowledgeable of the subject matter by teaching.

James had won about every shooting contest in Reynolds County. He had gotten the nickname, The Young Turkey Eye. Since turkeys were known for their keen eye sight, James was pleased with this nickname.

Reynolds County was blessed with an abundance of wild game. During the winter months, James and his brothers stayed busy trapping near Black Creek Ridge Mountain near Redford. Trapping was a way of life for most families living in the neighborhood. Wild game was plentiful and fur trading was a decent way of supplementing one's income, especially during the winter months when farming was at a standstill.

Several trappers in the Redford Community were experiencing a loss of income due to poachers problem. James and his brothers had also fell victim to the poachers as well.

The Barger brothers decided enough was enough and set out to catch the poacher. The brothers felt the poacher had to be someone who was well acquainted with the territory and who knew where the traps were being set. Henry, being the oldest, devised a plan. The brothers would divide into two parties and have two lookout stations which would overlook their trapping area.

Henry, William T., and George would make up one party while James and Jesse paired together. Each party would be located at a position overlooking their trapping area. It would be a joint adventure to trap the poacher and arrest him.

On the cold, snowy morning of December 17th, the Barger brothers set out to put their plan into action. After reaching their trapping area, they broke tops from young pine trees and used them to cover their trail. They settled in their designated areas to wait for the poacher. One hour passed and nothing happened. Everyone was shivering from the bitter cold. The second hour passed without any action. George, the youngest Barger, was getting tired and restless. He started complaining about being cold and wanted to abandon the project and return home. Suddenly, Henry saw something moving near one of the trap areas. He quieted George and instructed him to be still. Sure enough, it was the poacher, not just one, but two. The poachers were in the process of robbing the traps when Henry instructed George to go tell James and Jesse. When James saw George running toward him, he knew something was happening. As George got within fifteen feet of James and Jesse, he shouted, "Come on, the poachers are here! There are two of them!"

"George be quiet!" James whispered

"George, go back and tell Henry we are moving into our positions. Go on now and be quiet!" James said.

Henry's plan was to surround the poachers from all four sides. Henry would take the north side which would be in front of the poachers, William T. would take the west side, Jesse would come up from the south, and James would take the east side. George being the youngest would stay behind in case this plan didn't work and go for help should the plan backfire.

Once the boys were in position, they would wave at each other and make their move toward the poachers. Hoping to arrive at the poachers at the same time.

As the poachers were busy robbing the traps, the boys moved in. Henry arrived on the scene first and was waiting for the other three to close in. One of the poachers spotted Henry and started for his gun. Henry shouted, "Get your hands up. You are surrounded."

The poachers didn't believe Henry, and went for their guns. Henry didn't want to kill anyone, but he would if he needed to. The others heard the commotion but weren't close enough to help poor Henry.

One of the poachers picked up his gun and fired at Henry. Henry dropped to the ground.

James had seen his brother fall to the ground. Thinking Henry might be dead, James aimed his rifle and shot the poacher who shot Henry. The poacher fell to the ground. The second poacher turned in the direction of James with his gun in hand.

James shouted, "Drop your gun! You are surrounded."

By this time, William T. and Jesse began to shout, "Drop your gun or we'll shoot you!"

The poacher knowing, he was surrounded, dropped his gun and James, Jesse, and William T. converged on the two poachers from three directions.

Henry seeing that everything was under control stood up and made his way toward his brothers.

"Henry, are you okay?" William T. asked.

"I'm fine. The bullet just grazed my arm. I'm okay."

As it turned out, James had chosen to shoot the poacher in the arm so not to kill him. He could have easily killed both and confessed later that he almost did after seeing Henry fall to the ground. "For a split second, I was going to kill the poacher who shot Henry but decided against it."

Word passed quickly throughout the county how the Barger brothers captured the poachers. They were made heroes in Reynolds County.

A celebration was held in Centerville for the Barger brothers. They were all recognized for their bravery and courageous law enforcement.

During the same year the poachers were apprehended, James Barger and Sally Hampton developed a more-than-friends relationship. From the time James was fourteen years old, he had had a crush on Sally. Although, when it came to girls, he was shy and hadn't found the nerve to get down to serious business. It was only when he became sixteen that his hormones took over and gave him courage to approach Sally.

James and Sally's first real date came at a pie supper held at the Black Creek Baptist Church.

Allen instructed his boys to bid on a girl's pie. He said, "This is a fund raiser for our church and we all need to take part. You boys need to know what it's like to share a pie with a beautiful young lady." James wasn't sure he agreed with his father, but he would take part.

When it came time to bid on Sally's coconut pie, James bid four bits and was awarded the pie. This was the beginning of an innocent courtship. James and Sally enjoyed the church picnics together. They enjoyed going fishing together, but not the company of their brothers and sisters who were instructed to tag along.

On Saturday nights, James and Sally square danced with the adults at the weekly square dances in Centerville.

For several weeks, James thought he might be falling in love with Sally. His heart and mind told him she was everything he wanted in a girlfriend. He had dreamed of being alone with her several times and wondered what it would be like to kiss her.

The opportunity to kiss Sally finally came during a Saturday night square dance in Centerville. James and Sally had danced every dance the fiddler had played. Being exhausted they decided to get some lemonade and take a stroll down by the horse corral.

"Sally, I've been thinking a lot about you lately," James said.

"In what way, James."

"Well, I, I, ...," James stumbled.

"James, what are you trying to say?"

"What would you say if I asked you if I could kiss you?" James finally got it out of his mouth.

"I thought you were never going to ask me," Sally said with a smile.

"Then, you don't mind?"

"No, James, I don't mind."

James moved close and pulled Sally near him. He had never kissed a girl and wasn't sure how to do it.

"You will be the first girl I've kissed," James said with a little fear in his voice.

"I've never been kissed either," Sally quickly said.

James gently took Sally's face in his hands as their lips met. The warmth of Sally's lips told James that this was a good thing.

"Did you like it?"

"Yes, I liked it," Sally said with a smile which melted James' heart.

"Can we try it again?"

Sally responded with a big, "Yes."

A moment later, Sally pulled away and said, "We have to stop kissing, James."

"Why?"

"James, I have this funny feeling which comes over me every time we kiss. I'm afraid we will do something which God doesn't approve of."

"Sally, I'm having the same feelings. It feels really good to me."

Sally looked at James with a big smile. "I think we need to go back to the dance," Sally said as she grabbed James' hand and took off in the direction of the dance.

James and Caleb Hampton also became the best of friends during James and Sally's courtship. The fight which occurred earlier in their lives was the last conflict the two had.

On March 7, 1856, Nancy gave birth to John Wesley Barger. He was their ninth child and their sixth son. John would be the last child born to Allen and Nancy.

In June 1856, the St. Louis-Iron Mountain Railroad reached Pilot Knob. The opening of the railroad to St. Louis and Saint

Genevieve proved to be one of the greatest things to happen to Reynolds and Iron counties. The farmers were now able to transport their supplies to Pilot Knob where the train stopped. They no longer had to make the long, tedious two or three-week trips to St. Louis by wagon to sell their crops and buy supplies. The railway proved to foster the economy for both Iron and Reynolds Counties.

Henry got a job working with the railroad. This was his first job away from home. He was hired as a loading dock employee. Although his job was hard, he enjoyed getting to know people and most of all the money.

The railroad boosted both the population and economy in Reynolds and Iron counties. A large segment of the growth came from the Northern states. The new settlers coming to Reynolds County believed slavery should be abolished. Their beliefs clashed with the older settlers living in the County. Slavery became the hottest issue at the Reynolds county government meetings.

Besides the issue of slavery, came the question of whether Missouri should secede from the union. Some felt the County should remain neutral. Others felt they should stay a part of the union, and others felt they should secede. The county was in turmoil.

Allen grew tired of the constant debating and bickering of the people. He became frustrated trying to serve in a county government which was also split in their views.

Another issue confronted the family. William T. had been caught with a neighbor's daughter in an unbecoming, compromising situation. The neighbor was outraged and threatened to kill William T. if he ever set foot back on his property. This incident was causing the family a great deal of grief.

Jacob Brooks, a good friend of Allen's, had left Reynolds County in 1853 and bought a farm in Moniteau County, Missouri. His letters to Allen described the farm land in Moniteau County as "flat, rich, and not rocky like the land in Reynolds County."

Mr. Brooks wrote letters from California, Missouri, encouraging Allen to join him in Moniteau County. These letters from Jacob Brooks encouraged Allen to sell his property and move to Moniteau County.

Allen had grown to love Reynolds County but the bickering and division between the people were getting worse. The incident with William T. made it even more important to leave. Allen had always put the safety of his family first and the issue with William T. was serious. He needed to get his family out of Reynolds County.

After a county meeting on September 15, 1858, Allen called his family together to discuss his plans to move to Moniteau County. As customary in the Bargers' household, all family members had an opportunity to express their opinions on family issues. This night would be no different.

Allen gave each member an opportunity to voice an opinion about moving to Moniteau County. He started with Henry who was the oldest. Since Henry had a job working for the railroad, Allen didn't know how he would feel about leaving his job.

"Henry, since you are the oldest, how do you feel about moving?" Allen asked.

"Father, I trust your judgment. If you think it's best we move on, I'm ready to go."

"What about you, Martha Jane?" Allen asked.

"It's all right with me, Father," She replied.

"William T., what about you?"

"I know I'm partly the reason you feel we need to leave. I'm sorry for bringing shame on this family. I need a new beginning. I'm ready to go," he said.

"James, what are your feelings?" Allen asked.

Before James could answer, Jesse said, "Will he be able to bring Sally Hampton with him?" Everyone laughed.

"That's very funny, Jesse," James said as he gave Jesse an evil look.

"Well, Son, what do you think?" Allen asked.

"Will there be some good hunting and fishing in Moniteau County?" James asked while everyone chuckled.

"I'm sure there'll be plenty," Allen said with a smile.

"Jesse, what do you think?" Allen asked.

"I'm ready!"

"What about the rest of you?" Allen asked.

"Pa, when do you suppose we'll be leaving?" Henry asked.

"I'm going to Centerville tomorrow and spread the word that our farm is for sale. When the farm sells, we'll leave," Allen said.

Two weeks later, Allen found a buyer who would pay him market value for his property.

The Bargers attended their last Saturday square dance in Centerville on October 1, 1858. It was at this square dance that James and Sally said goodbye.

James really didn't know how to approach Sally with the news of his family leaving. He had struggled for days trying to find the right words to say to the girl he loved and wanted to marry. Ready or not he realized he must tell Sally.

"Sally, let's go down by the old corral. I need to talk to you," James whispered in her ear. Sally was more than ready to follow James A. Barger anywhere.

"You've not been yourself tonight, James. What is it?" Sally asked.

"Pa is moving us to Moniteau County next week," James said.

"You and your family are leaving?"

"I'm afraid so," James said as he reached out and grabbed both of Sally's hands.

"James, I don't want you to leave. What about us? What about our plans?" Sally said with tears beginning to run down her cheeks.

"Sally, we can write each other and someday I'll come back for you and we'll get married."

"O, James, I don't think I can stand this," Sally said as she began to cry.

James put his arms around her and held her tight. "Sally, I wish I could stay here and be with you for the rest of my life, but I must go with my family. Pa has already sold the farm, and we leave next Tuesday."

"I love you, James. What am I going to do without you?"

"I love you too, Sally. I'll write you often. You can write me, and when I get older and on my own, I'll come for you," James said convincingly.

"I wish I could believe that, James."

"You can, Sally! I promise you."

"James, you'll always be my first love. Whatever happens I want you to know that. I don't want you to make me a promise that you can't keep."

"I love you, Sally, and I'll keep my promise."

CHAPTER 17

On October 15, 1858, Allen loaded up his two wagons with his family belongings and headed out for Moniteau County. He would drive one wagon while Henry drove the other. The younger boys herded the family's livestock behind the wagons. It took them two-weeks to make the trip. They arrived in the city of California, the county seat of Moniteau, County, exhausted and shivering from an early frost.

Jacob Brooks and his family came to meet them. Allen and Jacob's friendship went all the way back to Tennessee, but he had not seen his friend in about four years, and it took him a minute to realize that this stranger hollering "hello" was Jacob.

Jacob's wife Carolina had hardly changed, but the Brooks children had grown so much that the Barger youngsters took a moment to recognize their old playmates. The Brooks family farm was prosperous and his house, a frame house, and not a cabin, had a second floor. The two families settled down to a feast of ham, roasted potatoes, and succotash served on porcelain plates, not on wooden dishes, or on tin. Clearly life in Moniteau County had been prosperous for the Brooks family.

Over dinner Allen asked Jacob about the county.

"Farming here is much easier than in Reynolds County. It is bottom land not the hilly ground you have in Reynolds County, and the soil is much more fertile. The Missouri River runs along the boundary between Moniteau and Cooper County and you have a lot of rich river soil for farming. I swear, Allen, when I plant here I put a seed down then run to get out of the way of the sprout. It is incredible farmland. The farm I have got picked out for you is some of the best in the county, too."

"Is it close?"

"Just down the road a piece and not too far from Centertown. It's about one hundred acres, and fine acres they are. Best of all, you don't have the backbreaking work of starting a new farm. About sixty acres are already cleared. There is a fenced pasture, and there's a cabin, a barn, and a good spring on the place. It's ready for planting in the spring, with no clearing to be done!"

"Excellent," Allen said.

"I can't wait to see it! Would you come along and introduce me to the owner? I'm thinking he might give me a better deal if my neighbor was present."

"Well, that won't be possible," answered Jacob. "The owner left town. He couldn't make his mortgage payments, so the bank had to foreclose. I know the banker, Mr. Winfield Billings, who is a resident of California. I told him he had a buyer and not to let the land go to anyone else, and he won't."

"But if the land's fine why could the owner not make his mortgage payments?"

"Strong drink," answered Jacob. Then in a louder voice so that the youngsters at the other end of the table could hear, he added, "Strong drink has been the wreck of many a good man," Jacob said.

"I fear that's true," Allen said.

"As soon as we get the dishes cleared away, let's go see the farm."

"I'm not sure about that. It gets dark here early and I want you to be able to explore the house and farm a little before we head over to talk to Winfield. I recommend we wait until tomorrow. I'm sure Winfield has already closed the bank and gone home for the day. Ya'll can bed down here tonight. It's going to be tight quarters, but we can make it. Tomorrow we'll go to California and talk business with Winfield," Jacob said.

After a good country breakfast, prepared by Agnus Brooks and Nancy, the Jacobs and Bargers were prepared to go see Allen and Nancy's future home.

"Since I know Winfield is going to sell you the property, we will take Nancy and the children by and let everyone look at the property before you and I go see Winfield. How does that sound?"

"That sounds good to me. I would like to see the house before Allen goes and puts his 'John Henry' on the bank note," Nancy said.

"Allen, you and I will ride horses into California. I had Samuel saddle two horses. They are hitched to the hitching post out front."

"That sounds like a good idea," Allen said.

Henry and William T. had already hitched the mules to the two wagons and were ready for Jacob to take them to the farm. Upon arriving at the farm house, Nancy looked at Henry and said, "This house is going to be a challenge. It's going to take a lot of repairs before we can comfortably live in it. I can see right away that we're going to need to add some rooms also," Nancy said.

The house was much smaller than the one they had grown accustomed to back in Reynolds County. The living room and kitchen was one big room together with a large dining table in the middle. It had a loft where the boys could sleep and two rooms, one for Allen and Nancy, and one for the girls.

Some of the windows were broken and the kitchen door didn't close properly. However, everything else seem to be in pretty good shape. There was a dug well close to the house which Nancy liked, and another plus was it had both a front porch and a back porch which appeared to be in good condition.

The outhouse wasn't far from the house which was another plus, and it could accommodate two people, meaning it had two holes.

Nancy, being a tidy housekeeper, after seeing the leaves and rubbish all over the living area, quickly started barking orders to the children. Within ten minutes of arriving Martha, Mary Ann, and Delilah were sweeping and picking up the leaves and rubbish while Henry and William T. checked out the condition of the roof.

James, Jesse, and George were ordered to check the corral to see if it needed any repairs before the stock was put in the corral. Nancy also ordered them to check the fencing around the one hundred acres to see what condition the fence was in.

Allen chuckled to himself realizing that Nancy had made the place home even before he had bought it. Allen was convinced they could live in this house. It would be hard at first, but they could adjust to the inconvenience until he could add additional rooms to the house. Before taking off to see Mr. Billings, Allen took Nancy off to the side and whispered, "Are you going to be all right with this house?"

"Allen, we will make do for now. I still have the money my father left me. I may want to use some of it to build some more bedrooms," she said.

Jacob Brooks came over to Allen and Nancy and said, "Allen, are you ready?"

"Yes, I'm ready." He gave Nancy a kiss and hug and he and Jacob left to see Winfield Billings at the California Bank.

Mr. Billings was an imposing figure, in a stern black suit with a gold watch chain, and white side whiskers which rimmed his face. His New England accent was distinct and odd to Allen's ears.

"So, you are the man that Jacob speaks so highly of?" Billings said as he grasped Allen's hand with a firmness that concealed his years.

"I am honored that such a fine man as Jacob speaks well of me," Allen replied.

Billings smiled and motioned them into a smaller office where a massive desk faced several comfortable chairs. A cheery fire crackled in the stove, driving away the intense cold of this early winter.

"As Jacob has probably told you, the land that you're interested in was foreclosed several months ago. The former owner and his family ran the place into ruin, taking a perfectly prosperous farm and running it into heavy debt in three years. I'm offering it for three hundred dollars."

"Mr. Billings, I can pay you half of what you're asking. Could you carry me for the other hundred and fifty dollars?" Allen asked.

He turned to Brooks and said, "Jacob, is your friend Allen Barger, good for his word?"

"Allen Barger is a man of his word," Jacob replied.

"In that case, I believe we can make a deal," Mr. Billings said.

"Thank you," Allen said reaching across the desk to shake Mr. Billings' hand.

"We will set your bank note for three years. You'll be paying the bank fifty dollars a year plus interest for three years. How does that sound to you?" Mr. Billings asked.

"That sounds fair to me," Allen replied. The deal was sealed with a firm handshake.

One week later Allen was on the roof of their new cabin nailing down shingles to stop the leaks when he saw a dozen wagons approaching. As he climbed down he hollered for Nancy to come out. They both stood peering into the gloomy November light to try to make out who it was. They were only fifty yards away when Allen recognized Jacob Brooks on the lead wagon and saw that the wagons were loaded with logs, lumber, saws, nails and everything needed to increase the size of Allen and Nancy's house. Behind Jacob, the Bargers' new neighbors shouted their hellos as they drew their wagons to a halt in front of the house. Allen and Nancy were not expecting this type of generosity. They were humbled by the show of Christian love and respect from their new neighbors. In five days, the neighbors constructed an add-on that was two times the size of the original house, plus patched the barn and worked on the fences.

Allen and Nancy were thankful for the kindness and generosity of their new neighbors. On the day the house was completed, Allen called together all the neighbors who had worked on the house. "Nancy and I are ever so grateful for the help you've given us. We would like to ask you and your families to come over tomorrow night for a social. My wife fixes wonderful fried chicken, and I expect if we move the furniture back against the wall there'll be enough room for some dancing."

Nancy and the girls worked all day and fixed a meal fit for a king. That evening, the cabin overflowed with the Brookses, Hartsfields, Millers, Garnetts, Clarks, and the Stockdales. Much to Nancy's surprise, the ladies had also brought food items to go with the chicken, and enough dessert to feed an army. Everyone ate to their hearts and stomachs content. There were some who took Allen up on dancing.

That evening, James and Jesse were sitting in the corner enjoying another helping of coconut pie and talking about hunting with the Hartsfield brothers. Nancy approached and said, "Jesse, James, I hate to tear you away from your conversation with these nice-looking young men, but I need you for a few minutes."

Leading her sons across the room she paused before two attractive young ladies. "Jesse, James, this is Margaret and Christina Ann Miller who live on the farm east of us. Ladies, this is Jesse and James," she said, gesturing. Then she added, "Their parents are George and Hannah—you two met George when he was working on the house. Anyway, Mr. Garnett is about to strike up another tune on his fiddle, and neither Margaret nor Christina has anyone to dance with. You two be good hosts and keep them company." Then, as if by prearrangement, Nancy was called away by Allen leaving Jesse and James to get acquainted with the Miller sisters.

During the dance that followed, James noticed that his mother was engaged in conversation across the room with Mrs. Clark and Mrs. Stockdale but seemed to be keeping an eye on her two sons. By the end of the evening, the four young people were as close as old friends.

Allen and Nancy loved their new home. They both felt God had led them to Moniteau County. They immediately involved themselves in community activities. Besides going to square dances in California on Saturday nights, they attended New Hope Baptist Church between Marion and Centertown, Missouri.

It was at a church-sponsored pie supper, in February 1859, that Henry met Pamela Moon. The church was auctioning off pies made by the young ladies to be purchased by the eligible bachelors. The proceeds went to repair the roof, and the winning bachelor got to share the pie with the girl who baked it.

The Bargers attended and were astonished at the crowd. Not only had virtually the entire congregation turned out, but considering the winter weather, a surprising number of people from all over the township were there.

Henry, who was socializing with the young folks, felt a hand on his arm and was pulled aside by Elizabeth Stockdale.

"Henry, I have baked a special pecan pie just for you," Elizabeth said.

"When the bidding starts you be sure and buy the pie covered with a white napkin and topped with a red bow. That will be mine," Elizabeth said.

Henry infatuated with Elizabeth, promised he would bid on the pie.

The bids began. Henry who had just over a dollar to spend waited patiently for the pie with a white napkin and a red bow. Finally, the preacher who was doubling as auctioneer reached down into the basket and pulled out the pie. Henry's hand shot up "four bits!" he exclaimed.

From across the room a stranger bid five bits.

Henry immediately yelled out, "six bits!"

The stranger bid seven bits.

Henry who was exasperated that some stranger would be bidding on his girl's pie, shouted, "One dollar and twenty-nine cents!" Chuckles was heard throughout the audience. The stranger pulled some coins from his pocket and counted them, then shook his head, conceding defeat. The preacher marked Henry's name on the card and put the card on top of the pie to be given to Henry later.

The bidding started up again. Henry leaned back in his seat and whispered to William T. that he had just purchased Elizabeth Stockdale's pie. He was so excited to know that in a few minutes he and Elizabeth would be enjoying pie together.

Henry was taken back when the preacher picked up another pie with a white napkin and a red bow. "This one looks like it is pecan," announced the preacher. "Who will give me fifty cents?" The stranger on the other side of the room immediately bid and got the pie for seventy-five cents.

When the bidding was done, Henry took a deep breath, and walked up to the table full of pies to see which one he had purchased. His name, the price, and the name of the person who baked the pie was written on a card on top of the pie. The pie was baked by Pamela Moon, a name that Henry had not heard before. Out of the corner of his eye he saw Elizabeth introducing herself politely to the stranger with whom she would now share a meal, with pie for dessert. Elizabeth saw Henry looking at her and returned a glare that fired daggers at him.

Henry settled down to eat a picnic lunch with Pamela hoping to smooth things over with Elizabeth later.

By the end of the afternoon, however, all thoughts of Elizabeth were gone from Henry's mind. That afternoon saw the beginning of a two-month courtship that would lead to Henry and Pamela's marriage.

In early April, Henry found Allen sitting on the front porch. Taking advantage of his father being alone he decided to discuss his marriage plans.

"Pa, I asked Pamela to marry me, and she said yes."

Allen who had been expecting this news said, "Son, isn't this pretty sudden? Where will you live, Henry? You can't afford a farm."

"Well, Pamela has talked about that with me, and we've talked with her father. As you know, he's disabled, but has a good piece of land south of California. Right now, he's using hired men to run the place and barely making ends meet. But, with a son-in-law to take over the farm it could bloom. Anyway, Mr. Moon has invited Pamela and me to live with him when we marry."

"You're a hard worker, Son. If anyone can make the Moon farm into a profitable business, you can. I'll miss your work around this place, but I like Pamela, and if you love that girl, I'm not going to try to talk you out of this marriage. We best go now and break the news to your mother."

"I'll still be close enough, Pa. If you ever need me, I will be here."

Nancy liked Pamela and felt she would be a good wife for Henry and gave him her blessings.

The couple was married on May 15, 1859, in a ceremony attended by family and friends. In the audience was another young couple, Martha Jane Barger and her boyfriend, Thomas Barton Tull.

One month after Henry was married, Thomas, Allen and Nancy's beloved oldest daughter, Martha Jane, were married. The worst part about their marriage was Martha Jane would be living with Thomas in Cooper County just across the Missouri River. The closest way to get to Thomas and Martha's new home was by a ferry boat. By way of the ferry it would still be about six miles away from where Allen and Nancy lived.

The marriage of Henry and Martha Jane made the Barger household a little smaller, but still crowded. Allen and Nancy still had seven children to feed and clothe. William T., James, and Jesse were now old enough to help Allen with the farming responsibilities. All three were hard workers. Allen had taught his boys good work ethics which would remain with them throughout their lives.

William T. was now eighteen years old. James would soon be seventeen and Jesse was fifteen. James and Jesse attended school during the day and worked on the farm after school. After finishing their farm responsibilities, they fished and hunted until dark. To be sure, as long as James and Jesse were around, the family would have fresh fish or wild game for supper.

James and Sally Hampton continued to write each other, but as the years went by, the letters became fewer and fewer.

CHAPTER 18

King, James' coon dog, had turned into a fine hunting dog. He had been a big part of James life for two years. Everywhere James went, King was by his side. If ever a dog was a man's best friend, he was surely James' best friend. He loved to hunt as much as James did. As soon as he saw James come out of the house with his gun, he would take off in the direction of the woods.

In early October, James and Jesse went hunting for rabbits and squirrels. King trotted along beside them. It was exceedingly warm that autumn with summer like temperatures continuing well into October. They had been hunting for about an hour when they jumped a big swamp rabbit. The rabbit ran into a large hollow log with King hot on its heels. James checked the other side of the log to see if it had an opening. If it didn't he knew they could smoke out the rabbit. Instead of waiting on James, Jesse reached into the log to see if he could pull out the rabbit. As he reached into the log he felt a sharp sting to his hand.

"Gosh, James, something just bit me." James immediately knew what had happened. He looked at Jesse's hand and saw two small holes. James had seen this bite before when one of their neighbors in Reynolds county got bit. James knew right away it had to be a snake. He needed to find out what kind of snake and fast. He immediately took a long stick and started punching the stick inside of the hollow log. Out came a big copperhead. James knew right away that this was bad news. He immediately killed the snake. James then made a tourniquet utilizing his belt and a stick. As he was making the tourniquet he thought, why didn't I do this first? He then said to Jesse, "We've got to get that poison out of your hand before it gets into your blood."

"What are you going to do, James?" Jesse asked as he began moaning with pain from the bite.

"I'm going to have to cut you, Jesse," James said as he pulled out his hunting knife.

He took Jesse's hand and made a cross cut across the snake bite and began to suck the blood out of Jesse's hand. Allen had taught his boys all about the wilderness and what to do should one of them get snake bit.

As James continued to suck the blood from Jesse's hand, Jesse began to get sick at his stomach. He vomited and bent over with cramps. He began sweating and turning pale. The poison had already gotten into his system.

Jesse looked up at James and said, "I'm awfully sick."

"You hang in there, Jesse. I'm going to get you to the house!" James said as he picked Jesse up and put him across his right shoulder. Jessie was heavy and almost as big as James. It was all that James could do to pick him up. After picking Jesse up, James headed for the house as fast as his legs would carry him. King, sensing trouble, ran along beside them whining and yelping. Somehow, James found the strength to keep going. He knew he had to get help for Jesse or he could die. By the time he reached the house, he was about to drop. He laid Jesse on the front porch and opened the front door with a rush.

"Pa, come here! Jesse has been bitten by a copperhead," James shouted as he went back to attend to Jesse.

Allen sprang from his chair and ran to the front porch followed by Nancy, William T., and the other children.

"James, what happened?" Allen asked with fear in his voice.

"Pa, we jumped a big swamp rabbit and he ran into this big hollow log. Jesse reached in the log and a copperhead bit him," James explained.

"William T. go get Doc Bennett. Tell him to hurry," Allen said.

"Nancy, go get that bottle of whisky in the kitchen. James, give me a hand. Let's get Jesse inside," Allen said as he picked up Jesse from the shoulders as James picked up his feet.

They carried him inside and laid him on his bed. By this time Jesse was moaning and groaning.

Nancy handed Allen the whisky. Allen lifted Jesse's head and began to make him drink the whisky. Jesse coughed and began to vomit. After he vomited, Allen made him drink more.

Giving pure whisky was one of the best treatments for poisonous snake bites, so Allen continued to make Jesse drink the whisky.

"James, run and get me some red clay from the clay bank down the road. I need it fast. Go now!" Allen said with haste.

"I'll be right back, Pa," James said as he turned and ran out the door.

"Nancy, get me some vinegar and cloths. When James gets back, you'll need to make a clay poultice and put it on Jesse's hand. It will hopefully, draw the poison out." Jesse's hand had already swollen twice the normal size.

James returned with the clay, and Nancy mixed the vinegar with the clay and made a poultice to put on Jesse's hand.

"Pa, how's Jesse doing?" James asked with a quivering voice.

"We will have to just pray he's going to be all right," Allen said as he turned and put his arm around James.

"I feel it's my fault, Pa. I should've warned him not to be sticking his hand in hollow logs," James said.

"Don't be blaming yourself," Allen said.

About that time Doc Bennett and William T. entered the cabin.

"Doc, I'm so glad you're here," Nancy said with a sigh of relief.

"Let's look at you, Jesse," Doc Bennett said as he listened to Jesse's breathing.

"How much whisky did you give this boy?" Doc Bennett asked with a smile.

"I gave him all I could get down him," Allen replied.

"I believe the whisky worked," Doc. Bennett said.

"Praise the Lord," Nancy said with joy.

"Jesse, don't go sticking your hand in any more of those hollow logs," Doc. Bennett said with a big smile.

Jesse looked up at Doc Bennett and gave him a weak smile.

"Nancy, make sure Jesse drinks lots of water," Doc Bennett said.

"Thanks, Doc," Nancy said.

James walked over to Jesse and said, "You're going to be fine."

"James, tell me something. Was I heavy?" Jesse asked.

"You were pretty heavy. I thought I wasn't going to make it to the house, but something just kept giving me strength."

"The last thing I remembered was you carrying me."

"James, let Jesse rest now," Nancy said.

"I'll see you later," James said as he began to leave.

"Did we get that rabbit?" Jesse asked.

"No, but we'll get him next time."

James went out on the front porch and began to cry. He was an emotional young man, a lot like his mother. He had a genuine concern for people and always seemed to sense when someone was in pain.

Two weeks after the copperhead had bitten Jesse, he and James returned to hunting and fishing. This time, Jesse was a lot more cautious with each step he took.

CHAPTER 19

The annual Moniteau County Fourth of July Celebration brought people from all over Moniteau, Cole, Cooper, and the surrounding areas to California, Missouri. The day included horse races, wagon races, horseshoe games, sharpshooting contests, street dances, baking and weaving contests for the women, and lots of games for the children.

James decided he wanted to enter the sharpshooting contest. The rife his father had giving him for his fourteenth birthday was a real man's rifle and not a boy's rabbit gun. Old Faithful had never failed to shoot when he pulled the trigger. He could hit anything within three hundred steps.

About fifty men entered the sharpshooting contest and James was one of the youngest contestants. He put a hard-earned dollar down for the entry fee. The first round began at 3:00 P.M. in the grassy meadow behind Tom Garnett's general store, with a slope beyond a backstop for the bullets. As the contestants lined up, Doc Bennett, who would be the judge announced the rules.

"The first shot will be fired at fifty paces. The second shot at one hundred, the third at one hundred and fifty, and so forth until there is only one contestant left. The targets will be glass bottles on the stump down yonder," he gestured.

"The firing line for the first round will be here, this line in the dirt. As for the prize, there is $51 in entry money, so the winner gets $30, the second place gets $15, and the third place gets $6. Are there any questions? Then let's start shooting!"

By mid-afternoon there were three left. They were James, George Bennett from Cooper County, and Frank Blakely from Moniteau. Mr. Blakely had been the sharp-shooting champion for several years in Moniteau County. Two more rounds passed at 200 paces, then 250 paces, before Bennett missed. Doc Bennett consoled his cousin. "Better luck next year, George." Now the shooting contest found Frank Blakely and James in the finals. Word spread throughout town that Frank Blakely was being challenged by a seventeen-year-old sharpshooter for the championship. Many people left other activities to see the final round of competition.

Frank and James paced off another fifty paces back from the stump, which was now three hundred paces away. Doc Bennett drew another line in the dirt with his cane. Another whiskey bottle was placed on the old stump. A coin was tossed to see who would get to go first. Mr. Blakely won the toss. Everyone just knew that Mr. Blakely would hit the whiskey bottle on his first attempt. He had earned the name as the best shooter in the state of Missouri. Frank Blakely, about forty years old, was about six feet tall, weighed about two hundred pounds, and was a handsome man. He was one of the most respected gentlemen of Moniteau County. He owned a large farm north of the city of California. He had won the sharpshooter contest for the past ten years and was very confident about his shooting skills. As he walked to the shooting stand, he looked at James and winked.

To everyone's surprise, James winked back at Mr. Blakely. Everyone laughed!

Mr. Blakely raised his gun, took aim, held his breath, and pulled the trigger. To everyone's surprise, he missed the target.

After Mr. Blakely missed the whiskey bottle Jesse ran up to James and said,

"James, you can hit that whiskey bottle. I've seen you do it. Don't give that Blakely fellow another chance," he said with encouragement.

Allen walked over to his son and said, "James, remember to check the wind. Remember what I've taught you about how the wind affects the shooting. Allow some lead way in how the wind is blowing. You can do it, Son," Allen said as he patted him on the shoulder.

James walked to the firing line. He did as Allen suggested. The wind was blowing from the north. He would need to allow a little to the right of the whiskey bottle because of the wind. He looked at Mr. Blakely and gave him a nod. Mr. Blakely gave him a nod back. James aimed, held his breath, pulled the trigger on Old Faithful, and the whiskey bottle exploded. There would be no need for another round of fire. James had just become the new sharpshooting champion of Moniteau County.

Several people rushed up to congratulate James on his honor. Nancy gave her son a hug. Mr. Blakely came over and gave him a hefty handshake as he complimented him on his shooting. "Son, that was some mighty good shooting. Where'd you learn to shoot like that?" Mr. Blakely asked.

"Hunting wild game," James replied.

Mr. Blakely didn't cherish losing to a seventeen-year-old boy, but he was a gentleman and reacted as one.

James was handed thirty dollars for his winnings in the sharpshooting contest, the most money he'd ever held in his hand.

"What are you going to do with that money, James?" Jesse asked.

"I'm going to put this money in the bank for my future farm," he said.

As the crowd broke up, James noticed Christina Miller standing near her sister, Margaret. They had come to watch James compete in the sharpshooting contest. James, Jesse, and the Miller sisters were already good friends. They had been going to the same church and school and lived in the same community. The Millers' farm was next door to Allen and Nancy's farm.

"James, that was some really nice shooting," Christina said with a smile.

"Thank you, Christina. I was scared, but Old Faithful didn't let me down. Isn't she a beauty?" James asked as he lifted the gun.

"I don't care much for guns, James," Christina said as she backed away.

"This gun won't hurt you, Christina. It's not even loaded," James said as he chuckled.

"Are you going to the square dance tonight?" James asked.

"Are you asking to escort me?" Christina asked.

"Well, I guess you might say that."

"I would be most honored to go to the dance with the best sharpshooter in Moniteau County," Christina said smiling as she grabbed James's arm.

CHAPTER 20

That Fourth of July was one that James would always remember. He had brought recognition to himself which would remain for years to come.

The city of California and Moniteau County were beginning to show considerable growth during the year of 1858. In September the first city government elections were held in California, Missouri. William F. Lansdale was elected mayor of the city of California. Mr. Lansdale's office was in an old two-story, redbrick courthouse. The courthouse, located in the center of town, became the center of several political debates on slavery.

Prior to 1858, commercial transportation was limited to the stagecoach. The stage line ran from Jefferson City, Missouri, to Bonneville, Missouri, through California. The stage stopped in California at Wood's Hotel which was across from the new railroad depot.

In October 1858, the Pacific Railroad was completed through California and went as far west as Tipton, Missouri. The arrival of the Pacific Railroad was an economic boost to Moniteau County and the city of California.

The Weekly California Newspaper printed its first edition on September 18, 1858. At this time the city of California had a population of 714. The city had ten dry goods stores, two drug stores, a tobacco factory, a large steam flour mill, a high school, a printing office, one bank, and a courthouse. The Weekly California Newspaper began to print news articles on the issue of slavery. The question of slavery became the number one issue in Moniteau County.

Some of the farmers in the county who owned and operated larger farms owned slaves. They continued to believe that it was their constitutional right to own slaves. Others in the county believed it was wrong to own slaves. The debate over the slavery issue was never ending.

On September 15, 1859, William T., James, and Jesse attended their first political meeting with their father in the city of California. Allen wanted his boys to be exposed to the issues of the day which included slavery. The debate was between Mr. Frank Blakely, the man James had beaten in the shooting competition, and Jacob Brooks. Both were running for the state legislature. Blakely ran as a Democrat and Brooks was a candidate of a brand-new party that Allen and his sons were not too familiar with, the Republican party. While the two candidates had debated several times that autumn, this debate, was focused on slavery and had attracted the most attention. A large crowd turned out on the courthouse lawn. A wooden platform had been erected with several chairs and a podium. On the platform, Mr. Blakely, Mr. Brooks, and Mayor Lansdale solemnly scrutinized the crowd.

Mayor Lansdale first recognized Mr. Frank Blakely. "My friends," began Lansdale, "our first speaker needs no introduction. Many of you know him as a good neighbor and as one of the most prosperous farmers in these parts. Many of you know him as the undefeated champion of our annual Fourth of July sharpshooters' contest."

In the audience, James could hardly restrain himself from correcting the mayor. Jesse chuckled under his breath, and James noticed various friends in the audience glancing over their shoulders at him, grinning and whispering among themselves. Allen leaned over and whispered "Well, so much for Lansdale's memory!"

Lansdale meanwhile was continuing his introduction. "Many of you may not know, however, that Mr. Blakely himself is a slave owner. This makes it entirely appropriate for Mr. Blakely to be here today on this platform to address this important issue. Let me add that I have known Mr. Blakely for more than twenty years. He's a good man who stands up for his constitutional rights.

"Mr. Blakely has prepared a printed hand bill that list the major points of his argument, and several young men are now passing them out to the crowd. I ask you to give your closest attention to Mr. Blakely."

Allen leaned over and whispered, "Well, so much for Lansdale's impartiality." Just then, a young man handed one of the hand bills to Allen. The four sons crowded close to peer over their father's shoulder. The title, in large letters read, Biblical, Charitable, Evangelistic, Social, and Political reasons why Christians and others should support slavery.

As the sheet was passed around, disgruntled remarks could be heard throughout the crowd. Mayor Lansdale reminded the opposition that they would have their time to speak later. Allen and his sons paid little attention to the murmuring and read the text of the handbill:

Biblical Reasons

*Abraham, the father of faith, and all the patriarchs held slaves without God's disapproval. (Gen. 21:9-10)

*Canaan, Ham's son, was made a slave to his brothers (Gen. 9:24-27).

*The Ten Commandments mentioned slavery twice, showing God's implicit acceptance of it. (Ex. 20:10,17)

*Slavery was widespread throughout the Roman world, and yet Jesus never spoke against it.

*The apostle Paul specifically commanded slaves to obey their masters. (Eph. 6:5-8)

*Paul returned a runaway slave, Philemon, to his master (Philemon.12).

Charitable and Evangelistic Reasons

*Slavery removes people from a culture that worships the devil, practices witchcraft and sorcery, and other evils.

*Slavery brings heathens to a Christian land where they can hear the gospel. Christian masters provide religious instruction for their slaves.

*Under slavery, people are treated with kindness, as many northern visitors can attest.

*It is in slave holders' own interest to treat their slaves well.

*Slaves are treated more benevolently than are workers in oppressive Northern factories.

Social Reasons

*Just as women are called to play a subordinate role (Eph. 5:22:1 Tim. 2: ll-15), so slaves are stationed by God in their place.

* Slavery is God's means of protecting and providing for an inferior race (suffering the "curse of Ham" in Gen. 9:25 or even the punishment of Cain in Gen. 4:12).

*Abolition would lead to slave uprisings, bloodshed, and anarchy. Consider the mob's "rule of terror" during the French Revolution.

Political Reasons

*Christians are to obey civil authorities, and those authorities permit and protect slavery.

*The church should concentrate on spiritual matters, not political ones.

* Slavery is mentioned in the United States Constitution. Our founding fathers condoned it.

* George Washington held slaves.

* If slavery is abolished, society would be burdened with a class of destitute former slaves who would become a burden lest they starve.

Mr. Blakely's arguments were uninspired oratory, tracking the points listed on the handbill, without too many deviations from the printed page. After Mr. Blakely finished, Mayor Lansdale rose.

"My friends, let us give a hearty round of applause to Mr. Blakely. I have seldom seen such clarity of thought, such insight, such logic, coming from a candidate for public office." He paused to allow the audience to clap. Some clapped enthusiastically, some clapped politely. Then, Lansdale continued: "Before we go on, I might point out that Mrs. Lansdale, my wife, and some of the other fine ladies of our community have prepared lemonade which is available across the street in the yard of Widow Simms' boarding house. And now, Mr. Jacob Brooks, the candidate of the so-called Republican party, will speak."

Ignoring the fact that several members of the audience were already heading for the lemonade, Jacob rose and solemnly addressed the audience.

"My fellow friends and countrymen. Mr. Blakely has certainly done his research. But let me remind Mr. Blakely that we are no longer living under the Mosaic Laws of the Old Testament. My Bible teaches me that we are to love our neighbors as we love our selves. We are to treat others as we would want to be treated. These are also commandments of Jesus Christ our Savior. I don't think that Mr. Blakely, or anyone else who owns slaves, looks upon their slaves as Jesus has instructed us to do in his Holy Word." A large segment of the crowd applauded. Several people booed. James never witnessed anything like this. This was exciting but a little scary.

Jacob ignored the boos and continued, "My dear friends, in 1807 a provision was written into our law that abolished slave trading. This law was not carried out completely, although it has slowed the further importation of slaves to a trickle. I have always agreed, and still do with the Abolitionist, William Lloyd Garrison, that all slaves in the United States should be emancipated at once. It is, in my opinion, a moral Christian obligation to do so. Most of the Northern states have now done so and have done so without the anarchy, the riots, or the other evils that Mr. Blakely hints would follow abolition. We should follow suit."

After Jacob finished speaking, Blakely rose to give his rebuttal. "Gentlemen, please don't get confused by what my well-intentioned, but ill-informed friend, Jacob Brooks, has said about slavery. I believe Mr. Brooks stated that our law makers wrote into the laws a provision which abolished slave trading. He's correct on that, but the right to own slaves was written into the United States Constitution in 1787. It's true that the Northern states abolished slavery between 1777 and 1804. Their actions had no influence on us here in Missouri. In my opinion, the North abolished slavery because they did not want a large negro population living in their midst. The constitution of the United States gives us the right to own slaves, and that's the way it's going to be." Mr. Blakely sat down to the applause of his supporters.

The debate had made an impact on James. He felt, as most of the people did, slavery was wrong. He, too, hated to see friends turning against each other because of their different beliefs.

"Pa, do you think we will go to war over this slavery issue?" James asked Allen as they traveled home from the town meeting.

"The issue is certainly dividing our country, but I doubt there will be a war," Allen said.

"It appears to me that it's a moral issue. Is that what it's about?" James asked.

"According to what I know from reading The Weekly California Newspaper and listening to those who seemed to make this their daily conversation, I think there must be other issues involved. The moral issue is one thing, but the other issue is the disagreement between the Northern states and the Southern states over free and slave states. There seems to be a political reason here also. The South wants more slave states where the North wants more free states. The North wants more land and power in the Senate. The South fears the North's growing power in the Senate. The North is heavily involved in manufacturing and wants high tariffs to protect its factories from European competition. The South wants to export its cotton and tobacco to Europe and wants low tariffs. We really have two countries, I fear, with two different views on every issue, not just slavery.

"I do worry that the country will split up, but I doubt there'll be a war," Allen said hoping he was right. If he was wrong, he would have three sons old enough to go to war, and he didn't want his sons fighting in a war.

"Do you think the hostility is as great in other places as it is here in Moniteau County?" James asked.

"Yes, I do. Can you remember how the hostility was getting in Reynolds County before we moved to Moniteau?" Allen asked.

"I do recollect you being upset over some slavery issues at the town meetings," James said.

"There are those who believe in complete abolition of slavery, those who are against the expansion of slavery but who are willing to let slavery exist in those Southern states where it already exists, and those who are pro slavery as you heard tonight," Allen answered.

"Even those who oppose slavery cannot agree. Some want it to end immediately, like Jacob Brooks. Others want to end it gradually, in twenty or thirty years. Some Northern abolitionists want to end it and return all slaves to Africa. Other Northern abolitionists want to end it, allow the freed slaves to remain in the country, but forbid them from moving up North."

"Are we Republicans or Democrats?" James asked.

"Why are you asking?" Allen asked.

"It appears the Republicans are more sympathetic with the abolishment of slavery than the Democrats," James replied.

"I believe you're right, James. The Republican Party was formed in opposition to Southern expansion. Their platform was Free Soil, Free Men and Free Labor. The Republicans were anti-South, but they were in no way an abolitionist party. They believed slavery was a flawed system which made the South inefficient and that the North's free labor system was superior and must be defended from Southern aggression."

" Who is this Abe Lincoln I kept hearing about tonight at the town meeting?"

Jesse asked.

"Some people think he may be the next President of the United States," Allen answered.

"I've been reading about him in The Weekly California Newspaper lately. I really like him, Pa." James said.

Allen knew James read a lot and had always showed an interest in politics, but he was amazed how James comprehended so much from the debate. Allen was aware that James was gifted in history. He had read several reports James had done for his history assignments at school. James always made excellent marks in his subjects.

James and Jesse had Negro friends in both Reynolds and Moniteau Counties. They always felt sorry for their slave friends.

James mentioned from time to time how hard the slaves were worked and how horrible their living conditions were. He would never forget Joe, the slave boy in Reynolds County, who was whipped so badly by his owner, Mr. Steagall. Ever since his experience with Joe, James had been sympathetic toward the slaves.

On November 20, 1859, Allen was able to pay First Bank of California the last installment on the farm note. The farm was now free of debt. It was paid off earlier than expected, which called for a time of celebration for the Bargers.

On November 30, 1859, Allen, Nancy, and other family members were present for the birth of Martha Jane's first son. As they arrived at Martha's home in Lamine Township, Cooper County, they found Nellie Barker attending Martha. Mrs. Barker had the reputation of being one of the best mid-wives in Cooper County. This was the first time that Thomas Barton Tull had faced being a father. He was like most new prospective fathers, as nervous as a cat.

"You remind me of myself when Nancy was giving birth to our first son," Allen said.

"It's taking a long time for Martha to have that baby. Do you think she's all right?" Thomas asked impatiently.

Finally, they heard the cry which they had been waiting for. It was a strong cry, one that told Allen it was a boy. The door opened from the bedroom and Nancy came out holding the baby.

"Thomas, you have a big, healthy son," Nancy said with a smile.

Thomas immediately went over to where Nancy was holding the baby and gazed down at his son.

"He is a big one, isn't he?" Thomas said with a big smile.

Thomas had wanted a boy. He and Martha had decided to name their first son Allen Franklin Tull. It was Martha's suggestion that the first son be named after her father, Allen.

It was a custom for women to spend three to four days in bed after giving birth to a child. It was also a custom for the mother not to lift anything weighing more than ten pounds for the first seven days after giving birth.

Nancy volunteered to stay with Martha Jane until she got back on her feet.

On July 4, 1860, James repeated as winner of the sharpshooting contest at the Annual Moniteau County Fourth of July Celebration. He again defeated Frank Blakely in the final round of the competition.

On November 9, 1860, Martha Jane Tull gave birth to her second son, Joseph Henry Tull. Things continued to go well with the Bargers in Moniteau County, in spite of the county's being divided on the slavery issue. Since Allen and Nancy didn't own slaves, they tried to distance themselves from the controversy which had split friendships within the county. The issue of who would be the next President of the United States of America became the immediate concern throughout the country.

On December 12, 1860, James received the following letter from Sally Hampton.

My Dear James:

In a few weeks it will be Christmas. I hope you and your family will have a good Christmas. We are planning a Christmas celebration at church tonight. We are having a short play about the birth of Jesus. I'm going to be Mary and Matt Brawley is going to be Joseph.

James, I've got something very important to tell you. This is not going to be easy, but I feel it's the Christian thing to do. Matt Brawley and I are planning to marry in the spring. I never thought I would love anyone but you, but I've fallen in love with Matt. He treats me well, and I know he will be a good husband.

James, I've thought about your promise that someday you would return to Reynolds County and we would be married. I'm now releasing you of that promise. Maybe if you had stayed in Reynolds County we could have had a life together, but you didn't and over the course of two years I've been courted by Matt Brawley. He is a good man and has been good to me.

I know you would want me to be happy and I do hope you will understand. I know beyond any doubt there is another girl out there who will steal your heart away. Just be ready when she does.

You will always occupy a warm spot in my heart. Please know that! I will always treasure the good times we had together and hope you will do the same. I want you to be happy, and I don't want you to feel bad toward me. You were my first love, and I will always remember you.

Please be happy, and please be ready when that special person comes into your life. You are a very special person, and you will make a wonderful husband.

I regret to inform you of this news right before Christmas, but I felt it was the Christian thing to do. Please forgive me if I've caused you grief. Time will help both of us.

I pray you and your family will have a Merry Christmas and a Happy New Year. God bless you!

Sincerely yours,

Sally Hampton

After James read Sally's letter, he folded it and placed it back in the envelope. There was some disappointment, but in a way, James felt relieved. Sally was right. There was a girl who was stealing his heart away and she was Christina Ann Miller.

CHAPTER 21

On May 18, 1860, Abe Lincoln was nominated for the President of the United States by the Republican Party. He was opposed by Senator Stephen A. Douglas from the Democratic Party, John C. Breckinridge from the Southern Party, and John Bell from the Whigs Party.

When the votes were counted on November 6, 1860, Abe Lincoln had won most of the electoral votes and was declared the sixteenth President of the United States of America.

He was sworn in as the sixteenth President.

The Southern states had already stated that if Abe Lincoln, the candidate of the anti-slavery Republican Party was elected President, they would withdraw from the Union. The South held to their promise and on December 20, 1860, South Carolina promptly seceded from the Union.

Several attempts were made to try to keep the Southern states from seceding from the Union. When efforts of compromise failed, other Southern states followed South Carolina's example.

Those states seceding from the Union in chronological order were South Carolina on December 20, 1860; Mississippi on January 9, 1861; Florida on January 10, 1861; Alabama on January 11, 1861; Georgia on January 19, 1861; Louisiana on January 26, 1861; Kansas on January 29, 1861; and Texas on February 1, 1861. As each state seceded, it seized all federal properties within its borders. These properties included forts, posts, camps, arsenals, customs, houses, and post offices. Most United States military establishments surrendered without resistance.

On February 4, 1861 the Southern states held a convention in Montgomery, Alabama, which became the first capital of the Confederate States. The seven seceding states created the Confederate Constitution, a document that was like the United States Constitution but stressed more local autonomy for each state. The Southern states appointed Jefferson Davis as Provisional President and Alexander Stephens as vice-president until elections could be held.

The Confederate capital was moved from Montgomery, Alabama, to Richmond, Virginia, in May 186l, when Virginia seceded from the Union. The Southern states under President Jefferson Davis counted on patriotic fervor, the strategic advantage of interior lines of communication, and the international importance of their chief cash crops cotton and tobacco to win a short war of independence.

The Northern states of the Federal Union under President Abraham Lincoln commanded more than twice the population of the Confederacy and held even greater advantages in manufacturing and transportation capacity.

In February 1861, the Southern states had called on President James Buchanan to surrender the Southern forts to the seceding states. When Buchanan refused the Southern states began to stop supply ships from New York bringing supplies to Fort Sumter. All ships that made attempts to enter the harbor were turned back. The conflict between the North and South had started.

In Lincoln's inaugural address held on March 4, 1861, he stated, "I have no plans to end slavery in those states where it already existed, but I also will not accept secession." He had hoped to resolve the national crisis without warfare.

On April 7, 1861, President Lincoln alerted the state of South Carolina that he planned to send supplies to Fort Sumter which was under Union control. He alerted South Carolina in advance in hopes it would avoid hostilities. However, South Carolina feared it was a trick.

It was at this time that President Jefferson Davis ordered Brig. General Pierre Gustave Toutant de Beauregard of the Provisional Confederate forces at Charleston, South Carolina, to fire on Fort Sumter.

Fort Sumter was under the command of Major Robert Anderson who was born in Kentucky and graduated from the U.S. Military Academy, at West Point in 1825. Anderson was a strong-willed person who had previously served in the Black Hawk and Seminole and Mexican Wars. Although Anderson had a small force of some seventy-five men, he had no intention to surrender Fort Sumter to General Beauregard.

On April 4, 1861, at 4:30 A M., the first signal rocket was shot into the sky over Fort Sumter. Many rockets followed, lighting up the sky over Fort Sumter. Following the rockets was a barrage of shells from Major Beauregard's artillery from the shoreline. Fort Sumter soon was surrounded by smoke from the exploding missiles and artillery fire. The Civil War had begun.

The battle raged on for thirty-four hours before Major Robert Anderson surrendered Fort Sumter to Major Beauregard. The flag of the United States was lowered, and the red and blue confederate flag was raised in its place.

Eighty-five years after the Declaration of Independence had announced that Americans were free from English rule, the United States found itself battling for survival in the grip of a terrible Civil War that would divide states and families.

The Confederates had committed an act of war that President Lincoln could not ignore. He immediately issued a call for 75,000 Union soldiers and ordered a blockade of Southern ports.

"If the South wants war, then war is what they will get," he said.

The attack on Fort Sumter prompted four more states to join the Confederacy. On April 17, 1861, Virginia seceded from the Union. Virginia was followed by Arkansas on May 6, 1861, North Carolina on May 20, 1861, and Tennessee.

The state of Missouri sat on the border between North and South. Most of Missouri's American-born settlers were from Southern states and were Southern in sentiment. Generally, they lived on farms, and many owned slaves. But the state also had a larger foreign-born population most of whom were strongly in favor of the Union. A convention was called in St. Louis, Missouri, to decide what course Missouri should take in the war.

The state took a position of armed neutrality. It was determined that neither the North nor the South should invade Missouri.

Missouri would raise its own army to protect itself against the government in which it was a part and against its neighboring states which had seceded from the Union. The Missouri State Guards were organized for this purpose.

The tide of feelings on both sides would rise to the extent that they would not be able to stay neutral.

The Weekly California Newspaper was filled with stories about the Battle of Fort Sumter. The citizens of Moniteau County began to be caught up in the issue of the Civil War.

Allen and Nancy couldn't go anywhere in the county without hearing something about the Civil War.

On May 12, 1861, at a square dance in California, William T. Barger met Rutha Letty Gouge. She was twelve years older than him, but this didn't seem to matter to either of them. Rutha's husband of ten years had died of typhoid fever and she had been left alone for the past two years. Her husband had left her a fifty-acre farm that was about three miles south of the city of California. Rutha was a lovely woman who needed a man's companionship as well as someone who could run the farm. William seemed to meet those requirements in Rutha's eyes.

William was strong and handsome. He stood about six feet tall and had dark eyes and black hair. His parents had taught him how to respect a woman and his gentlemanly manners pleased Rutha. She was immediately attracted to him.

On July 6, 1861, William and Rutha Gouge were married in the New Hope Baptist Church outside of Marion, Missouri.

Allen and Nancy were not pleased with William's decision to marry Rutha. They felt he was making a big mistake marrying a woman twelve year older. Although they were not pleased with his decision, they decided they would honor his decision and support the marriage.

After the wedding, William and Rutha returned to her farm south of California.

Allen and Nancy saw very little of William and Rutha during their first year of marriage. They stayed to themselves.

The Allen Barger household now consisted of Nancy, James, Jesse, Mary Ann, George, Delilah, and John Wesley. James was now the oldest child at home. He turned eighteen on September 4, 1861. Jesse was seventeen, Mary Ann was fifteen, George thirteen, Delilah eleven, and John Wesley seven.

James and Jesse were no different from the other young men of Moniteau County. They were anxious to get involved in the war. After all, it was going to last only a few months, and if they didn't hurry and enlist, they might miss it.

In early October, James and Jesse were in California buying supplies when they saw a huge crowd gathering in front of the Moniteau County courthouse. The crowd had gathered to hear George Boomer, a recruiter and resident of Castle Rock, Missouri.

"My friends," said Boomer, "I have been authorized by General John Fremont to raise a battalion of Missouri Sharpshooters, for immediate service in suppressing the rebellion. I am only looking for the best recruits, the cream of the crop. I am looking for strong, energetic young men, who are not afraid of rough service. And most of all, I am looking for good shots. This afternoon in the pasture behind the feed store there will be a target practice session. Now, any man who has some interest in joining my battalion come on down and try your hand. There is no finer regiment about to take the field. I am sure that Moniteau County has a lot of steady shots who are eager to teach Jeff Davis a lesson, and I want to see them at 2:00 P.M. Come for the Union!" Col. George Boomer said.

The crowd responded with enthusiastic cheers. James, who had been toying with the idea of enlisting as soon as the harvest was over leaned over to Jesse and said, "I think I will try a hand at that. The pasture where they are shooting is the one where the Fourth of July shooting competition is held, and I have already practiced there. I should have an advantage because I know the range pretty well in my head."

Jesse grinned, "As long as Frank Blakely doesn't show up, you should be the best shot. But I hear Frank Blakely joined the Rebel army, so I doubt he will show up!"

At 2:00 P.M., James was waiting eagerly in a crowd of young men. Mr. Boomer was seated in a chair in the back of a wagon where an impromptu spectators stand had been set up. Several of the distinguished citizens of Moniteau county sat with him. James was only disappointed that he had not had time to go home and get Old Faithful. Still, he could make do with the Army rifles that were arranged on a table in front of the crowd.

A man in uniform with stripes on his sleeves stood next to the table. James was casually wondering about the rank of someone with three stripes.

James didn't have to wonder long before a man with a bushy mustache came up to him and introduced himself.

"I am Sergeant Mason. To become a sharpshooter a candidate is required to shoot a qualification test using a rifle either brought by you or one that is provided. The course of firing consists of shooting ten rounds into a target as rapidly as the shooter can reload. The target is ten inches in diameter at two hundred yards. All ten rounds must hit the target and the average distance the shot falls cannot be further than five inches from the center of the bull's-eye. This will be measured by a fifty-inch string.

As James listened to the criteria, he thought, I can do this. I know I can.

Sergeant Mason continued, "In the sharpshooters, you will be expected to aim at and kill Confederate soldiers. For you farm boys that is a lot different from hunting and shooting wild game. It is especially not an easy thing to do with the roar of a battle all around you, bullets buzzing past, smoke and dust obscuring your vision, and you so nervous you cannot hold your rifle steady. I was in Mexico with Winfield Scott. Believe me, I know.

"It is important, however, to have a good unit of sharpshooters with the Army. The unit is organized to serve primarily as skirmishers and long-distance marksman. As skirmishers you will operate either on the flanks or in advance of the main body of troops, compressed into mass line formation. Instead of the soldiers being shoulder to shoulder in a mass line the sharpshooters will be about five to ten yards apart spread out in the woods."

To James spacing soldiers five to ten yards apart made more sense than the type of shoulder to shoulder formations which he had heard the Army used. He thought making soldiers march shoulder to shoulder would make them sitting ducks for the Johnny Rebs.

"During battle the sharpshooters play two important roles. First, they are responsible for trying to kill as many Confederate officers as possible, from long range. The shooting of a Confederate officer will slow an attack and create a break in the line of defense if men run after seeing their officer shot.

"Second, the sharpshooters are responsible for trying to kill the enemy crews who man the artillery pieces. The sharpshooters' fire will enable the Union troops to move in mass in an attack or hold strong in a defense when the sharpshooters suppress the Rebel artillery.

"As a sharpshooter, you will wear a special green wool uniform which is made to blend in with the green vegetation. The rebels will not be able to see you in the forest. Also, as a sharpshooter, you will receive special target rifles imported from Europe. Have any of you ever heard of Whitworth Rifles?"

Mason paused while waiting for a response, but there was none.

He continued, "Well, it is the most remarkable rifle made. A good marksman can kill at a thousand yards with it." Gasps could be heard from some in the audience at this announcement. "Each Whitworth has a scope. You do know what a scope is? It is mounted on top of the barrel and runs the length of the barrel. With that, you can see a target a mile away."

One hundred and five men tried out for the Missouri Sharpshooters that day. The shooting took several hours. There were ten men shooting at the same time.

Sergeant Mason said it was important to see if each candidate could load and fire quickly and coolly while the noise and smoke of nearby gunshots distracted him. At 5:00 P.M., exactly twenty-one of the men who had started the competition had completed it successfully and qualified for the Missouri Sharpshooters.

Mr. Boomer who had sat watching closely from the back of the wagon now rose and complimented each soldier for his unique shooting ability.

Boomer when on, "Within the next few days, I shall receive a commission in the Missouri sharpshooters, and the battalion will officially come into existence. But now is your chance, each of you twenty-one successful candidates, to become a part of the best unit about to take the field! Now begins the adventure that you shall tell your grandchildren about! Join the sharpshooters! March with me to glory! On to Richmond!"

The shouts and cheers almost drowned out the last words of Boomer's speech. James and Jesse wanted to enlist at that moment but decided to wait until they talked with their parents. One troubling problem was that, while James had easily qualified, Jesse had not even tried his hand with the rifles. Both James and Jesse knew while Jesse was a fair shot, he would never be able to put ten shots in a target at two hundred yards. Both wanted to enlist together, but neither could see a way around this obstacle.

James got the attention of Sergeant Mason and asked him about the problem.

"Sergeant, my name is James Barger and I was one of the twenty-one who qualified. I am very much interested in joining your sharpshooters, but my brother, Jesse, who is a decent shot is not going to be able to qualify. But I want to join the same regiment as my brother. What should we do?"

The sergeant responded, "Don't worry. The sharpshooters need every good Union man we can get. I saw you, Barger, during the competition. You did very well. To get a marksman like you into the Missouri Sharpshooters, I think we can look the other way, and let a decent shot in." James and Jesse grinned at each other at the news.

CHAPTER 22

It was the night of October 10 when the Bargers took their seats around the supper table that Allen noticed James and Jesse were acting different from normal. As they began to eat, Allen noticed James and Jesse sending eye and head signals to each other.

"What's going on with you boys tonight?" Allen asked.

James looked at Jesse and then he looked back at Allen.

"Jesse and I want to join the Union Army, Pa," James said.

"So, you want to join the Union Army?" Allen asked as he reached for the potatoes.

"That's right, Pa!" James said as he looked at Jesse.

"Jesse, is this what you want to do?" Allen asked.

"Yes, Pa," Jesse answered.

"Son, you are not quite eighteen years old. Do you really think you are old enough to get involved in this Civil War?" Allen asked as he laid his fork down.

"I'll be eighteen on June 17," Jesse replied.

"Do those recruiters in California know how old you are?" Allen asked.

"They didn't ask my age, Pa," Jesse replied.

Allen's gaze panned from one boy to the other and the boys felt the intensity of his eyes on them. Neither had ever had such an important topic to discuss with their father and mother. At least nothing before seemed as important as going off to war to fight for a cause.

Nancy couldn't stand it any longer. She placed her fork quietly on her plate, set straight up in her chair and said, "I'd like to speak."

Everyone turned their eyes upon Nancy. Normally, Nancy didn't have a lot to say during meal time, but tonight, she would have plenty to say.

"Boys, this is certainly a shock to me and your father, to everyone at this table I'm sure. I can't believe you would even entertain the thought of getting involved in this Civil War. I'm going to tell you both right now, I'm against you even thinking about it. There will be hundreds of men killed in this war. I don't want my boys to be two of them," she said as she sat back in her chair.

Allen turned his eyes back at James to get his undivided attention. "James, you and Jesse just heard your mother speak. Now, I want to hear from you. I know you have done some serious thinking about this, and now I would like to hear your final thoughts or conclusions."

James hesitated. He was not prepared to offer a good rhetorical argument to back up his decision. So, he started off with some trepidation. "Well, Pa, I thought a lot about what they said at the debate on the court house lawn. You do remember the debate, don't you?"

Allen shifted in his chair and said, "I don't fully understand what you're saying, James. My original question to you is why you want to join the Civil War?"

"Well, Pa, the way I see it a man has to look into his heart and not his head." James said as he glanced at his mother and Jesse who seemed transfixed by his remark. James continued. "What I mean is that it has more to do with how you feel than how it appears logically."

Allen nodded. "And how do you feel? What does your heart tell you?"

"Well." James stared at his feet for a minute. "Well, Pa, I don't think it's right for a man to own another man. Not only that, but when they tell you they are treated well, and you know that's not the truth, then you have to go with your heart, and my heart tells me I could make a difference in proving my point in this war."

Jesse, out of nowhere, burst in. "Yeah. I was thinking that too."

Allen coughed and stared at the boys.

"Boys, I have to say first how proud I am of you that you can think as well as you do. And, that you think from the heart. But one day you will be fathers, and I must tell you how, as a father, I am thinking."

He coughed again to clear his throat. For country people none of them had ever done so much sustained talking.

"From a father's point of view, I have to say I'm with your mother on this, I'm against it. It's not that you boys don't have good reasons because you do. It's just that I've lived longer. It's like your hunting dogs. The ones that's been around more know where the game is and doesn't fall for any of his tricks. The young'un's do. That's what I'm saying here. It's not that I'm smarter or anything like that, but boys, them politician fellers don't care about a man's sons. They care about other things. Things like power and money and control. They don't care if a lot of people are going to get killed, and that's wrong. War is wrong. Think about it, boys. Killing a man is not like looking down the sights and pulling the trigger on a big fat rabbit for dinner. No, you're killing some mother's son. Some woman's husband. Some little child's father. Boys, that's a big difference."

Silence filled the cabin. The fire crackled. The dog whimpered as he curled his body into a more comfortable position.

"I know you boys are mighty fond of all that fife and stuff, the marching and the flags, and the bugle calls. But those are just the trapping. The glory men talk themselves into. But, boys, it's not a good reason to go off killing your fellowman. No, as a father, I am against it. Now I think we ought to pray on it, and then I'll trust each of you to follow not only your hearts but your conscience. Do what you think God is telling you to do. Now let's pray.

"Our Heavenly Father, which art in Heaven, we praise you for the almighty God you are. We recognize you as our Father and Savior. We thank you for all your goodness and kindness, and the many blessings you send our way

"God, I come to you with a heavy heart. Our country is in a state of turmoil. Our young men are enlisting in this Civil War in great numbers. Some will leave and never return home. Some will leave and return crippled and scarred. God, some are just babies!

God, I lift my boys up to you and pray they'll not become casualties of this war. If tomorrow they still want to join the Union Army, give me and Nancy the understanding to accept their decision. I have always trusted you in my decisions. I know you love us, and I know you will guide James and Jesse in their decision. Thank you, God, for everything. It is in Jesus Christ's name I pray, Amen."

This was certainly a sad time. Although it was sad, James loved to hear his pa pray. He always felt that his pa had a direct line of communication with God in Heaven. James' faith was not as strong as his father's, but he did believe in prayer. He promised his father that he would sincerely pray about his decision to join the Union Army.

James and Jesse excused themselves from the supper table and went outside to sit on the front porch. They both were troubled over their pa's and ma's reaction to their wanting to join the Union Army. King lay sprawled at their feet.

"James, what should we do?"

"I think we should pray about it as Pa suggested."

"I didn't realize pa and ma would be so upset with us wanting to join the Army. I thought they would understand we'd be fighting for a good cause. Especially, since they feel the same way we do about slavery," Jesse said.

"I don't think it's got anything to do with the slavery issue. I think they are just concerned about our well-being.

"What if the recruiters ask me how old I am? Should I lie to them?"

"Don't lie, Jesse. Tell them the truth. I heard they don't really care about how old you are anyway. I really don't think Sergeant Mason cares. He was chomping at the bit to enlist both of us this afternoon. Heck, I think he would enlist Mary and George if he could," James said as both brothers laughed.

James and Jesse sat on the front porch until about midnight. They prayed and found peace with God. They both agreed that joining the Union Army and fighting for the end to slavery was what God wanted them to do. James believed that God created all men to be free and should never, under any circumstances, be owned by another human being. This one thing would be worth fighting for.

The next morning James awoke smelling the aroma of his mother's cooking. The smell of bacon had filled the entire cabin. Soon he and Jesse would be sitting at the table telling the family what they had decided to do. It wouldn't be easy, but they had a sense of peace about their decision.

"Good morning, boys," Nancy said as James and Jesse climbed down the ladder from the loft.

"Good morning, Ma," they said at the same time.

"Get washed up and take your places at the table. Breakfast will be ready in about five minutes," Nancy said.

At this time Allen came in through the front door carrying two buckets of fresh water.

"How's everyone this morning?" Allen asked as he took his place at the table.

"Just fine, Pa," everyone responded at the same time.

Allen asked everyone to bow their heads for prayer. He called on James to offer the morning prayer. James didn't mind praying. He had prayed in public in church and at home many times. Praying was something his father had required of all his sons.

James's prayer was one of thanksgiving. By the time he finished Allen felt he already knew what James' and Jesse's decision was going to be.

"James, did you and Jesse pray about your decision to join the Union Army?" Allen asked.

"Pa, God has given us a peace of mind about our decision. We feel it's what we need to do for our country. Please try to understand and support us in our decision," James said looking straight at Allen.

Allen looked in the direction of Jesse.

"That's how I feel too, Pa," Jesse said.

"Although I'm still against you going off to war, I'm not going to stop you from doing something you feel is right. I've taught you to stand up to what you feel is right, and we will just have to trust God to protect you every step of the way," Allen said as he gazed at both boys.

"Thank you, Pa!" James said.

"There is one thing I want to do," Allen said.

"What's that, Pa?" James asked.

"I want to go with you to town when you enlist. I want to know where my boys are being sent and who they will be serving under."

"That's good with me," Jesse said.

James agreed.

James had one other thing he had to do before enlisting in the Union Army. He had to break the news to Christina Miller. He and Christina had been falling in love since the first day they met. They had planned to marry and live in Moniteau County. These plans would have to wait until after the Civil War.

The night before James enlisted in the Union Army he broke the news to Christina while they were standing on the front porch of George Miller's house. As he expected, Christina was saddened by his decision.

"How long do you think you'll be gone?" Christina asked.

"I don't rightly know. Some thinks the war will not last long," James answered.

At this time, Mr. and Mrs. Miller and other family members joined Christina and James on the front porch.

James shared his decision with the Millers. Mr. Miller revealed that his son, Hiram, was going to join the Union Army also. After visiting for a spell, James and Christina asked to be excused for a stroll down to Miller's Creek.

James and Christina's favorite place on Miller's Creek was a big rock located near the creek. They had spent many hours on the rock during their courtship. They had shared their dreams and plans for a future together.

This time was very different. Their hearts were breaking at the thought of a long and dangerous separation.

As they sat with their arms around each other, they renewed their pledge to remain pure and to save themselves for each other. Even though it was hard, they each knew in their hearts that it was God's plan for their lives.

They finally stood, and after a good night's kiss, they walked hand in hand back to the house. On October 12, 1861, Henry, James, Jesse, Thomas Tull, Hiram Miller, and James Brooks enlisted together in the Union Army at California, Missouri.

Sergeant Mason who had been so determined that only the best marksmen should join the Missouri Sharpshooters did not question the qualifications of a single man as they raised their right hands and swore an oath of allegiance. Most importantly, for Jesse, was that the sergeant did not ask anyone's age. Besides the Barger brothers and their friends, about sixty others enlisted that day. The whole county of Moniteau turned out to see the soldiers off. The women had prepared a meal to be served on the courthouse square. The politicians made farewell speeches while many of the soldiers spent the last few hours with their relatives before bordering the train to St. Louis.

It was an exciting day as well as a sad day. The Moniteau County politicians were grateful that the county had so many young men who chose to fight for the Union Army.

Allen and Nancy were sending three sons and one son-in-law off to a bloody and brutal war which would last longer than anyone had expected. Like other parents, they had no assurance their sons would return home alive.

James and Christina spent the last thirty minutes reassuring each other of their commitment and love for each other. They promised each other that they would write as often as time permitted.

"Christina Miller, promise me you will wait for me, and marry me when I return from the war," James said as he wrapped both arms around her and pulled her close to him.

"James Barger, I will marry you and I'll pray every day that God will bring you home safely to me," Christina said as she looked up at him with her beautiful blue eyes while tears ran down her cheeks.

"You're not getting sentimental on me, are you?"

"James, I love you more than life itself. You find a way to stay alive," Christina said as she kissed him.

"Christina, I promise you I'll stay alive."

The chapel bell on First Baptist Church began to ring. This was the signal that everyone was to meet at the train depot. James took Christina by the hand and led her toward the train depot. As they arrived, they found their families waiting.

The train depot was crowded with several families saying their goodbyes. It was a sad day for family members who were staying behind. Fathers and mothers were sending their sons off to a war that would prove to be the most crippling war of all times. Some of the young men leaving for the war would return to California in caskets, compliments of the United States Government. Others would return wounded and scarred for life.

Allen assured Thomas Burton Tull that he would keep a watch on Martha Jane and the boys. He also assured Henry he would check on Pamela as well.

It was difficult for Henry to leave Pamela. They had been married for only a short time, and to him it felt like every day was a honeymoon.

It was even harder for Thomas Burton Tull to say goodbye to Martha Jane, who was pregnant with their third child. He and his boys had built a strong relationship. He would miss seeing and playing with them daily.

As the train pulled away, soldiers stood waving in the train doors and hanging out windows, shouting their last goodbyes to their loved ones. James leaned out the window and watched his parents and Christina as far as visibility would allow. King, loped along beside the train for a few hundred yards and then, despairing of keeping up with his master, turned for home. Most of the families remained at the depot until the train passed out of sight.

CHAPTER 23

The train arrived at Benton Barracks near St. Louis, Missouri, around 6:30 P.M. on October 13, 1861. The company from Moniteau County was assigned to one of the brick barracks. This pleased the boys from Moniteau County. They were glad they were not out in the weather. The brick barracks were extremely overcrowded, but many newly arrived companies were living in tents. James figured they would be in tents soon enough, so they would appreciate every day spent indoors.

James and Jesse had never been apart. Everywhere you saw one, the other was not far away. It wasn't like Jesse couldn't do anything on his own, but if James was around, Jesse let him make the decisions.

The day after arriving at Benton Barracks, the soldiers of James' company were mustered in. A large chart, called a muster roll, was prepared listing the names of each soldier, along with other information such as age, height, and occupation. An officer then stood before the new soldiers, called the roll from the list, and swore in the new company.

Soon, the new soldiers started to become familiar with the routine. Each day at Benton Barracks started with Reveille at 5:30 A. M. After roll call, the soldiers had a few minutes in the barracks before the fifes and drums sounded breakfast call. Breakfast was served at 6:00 A. M. At 7:30 A. M. the fifes and drums again beat, calling for the guard details for the day to assemble and be inspected. Shortly after, the musicians again played, this time sounding sick call, a time soldiers could report to the infirmary. At 7:30 A.M. the musicians again played, this time sounding sick call. Sick call was a time soldiers could report to the infirmary. At 8:00 A.M. the fifes and drummers played "drill call" which summoned the soldiers for drill. A few minutes before noon, after four exhausting hours of drill, the troops were dismissed. Dinner was served at 12:00 and, as always, began with a fife and drum call. The afternoon consisted of more drill, which started at 1:00 P. M. At 3:00 P. M. the soldiers were dismissed to get a little rest and clean camp before parade. The soldiers then filed into formation for a formal inspection and review. At the end of the evening parade, the fifes and drums played "retreat" while the flag was lowered. This also signaled the end of the work day. At 5:30 P M. supper was served. After supper the soldiers were free for several hours, and many took the time to write home. At 8:30 P. M. lights were ordered out in every barrack. At 8:45 P.M. taps were played. Every soldier was expected to be in bed.

On the third day at Benton Barracks, James and the other Moniteau County soldiers were sent to the quartermaster to draw their equipment. James who had been dreaming over the prospect of holding a Whitworth rifle in his hands, with a telescope mounted on the barrel, could hardly contain himself. The first item of business, however, was to issue clothing. An Irish sergeant presided over this.

"It is against the regulations of the United States Army for a soldier to possess or wear unauthorized civilian clothing. I am going to issue your uniforms now. On Tuesday a rag dealer from St. Louis will visit. He will buy your civilian clothing. Any civilian clothing you do not want to sell must be shipped home immediately. Any questions? Good. Now line up here."

The procedure was simple. The sergeant had each soldier step up against a wall with markings for feet and inches on it. He glanced at the man's height, judged the man's size, then began handing--actually, throwing--articles of clothing at the soldier. When James stepped up to the wall, he asked for clarification as he eyed the blue wool that was being passed out to his comrades.

"Sergeant Mason said we would get green uniforms," James said.

"Sergeant who? I suppose he also promised you a parasol? You will get the blue uniform of the United States Army, soldier, and you will wear it."

"But we are sharpshooters. We are supposed to wear green uniforms."

"Look around. Help yourself to every green uniform you find."

Giving up, James took the blue clothing that was handed to him and went back to his place in the line. A corporal came down the row handing out blankets, and a third soldier followed handing out caps.

"Now, "continued the sergeant," this issue is on Uncle Sam. From now on it costs you. If you lose it or wear it out, you replace it. There is a regular schedule of prices. You will each have an expense account with $3.50 added to it each month. If you are careful with the clothing it will last you, and at the end of the year you will receive whatever cash is left in your clothing account. But if you overdraw your clothing account, it comes out of your pay. Any questions? Good. The corporal over there will take you to the armory to draw your weapons."

Well, thought James, at least I will get my Whitworth.

Arriving at the armory, his company was lined up while a second sergeant, this one with a German accent, handed out firearms, cartridge boxes, bayonets, and belts. James was astonished to see that the sharpshooters were receiving battered, rusty old muskets. When James was handed his, he looked at the plate by the trigger and read "Springfield 1842." It was an antique that had probably been carried in the Mexican War. There was a great deal of grumbling and hushed complaining in the ranks of the sharpshooters as they eyed the relics that they were being issued, but only James had the temerity to step forward and demand an explanation. Spotting a captain who seemed to be supervising the issuance of the weapons, James stepped forward.

"Captain, Sir, there seems to have been some mistake. This is a company of sharpshooters. We tried out and proved our marksmanship as a condition of enlisting. Each man here is a crack shot," Well, most of us are crack shots anyway, and we were promised Whitworth rifles with telescopes on them when we enlisted."

The Captain seemed momentarily angered when James stepped forward, but his manner quickly softened. His answer was patient and almost apologetic. "You are the second group to come through with that same complaint in the past couple of days. I was very much perplexed when I heard from some soldiers the other day that they had been promised Whitworth rifles. Well, I am afraid I must tell you that there are no Whitworth rifles. There is a severe shortage of weapons, and the muskets that you are being issued will have to do for now. Hopefully, within a few months, those rusty antiques will be replaced. Perhaps they will be replaced with Whitworth rifles. I don't know. In the meantime, I do know that the Missouri Sharpshooters Battalion has been discontinued. The companies recruited for it have been reassigned to the 26th Missouri Infantry. The gentleman who recruited the sharpshooters, I think his name is Boomer, has been commissioned as the Colonel of the new regiment. You are a part of that regiment."

James, Jesse, Henry, Thomas Burton, James Brooks and Hiram Miller were assigned to Company "G" of the 26th Missouri Regiment.

In James's first letter to Christina, he described how it felt to be a soldier and related his feelings as a soldier.

My dearest Christina,

I have now been assigned to Company "G" of the 26th Missouri Regiment. I am very disappointed I will not be carrying a fancy sharpshooter's rifle. The musket that they have given me does not even compare to Old Faithful, but I hope this will only be temporary and that I will soon have a better gun.

I do like Col. George Boomer who is commander of the 26. He inspires me. I want to be more like him. He keeps telling us that we should receive our orders soon, but so far we've not heard anything about going into battle. Although, the thought of going into battle is a little frightening, I still look forward to an opportunity to do battle with the Rebs. We continue to hear that things are getting pretty heated up down in Mississippi. According to rumors, Mississippi may be where we are headed.

Every night I lie awake thinking about you. You are the reason I live. I love you more than I can possibly tell you in a letter. I love you more than life itself. Please pray for me every time you have an opportunity.

I guess I better get this ready for mailing. Please write me and let me know how things are going back home.

With my deepest love,

James

As the 26th Missouri continued their training at Benton Barracks, the Bargers back in Moniteau county were experiencing a horrible and embarrassing trial. James learned about it in a letter from Christina, which caused him much anxiety:

> *My Dearest James,*
>
> *I am afraid that I have most distressing news. William T. went on an expedition with the Missouri militia to look for Rebels reported in Clay County. While he was gone, Rutha became most gravely ill, and took to her bed unable to move or to call out for help. She lay there for days with no food and no water until, thankfully, a neighbor thought to check on her and found her in her pitiable condition. The flies had covered her body, James!*
>
> *Some of the well-meaning neighbors tried to get her some money from the county and petitioned the judge for assistance, saying that she was a pauper. The judge, who I think is a secession sympathizer, refused to allow her to get county money saying she was the wife of an able-bodied man, and that he should support her. When William T. came back from his expedition with the militia, he was horribly distraught over his wife's condition. Some of Rutha's family, however, see it differently. You may remember that some of the Gouge*

family were not happy when William T. married Rutha and thought he was after her for her property, her being an older woman. Well, some of them saw their chance and they hired a lawyer named John P. Scott to sue William T. as a vagrant. If he is convicted, he could be sold for a six-month indenture to the highest bidder! The lawyer tells me that vagrancy is grounds for divorce in Missouri, and I fear that some of Rutha's relatives are trying to impress upon her, in her enfeebled condition, that she should divorce poor William T.

The trial is set to begin in a few days, and I will write presently with word of its progress. Do not be afraid for William T. because your father has seen that he has a good lawyer, and the Bargers have many friends in this county.

I love you,
Christina

Two weeks later, Christina wrote again. After two days the trial had ended in a hung jury. William T. found sympathy with the jury because of his commitment to serving in the militia. Several of the officers of the militia gave testimony for his behalf. The jury could not arrive at a decision against a young man who had committed to serving his county during a time of war.

James was relieved as he read the letter until he reached the last sentence. The Gouge family had not given up and there would be a second trial of the case.

During the second trial, John P. Scott enlisted the services of his attorney friend, Samuel H. Owens.

Edmund Burke and Charles Drake, two of the best lawyers in Moniteau county defended William. The trial lasted three days and was the most hotly contested trial ever recorded in Moniteau county up to that time. During the trial William stayed with Allen and Nancy. The whole trial was embarrassing to both William and his parents, but they kept their heads high and relied on God for strength.

Christina again wrote to James:

Dearest James,

I'm afraid I don't have any good news for you.

The outcome of the second trial was not good. Your father hired two of the best lawyers in the county, and they did their all to try to win an acquittal for William T., but the lawyers for the Gouges called some of the neighbors, the Gouges' friends who testified that William started neglecting Rutha right after they were married. The judge let in rumors that William T. was chasing after other women. I do not think it to be true, James, and I hope it is not so, but they said truly horrible things about your brother.

The mood of the jury quickly changed from supporting William to supporting Rutha. The jury was made to believe that when William T. signed up for the militia and agreed to go on the expedition to Clay County that he already knew his wife was bedridden but left her anyway without even a word to a neighbor. This time the jury convicted William of vagrancy.

He was confined in jail for a week until he was sold on the front steps of the Moniteau Courthouse. Sheriff Hoge sold him to H.C. Finke, a friend, for five cents. Naturally, Finke will not make William T. work off the debt, so William T. is a free man.

I am afraid, though, that the Gouge family is about to have their way with Rutha. She is gravely ill, and her mind is much affected. I fear she will be coerced into suing William T. for divorce over this matter. While William T. was in jail, the Gouges filed a petition to have her declared a ward of the county saying that she was destitute and in need of support. Your father went and asked the court to allow him to support her believing that the family honor demanded no less.

The Gouges would not hear of it. Worst of all, rather than taking her into their homes, they allowed her to be lodged in the county almshouse like a common pauper.

She is reported to be much under the influence of her relations now, and I believe that she will presently sign the petition for divorce. Your father believes that the Gouges fear that Rutha will soon pass from this world and if she dies married to William T., he will inherit her farm where William T. and Rutha have resided. So, they want to make sure she divorces him before she dies, so that her land will return to them upon her death. I fear, James, that your father is right and that dear Rutha is not long for this world.

How are Jesse, Henry, and my brother, Hiram, doing? Hiram hardly ever writes. My folks worry about him. Please tell him to write us. If he doesn't, would you keep me informed? I will pass the news on to the folks.

Tell Jesse that Margaret expects a letter from him soon. I believe he's a lot like Hiram when it comes to writing letters. Margaret talks about Jesse all the time. I really think she's in love with him. After the war we may have two Barger boys marrying two Miller girls. What do you think about that? Please tell Jesse, Henry, Hiram, and all the other boys from Moniteau County that I send my regards.

By the way, I've been practicing my baking skills. Maybe next time I will send you a batch of my oatmeal cookies. How does that sound?

We continue to meet every Wednesday at New Hope Baptist Church to make supplies for the army. Mostly bandages which I pray you will never need.

This letter has become longer than I had intended. Please know, my love, that you are always close to my heart. I love you so very much. When and if you do go into battle, I pray you will find a way to stay alive. I want this war to end soon. Please take care of yourself. I hope my sad news is not too heavy a burden for you to bear so far away.

Please know that our prayers are with you, and that the troubles here in California will presently pass. Do not worry and remember always that I love you.

I will love you always,

Christina.

Rutha Barger died shortly after the trial ended. Not long after Rutha died William sold the farm and left Moniteau County to live in Ray County, Missouri. His actions were partially motivated by shame over his conviction, but in part he feared further harassment from the Gouge family and wanted to remove himself to a safe distance.

James was saddened by the news about William T., but realized that neither he nor anyone else could do anything about the results. He would do as everyone else, trust and pray that God would provide a new life for William T.

CHAPTER 24

On December 19, 1861, Company B of the 26th Missouri skirmished with a Rebel detachment near Middleton, Missouri. The next day, the same Company raided a private residence and arrested several men accused of forming a company for service in the Confederate Army. That was the beginning of the 26th's involvement in the Civil War.

On December 23, 1861, James A. Barger wrote home to his parents.

Dear Folks,

In two days, it will be Christmas. I just now realized this will be the first Christmas our family will be apart. I will miss being there with you to celebrate Christmas. How are things going with William's difficulty? How are Martha and the boys? Tell her that Thomas is getting fat on "hardtack." Ha! Ha!

Jesse said to tell you both he would write after Christmas. You know he's not too much on writing. Jesse, Henry, and Thomas are well. We are all assigned to Company "G" I am disappointed about the Missouri Sharpshooters, but I still hope to someday have a fine sharpshooter's rifle.

Only Company B has seen any action. They were involved in a skirmish near Middleton, Missouri, several days ago. No one was hurt, and they arrested several men who were accused of forming a company for service in the Confederate Army.

We're getting tired of the food here. We've had plenty to eat, but it's been hardtack, salt pork, and white beans.

Ma, your biscuits beat the heck out of hardtack. I know how hardtack must have gotten its name. It's like worm castles or jaw breakers. I guess it's better than nothing. All in all, things are satisfactory, except for the food.

I'm ready to see some real action. I believe my feelings are shared by every soldier in the 26th. We've been here since October and we're ready to "see the elephant."

I trust everyone is doing well there in Moniteau County. Tell our brothers and sisters we send our love. I want to wish everyone a Merry Christmas and a Happy New Year. I Love you all.

Your son,
James

On December 24, 1861, James received a package from Christina Miller. The contents of the package consisted of wool socks, oatmeal cookies, and a letter.

My Dearest James,

I hope you get this package before Christmas. I made the wool socks to keep your feet warm this winter. I hope you like them. I also made you some oatmeal cookies. Mama says they are quite tasty. She is a good cook as you are aware. I trust her judgement.

Things are going well here at home. We ladies still make supplies for the Union Army on Wednesdays at the New Hope Baptist Church. We knit socks and scarves, and I hope that some of them make their way to you.

Christmas won't be the same without Hiram, Jesse, Henry, Thomas and you. We've been celebrating Christmas together since your family moved to Moniteau County.

Margaret is sending Jesse a letter in this package. She told me to tell you to tell Jesse that she helped make the cookies and for you to share them. It's fine to share them with Jesse and Hiram. That is, if you choose to do so!

I miss you something awful. It's been three months since we last saw each other. I do hope this war ends soon. What do you hear about the war? The local newspaper says most of the fighting is taking place in the East. Do you think the 26th will have to go where the fighting is happening?

Please keep writing. I enjoy your letters. I will keep every letter I get from you. Someday you may want to write a book about your experiences in the Civil War.

Please know I pray daily for you, Hiram, Jesse, Henry, and Thomas.

My love always,

Christina Ann Miller

James answered Christina's letter on December 31, 1861.

Dear Christina,

Thank you for the oatmeal cookies and the wool socks. I'm wearing the wool socks as I write this letter. It is so cold here. We were in a warm barracks for a while, but just when the weather turned cold they moved us to tents. I'm sitting here wrapped up in my wool blanket trying to write this letter. My hands are freezing cold. If you can't read some of my writing, you'll know why.

Did you and your family have a good Christmas? Jesse, Henry, Hiram, Thomas, and I got together and had a family Christmas. We chipped in and bought two cans of peaches. They cost one buck. We bought some sugar cakes and apples for five cents each. It was so good to have something different from hardtack and salt pork.

Tomorrow is New Year's. I don't know how we will spend it. If I was at home in Moniteau County, I think I know how I would spend mine. I would be assured of a good hot dinner.

Christina, it's too cold to write anymore. Even the ink is frozen. I'm going to stop now and get this envelope addressed. Mail won't go out tomorrow because of New Year's Day. I may write more tomorrow.

My Love always,
James

Christina, the 26th Missouri was divided during the month of January 1862. Companies A and C were in St. Louis, while Company B was at Sturgeon, Missouri. The largest contingent, Companies D, E, F, G, H, and I, were guarding railroad lines and scouting near Pacific, Missouri.

Goodbye for now, my love,
James A. Barger

On January 29, 1862, James writes Christina.

Dear Christina,

I'm getting more impatient daily. We have done nothing this month but guard railroads and scout near Pacific, Missouri. I joined this army to fight for a cause, but so far, I've done nothing.

I guess the best part of being here is that I'm making good friends. I really like Col. George Boomer, our Commander of the Missouri 26th. He's not high and mighty like some officers I've seen since being here. He inspects each Company at least once a week. He samples the cook's fare and makes sure it is good. I think he's trying to keep our spirits high. I think he knows we are ready to get involved in this war, and he doesn't want us to get discouraged.

I have gotten to talk to Colonel Boomer which is more than most privates can say. About two weeks ago Captain Hoops came to me and asked if it was true that

I could write well. I told him that I could do it pretty good. He asked me to work as a clerk at the regimental headquarters. I don't get any more pay, but at least I am indoors most of the time out of the cold, and I drill with my company once a week. And no guard duty! I almost told Captain Hoops no that I wouldn't do it. I was afraid I would not get my chance at the Rebels when the fighting came if I was stuck someplace in a corner with a loaded inkwell instead of a loaded rifle. But Capt. Hoops said I would only be on duty as a clerk when the regiment is in camp, and that is fine with me.

It has been a passel of trouble to learn to be a clerk! The quartermaster cannot teach me because he is as new as I am at doing this, and he is just as confused by all the forms as I am. I stay up late reading up on how to do it, and it is starting to make sense to me.

Anyway, about a week ago I was in the little shed we use for a quartermaster's office working away when the door opened, and Colonel Boomer came in to get out of the rain. I jumped right up to salute him, and when I did, I accidental knocked over my inkwell. The ink went all over the papers I was working on. I became more at ease when Colonel Boomer laughed and helped me clean my mess up. I realized then and there that a strong relationship was beginning between the two of us.

He sat down and talked for a few minutes before he left. He has been in once or twice since then to talk. He says that as Colonel, he cannot have regular conversations with the enlisted men, and he is wondering how they feel about the endless drills and the rations, and what not. So, he appreciates the chance to sit and talk to me occasionally. When he stops being so formal and so military, he is a fine gentleman. He tells me that he is as new at this army business as anybody, and he is not comfortable being the Colonel just yet. He's not sure how to act in front of the regiment, so he stays very stiff and somber in front of the men.

I also like Captain John F. Hoops. He commands Company H, which is my company now. Capt. Hoops was born in Germany. He looks and talks differently than we farm boys from Missouri, but he's a fine fellow. I am starting to get used to hearing all these Germans talk, and I can understand what they are saying sometimes. I pride myself in knowing that I'm of German descent and wonder what it was like in Baden Wurttemberg, Germany, before my grandfather, Henry Barger, came to America.

Some other officers that I'm getting acquainted with are Lt. John Price, and Lt. Larimer Schemer. I hope I spelled Lt. Schemer's name correctly. He was born in Bavaria, and he also talks funny. I suppose my favorite Lt. is Charles A. Myer. You've heard me mention his name in my previous letters. He was born in Frankfort, Germany, but he lives now in St. Louis, Missouri. He took me and a dozen members of his company into St. Louis which is not too far to pick up some supplies. We stopped at his house coming back, and Mrs. Myer served us preserves and cake that she had made. I suppose she must have known we were coming because she had enough for all.

I guess my favorite Sergeant is Charlie Dallas from Osage County, Missouri. He was born in Virginia but doesn't have any ties left in Virginia. As you know, Virginia is a Confederate state.

My messmates are Silas Laughlin from Osage County, Missouri; William Kinsmen from Cooper County, Missouri; Joab Barton and William Clark from Cole County, Missouri; and Christopher Fick, Henry Jackson, and Jacob Johnson from Osage County, Missouri. By the way, Jacob Johnson is also a German.

I guess my best friend is Simon Keeler of Cole County, Missouri. Simon keeps me laughing. He's a real circus! I don't think Simon is afraid of anything or anybody. His biggest problem is that he drinks too much whiskey. I don't know where he gets it, but he's always got some around. I must admit, I've sinned since knowing Simon. He challenged me to drink with him one night and I took the challenge. That was the worst mistake I ever made. The last one too! I tell you, Christina, I'm not a drinker. I hate that stuff. It made me sick as a dog. When the drums started playing the next morning, I thought someone was using my head as a drum. It was something awful. Please don't mention any of this to Pa and Ma. They would think I'm going to the dogs!

The food hasn't improved here since the last time I wrote. I think I'm losing weight. I can hardly stand hardtack any longer. Maybe you and your mother could make up a batch of biscuits and send them to us. I know they will not be fresh, but neither is hardtack. You might throw in a jar of sorghum molasses.

I trust your family is doing well. I see Hiram almost every day. I am two tent rows over from Company G. He's doing fine, and so are Jesse, Henry, and Thomas.

We still don't know when we will be leaving for the South. There is some talk we will be joining General Ulysses Grant in Tennessee. When, I don't have any idea.

I guess I'll stop now and get this ready for the mail tomorrow. I love you today more than yesterday.

My love always,

James

The Missouri 26th spent the first two weeks in February 1862, in St. Louis. On February 16, they got their orders to move by steamboats to Bird's Point, Missouri. James was so excited he was nearly beside himself. They left on February 16 and arrived by boat on February 18. Rumor had it that the regiment was going to join General Ulysses S. Grant's forces besieging Ft. Donaldson on the Tennessee River. The fall of Ft. Donaldson ended the need to go to Tennessee. The regiment ended the month of February with headquarters at Bird's Point, Missouri.

After the Confederates surrendered Forts Henry and Donaldson, Tennessee, and evacuated Columbus, Kentucky, they looked for a strong point where they could best defend the Mississippi River.

General Pierre G. T. Beauregard, commander of the Confederate Army in the area, chose the city of New Madrid, Missouri, and Island No. 10 as sites to defend the river.

After fortifying both New Madrid and Island No. 10, he placed Brig. General John P. McEwin in charge of defending the Mississippi River.

It was the objective of the Union Army to break the Confederates' strong hold and take New Madrid and Island No. 10. On March 1, 1862, the Missouri 26th Regiment, along with the rest of General John Pope's Army, left Bird's Point, Missouri, for New Madrid. They marched overland through swamps, lugging supplies and artillery. On March 3, they arrived at New Madrid. The Union soldiers had marched thirty-eight miles in two days without tents or baggage, and with scant rations. They were tired, sleepy, and hungry.

Brig. General John P. McEwin instructed Brig. General Jeff Thompson, commander of a Missouri State Guard to defend New Madrid. General McEwin brought up heavy artillery to bombard the Union Army. On March 13, the Confederates bombarded the Yankees with heavy artillery and gunboats. This heavy bombardment did very little damage to the Union Army. After two days of artillery exchange, Brig. General Jeff Thompson realized he could not defend New Madrid. He issued an order for the Confederate Army and gunboats to evacuate to Island No. 10 and Tiptonville, Tennessee.

On March 14, General John Pope's army discovered that New Madrid was deserted and moved in to occupy it.

On March 16, 1862, James wrote home to Christin.

My Dear Christina,

As of March 16, I am still alive. It has been really exciting here. The 26th Missouri Regiment is now headquartered right here in New Madrid, Missouri.

Our camping conditions haven't been very pleasant. Nothing like what we experienced in good old St. Louis. Our clothes are dirty, and we smell awful. Food is scarce here. I had cold potato soup for dinner. It wasn't very tasty. The meager rations we get hardly fill our stomachs. But whatever you do, don't tell my parents! It will worry them. I really don't enjoy this part of being a soldier. I hear it's worse for other soldiers in the south.

I hope things are well with you and your family. We folks from Moniteau County are doing well. I saw Jesse and Hiram this morning. They looked as bad as I do. None of us have had an opportunity to shave. Believe it or not, Jesse is growing a nice-looking mustache. I look handsome myself in my new beard. Ha! Ha!

I don't know about mail from home. I don't think we will be here at New Madrid very long. The word is that once we take Island 10, we will be moving to Fort Pillow, Tennessee. I wish I could be more precise, but we privates aren't informed on the more important decisions!

Please know that you are always in my thoughts. I love you so much. I guess I had better get this ready to be mailed. Please keep writing. Your letters will catch up with me somewhere. Give my regards to your folks.

My love always,
James

James was right about taking Island 10. On March 17, a U.S. Navy flotilla, under the command of Flag officer Andrew H. Foote arrived upstream from Island No. 10. The ironclad, Carondelet, on the night of April 4 passed the Island No. 10 batteries and anchored south of the island. A second ironclad, the Pittsburgh, followed on the night of April 6. The two ironclads helped to overthrow the Confederate batteries and guns. The heavy bombardment of the two ironclads helped General Pope's men to cross the river and block the Confederates' escape route.

On April 8, 1862, Brig. General William W. McCall, who had replaced McEwin, surrendered Island No. 10 to the Union Army of Mississippi. The surrender of Island 10 and New Madrid made it possible for the Mississippi River to be opened all the way to Fort Pillow, Tennessee.

On April 8, Tiptonville, Tennessee, was captured by the Northern Army. The capture of New Madrid, Island 10 and Tiptonville, Tennessee, greatly weakened the Confederates' stronghold in Missouri and north Mississippi.

On April 13, after the fall of New Madrid, the 26th Regiment began an advance by steamboat downstream to Ft. Pillow, Tennessee. Ft. Pillow was about forty miles north of Memphis, Tennessee.

On April 6 and 7, the Battle of Shiloh was fought in western Tennessee. The 26th was ordered to move immediately to Tennessee and reinforce Grant's Army. Grant's Army was encamped near Shiloh Church at Pittsburgh Landing, Tennessee, on the west bank of the Tennessee River and about twenty miles north of Corinth, Mississippi.

General Grant's superior, Henry Halleck, had arrived at Pittsburgh Landing and taken over for Grant. Halleck was best described as "in an army filled with incompetent generals, he towered above the rest." Halleck, who detested Grant was amassing a huge army in the Shiloh area, eventually something more than 100,000 men. The 26th Missouri became one part of this vast army. Grant was in favor of a bold and forceful move using the huge force. Halleck was more cautious.

The Missouri 26th ended the month of April near Shiloh, Tennessee.

On May 2, General Halleck began his glacier-like advance from Shiloh. By May 6, his advance had slowed to a crawl, although he was only a few miles north of Corinth, Mississippi. During this time, there was constant skirmishing between Halleck's troops and the Confederates. Halleck's advance on Corinth became more of a siege, as heavy artillery was brought up and his troops began entrenching.

On May 26, the Missouri 26th drove back the Rebels. One man from Company A was wounded. Company A was compelled to pull back when Confederate reinforcements approached. Companies A and B of the 26th played a critical role in this skirmish.

During the night of May 29, the Confederates quietly evacuated Corinth. The next morning, Halleck's troops occupied the city which was a key railroad center.

James received a package and letter from Christina on May 30, 1862.

My Dearest James,

I received your letter dated April 28. It was so good to hear from you. The distances between our letters seem to grow further and further apart. Maybe it's because you are getting farther from Moniteau County. I miss you something awful. I wish this war would end.

I'm glad the wool socks are still holding up. I'm sorry about the food situation. I wish I could be there to cook for you. I'm sending you some of my oatmeal cookies and I've included some molasses cookies. Margaret helped make these cookies, so please share them with Jesse. She's included a letter to Jesse. Does Jesse ever say anything about Margaret's letters? Margaret doesn't tell me anything about what she writes. I was just curious to know if he talked about her letters.

My mother has been sick for two months. The doctor doesn't seem to know what's wrong with her. She doesn't have any energy. Catherine, Margaret, and I have started doing all the cooking and housework. I'm worried about Ma. Pa and the boys continue to work on the farm. Pa seems to be in pretty good health.

I saw your father at Centertown yesterday. He looks good. He said they hadn't heard from you in over a month. You might want to write them a letter. I know they worry about you.

I hope you enjoy the cookies. Since Ma isn't feeling good, we decided cookies would be better than biscuits. To be perfectly honest with you, I've not perfected biscuit making.

You stay healthy, James. I want you to stay alert and watch out for those Rebels. Please know that my love grows for you daily.

With all my love,

Christina

The 26th began the month of June camped about three miles southeast of the recently captured town of Corinth, Mississippi. A portion of General Halleck's army, under John Pope engaged in a half-hearted pursuit of the retreating Confederate forces. They arrived in Booneville on June 12. The 26th was near Rienzi, Mississippi, by mid-month, then moving further toward Ripley. The month of June ended with the 26th Regiment near Ripley, Mississippi.

During the month of June, General Grant and General Halleck continued to have their disagreements. Grant was eager to press on into central Mississippi, while Halleck was content to dissipate the available forces to form various garrisons and expeditions into northern Alabama and Western Tennessee.

The month of July was basically a quiet month for the 26th. The Regiment spent from July 3-8, 1862, at Rienzi, Mississippi. On July 9, they moved nine miles to a new camp on Clear Creek where the Regiment remained until the end of the month.

On July 14, the Regiment received four months back pay. The money was a welcomed sight.

On the same day that the Regiment received back pay, James visited Jesse, Henry, and the Moniteau County boys in a grove of trees near Company G's camp.

"Fellows, what are ya'll going to do with your money?" James asked as he walked up to where Jesse and the others were setting.

"I'm going to mail the biggest portion of mine back to Pamela," Henry said.

"I'm going to send Pa my money. I'm going to have him open a bank account for me. I plan to buy a farm when I get out of this war," Jesse said.

"I was thinking about doing the same thing," James said as he sat by the big oak tree that Henry was leaning on.

"I sure would like to have some good home cooking," Hiram said.

"So would I!" Jesse said.

"Jesse how did you like those oatmeal cookies Margaret baked?" James asked as he winked at Henry.

"Them cookies were the best I've ever eaten," Jesse said with a smile.

"Do you think of Margaret very often?" James asked

"I like Margaret, but I'm not hung up on her like you are Christina," Jesse said with a big smile on his face.

"Christina says Margaret talks about you all the time."

"Is that right?" Jesse asked.

"That's right. She said Margaret daydreams about how you and she are going to get married and have at least ten children."

"Now I know you're lying to me," Jesse said as he threw a stick at James.

"Would I lie to you, Jesse?" James said as he laughed.

"Yes, I believe you would," Jesse said.

"Henry, have you heard from Pamela lately?" James asked.

"I got a letter from her last week. She's doing fine," Henry replied as he stood up.

"What about Christina?" Jesse asked.

"Christina is doing fine. Mrs. Miller is sick, and Christina and her sisters are doing most of the cooking and housework."

"Pa thinks Ma might have the dropsy!" Hiram said as he lowered his head.

The conversation shifted to talking about the 26th.

"What's being said over here in "G" Company about the war?" James asked.

"We don't hear much," replied Jesse.

"We just drill and wait," Henry said.

"I'm ready for some action," Hiram said as he kicked the ground.

"Me too!" James Brooks said.

"I wish this war was over. I miss Pamela so much. It's been too long," Henry said as he sat back down by the oak tree.

"Col. Boomer keeps telling us it won't be much longer," James said as he stood up.

"I've got to get back to camp. It's my time to cook tonight. We are going to have potato soup and hardtack. Doesn't that sound good?" James asked jokingly.

After cooking supper, James wrote the following letter to his parents.

Dear Folks,

Today is July 14. I've just cooked potato soup for supper. It wasn't that bad. Although, we are so hungry here that anything tastes good. I sure miss your home cooking, Ma. I'd give about anything for some of your fresh bacon and flapjacks. I can almost taste them!

There isn't much going on here in Rienzi, Mississippi. We look forward to the day we will be called into action to fight the Rebs. So far only Company A has seen action in our Regiment. It was a skirmish with some Southern sympathizers. Only one man in Company A was hurt.

I visited with Henry, Jesse, and the other boys from Moniteau County this afternoon. Everyone is doing well. We all share the same thoughts. We want to see this war end, and we want to have our bellies full again. None of us are gaining weight. I am still sharing a tent with the same guys from Osage County, Missouri. We take time about in cooking. I'm turning out to be a pretty good cook.

Pa, how are things on the farm? Jesse and I are sending you some money. Jesse wants you to open him a bank account. I would like for you to deposit my money in my account. We are hoping we can save enough money to make down payments on farms.

Ma, how are things with you? How are our brothers and sisters doing? Has Mary Ann started dating yet?

Jesse and Henry send their regards and love. They said to tell ya'll they would write another time.

I hear Mrs. Miller is ill. How is she doing? I hope she gets well soon. There isn't a lot going on here now. We continue to drill and guard railroads. It's boring.

Pa, please ask God to speed things up in this war. I don't want to spend my entire life in this army. We are homesick. We are committed to what we came here for, but it's no fun just waiting.

Ya'll take care of yourselves. I love you all.

Your son,

James

The 26th camped at Clear Creek, Mississippi, until August 5. On August 5, 1862, they moved to Jacinto, Mississippi. They encamped about one and a half miles southwest of Jacinto and remained there until September 18.

On September 16, 1862, James wrote to Christina.

My Dearest Christina,

We are now encamped about two miles from Jacinto, Mississippi. I don't know how long we will be here. Col. Boomer has informed us we may be in battle soon. I think I can feel it. We've waited so long for battle. I must admit, I'm a little scared. Not of getting shot so much, but the thought of shooting or killing another man bothers me.

Col. Boomer continues to amaze me with his encouragement, energy, and humor. He is admired and respected by the entire 26th. I would like to be more like him.

A day's duty here at Jacinto is spent drilling and performing routine patrols of the vicinity.

Jesse, Hiram, Henry, and the other boys from Moniteau County are all doing well. I see them in formation about every day. Hiram is doing well. He told me to tell you hello and that he misses you.

Christina, you don't have to worry about me gaining weight. We are starving. We go to bed hungry and wake up hungry. Your last batch of cookies was delicious. Jesse bragged and bragged on them. Every time he took a bite, he would say, "These are the best cookies that I've ever eaten." I think he was thinking of Margaret every time he took a bite.

In your last letter you mentioned that your mother was ill. How is she doing? I hope she's better by now. She is such a great lady, just like her beautiful Christina!

We recently received four months of back pay. It was a welcome sight. We have been flat broke for so long. I've sent most of my money home for Pa to put in my bank account. We will someday use this money to purchase a farm. How does that sound to you? I can't wait!

I'll be right back!

Christina, I will now try to finish this letter. I had to stop to attend a roll call. Col. Boomer just informed us that it looks like we will be leaving soon for Iuka, Mississippi. This may be our first battle experience. I'll write you again after the battle. Yes, I plan to stay alive.

Please know I love you more each passing moment. I sometime wake up in the middle of the night calling out your name. I continue to remember the last night we spent together on Miller's Creek. I miss you something awful. Please pray for us all.

I love you,
James

CHAPTER 25

It was now September 19, 1862. James dropped down beside the dusty road and slipped his pack off his aching back. "How much farther can it be to Iuka? It seems like we have marched fifty miles today!" James said to Jesse.

Jesse laughed. "We will be in Iuka soon enough. I think it cannot be much farther. I was down the column delivering a message to Captain Hooper, and I heard him say that Companies A and B are going to move out to scout for Rebels ahead of us. I think we will finally see some action!"

James did not know whether to be eager, at long last, to see a real fight or not. At this moment, though, his feet and back hurt too much to care. He leaned back to try to rest. At least he was better informed than the average private in the ranks. As he slipped closer and closer to sleep, he thought back to the events of the night before when it was his turn to stand guard duty, a very serious proposition, since the Rebels were somewhere out there in the darkness. As he stood squinting into the darkness, a figure on a horse approached down the road.

"McDowell!" called out James, giving the name of a Union general.

"Pope!" answered the figure, who dismounted and advanced.

In the darkness the officer came within three feet before he and James recognized each other. "Barger!" said Colonel Boomer, "Are you not using your pen and inkwell tonight?"

"There is no need for an extra clerk while we are in the field. I'm itching to see action, Sir."

Boomer was in a friendly mood and leaned against a tree trunk to chat. After several minutes of small talk, James worked up the nerve to ask, "Sir, what is going on? Why this sudden marching?"

Boomer looked momentarily surprised at the question, then said "Well, it won't do any harm to tell you, I suppose. But keep this to yourself. Several days ago, a Confederate force seized the town of Iuka, which is up that road a piece. We have a deserter who says it is Sterling Price's force and that his orders are to raise hell in north Mississippi. Old Braxton Bragg and the main Confederate Army are up in Kentucky, and if Price can cause enough trouble down here, it will prevent us from sending reinforcements up to Kentucky to help fight against Bragg."

"So, there's really going to be a fight," James said.

"It looks that way. Grant has sent two forces against Price. We are here," James squinted in the darkness at the mark that Boomer scratched out in the dirt road. Here is Iuka, just north of us. That is where Price is reported to be. Our force under General Rosecrans is to march north to Iuka tomorrow to engage Price. The second force is under General Ord. Together, our force and Ord's will have enough troops to beat Price."

"Excellent!" said James.

"There is a problem, James. Don't tell anyone I told you this. But we don't have any contact right now with General Ord. He is just somewhere out there. Hopefully, tomorrow we will meet up with him, or perhaps when he hears our guns, he will attack Price from the other direction. I have just come from meeting with Rosecrans, and he plans to fight tomorrow no matter what happens with General Ord."

Boomer yawned. "How much longer do you have on duty, James?"

"I am relieved in about an hour, Sir."

"Well, get as much sleep as you can. You will need it tomorrow. Good night, James."

"Good night, Sir."

The colonel turned away, mounted his horse, and disappeared into the darkness.

Suddenly, James was shaken back to the present. Jesse, vigorously shaking his arm, was hoarsely whispering, "Wake up, James!" James was momentarily startled and then realized that he had dozed off and, in his dream, he had been reliving the conversation of the prior evening.

He sat up by the dusty road, "What's wrong, Jesse? Why won't you let me sleep? I was up half the night last night on guard duty."

"Somebody is shooting, and it's not too far up the road. Companies A and B pulled out to scout just a few minutes ago, and they have not had time to get far."

James, returning slowly to his senses, saw a flurry of activity along the road as resting soldiers stood, their weapons in readiness. More shots could be heard from down the road.

Lt. Colonel Holman rode up on his horse. "Stand to now!" he shouted, then to the fife and drum corps, he added, "Boys, the long roll, now!" The boys began to play the long roll, the battle alarm of the soldier, its pulse-quickening beat slowly mounting to crescendo. James slipped his pack back on, his aching back forgotten, and fell in with the rest of the company.

Holman wheeled his horse at the sound of an approaching rider. Colonel Boomer reined in his excited mount just feet from where James was standing. Over the shouted commands, the roll of the drums, and the drone of soldiers falling into line and preparing for battle, Boomer had to shout to be heard by Holman, and James could hear most of what was said.

"We are in a tight place now! The whole Rebel force is only about 400 yards ahead. The scouting party ran into them almost immediately."

"Damn!" answered Holman. "We aren't in battle line! The force is straggled out for two miles along the road. Damn! If the Rebels hit us now, they will just roll us down the road! We are too strung out to stop them! That bastard, Rosecrans! Has he never heard about scouting? Did he ever think about deploying before we got too close?"

"It's worse than you know," answered Boomer. "Stanley's division has fallen behind us. He is several miles away still. Only Hamilton's division, half of Rosecrans's force, is here with us."

"Damn!" answered Holman. James was somewhat amused by Holman's repetitive cursing, although the severity of the situation was beginning to dawn on him.

"Where is Ord?" said Holman.

"I don't know. Rosecrans has had no contact with him. We are on our own. Take the four companies in the lead forward. I will hold the remaining four companies here. If you run into Companies A and B, send them back to me. I will commit the reserve only when the Rebel's intentions develop. Hamilton is sending more regiments forward, you won't be on your on."

"Just pray that Price holds off twenty minutes! Twenty minutes! If we have that, we might be able to get enough on line to hold them!" Without another word, Holman wheeled his horse and galloped off.

Colonel Boomer turned, seeing James, shouted "Didn't I tell you we would have a fight?" Then, Boomer spurred his horse and rode off at a gallop too.

"Out of the road! Get out of the road now!" James and the rest of the 26th scrambled for the ditch, just in time as a battery of artillery galloped by. After a momentary lull, the firing ahead of them had become more intense. The 5th Iowa Infantry double- timed past the 26th.

As the 5th Iowa Infantry passed by, James couldn't help noticing the grim expressions on the soldiers' faces. They were scared, he thought. He too was scared, and he had not yet been called into battle. As they passed by him, he wondered how many of those men would fall by a Confederate bullet or a cannon shell. How many would die? He wondered if this might be the time he would be wounded or die. Would it be Jesse's, Henry's, or Hiram's time to die, he wondered? He lowered his head and prayed. He finished his prayer in time to see Lt. Colonel Holman off to his right summoning four companies forward. Companies D, G, I, and K formed up on the road and trotted toward the cloud of smoke beginning to form just down the road. Jesse and Henry passed near where James stood, heading for the front. James could not help thinking, even as the roar of battle grew closer, that he would never hear the end of it if Jesse and Henry got into a fight without him.

An endless wait followed. Ambulances raced past on the road, and James strained to see if he could recognize the occupants. The smoke, drifting from the fighting only a few hundred yards away, began to thicken as dusk fell. Not knowing what was happening only a short distance away was the worst of it. Boomer, chewing a cigar, paced up and down irritably, casting frequent glances toward the fighting. Nervous soldiers made small talk, and nervous laughter could be heard in response to hollow attempts at humor.

Finally, a horseman approached. He paused, looked, then rode straight to Colonel Boomer. James could not hear what was said, but the agitated horseman was gesturing straight into the thickest cloud of smoke directly up the road. Boomer nodded and mounted his horse, then calling out to the messenger, said in a voice loud enough for James to hear, "Where have my other companies gone? I only have four companies here?"

The rider responded with a shrug and a vague gesture into the smoke before galloping off. Boomer turned to his diminished regiment and shouted, "The 26th! There is a battery! There!" He pointed his sword into the smoke with a dramatic flair. "And we must save it. Now! Forward! Forward!"

With a yell the 26th surged forward. James trotted in the densely packed ranks, with the inferno ahead getting closer at every step. He stumbled and then realized he had almost tripped over a body. A bee buzzed past his head. Then another and another hummed past. James pondered where the bees could be coming from then, with a start, realized that the bees were bullets. The ground fluttered with little bits of paper, bitten off from cartridges with the teeth of countless soldiers who had already fought across this ground. The roar was like a train, but a thousand times louder, and it grew more intense with every step forward.

Suddenly, ahead of him, figures loomed through the smoke. He halted, lowered his musket, and fired. The shock of scores of muskets firing at once racked him. So, this was what a volley was like. Over the echoing ear throbs of the volley, he heard an officer shouting, "Damn it! Those are friendly troops. Hold your fire! Reload! Forward!"

The regiment now encountered more friendly soldiers, heading for the rear, staggering with wounds, helping limping comrades along, many in shock, staring off into the air. Suddenly, out of the smoke and darkness loomed the squat shapes of a row of cannon. A group of men were struggling to turn the cannon and at the approach of the 26th, they fired. James saw the muzzle flashes but could not make out their shots above the general din. Without orders --- for no orders could be heard in this roar--- the 26th unleashed a second volley. A soldier near James grabbed his leg and dropped to the ground, rolling in agony. A second staggered back, clutching a bloody hand.

Another volley! Now it was impossible to see anything but the soldiers next to you. The buzz of bees, incessant now, could be heard even through the constant thunder. Someone next to James yelled in his ear, but James could not hear what was said. There were moving figures in the smoke. Were they friend or foe? James loaded and fired mechanically, into the smoke and gloom.

Suddenly, a group of figures appeared out of the muck in front of him. James fired, not realizing that others fired in the same instant. He saw a figure pause before him, and saw a muzzle flash, there was a sharp tug at his jacket, and then the figure faded into the gloom again. Only then did James realize that he had almost been killed in that split second.

There came a moment's lull in the thunder, like a conversation at a party suddenly falling silent. Taking advantage of the relative calm, Boomer shouted "Forward, now! To the guns!" James, not knowing how many others in the darkness and smoke heard and obeyed the same cry, started forward. There were more muzzle flashes ahead, and the noise level again increased. James paused beside the wheel of a cannon, which offered only a little protection. Two gray clad figures sprawled nearby, one of them moving spasmodically. James aimed into the darkness and fired again and again.

Boomer was there, beside him, pistol in hand. James did not know where he had come from but saw there was blood on his jacket. James wanted to ask if he was gravely wounded, but in the next instant, turning back from firing a shot, Boomer was gone.

Suddenly, out of the gloom to his right, James caught a glimpse of a moving figure. Turning from his latest shot, he was stunned when a musket butt, wielded like a club, grazed past his head. Knocked off balance, he half crawled, and half crabbed away from the figure, leaving his own musket on the ground. The gray clad soldier, swinging his rifle by the barrel, limped after him, favoring his right leg. A second swing grazed James's knee. A third dealt a glancing blow to his arm, raised in a defensive posture, and knocked James on his side. James rolled back desperately trying to avoid another blow. The gray clad figure was gone. James had only a split second to wonder whether the man had been shot or had simply staggered off into the smoke again. His hand came to rest on the muzzle of a gun, which he wrenched from the hands of a fallen Confederate. Taking the dead man's cartridge box, James was stunned to realize this man carried an Enfield rifle, infinitely superior to his own battered old musket. He turned toward another figure emerging from the smoke, backlit by muzzle flashes. James fired, the figure spun in a complete circle, then fell not five feet from where James stood. With trepidation, James approached. He had never killed a man before. In fact, he had never even deliberately hurt anyone before. He inched forward and looked down on the face of a boy of fourteen or fifteen. The figure gasped for breath, his eyes locked on James's face, then faded to a non-comprehending stare. Then the breathing stopped.

James, overcome with emotion, staggered backwards and began walking in a daze through the whirlwind toward the rear. Figures loomed around him. Somebody yelled, "Don't shoot! It's Barger! He's one of us!" Shaken back to reality, James found himself during a score or so of 26th Missourians mixed in with a few others that he recognized from the 5th Iowa. Among them was Colonel Boomer, who now leaned weakly against a tree. Raising his sword, Boomer shouted "We have to try once more! We must get to those guns! We must take--" The last was cut off in a deep explosion of breath. James looked over to see Colonel Boomer slump to his knees, his jacket covered in blood. James knelt by him, supporting him. Boomer moaned, then opened his eyes. Blood trickled from his mouth. "Move forward" he whispered. "Leave me here. Move forward." Then he passed out.

Some of the soldiers began to creep, firing and loading as they went, toward the muzzle flashes, which now seemed as many as the stars on a clear night. James, with three others, grasped Boomer's limp form and began to drag him through the brush toward the rear. Only after two hundred endless yards, did they feel safe enough to stand up, and carry their fallen leader.

A few hundred feet further, an ambulance was encountered. Boomer, still unconscious, was placed on the wagon. Built for four stretcher cases, the wagon now held twelve wounded men, piled in three deep. It jolted off to the rear, with each bounce bringing a chorus of groans.

James turned back to the fight, but paused, exhausted, to catch his breath leaning against a tree. The firing had slowed considerably, he noticed. The moon was high in the sky. Had it been hours since the battle had begun? He gradually became aware of many figures plodding and limping from the woods to the rear. The firing played out, except for an occasional scattered shot.

One of the figures passing in the darkness, suddenly drew James' eye. It was Jesse.

"Jesse, over here," he cried, then was embarrassed at how loud his voice sounded in the newfound quiet.

Jesse glanced up, as if awakening from a trance, and focused on James.

"Henry is dead," said Jesse with a lack of emotion born of exhaustion. "He was standing right beside me. He grabbed his chest, and I got splattered with his blood. And he said 'Jesse, help me' and there was nothing I could do. I tried to carry him to the rear, but he was too heavy, and it hurt him so to pull him on the ground, James. But I tried, James! I tried." Jesse suddenly broke down in sobs.

"I hollered for help, but nobody heard over the noise. He grabbed my shirt and he said 'Jesse, don't leave me. I know I'm not going to make it. Please promise me you will send me back to Moniteau County. I don't want to be buried here in this strange place.' I wouldn't promise him, because I did not want him to think of dying. Then he said 'Promise me, Jesse. You got to promise me.' And I promised him. I promised him, James. Then he says 'Please tell Pamela that I loved her with all of my heart. Tell her I want her to be happy and not to stay a widow. She will need someone to take care of her. Promise me, Jesse.' So, I promised him this, too. Then he just put his head down and died."

"He's still back there, somewhere, James. We've got to go and look for him. I promised him, James."

James, choking back his own emotions, said "I know, I know, but there are Rebels in the woods and it's dark. We'll go get him in the morning. I promise, too."

Together, the two brothers staggered in exhaustion and grief to the rear.

As James lay down to sleep, he could not get Henry off his mind. He agonized with pain. His heart felt it would explode. He had never lost a relative and it hurt like hell. What he hated most was knowing he was in a dry warm bed and Henry's body lay cold and lifeless on a bloody battlefield. He wondered if Henry body would be disturbed by wild dogs before they could find him.

His father and mother's words kept creeping into his mind. He could hear them both saying, "I'm against this war. I'm against you boys going to war. War is for the rich folks not us poor folks. Soldiers will kill other parents' sons, women's husbands, brothers." Everything his father had warned against was true. He asked himself over and over, could this be a mistake.

The next morning, James, Jesse, Hiram, James Brooks and several friends searched the battlefield for Henry's body. The

Rebels had slipped away in the night, and parties of Union soldiers crisscrossed the shattered woods, collecting wounded, weapons, and dead. They had trouble finding the body because Jesse was not sure where he had left Henry amid the smoke and confusion. Finally, Hiram found him just ahead of the burial detail.

"We lost a good friend today," Hiram said as they viewed Henry's body.

"A good friend and brother," James replied.

"How are we going to get him back to Moniteau?" Jesse asked.

"There is a church about a mile down the road. Captain Hoops said that we could take his body there for burial. At least, that way he won't end up in a mass grave. We can mark where he is and return for him after the war," James explained.

Wrapping Henry in an army blanket and borrowing a stretcher, they began the slow, sad walk toward the church. Luck, however, smiled upon them that day. Coming up the road toward them was a wagon, painted with the words "Anderson and Son, Mortuary Embalmers, Corinth, Mississippi."

They flagged down the driver. Much haggling followed. The driver, Mr. Anderson, had only a limited supply of coffins, and most were already spoken for. But, pooling their money, they scraped together enough to pay the man. Mr. Anderson agreed to ship Henry's body back to Moniteau County.

James promised to repay Hiram and James Brooks, but both shook off his promises.

Three days later, back in camp, James took pen in hand to write a difficult letter,

September 19, 1862
Dear Folks,

My heart aches with pain to bring you this news, but there is no easy way to say it. Henry is dead. I want you to know that Henry fought with courage and died with honor. He was killed instantly and did not suffer any.

I experienced my first taste of battle and death. It just happened that my brother was one of the victims.

We won the battle, but we paid a great price. Over a hundred members of the 26th are dead or wounded, but Jesse, Hiram, and I are all right. I don't think I've ever seen anything so brutal. The way the armies line up and fight in columns, shoulder to shoulder is awful. I don't understand why we must fight that away. We are sitting ducks for the enemy. Anyway, we do as we are told and as a result, several soldiers have died.

Jesse and I have decided to send Henry's body home. The undertaker in Corinth is going to have him shipped via Adams Express Co. I hope that my letter reaches you first. I know Henry's death will be hard on you because he was your first. Please know he loved all of you. Please tell Pamela that Henry loved her with all his heart. He wanted her to know that. He didn't expect her to be a widow for the rest of her life. He also wanted ya'll to know he was ready to meet his maker. He credited ya'll for leading him to the Lord.

I don't know anything else to say currently. I will say that Jesse is remaining strong. He has taken Henry's death hard, but he is strong. He is in good health and so am I. We will survive this brutal war. I'll do everything I can to look after Jesse.

Please write us as soon as you can. We want to know if things went well with Henry's body being shipped back home.

I don't know where we will go from here, but your letter should catch up with us somewhere here in Mississippi.

Please know I love you, and please continue to pray for our safety. Also, pray that God will bring this war to a close soon.

Your son, James

It was not all true, he thought to himself, but it was better to tell a little lie than the full truth sometimes. Next, he wrote to Christina.

My Dearest Christina,

By the time you get this letter you will likely have learned that Henry is dead. I regret that I could not be there when you get the news. Jesse and I requested permission to bring Henry's body home, but our request was turned down.

After seeing Henry's body, I realized my bullets cost the lives of at least one, and maybe several Confederate soldiers who would be sent home in a box, like Henry. This doesn't give me a feeling of glory. In fact, I hate this war. I hate the killing. I know it's going to continue, and I know that I will continue to be a part of it, but I don't like it. My pa was right about this war. We are killing sons, husbands, and brothers. I'm afraid this is only the beginning of many more killings.

Let me tell you that Hiram is a good soldier. Jesse tells me he was out front in the charge against the Johnny Rebs before Company G was ordered to the rear. He and Jesse both are doing well. As far as I know at this time, Henry is the only soldier from Moniteau County who lost his life in the battle of Iuka.

Please know that as I fought, I thought about you. You are the reason I live. I will continue to cling to what we have together. I will continue to pray that God will take care of me. I know you are praying for me too.

I don't know what's going to happen next. We've heard that the Confederates are on the run, but I don't know for sure. We may do battle again soon.

Tell your folks hello for me. Remember, I love you with all my heart and soul.

Love you always, James

The Battle of Iuka, Mississippi, was the opening battle of the Iuka-Corinth Campaign. Union Maj. Gen. William Rosecrans was successful in stopping the advance of the Confederate Army of the West commanded by Maj. Gen. Sterling Price. After an afternoon of fighting, entirely by Rosecrans's men, the

Confederates withdrew from Iuka on a road that had not been blocked by the Union army. The Confederates later joined up with Confederate Maj. Gen. Earl Van Dorn.

Both the Union and Confederate Armies suffered many casualties during the battle. The Union had 790 casualties, 144 killed, 598 wounded, and 40 either captured or went missing.

The Confederate army had 1,516 casualties of which 263 were killed, 692 wounded and 561 either captured or missing. Henry was the only Moniteau County soldier who lost his life in the battle.

CHAPTER 26

After the Battle of Iuka, Maj. Gen. Sterling Price marched his army to meet with Maj. Gen. Earl Van Dorn's Confederate Army for retaking the city of Corinth, Mississippi, which had been a critical rail junction for the Confederates until Corinth fell to the Union Army during a one-month siege which lasted from April 29 to May 30, 1862.

At the beginning of the battle to retake Corinth on October 3rd, the Confederates pushed the Federal army from the rifle pits originally constructed by the Confederates. The Confederates exploited a gap in the Union line and continued to press the Union troops until they fell back to an inner line of fortifications.

It was on this day, October 3, 1862, that the Missouri 26th Infantry and other Union soldiers found themselves in the trenches waiting for instructions from General Rosecrans.

October 3rd was very hot, too hot to think, too hot to write Christina. James slipped the pencil and paper back into his pack and slumped down into the trench. He casually picked up a clod of dirt and crushing it, let it fall through his fingers. Perhaps a Confederate soldier had dug up that dirt clod? After all, the Confederates had originally dug this line of trenches to defend Corinth and now, ironically, they were the ones attacking it with the federals sitting in the very trenches that the Confederates had first dug six months before.

In front of him for several hundred yards, several trees had been felled. The jumble of logs now served as obstacles to trip attackers. The upper portions of trees had been felled toward the route of an anticipated attack, creating a jumble of branches called "abatis" which would also delay an attack. James could not help but think that a horde of insane beavers had been loosed upon the land and their handiwork left where it fell.

The drummer boys were back now. They had gathered up the soldiers' empty canteens and carried them to a spring they had located. Now, staggering under the weight of the full canteens they passed them out to the parched soldiers. James gulped eagerly.

Most of the soldiers lounged on the grass near the trenches now. Since there was no sign of Confederate activity in front of their position, there was no reason to be uncomfortable in the dirt and rocks. To their north, stretched across the barrier of felled trees and into the woods beyond, the Purdy Road was empty.

Refreshed by his drink, James turned back to his letter to Christina, forcing himself to write.

> *"There is a lull in the battle right now, but I am not involved in it. You will be happy to know that I am at a good, safe distance from the fighting. Last night we were ordered into the trenches a couple of miles north of Corinth. The 26th Missouri is in General Hamilton's division, and General Hamilton's division was sent to guard the Purdy Road northeast of Corinth.*
>
> *"This morning the Confederates attacked, but they came down the Chowilla Road, which approaches Corinth from the northwest. We have been sitting here in this trench all morning listening to the battle going on a mile and a half or two miles to the west, but nary a Confederate has come down that road from Purdy.*
>
> *"The rumor is that our boys over on the Chowilla Road are getting driven back by the Confederates, and judging from the sound of the firing, I think that may be true. I have been expecting the order to march to the fighting for hours, but we are still sitting here watching the Purdy Road. Some of the fellows say that we have been forgotten by General Rosecrans or that the Confederates are already behind us and between us and Corinth. Most of the fellows seem happy enough to stay at a safe distance from this fight."*

James laid his pencil aside again. The truth was he was totally mystified by what was going on. If Colonel Boomer were here, James could perhaps catch a moment with him and find out what was going on. But Boomer was still recovering in St. Louis from his wound at Iuka. It was a miracle that he had survived, and James had missed the occasional conversations when he worked in the headquarters. Now, he really wished that Boomer was there. Why was the 26th just sitting and watching, while a huge battle waged just a mile away?

It did no good worrying. James pulled his cap down over his eyes, and tried to sleep, hoping to escape the heat of the afternoon.

He was rudely awakened by a poke in the ribs. Hiram Miller whispered hoarsely "Get up! You will never believe what I heard!"

James sat up, rubbing the sleep from his eyes, while Hiram rattled on without pause. "One of the fellows over in D Company heard from somebody in the 5th Iowa who talked to a messenger on General Hamilton's staff!"

"Heard what?" moaned James.

"Have you heard a word I have said? This messenger said that messages have been going back and forth between General Rosecrans and General Hamilton all day! He heard General Hamilton cussing up a blue streak and saying that Rosecrans was not fit to command a dozen pack mules! That's exactly what he said, James, a dozen pack mules."

"What?" James said, slowly starting to piece this conversation together. "What made Hamilton say that?"

Miller sighed with exasperation. He calmly and patiently started over again like he was explaining to a child.

"Look, James, I have it good. This came from a messenger on Hamilton's staff. General Hamilton has been nagging at Rosecrans all afternoon. We have been sitting watching this road" he cast a derisive glance at the Purdy Road, "and nobody is coming down that damned road. The battle is over there," another derisive glance, this time to the west, and everybody from General Hamilton down to the drummer boys knows it. Only General Rosecrans doesn't seem to understand it. He won't give Hamilton permission to pull out of these trenches, wheel left, and attack. And you know what, James? The Rebels are behind us now! No, I don't mean it like that! What I mean is that if we turned and attacked now, we would attack the Rebels on their flank and from behind. Hamilton is chomping at the bit to attack them, but old Rosy keeps sending him these long, drawn out messages that say just about everything in the world except you can attack now."

"So, then this battle is going to pass us by?" James said.

"I don't believe it. Rosy will surely use us to attack that Rebel flank."

"Sure, don't look that way. This will be the end of Rosecrans. He is going to lose Corinth with a whole division! just sitting here watching. After all the trouble we went to, just to take this place."

Miller's last comment was cut off by shouted commands echoing down the line. "Fall in!" shouted the officers. "No drums! Keep it quiet! Stand to!"

James glanced at Miller with an "I told you so" expression then grabbed his musket and fell in.

"By the left flank! March!" The regiment turned to the westward toward the sound of the firing, now more distant than before. "Double quick! Forward!" The sun was low in the sky now, bringing some relief from the heat of the day. Evening was upon them.

"Rosy may have been planning this all along, James," Hiram said. "He may have just been waiting until we were in a good position to hit the Rebels from behind. But I think he waited too long. It will be dark within an hour, and we won't even be in position to attack by then."

Hiram was right. Darkness fell, and the 26th was ordered back to the inner defenses around Corinth.

The next day brought another hot day. The day proved to be equally as hot as the day before. As fate would have it, it was late that evening before James could continue his letter.

"Christina, It is now evening on the 4th of October. At this rate, I will never get this letter finished and mailed to you. It was a hot day today in more ways than one! The 26th was lucky though and lost very few men. The

Confederates attacked our lines with great ferocity about 11:00 A.M. and soon fought their way into the streets of Corinth. I was in a second story window of somebody's home firing at Confederate soldiers in the houses down the street. From where I was, I could see a desperate fight going on for Battery Robinette. Swarms of Confederates were sweeping over the fort, and I thought it would most surely be captured, but at the last minute one of the Ohio regiments charged and retook it. Then, Lt. Colonel Holman (he is commanding while Colonel Boomer recovers from his wound) came riding down the street shouting for the 26th to go forward! I ran out of the house and joined a bunch of the fellows in charging, but it was the strangest charge you ever saw. We went into back yards and over picket fences and through houses and around and in and out, chasing the Rebels all the way out of town. Poor John Stutter tried to hide in an outhouse, figuring that he could load his musket where it was safe, but somehow, he slipped and fell in! He was the most awful mess you ever saw coming out of that outhouse, and I swear, Christina, with the battle raging all around us, half the 26th Missouri stopped dead in their tracks with laughter!

"Colonel Holman is wounded, but I do not think it is too serious. Companies A and B of the 26th found a bunch of Rebels hiding in a barn after the battle and took them all prisoners.

"Captain Hooper told me that he was going to write me up in his report for my 'coolness under fire' and for the way that 'my accurate firing from a house kept the Rebels pinned down in the adjoining building' or something like that. He said that he may ask Lt. Col. Holman, or maybe Boomer when Boomer gets back, to make me a corporal. I hope Boomer gets back quickly because Holman doesn't really know me.

"It's late, and the word is that we will march at daylight in the morning in pursuit of the Rebels. I'll finish this after we return."

When the 26th Missouri returned to Corinth on October 9th, after a fruitless pursuit of the fleeing Confederates, James had a letter from Christina. He opened the letter as he slowly sat down.

My Dearest James,

I received your letter dated on September 19 after Henry's burial. I'm so sorry about Henry and your friends from Osage County. I know you wanted to be here for Henry's funeral, but I understand why you couldn't. This war has touched so many lives in Moniteau County. We have had five soldiers from Moniteau County buried in the last three weeks.

I'm afraid I have further bad news to share with you. Mama died on September 17, right before Henry's death. We buried her in the New Hope Baptist Church Cemetery. The doctors said she had dropsy. I hope I never again see anyone waste away like Mama did. She lost so much weight during her sickness. I loved her, and I miss her so much. My sisters and I are doing the cooking and housework. We also help Pa on the farm. Pa misses Mama a lot. I feel so sorry for him. He tries to be strong for us, but I know deep down how he must be hurting. I wrote Hiram a letter telling him of Mama's death. I don't know if he's received the letter yet.

Catherine is getting married to Samuel Caseman. He is from Cole County. She met him at a recent square dance in California. I like him. I believe he will be a good provider for Catherine. He's about ten years older than her, but that doesn't seem to matter. Pa likes him, and I guess that's all that counts.

I saw your parents at Henry's funeral. They are doing well. I felt so sorry for Pamela. She and Henry didn't have long together. She is such a pretty lady. I think she still plans to be a teacher. I'm sending you more newspaper articles from the California newspaper. It seems there is a lot of fighting going on in Mississippi right now. I pray for you, Jesse, Hiram, James Brooks, and Thomas Barton daily. Please know also, that our entire church is praying for you.

Your letter on September 19 said that the 26th Missouri might be going to Corinth, Mississippi. I hope this letter catches up with you in Corinth.

Please write me as soon as you get this letter. I want to know you are well. Please tell Jesse, Hiram, Thomas, and others from Moniteau County that I sent my love. Please know my love grows for you daily.

To the greatest man on this earth whom I love more than life itself.

Christina

After reading Christina's letter James pulled out paper and pencil and began to write.

Dear Christina,

I'm so sorry it's taken me so long to finish this letter. I started this letter during the battle of Corinth, and duty has not allowed me time to finish it.

I got your letter today. I am so sorry about your mother. She was a nice lady and a fine Christian. I too loved your mother. She will always hold a warm place in my heart. I will truly miss her.

I hope Catherine will be happy with Samuel Caseman. I don't know him but hope he will treat her well. Don't you get any ideas about marrying anyone!

I will now try to finish telling you about the battle of Corinth which lasted for two days.

I swear, Christina, I don't think I've ever been so hot. The temperature had to be over a hundred degrees. At one time, I thought the Johnny Rebs were going to retake Corinth. For some reason General Van Dorn stopped fighting for the day.

Christina, I've never seen anything like it. Both the Confederate and Federal cannons did great damage to both sides. Several of our boys had their limbs shot off. I saw one soldier with his head cut off. I hate to tell you these things, but you wanted me to describe what's happening here. It's just awful!

It still makes me sick to march shoulder-to-shoulder into combat against the enemy. Whoever came up with this method of fighting wasn't too smart. Anyone close to the exploding cannon balls is either killed or crippled for life.

As I mentioned earlier in my letter, I was able to knock out several Confederate gunmen who were operating the cannons. Killing still bothers me, but I find some comfort in knowing that when I kill a Johnny Reb, it saves us lives.

At one point during the day, the Confederates captured Battery Powell and were in pursuit of Battery Robinette when hand-to-hand combat fighting resulted. We were able to drive the Confederates back. We recaptured Battery Powell, and this forced General Van Dorn to retreat.

General Rosecrans chose not to go after General Van Dorn on October 5. I believe that this decision was because of soldier fatigue and the heat. This is one decision he didn't get criticized for.

On October 6, after a night's rest, we went after Van Dorn and Price. We were unable to catch them and returned to Corinth on October 9. I don't know just how long we will be here.

The keeping of Corinth is a major plus for the Union. There are two railroads crossing in Corinth, and we now control what comes in and goes out. Corinth has become a major asset to the Union. The Confederates will no longer be able to ship supplies to the South and that's going to hurt their chances in winning the war. I have heard for some time that the North's objective is to control both the railroads and waterways to the south. After they achieve this goal, they will be able to starve out the South as for as the south receiving supplies needed to fight the war.

I heard today that our Union Army during the Battle of Corinth had 2,520 casualties of which 355 were killed in action, 1,841 were wounded, and 324 are missing in action. The Confederates had 4,233 casualties of which 473 were killed, 1,997 were wounded, and 1,763 were either captured or missing.

Christina, you told me one time you keep all my letters because someday I might want to write a book on the Civil War. I mention the above numbers of casualties, so I will have a record of the number of men who gave their lives for a cause, one which I'm beginning to feel may be in vain. Deep down, I'm still holding out that someday there will be a reason why this terrible bloody war was fought.

Jesse, Hiram, and Thomas are doing well. I don't think Hiram has received your letter about your mother. He hasn't said anything to me about it. I will go see him after I finish this letter. I want to be there for him. We are still living on about half rations. The food isn't any better than the last time I wrote you. Please send more cookies when you have time.

Christina, I think I told you that Lt. Col. John Holman was wounded during the battle. He's going to live.

We also hear that Col. Boomer is recuperating very nicely in St. Louis.

Please know that I am doing well. I don't like this war, but I don't know anyone here who does. Anyway, we will continue to fight for what is right. Someday it will end, and I'll be coming home to Christina Ann Miller, the prettiest girl in Moniteau County.

Again, I'm sorry for not getting this letter written sooner, but in a way, I'm glad I didn't. Again, you and your family have my sincere sympathy in the loss of your mother. Mothers are our best friends. God only gives us one mother. I know you will miss her. Hang on to the fond memories. I'll be praying for you and your family daily.

All my love,
James

After James finished his letter to Christina, he went over to see Hiram. Upon his arrival he was told that Hiram was at the Tishomingo Hotel in Corinth. The Tishomingo Hotel was being used as a hospital. Jesse, Hiram, and some of the boys from Moniteau County had gone over to see their wounded friends. James walked to the Tishomingo Hotel where he found Jesse, Hiram, Thomas and others playing horseshoes on the west side of the hotel.

"Hello, James," Hiram said as James walked up.

"Hello, everyone. Who's winning?" James asked.

"Hiram and Thomas are beating all of us," Jesse said as he picked up the horse shoes and spit between the shoe for good luck.

"It might help, if you'd spit some of that tobacco juice on the horseshoe itself," James said as he laughed.

"That's funny, James," Jesse replied. "Why don't you show us how it's done, big brother!" Jesse said as he handed James the horse shoes.

"Is this all right with you boys?" James asked as he looked toward Thomas and Hiram.

"Sure, go ahead and show us what you can do," Hiram said as he clapped his hands together.

James' first throw was a ringer. His second shoe landed and leaned against the metal post. The ringer gave James five points and the leaner was worth three points.

"Private Barger, I think it would be best if you just watch while we finish this game," Hiram said with a smile as he removed the leaning horseshoe and the ringer from the metal post.

After the game, James asked Hiram if he could have a word with him. Hiram and James seated themselves on one of the wide steps leading up to the Tishomingo's front porch.

"Hiram, have you received a letter from Christina lately?"

"No, I've not heard from her nor my folks in some time now."

"I got a letter from Christina today."

"How is everyone?"

"I've got some bad news for you."

"Bad news? What kind of bad news?"

"Your mother died on September 17."

"Mama is dead?" Hiram asked in disbelief.

"I'm afraid so!"

"I was aware she was sick, but I thought she was getting better. How did she die?" Hiram asked as tears begin to creep out of the corner of his eyes and run down his cheeks.

"Christina said the doctor said it was dropsy," James replied.

At this point Hiram turned his back to James to avoid James seeing him cry.

James put his arms around Hiram, and said, "I'm so sorry, Hiram. I know this isn't easy for you."

"James, I need a little time to myself. I'll see you back at the camp," Hiram said as he turned and walked down the steps toward camp.

At this time, Jesse met Hiram coming down the steps of the porch. "What's wrong with Hiram?" Jesse asked.

"I just broke the news about his mother's death."

"His mother's death! When did this happen?"

"I received a letter from Christina today. She told me that her mother died on September 17."

"Gosh, what else is going to happen?" Jesse asked as he sat down on the step.

"Changing the subject, Jesse. What did you think about the battle of Corinth?"

"It was just awful, James. I hated every minute of it. I hate this bloody, cold war. My good friend, George Bradley died in my arms. He took a bullet to the chest, just like Henry. I saw other boys with their legs shot off. My friends George Mason and Thomas Crank are inside. They both were wounded. George may lose his arm. Thomas was shot in the shoulder. I think he's going to be all right. Time will tell. This is a terrible war, James," Jesse said with anger in his voice.

"Yes, I can agree with you about that. I think Pa may have been right about this whole war. At times, I think we should have listen to him," James said.

"Where do you think we will go from Corinth?"

"I'm not sure, but Captain Koop's said something about us joining General Grant at Vicksburg, Mississippi."

"Do you think this war will be ending soon?" Jesse asked.

"I don't think so. I hear we may be in for a long stay," James said as he got up from where he was sitting on the steps.

"I hope you are wrong, James. I don't know how much longer I can stand seeing men being killed and butchered so."

"I'll walk back to camp with you," Jesse said as he walked down the steps of the hotel with James.

On October 15, James and Jesse received a letter from Nancy Barger.

My dear James and Jesse,

We hope this letter finds both of you well. We are all doing well here in Moniteau County. We had a good crop of corn this year.

George, Mary Ann, Delilah, and John helped Allen get the crop in. George is really growing into a strong man. I don't know what we would do without him and the other children.

I want to thank you boys for arranging for Henry's body to be sent home. I know this is not a common practice for a soldier's body to be returned home after a battle. I don't know all the details, but please know we appreciate what you did.

We gave Henry a good burial. We buried him under the big cedar tree in the New Hope Baptist Church Cemetery. It was hard to part with Henry. He was a good son and a great young man. I know God knows what's best in our lives, but losing a son is mighty hard to bear.

Please stay alert and don't give those Confederate soldiers an easy target. I want you both home in one piece. I don't want another son coming home in a box. Don't take any unnecessary chances. We pray for you boys every day.

I assume Christina has written you of Hannah Miller's death. She died on September 17. We lost a good friend in Hannah. She, too, was buried in New Hope Baptist Church Cemetery.

I want you boys to know that New Hope is where I want to be buried. Keep that in mind when my time comes. I want to be buried by Henry. Allen wants to be buried there also. We have purchased a burial plot. There is ample room for several of us to be buried there.

Martha Jane, Allen, Joseph, and little Nancy have moved in with us. Martha couldn't run the farm by herself. Please tell Thomas that we are taking good care of his family. Little Nancy is so beautiful. She looks like Martha Jane did when she was a baby. I wish Thomas could see his daughter.

Pamela is teaching school in the city of California. She seems to be dealing with Henry's death. I guess being busy helps her. She loves to teach.

I see your adorable Christina often. I swear, James, if you don't marry that good-looking lady when you return home from the war, you should be horse whipped! I'm kidding about the horse whipping, but she is a beauty! I know you and Christina love each other, and your pa and I will be happy to have her as our daughter-in-law.

Jesse, Margaret Miller is turning out to be a nice-looking young lady. Maybe you two could get together someday. I would approve of her also as a daughter-in-law. I hear she has a crush on you. We are not the only family who has been affected by this cruel war. Several Moniteau County families have experienced a death of a son or relative. I pray God will continue to keep you well and safe as you continue to fight in this terrible war. It has lasted much longer than we thought. We pray daily that God will intervene and stop the killing.

Your father sends his love. He's doing well. Seems to be getting a little bossy in his old age. Ha! I love him just the same.

Our love to both of you,

Your loving parents

CHAPTER 27

The 26th Missouri left Corinth on November 2, 1862. On November 14, 1862, James wrote home to Christina.

My Dearest Christina,

We are presently camping near a small town of Holly Springs, Mississippi. I don't know how long we will be here. Col. Boomer told me that General Ulysses Grant is going to use Holly Springs as a temporary supply depot and headquarters in his quest of taking Vicksburg. Holly Springs is a booming little Southern town with the Mississippi Central Railway passing through it. There are several big plantations near this little city and a large population of slaves.

Colonel Boomer has told me he thinks General Grant plans to march straight down the railroad to Jackson and then turn west to Vicksburg. The Confederates had control of Holly Springs until yesterday, and we took it over. It was a small skirmish and the Rebels ran. We've been on the move since Corinth, so I have not had a chance to write you.

I'm so hungry! I've lost more weight too. You will have to fatten me up when I return to Moniteau County. The good news is that I believe we will be in Holly Springs for a few days. Since Grant is turning Holly Springs into a supply depot, we should be getting more food shipped here. Maybe we will be getting more to eat.

Jesse, Hiram, Thomas, and others from Moniteau County are all doing well. I see them almost every day. They are also losing weight and stay hungry. As we pass through some of the farms we help ourselves to anything that resembles food. I believe if we didn't do it, we would starve to death. The commanding officers realize our hunger and say nothing to us when we steal. I guess I'm sinning, but we need food for our bodies. The half rations we receive are just not enough to keep us going. There isn't anything worse than being hungry. When I return to Moniteau County, I'll never be hungry again, nor will I ever allow my family to be hungry. That is a promise!

I have some good news to share with you. First, I recently was promoted to the rank of Corporal in "G" Company. I'm excited about the honor. I just hope I can do it justice.

Secondly, On November 11, 1862, Colonel Boomer rejoined the 26th. It was so good to see him back. He walks with a little limp, but he looks good. He's brought inspiration and hope back to me and other soldiers. He seems to know what we need to hear. I've never met a man like him. I look forward to serving with him once again. There is talk that he may make general soon, and I hope this is true, although I would regret his leaving the command of the 26th. I admire and respect him a lot. If I was going to be an officer in this war, I would like to be like him.

How are things there at home? How's your father? You said in your letter that he was taking Hannah's death badly. Oh, Christina, I can't image losing you, and I know how he must feel losing Hannah after living with her all those years.

I know how caring you are, and I know you will do everything you can to lift his spirits.

I think of you all the time. Every step that I take, as we march from place to place, you are on my mind. I daydream of the time I will hold you close to me and kiss your soft lips. I can see and feel that right now. Christina, I miss you something awful. You don't know how much!

I worry at times that I will be wounded and crippled from this war. If that occurs, I wouldn't want you to live up to your promise. I wouldn't want you to have a cripple for a husband. I would rather be dead instead. But those thoughts enter my mind, especially since I've seen so many men with their legs and arms blown off. These men are sent home as cripples. I hate the thought of that ever happening to me.

This letter is one of my longest letters; and I probably could go on and on, but I must stop now and answer a letter that Jesse and I received from Ma while we were in Corinth. I'm sorry it's been a while since I've written, but as you can see, we've been on the move since Corinth.

I love you always,
James

After sealing Christina's letter, James glanced at the sky. It was around 3 o'clock, which meant he had almost two hours before evening inspection and roll call. Just enough time to write a letter to his parents. Pulling another piece of paper from his knapsack and placing it on the board in front of him, he began to write.

Dear Folks,

It's been a while since I received your last letter. I apologize for not writing sooner. My letter will explain why.

I hope this letter finds all doing well. Jesse, Thomas, Hiram, and the other boys from Moniteau County are doing well. We are still surviving on half rations. We are permitted to pick up some additional food here and there. Please don't ask what here and there means. You might not approve.

I was glad to hear George is being a big help. Christina tells me he's turned out to be quite a lady's man. Ma, you better keep a good eye on him.

By the way, Jesse promised me he'd write you. I trust he's done that. He's not much on writing, but when he tells me he will do something, he normally does it.

The last battle we've taken part in was the battle of Corinth. We are now in Holly Springs, Mississippi. I don't know how long we'll be here. It's rumored we will be going to Jackson and then on to Vicksburg. There is also discussion that we may go all the way to the Gulf Coast. I would love to go to the Gulf.

General Grant plans to make Holly Springs into a supply depot before we march further south.

I have some good news to share with you. First, I've been promoted to the rank of Corporal. I'm excited about that. I just hope I can do the honor justice. Secondly, Col. George Boomer has rejoined the 26th. He returned on November 11. He has already brought new life back to the Missouri 26th.

Ma, how's everything with you? Are you keeping Pa in line? Remember, he sometimes needs your firm hand. Ha! The next time you write, you might send a box of your molasses cookies. I'm craving your cookies. As you know, Ma, I kept your cookie jar pretty much empty all the time. Now you know the truth. I bet you thought Jesse was stealing those cookies, didn't you? Confession is good for the soul, isn't it?

Give everyone my love and I'll write again as soon as we relocate. Please take care of yourselves.

Your son, with my love,
James

After leaving Holly Springs the Missouri 26th Regiment advanced to Moscow, Mississippi, arriving on the 18th.

After arriving in Moscow, James was told by Col. Boomer about the previous Battle of Moscow that was fought on December 4, 1863.

The Battle of Moscow was another victory for the North. On December 4th, three thousand Confederate cavalries with artillery, led by Gen. James Chalmers, attacked the Memphis & Charleston Railroad bridge over Wolf River and ambushed Col. Edward Hatch's brigade of Union cavalry crossing the river on the state line road wagon bridge. Intense fighting ensued, and fortified Union artillery bombarded the Confederate rear. Union losses were 175 men and 100 horses. Near sunset, the Confederates withdrew, with a loss of 30 killed and 54 taken prisoners. Later, the Yankees burned the town of Moscow, leaving only two residences. As Col. Boomer related the details of the battle, James found it most interesting. It was the first battle he had heard of which included the involvement of negro troops fighting for the North.

Col. Boomer went on to say that the negro troops of the 2nd Regiment, West Tennessee Infantry, were instrumental in repelling the Confederate attack and holding of the railroad port at Moscow. He said that the 2nd Regiment had later been recognized by General Stephen A. Hurlbut, commander of the 16th Army Corps, for their gallant and successful defense of the important position.

James and Jesse had not seen each other in over a week. Jesse had been assigned duty away from camp. When he returned, he heard of James' promotion to the rank of Corporal.

"Hello, Corporal James A. Barger," Jesse said as he walked up to James near a big oak tree. He put his emphasis on the word "Corporal."

"Hello back to you, Private Jesse A. Barger," James said as he reached out his hand and smiled back, emphasizing the word "private" as he spoke.

"Corporal Barger. That sounds nice."

"It does sound rather nice, doesn't it?" James replied as he leaned up against the oak tree.

"You got any letters from the folks or Christina lately?" Jesse asked.

"No, not since we left Corinth. I wrote both Christina and the folks while we were camping in Holly Springs. Did you write the folks like you promised?"

"Sure did! You know I'm not as good about writing as you, but I did write. I even wrote Margaret Miller."

"Wow, Jesse! I'm really proud of you," James replied laughing.

"Anyway, I didn't have anything else to do." Jesse replied with a grin.

"How do you feel about Margaret?" James asked.

"I think about her a lot. I like getting her letters, and those molasses cookies she sends are delicious. Are they not?"

"Yes, they are. I think you're falling for Margaret." James said as he laughed.

"Maybe I am, and maybe I'm not. You don't know what's going on in my mind," Jesse said.

"No, but I can read your face."

"Let's change the subject. When do you think we'll leave Moscow? I don't like this place!"

"I expect it will be soon. Col. Boomer thinks it could be as soon as one week. Don't go and tell anyone. I could get in big trouble for telling you what Col. Boomer has shared with me.

"I won't tell a soul!"

"I hear Vicksburg is a stronghold for the Confederates," Jesse said.

"Yes, that's true. Col. Boomer says we need Vicksburg in the worst way."

"You like Col. Boomer, don't you?"

"In my opinion, he's the best officer in this Army. I've never met a man whom I respect and admire more," James said.

"Jesse, why don't you come and have supper with me and the boys tonight? We are going to have roast sweet potatoes. I know you like sweet potatoes," James said.

"Thanks, Corporal Barger, maybe another time. Since I've been gone for a week, I best be getting back to "H" Company."

"Jesse, I'm glad your back. I've missed you!"

"I've missed you too, James," Jesse replied reaching out and giving James a pat on the shoulder. "I'll see you tomorrow. Enjoy them sweet potatoes!"

James' prediction proved accurate. After only a few days in Moscow, Grant's army pressed on deeper into Mississippi. The next stop was Lumpkin's Mills, then on to Oxford, Mississippi. There James found time to write another letter to Christina:

My Dearest Christina,

I have little time, so this letter must be short. I am safe. So are Jesse, Hiram, and the boys from Moniteau County. The 26th Missouri is now assigned to the 3rd Brigade of the 7th Division of the 13th Corps. Please pass that information on to my folks.

Colonel Boomer has taken over command of the whole brigade, which means I see less of him now than before, although he has had me detailed to work for a day or two at brigade headquarters. He's told me I will be assigned to brigade headquarters on a regular basis.

Oxford, Mississippi

We are now in Oxford, Mississippi. After reaching Oxford, we received word that a force of Rebel cavalry under the command of General Van Dorn attacked our supply base at Holly Springs. We hear Van Dorn burned everything except for supplies that were useful to them. This is not the first time the Confederates have attacked our supply lines, but this is by far the worst. There are rumors that General Grant will retreat, but I do not know this to be a fact.

Colonel Boomer has certainly uplifted our spirits again. He arranged a huge Christmas dinner for us. I know it was his doing because I copied the requisition forms myself. We had beef stew, soft bread for the first time in months, vegetables and tea. It wasn't the usual turkey and dressing and was not anywhere near as fine as what Ma used to make but I enjoyed every bite. After dinner the chaplain preached a sermon and led us in prayer and then the whole regiment sang Christmas carols. I do believe Col. Boomer will have a crown in heaven. He's such a compassionate leader. One which continues to gain respect and admiration from his men. They would follow him into any battle.

They say Grant is going to pull back into Tennessee and then try something else to capture Vicksburg. I don't know what that can be.

I must stop now, we have drill in five minutes.

With Love,

James

CHAPTER 28

James didn't have to wait long to find out what General Grant's "something else" would involve. Orders were received on December 26, 1862, to march to Memphis, Tennessee.

The regiment arrived in Memphis on December 29, 1862. Two days later the 26th moved a few miles southeast of Memphis and ended the year encamped at Germantown, Tennessee.

On January 2, 1863, James received two packages, one from Christina, and one from his mother.

James found the following letter in the package from Christina.

My Dear James,

Merry Christmas! I'm taking a chance that this package will get to you before Christmas. If it doesn't, I hope you had a Merry Christmas. In the package you will find two pairs of socks and a wool scarf. I want you to be warm for the rest of the winter. I also hope you enjoy the oatmeal cookies. I wish we could have sent more, but the price of mailing items is costly. Please see that Jesse gets the molasses cookies Margaret is sending him. She is getting to be a good cook. You and Jesse can share the cookies, so you can have some of both.

We are getting ready for Christmas here. We plan to go to church on Christmas Eve. The church is putting on a religious presentation. I'm playing the Virgin Mary.

Father is doing pretty well. I think he's adjusting to Mama being gone. We've done everything we know to help him. He continues to go to church. He's also beginning to have something to do with his men friends again.

I see your folks at church and in town on Saturdays. Both your father and mother look good. Your father is still a handsome man, and your brother, George, is turning into quite a ladies' man. The girls are all over him at the dances. If he was a little older, I might be after him myself. Ha! Ha! You know I'm joking? Well, at least, you hope I'm joking! Although, he's good looking, he can't compare to you. You are the best looking of all the Bargers.

I'm sorry we won't get to spend Christmas together. I will miss you something awful. I wish your Col. Boomer could arrange a furlough for you. A few days with you would be just what the doctor ordered.

Please continue to let me know where you are and what's happening. Your letters give me comfort in knowing you are well.

Please give my love to Jesse, Hiram and Thomas.

Merry Christmas to all.

I Love you,

Christina

A letter from Nancy arrived also.

Dear James and Jesse,

I hope you don't mind sharing this letter with each other. What I would say to one of you, I would say to the other.

We are sending you some goodies. I hope they arrive before Christmas. We wish you could be here for Christmas but know that won't be possible. I trust God is taking good care of you both. We pray for you daily.

This war seems to be going on and on. I'll be thankful when it's over. It has affected a lot of families here in Moniteau County, including ours.

James, your pa and me were glad to hear about your honor of being named Corporal. Allen says a Corporal is very important. We are proud of you and know you will serve "G" Company well.

I visited with Pamela last Saturday in California. She is doing well. She says her teaching keeps her busy. She's a pretty lady and in time will find a nice man to love and care for her.

Your brother, George, has been a big help to your pa. He's grown up to be a fine-looking young man. He's very popular with the girls in this community. I'm afraid he's going to get himself in trouble someday. He's a good boy, but just a little on the wild side.

Lately, me and your pa have been gravely concerned about George. He's wanting to enlist in the Union Army. Your pa has flatly refused to listen to George's request. This time I'm in full agreement with your pa. We need George's help on the farm and not in this bloody war. I've lost one son, and I don't want to lose another. Pray that George will get this foolish idea out of his head.

Martha Jane, the boys, and little Nancy are all doing well. Martha Jane misses Thomas something awful, and she has her hands full with those two boys and little Nancy.

I'm glad we can help Martha Jane. She really gets depressed at times. We try to get her to go to California with us, but she goes nowhere except to church.

Allen buys The Weekly California Newspaper in hopes of keeping track of where you boys are. He says Mississippi is getting its share of the fighting. Please be careful and don't do anything to get yourselves shot. I want both of you home in one piece.

We are sending each of you two pairs of socks. I hope they keep your feet warm.

Your pa said he would write next time. He told me to tell you to keep your eyes wide open and watch your backs. He is still headstrong as ever, but my love grows for him with each passing day.

I've got to stop and get supper started. Mary Ann and Martha Jane are a big help to me. I'm glad they are here to help us. Mary Ann is being courted by Matthew Conant. I think they are falling in love. Allen has told her that she cannot marry until she is eighteen. He may have to change his mind.

I pray for you boys every day.

Love you both,

Mother

James and the 26th Missouri remained for several months in Memphis. The regiment's assignment was to guard supplies and the garrisons in Memphis during the cold winter months.

On January 15, 1863, James wrote to Christina.

Dearest Christina,

We are now camping near Memphis, Tennessee, a big town. I've never been in a town this size. The town has brick streets. We can walk down a street without getting our shoes muddy.

You've told me you wanted to know what's going on, so I may bore you with the following information. It's long but it will give you an idea of what General Grant's plans are. Vicksburg is well fortified and digging the canals may be the only way to win at Vicksburg.

Most of General Grant's troops moved on down the river taking up positions above Vicksburg on the west bank. Grant's forces have taken Fort Hindman, located at Arkansas Post. We hear that most of Grant's troops are now near Vicksburg.

Colonel Boomer says Grant's problem is getting across the Mississippi River. The Vicksburg batteries blocked the progress of Union ships south on the Mississippi, so he can't cross downstream from Vicksburg. Crossing north of Vicksburg was not a good idea, because the ground on the east side of the river is swampy and cut by many bayous.

General Grant has put his troops to work on a scheme to cut canals to bypass Vicksburg. He plans to link a network of natural waterways to allow a vessel to leave the Mississippi, pass through northeastern Louisiana, and reach the Red River which rejoined the Mississippi below Vicksburg.

Colonel Boomer thinks this might work, and since he is an engineer, he should know. He says that it will be very difficult to do in winter and in mud, so it will be much grueling work for Grant's soldiers. I am glad that I am in Memphis!

The 26th has been guarding a wagon train on the Memphis and Charleston Railroad. We hate this duty. Col. Boomer doesn't like it either. He had rather be engaged in battle somewhere in Mississippi! I share his same sentiments. It's boring here. Although I guess I shouldn't complain. I'm not dodging bullets right now. I guess that makes my odds of staying alive a whole lot better.

I think we are going to be here for a spell, so try to answer this letter right back. I want to hear from you before leaving Memphis.

I wish we could have one of those furloughs you mentioned in your last letter. Memphis is not far from Moniteau County. I could ride a boat to St. Louis and then take the train to California. Let's pray that someday they will give us a furlough.

Jesse, Hiram, Thomas, and all the others are doing fine. We all hate what we're doing right now, but we will deal with it.

Col. Boomer keeps encouraging us. He seems to know when we're down.

Things are not all bad. We are getting better food, living indoors in warm wooden barracks, and we are gaining weight for the first time since leaving St. Louis.

Please continue to pray that this war will end soon. Also give my regards to your father and family.

With my deepest love,

James

The month of January 1863 brought about three events which began to turn the tide for the North.

On January 1, 1863, President Lincoln issued the final Emancipation Proclamation freeing all slaves in territories held by Confederates and allowing the enlisting of black soldiers in the Union Army.

On January 29, 1863, General Ulysses Grant was placed in Command of the Army of the West with orders to capture Vicksburg.

On February 12, 1863, Col. George Boomer assumed command of a 3rd Brigade of the 7th Division of the 17th army corps. The Brigade consisted of 26th Missouri, the 5th Iowa, the 10th Iowa, and the 93rd Illinois. Most of these regiments had served together for over a year. To James, the change was simply another excuse to write home to advise of the new address.

James and Christina wrote each other several times while he was in Memphis. Their letters were full of encouragement and hope.

During the month of March 1863, General Grant continued digging canals and conducting a series of expeditions known as the "bayou experiments." These experiments were attempts to try to find a way through the morass north of Vicksburg. One of the most important of these four expeditions was the Yazoo Expedition which had begun in

February. A column of ironclads, escorting wooden transports, had been literally hacking their way through an almost impenetrable swamp for several weeks.

On March 3, 1863, the U. S. Congress enacted a draft which affected male citizens age twenty to forty-five years of age. The draft exempted those who pay $300 or provide a substitute. "The blood of a poor man is as precious as that of the wealthy," poor Northerners complained.

On the same day that the U. S. Congress enacted the draft, Col. George Boomer and the 26th Missouri left Memphis for Helena, Arkansas. After a few days' layover in Helena, transports were available for the force to move up the Yazoo, following in the path of other Union vessels who were, at that time, inching forward on the upper Yazoo.

It was several weeks before James could find the time to write Christina.

Dearest Christina,

I hope this letter finds you well. I'm presently cooped up aboard a tiny steamboat called the Natchez Warrior. It is crowded with about one-half of the 26th in here with me. For days we have been steaming through an ocean of huge cypress trees that seems to go on forever. We spend our days chopping and hacking and digging a passage through the swamp big enough for the steamboats, but the upper part of the Natchez Warrior is all battered to pieces from colliding with limbs and trees. Colonel Boomer has a bad cut above his left eye, which he got when a tree limb smashed the pilot house of his vessel.

At first, we saw little sign of the Rebels, but we were moving so slowly that they had a lot of time to prepare for us.

We are now stopped near Greenwood, Mississippi. Dry ground is so close that you can smell it! But there is a Confederate fort on the elevation ahead of us, and there is no way to attack it. The ironclads can creep forward single file through the narrow river, or the infantry can swim through the swamp. Either way, I do not think that we can capture it. There have been several efforts by the gunboats to shell the fort.

Two nights ago, General Grant sent a whole fleet slipping past the batteries of Vicksburg in the dark. Colonel Boomer watched from the shore, and said it was an impressive sight with all the "rockets' red glare and bombs bursting midair." I saw a little from a great distance but did not have a good view.

Then, yesterday, we had a dress parade and a formal review. The Adjutant General was visiting from Washington City, and we were reviewed by him. Whenever we have had a formal review, it has always been a sign that we were about to take the field, and now orders have come down to start cooking extra rations for our haversacks. We are taking the field. They say that Grant will use the steamboats which slipped past Vicksburg to cross downstream.

I was working at headquarters on the March returns last night, and Colonel Boomer was there and in a talkative mood. He told me all about seeing the gunboats slip past Vicksburg which I have already related to you. He says that Grant can use the gunboats to ferry us across the Mississippi south of Vicksburg, where the ground is firm, and we can march.

I must end this letter now because it is my turn to go on guard duty. I will write again soon. Give my love to my parents.

With Love,
James

The bulk of General Grant's army now departed from Millikan's Bend and marched or waded through twenty-rain-soaked miles to New Carthage, Louisiana, which was on the river below Vicksburg. Since Grant now had vessels below Vicksburg, he had the ability to ferry his troops across the river downstream from the city.

On April 29, 1863, Grant attempted to cross the Mississippi from New Carthage to Grand Gulf, with some of his troops being embarked on transports for this purpose. But after a prolonged artillery barrage failed to silence the Confederate batteries guarding Grand Gulf, these forces were returned to the west bank and disembarked again. The next day, Grand tried again, and on April 30, 1863, he successfully landed at Bruinsburg, Mississippi, without firing a shot.

Elsewhere, several key battles were fought in the month of May 1863. The Battle of Chancellorsville, Virginia, on May 1-4, 1863, brought defeat to the Union Army. The Union Army under General Hooker was decisively defeated by General Robert E. Lee's much smaller forces. Confederate General Stonewall Jackson was mortally wounded by his own soldiers. Hooker retreated from Chancellorsville. The Union had around 130,000 soldiers at Chancellorsville. After the battle ended, there were 17,000 men killed, wounded or missing. The Confederates had 13,000 men either killed, wounded or missing.

James and his friends in the 26th did not hear of this battle until some days later because Grant had completely severed communications as he marched east from the Mississippi towards Jackson.

The 26th Missouri, under the command of Col. George Boomer had left Millikan's Bend, Louisiana, on April 25, 1863. They marched over horrible roads for days before reaching Raymond, Mississippi.

CHAPTER 29

On May 12, 1863, Col. George Boomer and the 26th Missouri regiment joined Major Gen. James B. McPherson of the Union Army against Brig. General John Gregg of the Confederate Army in the battle of Raymond, Mississippi.

Lt. General John C. Pemberton, Confederate commander at Vicksburg, Mississippi, had sent orders to Confederate General Gregg to leave Jackson, Mississippi, and intercept the Union Army at Raymond, Mississippi. As the Union forces approached Raymond, they were attacked by Gregg's heavy artillery. At first the heavy artillery caused severe casualties in the Union army. Some Union troops broke, but Maj. General John A. Logan rallied a force to hold the line. Confederate troops attacked the line but had to retire. More Union soldiers arrived, and the Union force counter attacked. Heavy fighting followed for six hours. At the end of the battle, the Union forces had prevailed. General Gregg's men had to retreat and leave the battle field. Although General Gregg's men lost the battle at Raymond, they were successful in detaining a much superior Union force for a day.

The Battle of Raymond cost the Union and Confederate armies 1,011 soldiers. The Union army lost 442 men and the Confederates lost 569 men.

James, Jesse, and the rest of the group from Moniteau County were again safe. Although they engaged in the battle, they were spared any injuries or death.

James experienced his first assignment in battle as a Corporal from Col. Boomer.

After the battle, Col. Boomer congratulated James on his ability to lead out. This made James feel good and gave him a sense of accomplishment. He decided that being a leader was a good thing, dangerous, but good. He felt good that none of his men were wounded or killed in the battle.

Raymond, Mississippi, was a key area for the Union. By gaining control of the city and river nearby, the Confederates were stopped from using the river to ship supplies into Vicksburg.

The defeat in the Battle of Raymond gave General Ulysses Grant one step closer to meeting his goal of capturing every small stronghold of the Confederates who held cities around Vicksburg. Upon gaining control of all the areas around Vicksburg, he would take Vicksburg by starving them out.

The capturing of the surrounding towns and river ports would eliminate getting food, supplies, artillery, and ammunition into Vicksburg. It would also stop any reinforcement soldiers getting into Vicksburg.

If General Grant was successful in stopping any supplies and reinforcement coming in to Vicksburg, General John C. Pemberton, commander of the Confederate army in Vicksburg, would have to surrender. This would be only a short time, General Grant thought.

CHAPTER 30

On May 9, 1863, Gen. Joseph E. Johnston received a dispatch from the Confederate Secretary of War directing him to proceed at once to Mississippi and take chief command of the forces in the field. As he arrived in Jackson on the 13th from Middle Tennessee, he learned that two army corps from the Union Army of Tennessee, the XV under Maj. General William T. Sherman and the XVII under Maj. General James Bird were advancing on Jackson, Mississippi.

The Union Armies intended to cut the city and the railroads off from Vicksburg. Upon arrival in Jackson, General Johnston consulted with the local commander, General Gregg. He learned from General Gregg that only about 6,000 troops were available to defend the town of Jackson. General Johnston ordered the evacuation of Jackson and ordered Gen. Gregg to defend Jackson until the evacuation was completed.

By 10:00 A.M., both Union Army corps were near Jackson and had engaged the enemy. Heavy rain, desperate Confederate resistance, and good defenses prevented much progress until around 11:00 A.M., when Union forces attacked in numbers and slowly but surely pushed the enemy back. In mid-afternoon, General Johnston informed Gregg that the evacuation was complete and that he should disengage and follow. Soon after, the Yankees entered Jackson and had a celebration, hosted by Maj. General U. S. Grant who had been traveling with Sherman's corps,' in the Bowman House. The Union forces burned part of the town and cut the railroad connections with Vicksburg.

Gen. Johnston's evacuation of Jackson was a tragedy in a sense. If he had waited to evacuate Jackson until after May 14, he would have had 11,000 troops at his disposal and by the morning of the 15th, another 4,000. The fall of Jackson, Mississippi, the former Mississippi State Capital, was a blow to Confederate moral.

The battle of Jackson, Mississippi, took the lives of 286 Union soldiers and 850 Confederates.

Grant's army continued to be on the move. The army moved rapidly, despite rain-soaked roads, into central Mississippi. Grant deceived the Confederates concerning his true intentions by first going to Jackson, Mississippi, then rapidly back tracking toward Vicksburg. Grant also cut his own supply lines, forcing his troops to live on what supplies they were carrying and whatever supplies they could forage from farms in their path. The movement was too rapid to allow much foraging, however.

The Confederates were befuddled by this misdirection and by the speed of Grant's advance. Several divisions of Confederates were sent to attack Grant's supply lines, only to find that there was no supply line to attack.

Turning west toward Vicksburg, Grant's force fought the largest battle of the campaign at Champion Hill on May 16, 1863.

CHAPTER 31

It was weeks before James could find an opportunity to write again. Finally, on a sweltering May afternoon, James found himself sitting on a stump in the middle of a muddy camp in Mississippi penning a letter with one hand while swatting mosquitoes with the other. The crackle of musket fire in the distance mixed with the drone of mosquitoes.

My Dearest Christina,

Please do not be angry at me for not writing. I know that Hiram got a letter that said that you and my parents have been worried to distraction, not having heard from me in weeks. I have not had a chance to write, but I will try to make up for it now.

First, we have been marching constantly for a month. Grant slipped some steamboats past the Confederate forts at Vicksburg. Colonel Boomer had a good view from shore and said that the fireworks were spectacular. The steamboats carried us across the river, and we landed at a place called Bruinsburg, Mississippi. Grant cut off his supply lines and told us we would have only what we had in our haversacks, and what we could find to eat. When he cut off the supply lines, he cut off the mail, too.

We did some of the hardest marching I have ever done over some of the worst, muddiest roads in the world. The rain poured down on us. I thought we were going to Vicksburg, but instead Grant turned us east, and we marched to Jackson, Mississippi. We went to battle with the Rebels at Raymond, Mississippi. We fought for six hours under heavy artillery fire. Although I'm not one hundred percent sure, I think I took out several soldiers who were manning the heavy artillery. One never knows if it's his bullet or someone else's that drops a Rebel soldier.

At one point, I thought we were going to be driven off by the Rebels, but General Logan, who is our corps commander, rode up and waved his sword and shouted to us to fight on! His example gave us the courage to keep going, and the Confederates withdrew in the evening.

We did not have time to rest even then but pushed on towards Jackson. Did you know, Christina, that a man can walk in his sleep? I have seen it happen. Men were so tired that they fell asleep, but their feet kept moving until they stumbled and fell in the ditch, which would awaken them. We had to cross a rain-swollen creek west of Jackson, and I lost my knapsack. It had my pencils, paper and envelopes in it, which made it impossible to write even when I finally did get a chance.

By that time, I had pretty much decided that Grant had given up on taking Vicksburg. Rumors had it that we were going on east into Alabama after taking Jackson. I think even Colonel Boomer was puzzled by what Grant was doing. We got to Jackson in a pouring rain and attacked the Rebels who were entrenched outside of town. The Rebels held us off for a while then withdrew out the east side of town. A lot of our boys got a little crazy, and they burned a large part of Jackson, which I regret because it was quite a pretty little town. Now all that is left is chimneys sticking up like naked trees in a forest.

Not too long after we took Jackson, the chaplain told us that we could get some mail out. I borrowed some paper and a pencil and wrote you a letter to tell you that I was all right. The mail from the 26th went up the Mississippi on a steamer called the Choctaw Boy. I have heard tell that the Choctaw Boy caught fire up near

Arkansas. Everyone got off safe, as I understand it, but the 26th's mail was lost.

Anyway, we turned back west after Jackson and headed straight towards Vicksburg marching as hard as we could. We were supposed to be foraging off the local farms, but we were traveling too fast to do much of that, and we were down to a few biscuits of hardtack a day.

Colonel Boomer said that the Confederates were so befuddled by this misdirection, and by the speed of Grant's advance, that several divisions of Confederates were sent to attack Grant's supply lines, only to find that there was no supply line to attack.

I have just come through a battle safely. There was a big fight today at Champion Hill, which is about fifteen or twenty miles east of Vicksburg. I suppose you will read about it in the newspapers before this letter gets through to you. We were there, although we missed the first part of the battle. Champion Hill sits astride the road that we were taking from Jackson to Vicksburg. The Rebels were on top of the hill and were determined to stop us. The battle started not too long after dawn, after the lead division of our army collided with Confederates near Champion Hill. By late morning, Grant had brought up the bulk of his forces, and ordered a general assault on the hill, while a second column of troops tried to work their way around the northern end of the Confederates' line. The boys who were there say it was a formidable sight to see our fellows racing up that hill! They took the high ground, but then the Rebels struck back and counter attacked with great force. The 26th reached the battlefield at this point. Our brigade with Colonel Boomer in command and the brigade of General Holmes had already double timed about fifteen miles to reach the battlefield, and we were pretty much worn out by the time we arrived. But Colonel Boomer did not wait for a moment but ordered us right into the thick of it! The 10th Iowa and the 93rd Illinois were up front, and the 26th

Missouri and the 5th Iowa were held back in reserve on the second line.

Christina, they have thickets down here in Mississippi that you have never seen the like of in Missouri. We were fighting up hill and down through all this tangle. Suddenly, Boomer rode up and shouted that there were a bunch of Confederates making their way towards the brigade's right flank. There was a ravine there, and if the Confederates could get to it they could shoot right down the line at the whole brigade. Boomer ordered us to go, and we went. As played out as we were, we ran for that ravine, racing the Confederates to get there first! The 26th won the race by a hair, but Major Brown fell with a bullet in his chest just as we reached the ravine. He died several hours later. Just a minute after that, Captain Welker was shot in the head and killed instantly, so Captain Dean, who is a regular good fellow, took over the command of the 26th.

We had a hot fight in that ravine. The shooting was deafening, and the smoke choked us. The Confederates seemed like they were all around us, and there was no place to go in the ravine where we might not be shot. A good number of brave fellows were shot in the back, while valiantly battling the Confederates before them. I hope that no one will ever say that those of the 26th who were shot in the back did not uphold the honor of the regiment that day because the regiment fought as well as any ever have. We almost ran out of ammunition and took all the bullets from the cartridge boxes of the fallen. A few even dashed out to retrieve cartridges from fallen Confederates, but soon even that ammunition was almost exhausted. The situation looked serious.

Suddenly, the tide of battle turned. A fresh division of our boys attacked the Rebels. We may have been almost played out, but so were the Rebels! They took off running, and we took off chasing them!

We lost eighteen and about seventy were wounded. It would have been much worse, but that ravine we were in protected us. There were bullets buzzing around us like bees!

Now, I must tell you the bad news about the battle.

At this point James put his pencil down.

Christina had been devastated by Henry's death the year before, and he did not want to cause her too much of a shock with news of the loss of another friend from Moniteau. The Battle of Champion Hill had again touched the lives of the Barger family. He mentally reviewed the events of the past few hours.

Jesse, once again, had seen it happen. As soon as the firing had died down, James had gone searching for his brother, and for the other Moniteau boys. Jesse came running up to him crying, "O, my God, James, Thomas has been killed." Jesse grabbed James by the arms as tears ran down his cheeks.

"Jesse, are you sure he's dead?"

"I'm sure. I just got back from the hospital. He took wounds to the chest and legs. Oh, God, James, I'm so sick of this war. What are we going to tell Martha Jane?"

"Jesse, calm down," James said as he put his arms around Jesse.

"Hiram was wounded too, but not life threatening. He's in the hospital. He took a bullet in the arm. I think he's going to be fine. I helped carry him to the hospital and saw that he was taken care of," Jesse said.

"That's good news. Let's go see him," James said as he started to the hospital.

"James, I can't go back there right now. I'm so sick of seeing butchered up soldiers bleeding to death. Soldiers with no arms, legs, and sometimes not even a face. Oh, James, it's terrible. Please understand, I'm sick to my stomach. Please excuse me this time. I need some time to myself," Jesse said as he returned to Company "H".

The hospital was a barn full of hay filled to overflowing with wounded soldiers. The ground around was scattered with others, clustered anywhere that some protection from the Mississippi sun could be found. A surgeon moved mechanically from patient to patient, working quickly but efficiently. Drummer boys passed among the wounded, distributing water. Not fifty yards away, a burial detail dug a trench to be used as a mass grave of the dead while a second detail shoveled dirt on top of stacks of soldiers in a second mass grave.

As James reached the hospital, he soon had the opportunity to witness the horrible scene Jesse had described earlier. Wounded soldiers were everywhere, waiting to be treated for their wounds. Flies crawled on bloody bandages. The doctors had been taking the worst first. As James stood and looked at the sickening sight, he began to cry. He wondered how this could be happening.

As he stood there, he heard a voice call out, "I need some help over here." He turned to see an orderly struggling with a wounded soldier who had grabbed him and wouldn't let go. James rushed over to help. The soldier had a death lock, holding on to the orderly's wrist. James reached down and grabbed the soldier's fingers and forced them from the orderly's wrist.

The wounded soldier grew calmer but did not regain consciousness. The orderly again knelt by the soldier, took his hands, and placed them across his chest. "We won't be able to help this one. Heavens isn't this the worst thing you've ever seen?"

"Yes, it's awful! I've never seen anything like this in my entire life," James said.

"Since you are here, you had better help. The ones with the red flags get surgery. We move them over there. The ones in this group," the orderly motioned, "only need bandaging for now. That's my responsibility. The ones over there," he motioned again and lowered his voice, "are not expected to live. We give them laudanum and the drummers make sure they get drinking water, but not too much else can be done for them."

James helped the orderly for several hours, all the while scanning the faces of the wounded looking for Hiram Miller. Finally, in the shade at the rear of the barn, he spotted Hiram lying on a mound of straw. Hiram stirred and raised his head when James approached.

"I see you are still alive, Hiram," James said.

"James, it's so good to see you."

I'm glad to see you're still alive," James said with a smile.

"James, this is private Matthew Bentz from Iowa. Private Bentz this is my good friend, Corporal James Barger from Moniteau County, Missouri."

"It's a pleasure to meet you," James said as he reached out his hand to shake Private Bentz's hand. Tears began to stream down private Bentz face as he held up the bandaged stub of his right arm.

"I'm afraid I'll have to shake with my left hand," he said.

"I guess you know about Thomas?" Hiram asked.

"Yes, Jesse told me earlier."

"I was ten feet from him when he went down. We were running for the ravine but had not yet gotten there. The Johnny Rebs were bound and determined to keep us from taking that ravine. I don't think Thomas knew what hit him. He was butchered up something awful. I can still see him lying there. James, I don't know if I can take much more of this war. I just don't know if I can!" Hiram said as he began to cry.

"Hiram, you have got to be strong. This war shouldn't last much longer. Your folks would want you to be strong. You can do it. You have a lot to live for. How long do you think you'll be here?" James asked.

"The doctor said my wound should heal in about three weeks. I'm not going to be discharged. I'll be honest, James, I wish I was. I'm really sick of this war," Hiram said as he turned away from James.

James reached and touched Hiram on the shoulder and said, "My friend, I've got to be going."

Hiram turned with tears streaming down his cheeks and said, "Will you write my folks and tell them I'm okay? As you can see, I don't think I'm going to be able to write any letters anytime soon."

"I'll write your folks," James said as he said goodbye.

Now, sitting on a stump in a mosquito infested mud hole, James decided that the best approach was simply to be strong and positive.

James picked up his pencil and continued writing.

Christina, Hiram is hurt but he is going to be fine. His shoulder is scratched just a bit by a bullet, but it is nothing serious. I expect he'll be back on duty any day.

Well, an occasional white lie never hurt anyone, thought James. He continued:

The worst news, though, is that Thomas was killed in battle. Hiram said he saw him fall. He said he was only about ten feet away when he was killed. Hiram says Thomas didn't have to suffer. He died instantly.

I just returned from the hospital where I helped an orderly attend the wounded soldiers. Christina, I've never in my life seen such horrible conditions. I know you always told me not to leave out details, but this time I feel I should spare you the details. What I saw would make you sick at your stomach.

I feel God is blessing Jesse and me. Jesse is fine. I spent several minutes with him this afternoon. We both fought in the Battle of Champion Hill. We were exposed to the shelling and firing of the guns as everyone else, but we didn't get a scratch. I wasn't afraid. I did as I was commanded and took out as many Johnny Rebs as I could. I am beginning to hate this war. I'm not sure God ever intended this war to happen. I believe greed caused this war, and mankind will suffer for years to get over what man is doing to each other here on these battlefields. I hate it for Martha Jane. Her short marriage to Thomas Tull was good. She will desperately miss him in the days to come. Please be there for her as much as possible.

I don't know what lies ahead for us. I only know that I hope we don't continue to have battles like Champion

Hill. I swear, Christina, it was the worst thing I've experienced.

Even when it looked as though the Johnny Rebs might take the ravine, and when we were almost surrounded, I was thinking about you and how it was important for me to stay alive. Christina, I believe God means for us to be together. I'm going to hold onto that belief. You do the same, and you pray for me daily.

This has been my longest letter. There has been so much happening. I've got to stop now and write your father. I promised Hiram that I would write. I've got to write my folks also. That is going to be one of the hardest letters I've had to write.

I love you, James

James drew a deep breath, swatted a mosquito, and pulled another sheet of paper from his knapsack.

Dear Mr. Miller,

I regret to inform you that Hiram was shot in the Battle of Champion Hill today. He's going to be fine but has been wounded in the right arm and can't write now. I assure you, he will have a complete recovery.

You would be proud of Hiram. He is a very brave soldier who believes in the cause of this war. He, like the rest of us, would like to see it come to an end, but we all know we must keep the faith until the end. We are committed to finishing what we started out to do.

During the battle today, Thomas Tull was killed. According to Hiram, he was killed instantly. I'm glad he didn't have to suffer like many of the soldiers I saw suffering tonight at the hospital. Some of these soldiers will be crippled for life.

Many soldiers are being butchered something awful. Sometimes I think it would be better to die as Thomas did, rather than to be a cripple for the rest of one's life.

His death will certainly be hard on Martha Jane, and the kids. Thomas never got to see his little girl. How sad!

I trust that everything is going well for you after the death of Mrs. Miller. We all loved her, and I know you did too. Please know that I prayed for you during your period of grief.

I will continue to look in on Hiram as he recuperates from his wound. Please don't worry about him. He's going to heal just fine.

I'll say goodbye for now. You take care of yourself and make sure Christina behaves herself!

Your friend and neighbor,

James

With that chore behind him, James pulled another piece of paper, one of his last two, from his knapsack.

Dear Folks,

Today the 26th Missouri regiment fought in the battle of Champion Hill. It was the biggest battle we've been engaged in since entering the war. Today we were victorious but lost many good men. As you may already know, Thomas Tull was one of those good men. He was a brave soldier who we all loved and respected.

I know his death is going to be hard on Martha Jane and the children. I worry about how she will hold up under such pain. I know she loved Thomas very much. I'm glad you can be there for her and the children. They will need you.

I wish I could be there to help, but furlough is out of the question. The army is deep in Rebel territory and getting in or out is a tricky situation. I don't know how long it will take for this letter to be sent to you.

Hiram Miller was shot in the right arm today. He's going to be fine. I visited with him tonight in the hospital.

Jesse is taking Thomas' death hard. He's sick of this war. He asked me to give you his regards. He's in no mood right now to write. Although, he is sick of this war, he continues to be a good soldier. He doesn't do anything foolish. He fought well in today's battle at Champion's Hill. You would have been proud of him. Jesse amazes me by how he conducts himself. He is well respected in Company "H." Please don't worry about him; he's all right.

Please tell Martha Jane that I send my deepest sympathy to her and the kids. Tell her when I return, I will be happy to help her provide for the kids. Please tell her that Jesse and I love her and will be praying for her. Ma, about George wanting to join the Union Army. You and Pa do everything you can to prevent that from happening. George doesn't need to be in this war. Pa is right. Tell Pa to keep his foot on George and don't let him go into town along. Knowing George, he might just join up and leave on the spot. He's high spirited as you know.

Please tell him I said to stay put and help you and Pa on the farm. Tell him I'll do enough fighting for both of us. It upsets me to know that young men no older then George are dying daily in this bloody war. I don't want that to happen to my little brother.

I'll make this matter a priority in my prayers.

I don't know where we are going from here. It's been rumored we will be moving onto Vicksburg, Mississippi. Please continue to write us. Your letters will catch up with us somewhere.

I love you all,

James

CHAPTER 32

On May 19, 1863, arriving in Vicksburg, General Grant launched a hasty assault to smash through the entrenchments. The assault failed. He suffered several hundred casualties. The city of Vicksburg was well fortified, and the fortifications were on high ground.

On May 22, Grant launched a second assault on Vicksburg. Col. Boomer and the Missouri 26th were heavy engaged in this assault.

As usual, Col. Boomer completely exposed himself to the enemy's gun fire. Boomer believed that officers in command should participate in leading an assault rather than sending men into battle. His bravery was admirable but got him wounded in the battle of Iuka.

The Confederates were determined that Vicksburg would not fall to General Grant. Like the first assault, the Union Army suffered great damage. Union soldiers were falling left and right as they tried to press forward. Grant, seeing it was hopeless, sent word to retreat. The second assault had failed and with it several Union officers and soldiers were either wounded or killed. Among them was Col. Boomer of the Missouri 26th.

James and Jesse were fighting near Col. Boomer when he was shot and killed. James rushed to his side to try to help him, but it was too late. Col. Boomer died instantly.

James had lost a great friend, one who had taught him so much. James had always been afraid for Col. Boomer as he exposed himself out front with his soldiers. He was so brave, but in the end, he got himself killed by being brave.

The Missouri 26th infantry experienced a low morale from Col. Boomer's death. He had been with them from the beginning.

He had been their leader and friend. How could God let this happen? Who could replace him? These questions circulated throughout the camp.

General Grant didn't let Boomer's death pass unnoticed. As soon as things settled down after the attempted advance on Vicksburg, General Grant recognized Col. Boomer and those men who died along with him.

General Grant made sure that Col. Boomer and his brave soldiers were properly recognized in a special memorial service, during which James learned several things he didn't know about Col. Boomer.

Several hundred soldiers gathered around a platform that was erected to honor those who gave their lives in the Battle of Vicksburg.

General Grant's recognition of Col. Boomer and his fallen soldiers was touching to James and the other soldiers who fought alongside Boomer.

Looking out over the vast union army who came to pay their respect, General Ulysses Grant began to speak.

"We are gathered here today to pay tribute to Col. George Boardman Boomer. George Boomer was born in Sutton, Massachusetts, on July 2, 1832, and died on May 22, 1863. He attended Worcester Academy and graduated in 1847. At the outbreak of the Civil War, he raised a company which became part of the 26th Missouri Volunteer Infantry Regiment and by 1863 was promoted to Colonel. He distinguished himself at Vicksburg as Brigade Commander under Major General James B. McPherson.

"Col. Boomer will go down in history for his heroic representation of service during the heavy engagement of his brigade on May 16, 1863, at the Battle of Champion Hill, and for the second assault here at the battlefield of Vicksburg. During this battle, he courageously led his soldiers' straight ahead to Railroad Redoubt where he was mortally wounded. Only a few days ago, he was commissioned Brigadier General, but had not yet been told. I have never known such a brave soldier and commander. He faced death head-on and was a leader, not a follower. He believed in his soldiers and set a strong example as a leader.

"We will always remember his contributions made to this war. He accomplished so very much in such a short time. May his memories linger on in our minds in years to come. God bless Brigadier General George Boardman Boomer and these brave man of the Missouri 26th Infantry Regiment and others whom he led. He and his brave soldiers are now at peace with our Heavenly Father."

After these remarks, the cannon fired three rounds to commemorate the lives of these brave men.

James had lost both a great commander and a good friend. One who had inspired, encourage, and taught him courage. It would be hard to accept a new commander, James thought.

The Missouri 26th didn't have to wait long for Col. Boomer's replacement. Knowing he had to act fast, General Grant appointed Colonel Benjamin D. Dean, who had been wounded in the battle of Iuka, Mississippi, to replace Col. Boomer. Dean was born in Greenville, Ohio, on October 7, 1828. He was raised on a farm and later studied dentistry. He practiced the art of dentistry for several years in Ohio. He later went into the retail sales business which offered him a successful financial future.

In 1857, he moved to Lamar, Missouri, which is in Benton County. When the war broke out, he raised a company which eventually became Company "F" of the 26th Missouri Regiment.

After the second unsuccessful charge on Vicksburg, Mississippi, General Grant decided to settle down and wait the Confederates out. He felt confident that in time, he would take Vicksburg.

From June 1 to June 22, 1863, the 26th Missouri was involved in the siege of Vicksburg. Union regiments rotated out of the trenches every couple of days for rest. The trenches were dirty, wet, and dangerous. Sharpshooters were a constant hazard. The soldiers were kept busy with guard duty and digging further trenches. The most dangerous construction project was digging approaches which were trenches that zigzagged toward the Confederate lines. The intent of the approach was to get close enough to the Confederate trenches to allow a successful assault. Bundles of sticks, called fascines, were used to cover the approach trench and prevent Confederates from firing at Union soldiers. Blankets were also used to block the view into exposed sections of the trenches.

On June 11, after a hard day in the trenches, James and Jesse met on the banks of the mighty Mississippi river.

"I never dreamed I would be digging trenches, James," Jesse said as he sat down near a big tree that hung partially out over the Mississippi River.

"Neither did I, but I think this is our only hope in taking Vicksburg," James said.

"I got scared to death today. I almost got bit by a poison snake. He struck at me, but I moved fast enough to escape his strike. I hate snakes!"

"What are you laughing at? It's not funny, James."

"I'm not laughing at you Jesse, I'm laughing at the way you described the incident."

"James, are you aware there are more soldiers dying of disease and snake bites from digging these trenches than Confederate bullets," Jesse asked.

"I've heard that to be true," James replied.

"I'm telling you, I'm ready to get out of the trenches," Jesse said.

"What else has been going on with you, brother?" James asked.

"Nothing much. Oh, I did get a letter from Pa. Did you get one?"

"No! What did Pa. have to say?" James asked with interest.

"Pa got a letter from Uncle John Barger from Tennessee. Uncle John was telling Pa that their brother, Pointer, had three sons, Wiley, William, and Abraham fighting for the North. He said things were really heating up down in Tennessee."

"Did you know we had cousins fighting for the North?"

"No, but I've heard Pa mention Pointer several times."

"Do you think we will be going to Tennessee?" Jesse asked.

"If this war continues, I'm sure we'll end up in Tennessee," James said.

"I hope we do. I would like to meet up with our cousins," Jesse said.

"I'd like that too. I would like to see some of the counties where Pa lived before going to Missouri," James said.

"Do you remember where Pa was from?"

"Yes, he first lived in Morgan County. He was living in Bledsoe County when he moved to Missouri."

"What part of Tennessee is these counties?"

"East Tennessee," James replied.

"Jesse, I've got to get back to camp. I'm cooking tonight. Would you like to come and eat with us?"

"Thanks, Corporal Barger but I believe I'll pass."

"Suit yourself, little brother. Some day you will be hunger enough to eat my cooking. You will then know what you've been missing," James said as he left Jesse standing under the big tree.

On June 15, 1863,James wrote home to Christina.

My Dearest Christina,

We are now camping outside the city of Vicksburg. Since the battle of Champion Hill, we have had two unsuccessful assaults on Vicksburg. The 26th was involved in the second assault. Each assault has been painful for soldiers. I regret to inform you in this letter that my good friend and leader, Col. George Boomer, was killed in the May 22nd assault. It was a sad day. We miss him. He was a great officer and a friend to the 26th Missouri. We had only advanced about three hundred yards when the fire from the rebels became so intense we were forced down in a slight depression of ground. Everyone knew it was hopeless to go on, and I suspect even Col. Boomer knew that. But he started walking up and down the lines urging his men to get up and go forward. Several soldiers yelled at him to get down, but he ignored them. Just before he was shot, he looked straight at me. I started to yell to him to get down when he suddenly staggered to the side and fell forward, dead. I feel a certain part of me died with Col Boomer.

We remained pinned down until darkness fell. We found out during his memorial service that Col. Boomer had been promoted to Brigadier General. It's so tragic to know a man who worked so hard, was so faithful and sacrificed so much, died without knowing about his due recognition.

Col. Benjamin D. Dean has replaced Col. Boomer. He seems to be a respectable gentleman but not nearly as personable as Col. Boomer.

It's not going to be easy to take Vicksburg. Vicksburg is located on high ground and is well fortified. We are in the process of digging trenches in hopes of getting close enough for our guns to do damage to their fortifications.

Digging trenches is not my favorite pastime, I assure you. But someone must do it. We are under fire daily from sharpshooters' bullets. We use "fascines" and blankets to help shield us from the sights of the Confederate sharpshooters as we dig the trenches. In case you're wondering what, a fascine is, it is a bundle of sticks or tree limbs that are placed in front of the area which we are digging. This works most of the time, but we have lost a few men who got careless. Don't worry, I keep my head down.

I have a hunch that soon, I will be up front using my sharpshooting skills when we get close enough to get in the fighting.

I had no idea when I joined this army that I would be digging trenches. The conditions are horrible. The trenches are wet and cold at night. All day the sun beats down on us mercilessly. There are rats and snakes everywhere. The trenches stink and after a day in the trenches, we look like hogs, and smell like them too! You wouldn't want me near you. About every two days, we rotate out for two days to rest.

My dreams of you are becoming more frequent. Let me tell you of my latest dream. It was so real! I dreamed we were married and I was plowing our crop of corn. It was so hot, and I was sweating something awful. I stopped to wipe the sweat from my brow when I saw you coming across the field. You had your lovely polka dot dress on and you were barefooted. You were so beautiful! As you handed me the jug of water, I took a few swallows, set the jar down, wiped my lips with my shirt sleeve and reached out for your hands. I pulled you close and kissed your sweet lips. You didn't seem to mind that I was hot and sweaty.

As soon as this war is over, and I come home, I want us to get married and have some babies. I want at least six. All boys preferably! I'm only kidding. A few girls tossed in would be all right too. I've never asked you if you want children. I sure hope you do.

Someday, I know my dream will come true.

Please know you are my sunshine in the morning, my hope during the day, and my peace at night. You are the reason I stay alive.

Hiram and Jesse are both doing well. Hiram's wound is healing good. I see him and Jesse about every two days. They too are digging trenches, and like me, they hate it.

I pray things are well with you. I've been looking for a letter from you every day. Nothing yet, but I know I will receive one soon.

It's getting late here so I'm going to say goobye for now. Hope to hear from you soon.

Love James

On June 17, 1863, James A. Barger received a package from Christina. In the package James found his favorite oatmeal cookies, and the following letter.

My Dearest James,

I received your letter about the battle of Champion Hill. I'm sorry so many soldiers were killed. I'm so thankful you were not hurt. I continue to trust in your guardian angel.

I attended Thomas Tull's memorial service. Although his body was not actually there, it still was just awful. Martha Jane took it so hard. I'm worried about her. I've never seen anyone hurt so badly. She is now a widow with three small children. Your dad and mom are taking good care of her and the children, but how long can that last? Although, she is a beautiful lady, how many men will want to marry a woman with three small children?

The Weekly California Newspaper carries a list of soldiers weekly who have lost their lives or who have been released because of being crippled by the war. Moniteau County is having its share of those soldiers. First it was Henry and now it's Thomas Tull. Last week's paper carried an article about Benjamin Donaldson. I think you know him. He is the son of Thomas Donaldson. Anyway, he returned last week with no legs. Benjamin will need someone to take care of him for the rest of his life. What a shame!

I got a job working for Mr. and Mrs. John Hanover who live here in the city of California. I clean their house and make their meals. The Hanovers are one of the wealthier families in California. Mr. Hanover once owned the general mercantile store here in California. He is now retired and getting up in age. He and his wife don't have any children and need someone to help look after them. They have money and pay me well.

The Hanovers asked Pa if he would let me stay with them. I wanted to, so Pa let me. I like being here. I get to go shopping for the Hanovers. This gives me a chance to talk to other people. You would be surprised to hear what comes out of the mouth of some of the local town's ladies. I swear, they do like to talk!

I see your folks at church every Sunday. They are doing well. Your good-looking brother, George, has the girls hanging all over him. He's a fine-looking young man. I think he knows that also.

I hope you enjoy the cookies. I wish you were here, so I could fatten you up. After you return home, I will never let you be hungry again. That's a promise!

I've written about everything I know to write about this time. Like everyone else, we are ready for this war to end. Please know I do pray for you daily. My love grows for you each breath I take.

Please stay smart and watch your back. I look forward to hearing from you.

My love is yours,
Christina

Christina's letters gave James strength and hope. Hope of sharing his life with the girl he left behind.

By mid-June, General Grant was aware that another Confederate Army was assembling in east central Mississippi. Confederate General Joseph Johnston was in command of this force. Grant feared that General Joseph Johnston might launch an attack from his rear and cut him off from any Union help. To guard against General Johnston's threat, he detached several thousand troops, about a corps, to the Black River area where they constructed a network of fortifications to defend against any attack from the east.

On June 22, 1863, the 26th Missouri was ordered out of the trenches to join other Union forces at Black River. Fortunately, for General Grant, General Johnston was never able to muster enough troops to mount a serious threat to Grant's troops at Vicksburg. To James and the 26th, it meant more digging trenches but under conditions that were a lot better. With no Rebel sharpshooters, one could stand up while he dug, sleep in a snug tent every night, and eat hot meals every day.

On July 4, 1863, Vicksburg surrendered after some extended siege operations. This was the outcome of one of the most brilliant military campaigns of the war. With the loss of General Pemberton's army and this vital stronghold on the Mississippi, the Confederacy was effectively split in half. Grant's successes in the West boosted his reputation, leading ultimately to his appointment as General-in-Chief of the Union Armies.

General Grant's siege of Vicksburg started on May 18 and ended on July 4, 1863. The two principal commanders were Maj. Gen. Ulysses S. Grant, Union Army and Lt. General John C. Pemberton, Confederate Army. There were two major forces engaged in the battle, the Army of Tennessee, the Union Army, and the Army of Vicksburg, the Confederate Army.

The siege of Vicksburg claimed many lives. The Union had 4,550 killed, wounded, and captured, and the Confederates lost 31,275.

On July 12, 1863, the 26th Missouri was called back to Vicksburg to take part in an attack against Jackson, Mississippi, which Grant had briefly occupied in May 1863. The 26th was part of the force which advanced upon, and briefly besieged, Jackson. Confederate forces in Jackson evacuated their trenches and slipped out of town to the east on July 16. The Union forces occupied the town on the 16th.

The soldiers of the 26th Missouri regiment, who had been either marching, digging, or fighting since April, moved back to Vicksburg for a well-deserved rest.

On July 22, 1863, James wrote Christina this letter.

> *My Dearest Christina,*
>
> *We are still camped at Vicksburg. I'm sure you've heard by now that we are in command of Vicksburg. Confederate General Pemberton surrendered on July 4$^{th.}$ It was a long drawn out ordeal. Our victory at Vicksburg has severely damaged the Confederate states.*
>
> *We have been engaged in drilling, patrolling, and constructing entrenchments. One thing we are doing is filling in trenches that we dug during the siege. The generals are afraid that if the Confederates ever try to recapture Vicksburg, they might use our old trenches to do it, so we must refill all of them.*
>
> *The good news is that I now have a decent rifle. I have a .577 caliber Enfield that was made in England. The Rebels had thousands of these Enfield's brought in through the blockade, but many of our boys still had*

old muskets. So, as soon as Vicksburg fell, I got to turn in my old musket and was given a genuine Confederate Enfield. The whole 26th and a bunch of other regiments in Grant's army now have shiny new Enfield rifles. It is a fine rifle, but it is not as good as Old Faithful, my hunting rifle back home.

According to Col. Benjamin Dean, the siege of Vicksburg was the most important victory of this war. The Mississippi River is now ours. We will be able to control supplies up and down the river. This war will certainly go down in history as the bloodiest, cruelest, and most crippling war of all times. At least these are my thoughts. This war will certainly make up a big part of history books that will someday be read by many young people. I do hope what we are fighting for is within God's will. If it's not, we sure are paying a terrible price. We have seen a lot of desertions lately. The war is taking a toll on lots of our soldiers, including me. I would never desert. I feel that would be cowardly.

Jesse, Hiram, and the others from Moniteau County are doing well. Jesse has had a summer cold but seems to be doing better. I think it's due to getting wet and dirty in the trenches. Everybody has had a little malaria here, but the surgeons give us quinine and we usually get better.

I really don't have any information about what's next for the 26th Missouri. I have heard a rumor that we may be heading to Tennessee. If this is true it will be nice to see Tennessee. I hear Tennessee is a lot like Missouri. It would be nice to see Morgan, Overton, and Bledsoe Counties where my pa grew up. He has spoken so well of it over the years. Uncle John and his family now live in Cumberland County which boarders Bledsoe County It would be nice to see Uncle John.

I'm glad you have a good job with the Hanovers. They seem to be nice people. Do you stay on the weekends also? Tell my family that Jesse and I are doing fine. We miss them and long for the day when we can return.

Yes, I think of you daily. I love you more than I ever thought possible. I live for the day I can hold you in my arms and claim you as Mrs. James Barger. I'm hoping that won't be too long.

I'll stop now and get this ready to mail. Give my regards to your father, sisters, and brothers. I will always love you.

Sincerely,
James

The 26th spent the whole month of August in Vicksburg drilling, patrolling, constructing entrenchments and filling in trenches.

CHAPTER 33

James had plenty of time to write Christina and his parents as the steamboat Thomas E. Tutt slowly worked its way up the Mississippi River. It took four days to go from Vicksburg to Helena, Arkansas.

Dear Christina,

I am currently writing this letter on the steamboat Thomas E. Tutt as we travel up the Mississippi River to Helena, Arkansas. General Steele has an army trying to take Little Rock, and we are to join him.

When the regiment finally docked in Helena, James added a postscript to his letter: *We got here safe on the 15th of September. They say Steele captured Little Rock on the 10th. So, we are not going to Little Rock, after all, and hopefully will have a nice rest in Helena.*

James mailed his letters to Christina and his parents and settled in to what he thought was going to be several days of relaxing.

After arriving in Helena, the Missouri 26th set up camp just outside of Helena. James and Jesse were soon hard at work felling trees and building shebang's, the half-buried, half-log, and half canvas shelters that the soldiers occupied in the winter. After two weeks of intense work, the 26th Missouri had a snug warm camp to pass the winter away in Helena and had every intention of doing so.

Then, news arrived that changed the regiment's plans. There had been a major federal defeat at Chickamauga, Georgia, on September 20, 1863. Chickamauga was about ten miles south of Chattanooga. A Union Army under General Rosecrans, who had led the 26th at Corinth, had been defeated and compelled to retreat into the city of Chattanooga where it was now besieged and in a desperate situation. Rosecrans was relieved of his command and replaced by General George H. Thomas.

President Abe Lincoln ordered all available forces to move to the relief of the troops trapped in Chattanooga.

From the Vicksburg vicinity came General Ulysses Grant, General William Sherman, and most of their forces.

From Virginia, two corps of the Army of the Potomac began a roundabout railroad journey to northeastern Alabama. The 26th Missouri leaving from Helena was one small part of the huge troop movement.

On the 28th, saying farewell to the warm huts they had planned to occupy, the regiment boarded the steamer Rocket which, true to its name, got them to Memphis the next day. After several days delay in Memphis while other forces assembled, the 26th left Memphis on October 3, 1863. The regiment moved by train to Glendale, Mississippi. From this point on October 6, the regiment took a train to Burnsville, Mississippi. From Burnsville it was all on foot. From Burnsville they marched through Iuka, Mississippi, and areas that were familiar to the veterans of the regiment from the campaigns of the prior year.

James felt a tightness in his throat as he surveyed the battlefield of Iuka again. It had only been a year ago that he had fought there, but it seemed like an eternity. Iuka was a constant reminder to James of the death of Henry. He would never forget the look in Jesse's eyes and the pain on his face when Jesse told him of Henry's death. It made him very sad to pass near the battlefield.

The regiment crossed into northern Alabama on October 20 and ended the month at Chickasaw, Alabama.

During this time, Union forces inside Chattanooga grimly hung on, while rations dwindled. In late October a route was cleared to approach Chattanooga from the north. This supply line, dubbed the cracker line, kept the defenders fed until help could arrive.

In early November 1863, the 26th Missouri crossed the Tennessee River at Eastport, Alabama, on the steamer Anglo-Saxon. They then set off across country arriving at Bridgeport, Alabama, on November 15, 1863.

On November 20, the regiment arrived two miles above Chattanooga and on the far side of the Tennessee River from Chattanooga.

James wrote to Christina.

Dear Christina:

You would not believe how many soldiers are here! I have never seen such a large army. There are thousands of troops brought in from the Army of the Potomac in Virginia, and they say they are going to show us westerners how to fight. Naturally, we don't take this any too well. Most of the regiments we served with at Vicksburg are here too, plus the entire Army of the Cumberland under General Thomas. Thomas' soldiers are still inside the city, but we are hiding behind hills on the other side of the Tennessee River. The Confederates are on a line of hills south of town on the Chattanooga side of the river. The only way to get into Chattanooga is a pontoon bridge stretched across the river. I believe, Christina, there is about to be the biggest battle that I have ever seen.

I've got to stop now. I will write more later.

James couldn't share with Christina what was about to take place in a letter. If it was intercepted by the Confederates, it would be a disadvantage to the Union Army.

Under General Grant's plan, Joseph Hooker would lead one wing of the army in the assault on Lookout Mountain, south of town. Then, General William Sherman would cross the Tennessee north of Chattanooga and seize Tunnel Hill. The 26th Missouri will accompany General Sherman. Finally, Thomas' Army of the Cumberland would attack out from Chattanooga to seize Missionary Ridge, while Hooker and Sherman would strike the flanks of the Confederate position. If General Grant's plan works, the Union Army should be victorious. On November 23, Thomas army advanced out of Chattanooga. On the plain east of Chattanooga, Thomas' army deployed and advanced on a wooded knoll called Orchard Knob. With drums beating and flags waving, Thomas' men charged Orchard Knob, which fell after a brief fight.

Hooker's part also got off to a good start on November 24. In a dense fog, Hooker's troops advanced up Lookout Mountain. They overwhelmingly surprised the Confederates who were spread out to cover several possible approach routes. After a deadly fight in dense fog, Hooker seized the high ground by evening.

General Sherman, however, had problems. His force, a mixture of regiments newly arrived from "back east" including mostly German units, plus some of his troops from the Vicksburg campaign had been hiding behind a line of hills for several days. Just before midnight on the night of November 23-24 in a rain storm, Sherman began ferrying his troops across the Tennessee River in pontoon boats. James helped carry the pontoon boats down to the river, and then with muffled oars the 26th rowed across. Behind them, engineers were assembling other pontoons to make a pontoon bridge. While the engineers worked as quietly as possible, with no talking above a whisper allowed, James could not believe that the noise would not be heard, even above the sound of the falling rain. After disembarking from their pontoons, the 26th advanced a short distance and dug in to wait the rest of the army.

At dawn on November 24, James was astonished to see a pontoon bridge stretching like a ribbon all the way across the river and columns of federal troops crossing the bridge. Watching the rickety bridge buck up and down with the tramping of thousands of feet, James was glad he had taken the boat.

James had little time to contemplate the bridge. Hushed orders were passed down the line to fall in. The 26th became one small part of a solid wall of blue advancing up the wooded slope. There was a scattering of shots, but with a yell, the blue-clad wave swept to the crest of the hill. There they paused to cheer and celebrate an easy victory. James was so preoccupied with exchanging congratulations with his friends that he failed to notice the small knot of mounted officers.

General Sherman was enraged. The celebrations of the 26th Missouri and other federal regiments did not help his temper. "It's the wrong damn hill!" he screamed. "The map is wrong! We need to be over there!" He paused, fuming, while his staff contemplated the 3/4-mile-wide valley between the hill they presently held and a second, steeper hill in the distance, a hill flourishing with Rebel battle flags.

Meanwhile, Colonel Dean restored order to his unruly soldiers and directed them to "stack arms," go to a rail fence, dismantle the fence, and then use the rails to improve their hastily constructed defenses. Walking toward the fence unarmed, the regiment was startled when several dozen Confederates who had been hiding behind the fence suddenly jumped up and fled! It was the first time in the history of the 26th that it had ever routed the Confederates without a single shot.

On the 25th, after spending an uncomfortable night on the cold ridge crest, Sherman's army moved out to attack across the valley towards the second hill, known as Tunnel Hill. The terrain was rugged, and progress was slow. Halfway across the valley, the Confederates opened fire, and bullets and shell began raining down on the 26th.

James was forced to recall the assault on Vicksburg, only this was worse. Poor Colonel Boomer had been shot in an assault just like this one. Just as James was remembering Boomer's death, Brigadier General Mathies went down with a head wound. To James' relief, however, General Mathies was able to ride to the rear. At this time, the command of the brigade fell to Colonel Dean.

Despite the rain of bullets and shells, the 26th crossed the valley with only a few being killed; however, several were wounded. James's good friend, Fredrick Marshall, was one of those killed. He was close to James when he was shot in the chest and he died instantly. James stopped to attend him, but after seeing he was dead, James continued. Colonel Dean miraculously escaped injury when his insignia was shot away.

Reaching the base of Tunnel Hill, the waves of Union troops began working their way uphill, firing, moving from cover to cover, and then firing again. The smoke was more intense than James had ever seen it before, even at Iuka. The vicious Confederates fire caused the Federal assault to stall. James found himself with a score or so of members of the 26th and the 93rd Illinois, crouched in a slight ditch, partially protected by a large log. Here, the Union soldiers loaded repeatedly and fired at the line of muzzle flashes that could be seen through the smoke above them.

A figure dashed into the depression and crouched beside them. It was Colonel Dean. He surveyed the group then said, "You, there, isn't your name Barger? I think I have seen you clerking at headquarters."

"Yes, Sir, you have. I am James Barger, Sir," answered James, thinking this was an odd topic with a battle raging around them.

"Go find Major Holman. He is over there somewhere," Dean said gesturing vaguely. "Tell him to refuse our right flank! Do you understand me? REFUSE THE RIGHT FLANK! Tell him that the 26th and the 93rd are separated here, and I don't know where the rest of the brigade is, but I do know that our right flank is in the air. We've got to pull it back before it gets turned! Go! Hurry."

James would have been frightened if he had paused to think, but the urgency of Dean's voice caused him to spring from the ditch and scrambled down the slope in the general direction that Dean had indicated. James passed several knots of Federal soldiers, crouched behind any available cover who glanced at him as he sprinted by. There was no immediate sign of Major Holman, but there were still a lot of nooks and crannies on the hillside to check. James headed for a burning farmhouse. There he spotted a large group of Federal soldiers crouching behind it.

Before he was able to reach the farm house, a cry went up all along the Union line. Over the roar James couldn't understand what was being shouted by a thousand voices at once. Instinctively he knew it was a warning and crouched down. Out of the smoke, like gray ghosts, came a horde of charging, shouting Rebel soldiers. The Rebs had found the hole on the brigade's flank that Colonel Dean had been worried about. James lowered his rifle and pulled the trigger, but nothing happened. It was not loaded. He mentally called himself all kinds of stupid names for making such a childish error. The thought flashed through his mind that this was the first time since Corinth that he had really had a good shot at Confederates. Here he was, supposedly a sharpshooter, with a rifle that wasn't loaded. James could not help but laugh at himself.

A stampeding horde of Union soldiers dashed past James' position. There was nothing he could do but join them. When they reached the open plain of the valley, James could see thousands of Sherman's soldiers streaming across the valley back at the ridge where they had camped the night before. James winced, as he stumbled and turned his ankle.

Back in the safety of their own ridge, James and the 26th rested. James' ankle was soon swollen, and Jesse found some water and bandaged it with damp rags. "I don't think it's broken," said Jesse, "but it sure looks like a bad sprain."

Just then corporal Lemming of "D" Company wearily dropped down, next to James. "This may be a lucky sprain for you," said Lemming.

"How so?" asked James.

"I was filling my canteen at that well over yonder when Sherman and his staff rode up. At about the same time, a messenger came riding up and handed Sherman a note from Grant. Well, Sherman read the message from Grant and got all mad. You should have seen him! Anyway, Grant has ordered Sherman to attack again!"

A groan escaped from every soldier within earshot. They didn't have to worry much because Sherman launched a very half-hearted assault with a few hundred men who cautiously advanced a short distance and then called it a day. James and

Jesse, eating hardtack, watched with amusement from their high perch. A voice behind them brought Jesse to attention.

"Well, I finally found you, Barger! I was afraid you had been killed." Colonel Dean glanced at James' leg with some apparent concern, "Nothing serious I hope?"

"No, Sir," said James, "it's just a sprain."

"Well, I am going to be keeping my eye on you, young man. I know that Colonel Boomer thought a great deal of you. Now, I know why. I have been all over the face of that ridge looking for Major Holman. Four times I have tried to get enlisted men to help me search. Every one of them refused to leave his safe hiding place, except for you."

"But I didn't find him," stammered James, embarrassed by being praised in front of his friends.

"Well, neither did I," said Dean, with a chuckle." Listen, if your leg isn't too bad, there is a message that needs to be delivered to Orchard Knob. I have a spare horse, but no spare man to ride it. With a limp leg, you are perfect for the job."

"Yes, Sir. I will deliver it, Sir, but where is Orchard Knob?"

"It is that little hill down yonder," Dean pointed. "The whole Army of the Cumberland is drawn up around it. If you stick to this side of the valley, you should have no trouble from the Rebels. All right?"

"Yes, Sir."

Fifteen minutes later James galloped down the valley. Chattanooga was to his right, and Orchard Knob, a small knoll, was ahead of him. To his left the low, ominous rise known as Missionary Ridge was crowned with dozens of Confederate battle flags. James' ankle throbbed with every lurch of the horse and he regretted his eagerness to become a mounted courier.

Arriving at Orchard Knob, James dismounted. A young bugler offered to hold his horse. There was quite an assembly of officers there, Grant included, but James' message was addressed to General George H. Thomas. Unfortunately, James' didn't have the slightest idea what Thomas looked like. After making several inquiries he was directed to a robust man with a graying beard. He presented the letter to Thomas, who, noticing James' limp and his bandaged leg, asked if James had been shot.

"No, Sir. But I sprained it pretty good in the charge up Tunnel Hill this morning."

"Well, sit down over there and rest a spell. I want to write a reply, but I don't have time to do so right this moment. My boys are about to charge over to that ridge over yonder," he said by pointing to the Cumberland army.

James gave an exclamation of surprise and said, "You don't believe they can do it, do you?"

"Well, you don't know my boys! Anyway, we are not actually going up the ridge. Grant's orders are just to clear the outposts at the foot of the ridge. Have a seat and watch the show!"

What a show it was! With drums beating, fifes playing, flags waving, the Army of the Cumberland stepping off across the plain towards the ridge. James recalled reading, as a boy, an account of the spectacle of the Battle of Waterloo. It had been described as a vast panorama of thousands of soldiers. James had been disappointed as he realized real battles were not like that. This, however, was one like that.

The Confederates on the ridge were firing now, but Thomas' troops continued onward. When the troops reached the outposts at the foot of the hill, a collective sigh of relief was shared by every spectator on Orchard Knob. In a voice mixed with rage, astonishment, and disbelief, Grant suddenly shouted, "What the hell do they think they are doing?"

All eyes on the Knob turned their attention back to Missionary Ridge. Blue clad soldiers could be seen scrambling up the steep slope toward the main Rebel position at the top.

"Who ordered this charge? I will have me a court martial if this charge fails!" Grant was almost too angry to speak.

One of the generals standing next to Grant quietly remarked, "Those Army boys of the Cumberland just don't know when to quit."

Another officer replied, "When they get going good, it is almost impossible to stop them."

Grant, while still fuming, raged on, "They can't take that position by themselves! It's too strong! Damn! Is there any way to call them back? Damn! It will take that whole army, plus all of Sherman's troops and Hooker's corps to even stand a chance on taking that hill. Damn!"

Grant fell silent. The group of officers on the Knob stared at the ragged lines of blue crawling toward the top. Smoke rolled down and over them, but through gaps they could still be seen climbing up the hill.

Suddenly an aide shouted, "Look there! On the left!" The Stars and Stripes could be seen atop Missionary Ridge. Then a second and a third appeared. Finally, the top was covered with the red, white, and blue flags. Grant and his officers could hear cheers from the top of Missionary Ridge peak.

James had never seen a general dance before this moment. Grant, beside himself with joy, danced a jig shouting to no one in particular: "I knew they could do it! Didn't I tell you they could do it? They did it!"

The Battle of Chattanooga was over. The Confederate forces at Tunnel Hill, opposite Sherman's troops, pulled out and withdrew as darkness fell. The battle was over. With the fall of Missionary Ridge, the Confederates lost about 6,500 men, two-thirds of whom were captured.

Grant's forces suffered 5,800 men who were either killed or wounded. About half of the union soldiers who died or were wounded were from Sherman's force. The 26th Missouri had fifteen killed, and thirty-four wounded, and four men were missing. These casualties were heavier, in proportion, than the losses in earlier battles such as Champion Hill and Iuka. The much depleted 26th had paid dearly for the ridge.

It was much later that evening when James returned to the camp of the 26th Missouri, where he found Jesse.

"Hey brother, it's sure good seeing you standing there in good shape. You were gone so long I was getting seriously worried," Jesse said as he walked up to him.

"Boy, James, I thought we were goners today. I could just see them Johnny Rebels swarming down on us from all directions. I just knew we were going to die," Jesse said with excitement.

"I admit the thought of dying entered my mind several times today, too," James said as he sat down by Jesse.

"James, I lost two good friends today. Homer Davis from Osage County was shot in the head. I don't think he even knew what hit him. Melvin Douglas from Cole County took a shot in the stomach. It was just terrible!" Jesse said as he lowered his head.

"I lost a friend today, too. Fredrick Marshall from Osage County died near me. He was shot in the chest. Thank God he didn't suffer long," James said.

"Gosh all mighty, when is this war ever going to end? I don't think it ever will until all of us are dead. I'm really getting sick of this whole war. Good friends are being killed all around us. I don't know how much longer I can stand it," Jesse said as tears came in his eyes.

"Jesse, let me remind you that you've got to remain calm. You can't lose your head. When you lose your head, you are going to be dead too. You've got to stay strong and think about staying alive. Kill those Johnny Rebs before they kill you," James said as he laid his hand on Jesse's shoulder.

"Jesse, what's the talk about General William Sherman over here in Company H?"

"I've heard several soldiers talking about General Sherman. They say he is very ambitious and doesn't take no for an answer. He seems to have the respect of Col. Dean," Jesse replied.

"We hear that General Grant thinks a lot of him. I've only seen him up close once. He is a good-looking fellow. Other folks say that he is nervous and excitable," James said.

"How do you like our new commander, Col. Dean?" Jesse asked.

"He's no Col. Boomer, but you know how I felt about Col. Boomer. He was my friend and hero. I will never like another officer as well as I did Col. Boomer."

"I agree with you about Col. Boomer. I liked him too, and he was a good officer."

"I've got to go, Jesse. Remember what I've said to you. You've got to be strong and keep your head clear. You do that, and your chances of staying alive are a lot better. Goodbye, Jesse."

"Goodbye, James."

As James walked off, Jesse hollered at him and said, "James, don't let anything happen to you. If something happens to you, I don't think I could stand being in this war without you. Please take care of yourself."

A small grin broke James's powder blackened, tear stained face. He turned and said, "I'm going to do my best to stay alive, and thanks!"

After returning to camp and sharing a cold supper of moldy hardtack and beans with his tent friends, James settled down to finish his letter to Christina.

Dear Christina,

I'm back and will finish this letter I started days ago.

I'm writing this letter on the night of November 24, 1863, from our camp outside of Chattanooga, Tennessee. For the past two days we have been engaged in the Battle of Chattanooga. I'm happy to report that we were victorious, and Jesse, Hiram, and I are still doing well. No wounds from the battle. It appears that our guardian angels are still watching out for us.

Both Jesse and I lost good friends today. He lost two friends, one from Osage County and the other from Cooper County. I lost my good friend, Fredrick Marshall, from Cole County.

Sgt. Matthew Ryan of the Missouri 26th was killed today. He died right by me after being shot in the head. I tell you when I looked at him, it was all I could do not to get sick. He was a great man. He was always out front with his squad. Col. Putman of the 93rd Illinois was also killed in the battle. Another officer, Brigadier General Mathies, received a head wound. He was taken to the hospital, and I hear he's going to recover. Col. Dean of the 26th escaped injury when his insignia strap was shot away.

Things looked bad for us for a while. Just when I thought we were going to be defeated, the Army of the Cumberland, another part of Sherman's huge army launched a counter charge across the open ground towards a hill called Missionary Ridge. You should have seen them, Christina. It was a cheering tide of blue uniforms sweeping across the plains. I have read about battles like Waterloo and the vast spectacle it presented, but I have never seen anything like it until today. It was awe inspiring.

I was fortunate to get a bird's-eye view of the battle. Col. Dean had sent me to deliver a message to General George Thomas, commander of the Cumberland Army. General Thomas asked me to stay and watch the battle. It was exciting!

How's everything working out with your new job with the Hanovers? How's your father and the rest of your family? Have you seen my family lately? I enjoy the articles you sent me from the California Times. It's always good to read about what's going on in Moniteau County and other parts of the world. I'm glad they have a newspaper in California. I like to read, as you know. I want our children to be good readers. I'm meeting a lot of well-educated officers and soldiers here. I appreciate Pa and Ma making us go to school. It's been important to me, but there is still so much I need to learn.

I don't know where we'll go from here. We stand ready at any time. I like the Chattanooga area. Chattanooga is not far from Bledsoe County, and that's where Pa and Ma lived for three years before coming to Missouri. We are seeing some beautiful country here, but it's being tainted by death, blood, and suffering.

I had a long talk with Jesse this afternoon. He is very melancholy, but I think he's going to be fine. Please have Margaret write him a big letter and have her encourage him to think positive. He gets down when he sees his friends being killed. I wish we were in the same company, so I could keep an eye out for him.

The cookies you sent in your last package were a blessing. They always remind me of home. Please continue to send more.

It's bedtime and I've got to stop now and put out the light. I'll mail this letter tomorrow.

My dear Christina, there's not a night that passes that I don't dream about you. You are the reason I live. I love you so very much. You take care and let me hear from you.

I will always love you,
James

The next day, James received a message from Col. Dean to report to his headquarters. Colonel Dean had appropriated a log cabin and was conferring with two of the captains when he entered.

Colonel Dean saw him entering and said, "This is Corporal Barger. Do you gentlemen know him? At ease, Corporal Barger. I've heard a lot of good things about you. Colonel Boomer thought very highly of you. They also speak very highly of your bravery in battle. I need a good man like you to fill a vacancy as sergeant in the 26th Missouri Infantry. From all reports you would make an excellent Sergeant. We lost a good man in Sergeant Matthew Ryan yesterday. You come highly recommended to fill that position. How do you feel about becoming a sergeant, Corporal Barger?" Col. Dean asked as he puffed on his pipe.

"I would like to give it my best shot, Sir," James said with excitement.

"Well, consider it done. The orders will be written up by my clerk tomorrow, and it should be officially announced at roll call tomorrow evening."

"Thank you, Sir. I'll do my very best to make you a good sergeant," James said as he saluted Col. Dean.

James was received well by the men in his squad. Most of them already knew him and would gladly follow him into battle.

The Missouri 26th Regiment left Chattanooga on November 27 for Bridgeport, Alabama. After a cold march, they arrived in Bridgeport on December 5, 1863. The trip to Bridgeport was very hard on the Missouri 26th. Food was even more scarce, and several soldiers had become so weak from lack of food, they had to be supported by other soldiers to walk. After arriving in Bridgeport, they were fed, and it wasn't long before they had regained their strength. It was a hard march and one that James and Jesse would long remember.

The 26th Missouri remained in Bridgeport until December 22, 1863. On December 22nd, they moved to Larkinsville, Alabama, arriving there on December 26, 1863, where they celebrated a delayed Christmas party. Col. Dean had arranged for a good meal and plenty of hot tea, a rare beverage in an army where coffee was generally the only drink served.

On January 7, 1864, the 26th Missouri received orders to leave Larkinsville and move west to Huntsville, Alabama. The trip to Huntsville took the Missouri 26th three days to complete. The Missouri 26th would remain in Huntsville, Alabama, until April 30, 1864.

After arriving in Huntsville, James, Jesse, and Hiram were faced with a big decision. They had almost completed their first enlistment obligation. If they re-enlisted, they were promised a furlough and a bonus. They would each get an early discharge on their first enlistment, and would get $2.00 per month additional pay during the term of their second enlistment

James, Jesse, and Hiram had grown weary with the war at times. In fact, they hated the war. They didn't hate the cause behind the war but hated the long marches, the butchery, and the lack of food. Although they looked forward to going home, they still felt a strong need to re-enlist. They believed a man's freedom was still worth fighting for. They had saved money but not enough to buy the farms they wanted back in Moniteau County.

They also heard the war would soon end. A few more months would not make that much difference, they thought.

James also felt a need to re-enlist since he had just received his new rank as Sergeant. He needed the bonus money, which was $300.00.

The thirty-day furlough and believing a man's freedom was worth fighting for was the deciding factors in James, Jesse, and Hiram's decision to re-enlist.

CHAPTER 34

The long trip to California, Missouri, went without any incidents. Most of the regiment had re-enlisted. Those who did not remained on duty in Huntsville while the rest of the regiment was moved by train and steamboat to Jefferson City. There, they turned in their weapons to the local quartermaster and were instructed to be back in Jefferson City in exactly thirty days.

James, Jesse, and Hiram, and about twenty-five other Moniteau County veterans of the 26th Missouri, arrived in California by train at 2:00 on January 29, 1864. James, Jesse, and Hiram had chosen not to let their folks know they were coming home on furlough. They wanted to surprise everyone. Their arrival went without any notice as they stepped off the train. Other families had gathered to greet their loved ones, and the confusion of those tumultuous welcomes allowed James, Jesse, and Hiram to quietly slip away. They were ready for the six-mile trip home. Walking would not be a problem because of their fine physical condition.

"Jesse, if it's okay with you, I'm going to hang around here for a while. You don't mind walking home with Hiram, do you?" James asked.

"I bet I know what you're planning. You're going to see Christina, aren't you?" Jesse asked.

"Sure am!"

"Give my sister my regards and tell her I'll see her later," Hiram said as he and Jesse started down the street.

"Jesse, tell the folks I'll be home before dark," James yelled.

"I'll tell them, James," Jesse yelled back.

James picked up his knapsack and swung it over his left shoulder as he started down the street which led him to the Hanovers' home.

James walked up the steps that led to the front porch, laid his knapsack down, and knocked on the door. The door opened, and Christina stood looking at James. The expression on her face alarmed James. It was like she didn't know him. James had grown a full beard and was wearing his faded and tattered Union Army uniform. He looked completely different from the time she last saw him. In fact, it had been almost three years.

"Can I help you, soldier?" Christina asked.

"Yes, my beautiful Christina, you can help me by coming out on this front porch and giving me a big kiss and a hug," James said as he smiled.

"Oh, My God, James, it's you! I didn't recognize you! Oh, my darling, I'm so sorry," Christina cried as she pushed open the door and threw herself into his arms.

After a short hug, James pushed her back, took her hands and said, "You are so beautiful!"

"I've been keeping myself beautiful for you, James," Christina said as her face lit up in a big smile. "Oh, James, it's so good to see you."

James pulled her near again and they kissed. The kiss seemed to last forever. "Come on in, James. I want you to meet the Hanover's."

Christina grabbed James by his left hand and dragged him through the front door. As they entered the large parlor, Christina said, "Ya'll, I want you to meet my one and only love, James A. Barger. I mean Corporal James A. Barger." Christina then saw the stripes on James's uniform and said, "My gosh, James, you got another promotion. I stand corrected! This is Sergeant James A. Barger. James, this is Jack and Gladys Hanover."

"Pleased to meet you," James said as he shook Mr. Hanover's hand.

"It's a pleasure to meet you, James. Christina talks about you all the time," Gladys said with a smile.

"I hope it's all been good," James said.

"Oh, it's all good. You would think you were the President of the United States the way she talks about you," Jack said.

"James, what does the A stand for in your name? Mr. Jack asked.

"The A stands for Anderson. My middle name is Anderson. I believe Anderson came from one of my great uncles."

"Sit down a spell, James," Mrs. Hanover said.

"I'll make some tea while you all visit," Christina said.

"Have you been discharged from the Army?" Mr. Hanover asked.

"No, Sir, I'm just home on a thirty-day furlough. We must be back in Jefferson City in a month. From there, they will ship us back to Alabama," James replied.

"I know you're glad to be home," Mrs. Hanover said.

"Yes, Ma'am, I am," James said.

"Is the war as bad as the California newspaper reports?" Jack asked.

"No Sir, it's worse," said James.

At this point, Christina entered the room carrying a tray with four cups and a pitcher of hot tea. "Let me help you with that," James said as he stood up.

"Set the tray here on the table, James," Christina said after handing James the tray. Christina then poured everyone a hot, steaming cup of tea.

"This is so good. I've not had tea like this since I left California," James said.

"Did I hear you telling the Hanovers you will be here for a whole month?" Christina asked.

"That's right. Our furlough is for thirty days."

"Our furlough? Did someone else come with you?" Christina asked.

"Yes, Jesse and Hiram are both with me. They started walking home about thirty minutes ago. Hiram sends his regards and said he would see you later."

"Hiram is home. This is too good to be true. Oh, it will be so good to see him and Jesse. Have they changed as much as you? Do they also have beards?" Christina asked.

"Yes, both have beards. We don't have time to shave in the army. Almost all the men have grown beards. That's just the style."

After visiting for a while, Mr. Hanover said, "Christina, why don't you and James go out on the front porch and visit?"

"I know you two have a lot to talk about," Gladys said by following up on her husband's suggestion.

"That's a good idea," Christina said. She grabbed James by his hand and led him to the front porch. Before they sat down in the porch swing, they again kissed.

"Is there any way you can break away from your duties with the Hanovers?" James asked.

"Not tonight, James, but tomorrow night I'm free. On Friday and Saturday nights and all-day Sunday, I'm free to do as I please. I usually shop for groceries on Saturday, but after that I'm free."

"That sounds great!" James said. "I want to spend as much time with you as I can while I'm here."

"So do I, Sergeant James A. Barger," Christina said as she touched the stripes on his uniform.

Mrs. Hanover came to the front door and asked, "James, can you stay for supper?"

"No Ma'am, I best be getting along soon. It's about six miles to my folks' house, and I want to get there before dark," James said.

"You are more than welcome to stay overnight here," Mrs. Hanover said.

"Thanks, Ma'am, but I want to get on home and see my folks. I do appreciate your kind offer," James said.

"We will be seeing you again, I hope?" Mrs. Hanover asked as she closed the door. "Yes, Ma'am, you will be seeing me a lot," James said as he looked at Christina and smiled.

"Christina, I better be getting on home before it gets too dark," James said as he stood up from the porch swing.

"I wish you could stay longer," Christina said.

"I do too, but I need to get home. Oh, by the way, do they still have the Saturday night dances here in town?" James asked.

"Yes, they do, James, and you can take me to the dance on Saturday night," Christina said as she pulled James near.

"Tell your folks that I send my love and tell Jesse that Margaret will want to see him as soon as possible," Christina said as James turned and walked down the front steps of the porch.

Allen Barger's home was located off the main road that led to Centertown, Missouri. The house was in a valley with a small, narrow road leading to it. James had traveled this road many times, but he had never felt like this before. He looked forward to topping the hill that over looked the small valley below. This was his first real home coming.

The front porch of the log house faced the hill that James would be coming over. James remembered sitting on the front porch and watching people come down the road from the top of the hill. He could visualize the whole family sitting on the front porch with their eyes staring at the top of the hill, just waiting for his appearance.

As James stood on top of the hill looking down at the house, he could see several people sitting on the front porch just as he had pictured. Suddenly, out of nowhere, James heard voices calling, "Welcome home, James! Welcome home!" He turned and saw his brothers, George, John Wesley, and his baby sister Delilah running to him. They had been waiting under a big oak tree located near the road.

"It's good to see you, James," George said as he reached out his hand to shake James's hand.

"Gosh, George, you have grown up!" James said.

"I'm as big as you now," George replied.

Delilah stood jumping up and down waiting for her turn to greet James. "Delilah is that you?" James asked as he stood looking at her.

Delilah smiled back and nodded her head as to say, "Yes, it's me."

"Come here, beautiful," James said as he held out both hands.

Delilah quickly jumped into his arms and wrapped her arms around his neck. He gave her a big kiss on the cheek and swung her around and around. "Put me down, James. You're making me dizzy," Delilah said as she laughed.

"This can't be John Wesley, my baby brother?" James asked as he stood looking at his ten-year-old brother who stood about 4'5" tall. James walked over to John Wesley and gave him a big hug. "We could use you in the Missouri 26th Infantry as our drummer boy," James said in jest.

"Come on, James. The rest of the family is waiting anxiously to see you," George said. They started down the hill with Delilah holding one of James' hands and John Wesley holding the other.

When James got within fifty feet of the house, Nancy came off the porch and ran toward her son. Tears were running down her cheeks as she and James met.

"Thank God! Thank God! He has brought my sons home safely!" Nancy said as she placed both hands on James' face and gave him a kiss on both cheeks. James in turn gave his mother a bear hug and a kiss.

"It's so good to see you, Ma. I've missed you so much! You look as beautiful as ever."

"Why, thank you, James," Nancy replied.

By this time, everyone at the house was standing around James greeting him with warm hugs and kisses.

"Son, it's so good to see you," Allen said as he hugged his son.

"Pa, it's so good to be home. I've missed you all so much," James said as he wiped away tears.

It was a homecoming. One which everyone had looked forward to. Allen and Nancy's sons had come home. They were in one piece and in sound mind. God had protected them and allowed them to come home. What a glorious day!

Nancy and the girls had prepared a wonderful supper. It was James' and Jesse's favorite supper: fried chicken, mashed potatoes, white gravy, pinto beans, corn bread and milk.

"A meal fit for a king," James said as he sat down at the table with his family.

"I certainly agree with that statement," Jesse said.

It was like old times. Allen and Nancy sat at the ends of the big long table in their straight back chairs and the children sat on benches on either side of the table. “Let’s pause now and give thanks to God for sending us our boys home safely,” Allen said. Everyone bowed their heads and held hands as Allen begin to pray.

“Our loving Heavenly Father, we come to you praising you for being the almighty God and Savior that you are. Oh, God, tonight we thank you for this great blessing of having James and Jesse home with us. We praise you for answering our prayers. I ask your blessings upon this family as we are together during these next few weeks. Give us the true spirit of Christmas and remind us to keep our eyes on your son, Jesus. Thank you now for this good food. May it be used to strengthen us, so we might continue to serve you. In Jesus Christ name I pray, Amen.”

“Amen,” Everyone said as the food was passed around the table. It was a great homecoming for both James and Jesse.

After dinner the family sat on the front porch listening to stories told by James and Jesse. About 9:30 P.M., Allen announced that it was time for everyone to prepare for bed. Normally, everyone would have been in bed by 8:00 P.M.

“Ma, could you see to the children while I visit a while longer with James and Jesse,” Martha Jane asked.

“Certainly, let’s go children,” Nancy said.

“What’s on your mind, Martha Jane?” James asked.

“I wanted to talk to you about Thomas,” Martha said.

“Martha Jane, we were so sorry we couldn’t arrange to have his remains sent home for a decent funeral. The best we could do was to mark his grave. After the war, we will go and bring his remains home to Moniteau County,” James said.

“I fully understand why you couldn’t send him home for burial. We had a good memorial service for him at New Hope Baptist Church. I want to know if Thomas mentioned me and the children very often,” Martha Jane asked.

“Every time he got one of your letters, he was beside himself. Your letters were especially important to him. He shared with us the things you told him about what the children were doing. He looked forward to his return to his family," James said.

"How did he die?" Martha asked.

"I was there when he got shot. He was not far from me. He was fighting in the battle like the rest of us. He wasn't scared, and he was a good soldier. You have every right to be proud of him, Martha Jane," Jesse said.

"Did he suffer?" Martha Jane asked.

"No, he died quickly," Jesse said.

"Thomas loved you and the children very much. I'm sorry he didn't get to see his little girl. Nancy is a spitting image of you. She's beautiful!" James said.

"I miss him so much," Martha Jane said as she began to cry. James and Jesse both rushed to her side.

"I know you do, and so do we. He was not only our brother-in-law, but he was a good friend," James said as he held his sister in his arms.

"I don't know what I'm going to do without him. I can't live with Pa and Ma, forever."

"When I get out of the army, I will help you with the kids," James said.

"So, will I," said Jesse.

"That's awful nice of you both, but you will have your own lives to live," Martha Jane said lowering her head.

"It's our brotherly duty," James said.

Nancy came to the door and said, "I've made your beds. Breakfast will be ready at the usual time. Goodnight!"

"Goodnight, Ma," James, Jesse, and Martha Jane said at the same time.

"I guess I'll go to bed now myself," Martha Jane said as she went inside.

"It's so good to be home. I've dreamed of being here for months. It's hard to believe this is real and we're really here," Jesse said.

"It certainly is," James said as he sat in one of the rocking chairs.

"Isn't it peaceful here, James? No blood, dying, or war!"

"It's heaven!"

"What are you planning on doing tomorrow night, James?"

"I'm taking Christina to the Saturday night dance in California," James replied.

"I don't know yet what I'm going to do."

"You better get over and see Margaret. Christina told me that Margaret would want to go to the dance with you."

"I just might do that."

"I'm telling you, Jesse, Margaret has doe eyes for you," James said as he laughed.

"I'm going to bed!" Jesse said, as he went inside leaving James sitting on the front porch laughing.

King, who had been lying on the porch near the rocking chair got up and came over and laid his head in James's lap. "Old, friend, I've missed you so," James said as he gently stroked King's head.

"King, we'll get some serious hunting in during the next few days. You be ready!"

At that moment, James heard the front door open. He turned to see who had come out on the porch. It was his father.

"I thought you'd be sawing logs by now, Pa."

"I couldn't sleep. I guess I'm all worked up having my sons home."

"It is good to be home, Pa. You and Ma look good. How is your health holding out?"

"I'm doing pretty good. I can't do as much as I used to, but George and John Wesley have been a big help to me. They do most of the heavy work around here. George is strong as an ox."

"I hear he's getting to be quite a lady's man."

"That's right. All the young ladies want him to dance with them at the dances. He seems to be able to oblige all of them without creating a big fuss," Allen said as he laughed.

"There is something I want to discuss with you son," Allen said.

"What is it, Pa?"

"I've laid awake many nights praying for you and Jesse. I've asked God to bring my sons home safe and free from crippling injuries. He's done that. Our God is a great God, isn't He?" James nodded his head in agreement. Allen continued. "I was hoping you and Jesse was coming home to stay, but Jesse tells me that you have re-enlisted for another term. Again, I thought this was a bad mistake but after praying about it, I found peace. God protected you before and I believe He will protect you again. I've decided you are right about the reason you are fighting. No man should own another man. That's not right and I'm supporting you in your efforts to end this practice. It's not God's way, and I believe he will be victorious in the end."

"Pa, you don't know how much this means to me. I too have laid awake many nights thinking about what you said to Jesse and me before we enlisted in the war. I've wondered so many times if you could have been right. I do believe in what we're fighting for and knowing now you support us means everything in the world to me. Thank you, Pa," James said as he embraced his dad.

"I love you, Son," Allen said.

"I love you too, Pa," Allen replied with tears streaming down his cheeks.

"You have always been a strong force in my life. I'll always love and respect you. Please continue to pray for us daily," James said as he wiped away the tears with his shirt sleeve.

James and Allen sat down in the rocking chairs on the front porch.

"There's something else I want to talk with you about," Allen said.

"What is it, Pa?"

"I got a letter from your Uncle John in Tennessee. He wrote that three of Pointer's sons were captured by the Rebels and were being held in a prison at a place called Andersonville, Georgia. I was wondering if the Union Army has any plans to try to rescue soldiers that are being held at Andersonville."

"I don't know, Pa, but I'll try to find out once we return to Alabama."

"It would be nice if General Sherman would direct some of his interest to rescuing those soldiers being held prisoners at Andersonville. I understand there may be as high as fifteen thousand union soldiers being held there," Allen said.

"What three sons are imprisoned at Andersonville?" James asked.

"They are Wiley Morrison, William Henry, and Abraham Lafayette."

"That's awful! I bet Uncle John and Uncle Pointer are not taking this well."

"No, they both are very worried."

"I'll certainly try to find out what the Union Army's plans are concerning Andersonville when I return to Alabama. If my good friend, Col. George Boomer, were still alive I could find out. He would tell me. I believe I shared my close relationship with him in one of the letters I wrote to you and Ma. He was a great leader and shared lots of things. I miss him so. I'll will never again know a man like Col. Boomer. "

"If you can, I know John and Pointer would appreciate anything you can find out," Allen said.

"Pa, I'll do the best I can, but no promises. They usually don't share that information with sergeants!" James said.

"I felt you would want to know about your cousins."

"I hope General Sherman has plans for Andersonville. If anyone can take Andersonville, he's the man. He's a strong-minded man, and he doesn't step aside for anyone," James said.

"How was Christina?" Allen asked.

"She's as pretty as ever, Pa."

"You love that girl don't you, Son?"

"Yes, I do, Pa. I love her more than I can say. There's not many minutes in any day that she's not on my mind. She gives me a reason to want to live and return to Moniteau County. I don't mean to say you and Ma are not important to me, but do you understand how I feel?"

"I understand only too well. You are in love, and I can see it all over your face."

"It's that obvious, huh?"

"It's that obvious!"

"I'm going to marry her when I return from the war. How do you feel about that?" "I would be honored to have Christina as my daughter-in-law. She's the prettiest and sweetest thing in Moniteau County as far as I'm concerned," Allen said as he smiled.

"You and Ma do like her then?"

"We think she'd make you a wonderful wife, and, yes, we love her like she was our own daughter," Allen said, patting James on the shoulder.

"I'm taking Christina to the dance tomorrow night. Are you and Ma going to the dance?"

"Yes, we plan to go. We don't miss many of the social events in town."

"Pa, may I ask you a personal question?"

"What is it, son?"

"This is really hard for me to discuss with you, Pa."

"What's bothering you?"

"I'm crazy about Christina and she feels the same toward me. When we're together things happen to us. I know it's wrong to want to make love to a woman before marriage, but, Pa, I hurt so much for Christina. Would it be better for us to marry and be husband and wife than to sin before God?"

"My goodness, James! You do have it bad, don't you?"

"I'm sorry, Pa. I shouldn't have brought this up."

"No, son, it's all right. I don't mind talking to you about this. This happened to me, also. When two people love each other, they are going to have those feelings toward each other. To answer your question, yes, it's better to marry than to sin before God. But is it best to get married and in twenty-five days leave a beautiful wife behind? Twenty-five days wouldn't be a good start, I'm afraid," Allen said.

"But what am I to do? When Christina and I are together, things happen. We hurt for each other. We want to make love. Somehow this doesn't seem to be sinful to us. I know that may sound strange."

"Again, Son, it doesn't sound strange. I think God created that attraction between two people in love. I really don't know how to guide you in this, James. I only know that you should do nothing to embarrass, or cause shame to Christina. If she gets with child out of wedlock, you know what that will bring on her. You need to consider that possibility when these feelings come over you."

"Thanks, Pa, for talking with me."

"Any time, Son. I wish I could be more help. Let's try to get some good hunting and fishing in while you and Jesse are at home. What do you say about that?"

"That sounds great to me, Pa."

"Goodnight, Son," Allen said as he left James sitting on the front porch.

On Saturday night, James rode one of his father's horses into town. He would need a horse to ride home. He didn't relish the thought of walking six miles home in the dark.

The dance was like a homecoming for the Millers and Bargers. Both families were at the Moniteau County Saturday night dance.

George Miller, Christina's father, had started courting the widow Hazel Barnett, after his wife, Hannah, passed away. He enjoyed her companionship. Everyone expected Mr. Miller to announce that they would marry, but so far, he had not. He and widow Barnett loved to square dance. In fact, everyone enjoyed square dancing. It was a way of life on Saturday nights.

After dancing a few dances, James and Christina broke away. They took a stroll down toward the old corral east of the city of California.

After arriving at the corral, James pulled Christina near him. They embraced, kissing each other with total abandon. "Christina, I love you so much. I ache for you so bad."

"I love you too, James."

"Why don't we get married while I'm on furlough."

"Married! Do you mean it?" Christina asked with disbelief.

"If we were married it would not be wrong for us to make love to each other."

"James, I love you, and I want to marry you, but I want a big wedding, one I can plan for. When we marry, I want to invite everyone in Moniteau County. There just isn't enough time for me to plan a big wedding."

"Christina, I don't think I can stand to be with you without making love to you." "Then, let's make love. No one will have to know except us and God. I know it's not right in His eyes, but I want you to make love to me," Christina said as she put her arms around his neck and kissed him.

"Christina, what if you get with child?"

"If I get with child, I'll gladly have your baby, James," Christina answered with a smile.

"But what about the people, the talk, the shame that will come upon you?"

"I'll put my trust in God. If it's meant for me to get with child, so be it. I want you as much as you want me."

"Let's go back to the Hanovers," Christina said.

"Do you think that's a good idea?" James asked.

"I think it's a good idea," Christina said as she took James by the hand and started leading him back toward town.

"Won't the Hanovers think badly of you for bringing me to their house?" James said as he stopped.

"My room is on the other side of the kitchen. The Hanovers never come across to my room, and they can't hear what's going on. I've already asked them if it would be all right to have you over. They have given me their blessing. So, don't you worry!" Christina said with a big smile. "Now come, let's go!" Christina said as she again pulled on his hand.

"I hope you're right about this, Christina. I would feel bad if anyone caught us making love."

James knew in his heart and mind that this was wrong in God's eyes. There was too much of a chance that Christina would get pregnant. He didn't want to bring shame upon her and her family.

He remembered his talk with his father, and in his heart, he was convinced there wasn't any justification for going through with having sex with Christina before they were legally married.

After arriving back at the Hanovers, James stopped on the front porch and said, "Christina, I got to say something."

"What is it, James?"

"Christina, my love, I've come to a decision about tonight. I can't go through with making love to you. I want to so bad, but I've prayed to God for an answer and He's answered my prayer. We must wait until we are married. I don't want to carry around guilt with me all the time I'm here on furlough, and I certainly don't won't to put you through the same guilt. With God's help, we can do this."

After a minute to consider what James had said, she looked at him with tears running down her cheeks and said, "James, you are right. We can wait. I just want you to know how much I love you, and this decision tonight makes me fully aware that someday I'm going to be married to the most wonderful, intelligent, and spiritual man that walks this great earth. You are so special! There will never be another man like you in my life."

They sat in the front porch swing with James's right arm wrapped around Christina while her head leaned on his chest. They talked about their wedding plans, the type of house they wanted, the number of children they wanted, and agreed that their children would get a good education. They both listened to each other's heart beating and finely kissed goodnight.

As James turned to go down the front porch steps, Christian grabbed his hand and said, "James, I love you very much. You be careful going home and I'll see you tomorrow."

James got on his horse and headed home. On the way home, he thanked God for giving him the courage and conviction of resisting temptations of sin. He was thankful for a father who gave him good advice, and a heavenly father who loved and protected him in battle. He considered himself fortunate to serve both God and his country.

Someday when the war ends, he would again be blessed by returning to the girl whom he loved more than life itself. She would play a major role in his desire to survive.

The next few weeks were like a long vacation for both James and Jesse. Jesse spent a lot of time with Margaret Miller and James with Christina. They also enjoyed fishing and hunting trips with Allen, George, and John Wesley.

William T. came home from Ray County to visit with his brothers. It had been a long time since they all were together. William T. had left Moniteau County after his humiliating court trail and bought a nice little farm in the Camden Township of Ray County. While in Ray County he met and married Elizabeth Ellasaeser from Ohio. They were married in Clay County which borders Ray County. He and Elizabeth were happily married.

Elizabeth was a lovely lady. She was tall, had long black hair and blue eyes. Her complexion was like golden apricots. She smiled continually and made instant friends with everyone.

William T. had done all right for himself, James decided after being around Elizabeth for a while.

This was William T.'s first trip to Moniteau County since the trial which had left him in disgrace. It was hard for him to come home, but the love of his brothers outweighed any risk of criticism he might experience while visiting with his family.

Allen took advantage of having all three of his older boys at home. With their help, he was able to rebuild some of the old fences that were falling apart. To do this, several posts had to be cut and split. This was a hard job, but with four able bodied men, including George, they were able to finish the job in one week. They worked hard during the day and played hard at night.

James and Jesse didn't miss a Saturday night dance nor a Sunday worship service. They enjoyed being seen with Christina and Margaret. Both men had fallen in love and planned to marry after the war.

Jesse and Margaret had become a very close couple. One could easily see they were in love. It was going to be hard on both James and Jesse to return to Huntsville, Alabama.

James spent several nights visiting Christina in town. Christina had become a very good cook and invited James to eat with her and the Hanovers. James loved Christina's cooking. He bragged about her often to the Hanovers for the delicious meals she cooked.

"James, you are going to be one lucky man when you and Christina get married. She's not only the best cook in Moniteau

County, but she's the best-looking girl also," Jack Hanover said as he looked at Christina and smiled.

"Mr. Jack, you are just too sweet," Christina said as she smiled back at him. "James, if I didn't know Jack better, I would think Jack and Christina had something going on," Gladys Hanover said with a big smile.

"Do you think we better watch these two a little closer?" James asked.

"Just maybe you should," Jack said. Everyone had a good laugh.

After supper James helped Christina clear the dishes from the table. Christina washed the dishes while James dried them. After dinner they took a stroll down to the city park. This was a special time for Christina and James, and they savored it.

On February 27, 1864, James, Jesse and, Hiram attended their last Saturday night dance in Moniteau County. On Sunday afternoon, they would start their journey back to Jefferson City and from there back to Huntsville.

It was on this Saturday night that the town's people had planned a secret surprise party for James, Jesse, Hiram, and the other men who had come home on furlough.

After the third dance, Mr. Bradley, the Mayor of California, walked to the platform and asked for everyone's attention.

"Ladies and Gentlemen, may I have your undivided attention? Tonight, we want to honor several of Moniteau County's finest Union soldiers. These young men are a credit to both Moniteau County and to the Union. They have engaged in some of the bloodiest battles of this war. God has been with them and kept them safe. This hasn't happened to every soldier who left Moniteau County.

"James and Jesse have both lost a brother and a brother-in-law to this war. Let's pray that God will continue to bless them with His loving Grace. Men, would you come stand on this platform with me. We want to recognize you with some gifts donated by the merchants of the city of California," Mr. Bradley said.

As they made their way to the platform the crowd began to clap and cheer. "Men, it gives me great pleasure to present these gifts to you and proclaim this night as your night and Sunday as Pride Day. There will be a dinner on the grounds right here tomorrow after church service in your honor. We want you to know we are mighty proud of what you are doing and how you are representing Moniteau County," Mr. Bradley said as he turned and clapped.

"If any of you would like to say anything, please feel free to speak," Mr. Bradley said.

James Brooks said, "Sgt. Barger will speak for all of us. Right, James?"

This brought on a chant from the other soldiers, "Speak, James! Speak for us!" as they began to clap. It wasn't long before the crowd had joined in the clapping.

James stepped forward and addressed the crowd in this manner. "Folks, it is indeed a humbling experience for us to be recognized by your kind generosity tonight. We are grateful for your show of support. You have made us feel good tonight. I only wish my brother, Henry, and our brother-in-law, Thomas Tull, could be up here with us tonight. As you already know, they gave their lives for our country. They were brave men who believed in fighting for a cause.

"Every soldier on this stage has experienced a lot of heartaches, pain, and adversities, but God has seen fit to keep us alive. We are deeply thankful for your prayers. We know you are praying for us daily, and this truly means a lot to us. We would ask that you continue to pray for us and for this war to end. It's a war that needs to end. There are so many soldiers who have not been so lucky. Please know we love Moniteau County, and we look forward to making our homes here after the war. God bless all of you, and thank you again for the gifts," James said as he raised a pair of boots in the air.

The crowd applauded for several minutes as each soldier walked down the ramp from the platform and joined their loved ones in the crowd.

After the dance, James and Christina returned to the Hanovers. Christina went to the kitchen where she returned with a wet towel.

James pretended he was asleep in Mr. Jack Hanover's rocking chair. Christina came around behind him and placed the cold towel across his face.

"That feels good," James said as he reached up and grabbed Christina's hands.

"You are not getting sleepy on me, are you?" Christina asked.

"Who me?" James replied.

"I think it's time for me to go to bed, James. You best be getting on home. We have church tomorrow you know," Christina said in a flirtatious manner.

"Do you really want me to go?" James asked.

"You know the answer to that, but you also know you must. Good night to you, James."

It was hard for James to get out of bed on Sunday morning.

He heard Nancy below hollering, "James, your breakfast is getting cold."

Somehow, he managed to put his pants and shoes on and gradually, but slowly, stand up, walk across the loft floor to the stairway leading to the lower level. Everyone else had been up for some time, had eaten and now were enjoying visiting around the fireplace.

Nancy had put James' breakfast in the oven to keep his eggs and bacon warm. Although James' appearance made him look as though he had a hangover, no one kidded him about his looks.

As time came for everyone to leave for church, James came out of the house wearing a clean white shirt and brown pants.

"Son, you cleaned up very nicely," Nancy said.

"Thank you, Ma," James said as he gave her a kiss on the cheek.

The Bargers and Millers drove up to the New Hope Baptist Church at the same time. James jumped down from the wagon and helped his mother down while Jesse helped Delilah. He and

Jesse went immediately to help Christina and Margaret out of their wagon.

The Bargers and the Millers took up two pews during church service.

Immediately after service, they loaded into their wagons to attend the celebration in the city of California. It was a good day. Everyone was filled with a bitter sweet joy and the large amounts of food which had been prepared for the celebration. From the looks of the crowd, it appeared that most of Moniteau County had turned out for the celebration.

On Sunday afternoon, James, Jesse, and Hiram along with their parents, relatives, and a host of towns people gathered at the California train depot for the arrival of the 3 o'clock afternoon train which would carry the soldiers back to Jefferson City, Missouri.

All the other furloughed soldiers of the 26th were also there. There were no deserters. As painful as it was, their furlough was over. It was now time to say goodbye to the one they loved.

"Jesse, I want you to promise me you'll write me," Margaret said as she hugged Jesse's neck.

"I promise you, Margaret," Jesse said.

"I promise you that I'll be waiting on you, Jesse. I want you to know that I love you and I'll be here when you get back," Margaret said with tears streaming down her cheeks.

"I love you, and I will be back. I want you to marry me when I return. Will you do that?" Jesse asked.

"Yes! Yes! Yes! I'll marry you, Jesse," Margaret said as they held each other and kissed.

"Well, I hear the train coming," James said as he investigated Christina's cloudy, tear-filled blue eyes.

"James, this is so hard. I don't know if I can go on without you," Christina said as she began to cry.

"Hey, don't do that. You'll do just fine. This war can't last too much longer," James said as he lifted her chin and wiped the tears from her cheeks.

"If anything were to happen to you, I wouldn't want to live."

"Oh, Christina, my love. You are a part of me. You've got to be strong and have faith. I promise you, I'll return, and we will have a life together. A long life together!"

"I'm going to hold you to that promise, Sergeant James A. Barger," Christina said as she again touched James's sergeant stripes.

The train was slowly pulling into the depot. It was time to say goodbye to the family. "Pa, you keep praying for us. Jesse and I will do everything we can to stay alive, but your prayers make our odds a lot better," James said as he hugged Allen.

"I'll pray for you boys every day and night."

"Ma, you take care of yourself, you hear," James said as he kissed her on the cheek.

"James, I'm so proud of you. You find a way to stay alive and healthy," Nancy said as tears streamed down her face.

The train whistle blew giving one last warning for everyone to get aboard. James, Jesse, and Hiram rushed to get on the train. It was the hardest thing they had ever had to do. They waved goodbye standing in the door way of the box car as the train pulled away from the depot. They remained standing there until the people at the depot were merely specks on the horizon.

CHAPTER 35

On March 14, 1864, the soldiers of the 26th Missouri arrived back in Huntsville, Alabama. While there they followed a period of garrison duty, the boredom of which was reinforced only by a refresher course in drill. Several recruits had been added to the 26th, and they needed to learn the basics.

As soon as James got settled in, he wrote Christina the following letter.

My Darling Christina,

This will be short, but I wanted you to know we are safe in Huntsville, Alabama. We arrived today, which was one day earlier than expected. I still have some of my old squad members, but some new ones have been added. I believe I have a good squad to work with. I'm going to try hard to be a good sergeant.

I don't know exactly how long we will be here in Huntsville, although I've been told we may be here until the end of April. It is generally doubted that General Sherman will advance before that time, but I must tell you that when Sherman does advance, he will probably send for the 26th Missouri to join the main body of the army at Chattanooga. This will give you an opportunity to send us some of your oatmeal cookies. I can't wait to sink my teeth in them.

Christina, my furlough was just wonderful. You've made me the happiest man on earth. Thanks to you, my spirits have never been so high. I believe I can complete any chore I'm given. I have a great desire to help get this war behind us. I have a truly wonderful and beautiful lady waiting for me back in Moniteau County. Christina, please know that I've never been happier in my entire life. You can't know how much I love you and want to be near you, and how I'm praying this senseless war will end soon.

I've got to stop now and put the lights out. Jesse, James Brooks, and Hiram are doing okay. They are also settled in. Things are good right now.

I love you,

James

The 26th spent the month of March through April guarding railroad bridges and drilling.

On April 25, 1864, James received a package and letter from Christina.

My Dearest James,

It has been so lonely here in Moniteau County since you left. I sometimes think I cannot bear being without you any longer. I try to stay busy, but somehow, that doesn't help much.

I'm writing this letter on April 17, 1864. I hope you get this package before you leave Huntsville. I baked three dozen oatmeal cookies for you. If you like, you may share them with Jesse and Hiram. I ate some while they were cooling to see if they were good, and I even surprised myself. I hope you enjoy them.

Everything and everyone is doing all right here in Moniteau County. I see your folks at church every Sunday. We talk each time I see them.

Margaret is missing Jesse something awful. She came by on Saturday and spent the entire day with me. She loves him, almost as much as I love you. I'm glad they are planning to marry when Jesse returns home. Maybe we could have a double wedding. What do you think about that?

The Hanovers are doing pretty good. Although Mr. Jack has had a cold for three weeks. He hasn't been running fever but coughs a lot. Mrs. Gladys is doing well. She is as spunky as ever. We spend a lot of time sitting on the front porch. We like to watch people travel up and down the street.

The city of California has really grown since the railroad has come through.

Are you ready for some more good news? Pamela Moon Barger is going to get married again. She is marrying Brett Fletcher, the son of Mac Fletcher who lives over in Cooper County. I've seen them together in town. They seem to love each other a lot. I'm glad that Pamela is getting married. She grieved Henry's death for the past two years. It took her that long to decide she had to go on with her life. My father is also getting married. He is marrying Mrs. Nellie Parsons. She's the lady he's been courting and taking to the square dances. I'm happy for Father. He doesn't need to grow old by himself and us girls will have families of our own someday soon I hope. I believe Mrs. Parsons will be good to him.

I'm sending you the last four copies of The Weekly California Newspaper. I know you enjoy reading the paper. It appears things are really heating up down in Georgia. Do you think you will be going to Georgia?

Well, I've written about everything I can think of for this time. It's been very lonely without you. I cry and pray a lot. I want this war to end soon and for you to return home safely. Please take care of yourself and continue to write me when you find time.

My love always,
Christina

On April 30, 1864, the 26th Missouri left Huntsville for Decatur about thirty miles away. While at Decatur, they were busy doing picket and garrison duty and patrolling the vicinity of Decatur until June 15. While at Decatur they were frequently harassed by small parties of Confederate cavalry. Periodically, whenever there was a report of Confederate cavalry in the area, a signal gun would be fired and the garrison at Decatur would "stand to" until the danger passed. Many short patrols in the surrounding countryside also helped to fill the troops' time. Still, the stay in Decatur was described as pleasant.

James played baseball almost every afternoon and fished in the local creek. Fresh fish for dinner every night, plus some vegetables bought from local farmers was a lot better than army rations. Drill was increased to prevent boredom, and to allow another batch of new recruits just arrived from Missouri to learn to drill with the veterans.

While the 26th Missouri was stationed in Decatur, there were big things happening in northwestern Georgia. General Grant had returned to the east to take over command of all Union forces. This left General Sherman in charge in Chattanooga. Sherman left the Chattanooga area in early May and began working his way southward towards Atlanta, Georgia. To James' surprise, the 26th remained on garrison duty at Decatur.

Confederate soldiers under Joseph Johnston dueled with him every step of the way. In comparison to prior fighting in the Civil War which consisted of weeks and months of inactivity and maneuver, interjected by short, sharp battles, the Atlanta campaign was a constant day-in-day-out grinding battle which varied in intensity from day to day but never stopped. James and his comrades were shocked by reports from trainloads of wounded soldiers passing through Decatur about the fierceness of the fighting. Surely, James thought, the 26th would soon be called to the front since Sherman's casualties were staggering.

On June 15, the 26th Missouri left Decatur and moved about thirty miles to Huntsville, Alabama. Rumors circulated that the regiment was on its way to Georgia to join Sherman, and many of the recruits became nervous.

They left Huntsville on June 22 and traveled fifty miles to Stephenson, Alabama, arriving on June 25. The regiment marched from ten to fifteen miles a day in the hot June sun.

On June 27, the regiment moved by rail to Chattanooga, arriving very late in the night on June 28, 1864.

After a few hours' rest, the regiment marched five miles to Rossville, Georgia. At Rossville, they took charge of a herd of beef cattle and moved them southward. The recruits joked nervously that they could have just as easily stayed in Missouri and herded cattle. As they moved the cattle south, they made about ten miles a day toward Marietta, Georgia. The cattle kicked up thick, choking clouds of dust, which intensified the stifling heat. It was hard to identify each other because everyone was covered in a thick layer of dust. The route they took to Marietta went through Dalton, Resaca, Adairsville, Kingston, and Carterville. The regiment arrived in Marietta on July 9, where the herd was turned over to the local commissary. After a brief layover at Marietta, the regiment returned by rail to Kingston. From Kingston they moved to Carterville, arriving on July 13 and camping until July 23rd.

At Carterville, James and Jesse received a letter from Nancy Barger. The letter was written on July 5, 1864.

> *My dear sons,*
>
> *I hope this letter finds both of you doing well. We are all doing well here in Moniteau County. Your father and the boys have the corn crop planted. The tobacco plants will be ready to plant soon. They have worked hard. George and John Wesley have been a big help to your father. Allen could not have managed without them.*
>
> *Are you ready for some good news? Mary Ann is getting married. She is marrying John Conant from Jefferson City. He is a Baptist preacher. They met in May at the New Hope Baptist Church. He came and preached a revival. While he was here, he and Mary Ann met, and it was love at first sight! We like John and think he will make Mary Ann a good husband. They will be married next Saturday. After the marriage ceremony, they will be returning to Jefferson City where John will continue to preach at his home church. He pastors the Hill Top*

Baptist Church. He's a good preacher, and we like the way he preaches. I must admit I am a little sad knowing they will be living in Jefferson City, but that's not too far away. We can see them from time to time.

How are things going with you boys? Have you fought in any battles lately? I have been reading in the newspaper about Sherman's army fighting around Atlanta, and I suppose you must be in the thick of it. I pray for both of you daily and ask God to keep you safe and well. Please write us as often as you can. We want to know how you boys are doing.

James, I don't know if you've heard from Christina lately, but Mr. Hanover isn't doing too well. He's been coughing a lot and Dr. Holloway thinks he may have jaundice. It's not catching so you don't have to worry about Christina, but I do think it's life threatening. He's at home and Christina is taking good care of him.

That's about all the news around here. I'm sending you some back issues of The Weekly California Newspaper. You boys look out for each other. Let us hear from you soon.

Our love to you both,
Your mother

"I can't believe our little sister is getting married," Jesse said as James finished reading Nancy's letter.

"Our family is not going to be the same when we return to Moniteau County," James said as he put the letter back in the envelope.

"What do you think will happen to Christina if Mr. Hanover dies?" Jesse asked.

"I guess Christina will stay on and take care of Mrs. Hanover. She has no family," James replied.

"It must be awful not to have family," Jesse said.

"I can't imagine not having a big family. Christina and I want lots of children. We've already planned on having several."

"Me and Margaret want a big family too," Jesse replied.

"I believe that's the first time I've heard you mention marriage, Jesse Barger," James said as he chuckled.

"I love Margaret, and she loves me. When I first started courting Margaret, I was not seriously in love with her, but a month of furlough changed all of that. I've been unable to think of anyone but her since we left Moniteau County."

"I feel the same way about Christina."

"Did you ever think we would be marrying sisters?" Jesse asked.

"Not really, although Christina mentioned in one of her letters that we should make it a double wedding. What do you think about that?" James asked.

"I believe I'd like that," Jesse answered.

"I've got to report for fatigue duty," James said as he stood.

"James, when do you think this war will end?" Jesse asked.

"I don't have any idea, but I hear things are really happening down near Atlanta. I expect we will be going down there soon."

"What makes you think that?" Jesse asked.

"I overheard a conversation with Col. Dean and Cpt. Thompson yesterday. From what I could gather, that's what they were thinking would happen," James said.

"I'll talk with you again soon," James said as he left Jesse sitting.

"Goodbye, James," Jesse said as James walked toward his end of camp.

James and Jesse were both wrong and the regiment was not sent to the front.

On July 24, the 26th Missouri was assigned a new duty of guarding a stretch of the Etowah River. The assignment covered approximately ten miles in length which extended from Caldwell's Ford to Woolley's Bridge. This assignment continued until November 2, 1864.

While this was going on, General Sherman had finally reached the outskirts of Atlanta, Georgia.

General Joseph Johnston had succeeded in wearing down Sherman's forces while suffering comparatively light casualties among his men. It had been Johnston's strategy to delay

Sherman's advance to Atlanta and hold Atlanta until the November elections in hopes that Lincoln would be defeated as President.

In Richmond, Jefferson Davis did not see things the same way. He wanted a more aggressive General to take charge in Georgia. Relieving Johnston in mid-July, Jefferson sent General John B. Hood, who was foolishly aggressive to begin with, and who may have been addicted to morphine.

Hood launched a series of assaults on Sherman's army in late July. These attacks did nothing except to deplete the Confederate army. In a matter of days, Hood's tactics caused more Confederate casualties than Johnston had lost several months before. Hood, finally seeing the error of his ways, finally adopted Johnston's strategy of waiting--except he had a much weakened and demoralized army.

The main event for the 26th Missouri in July occurred on the last day of the month. A wagon train of supplies was attacked not very far away. The 26th Missouri marched to its assistance, but the Confederate attackers withdrew before the 26th arrived. The 26th staggered back to camp exhausted from a hot, dusty and useless march.

During the month of August, the 26th Missouri experienced some sporadic harassment by the Confederate cavalry, but nothing major occurred. The soldiers spent most of the month passing the time away fishing, swimming, and playing baseball.

CHAPTER 36

In early September, General Sherman, who had been besieging Atlanta since July, finally occupied Atlanta, the munitions center of the Confederacy.

General Hood's Confederates withdrew to the south. Sherman would remain in Atlanta for two-and-a-half months, giving his war-worn men time to rest and gather supplies for his march on through Georgia.

The 26th Missouri again spent the month of September guarding about a ten mile stretch of the Etowah River.

On October 3, 1864, James received the following letter from Christina.

My Dearest James,

A lot has happened in the last two weeks. First, Mr. Jack Hanover died on September 10. It was awful to see him suffer. He is better off going on to be with our Lord. Mrs. Gladys is holding up pretty well. She has asked me to stay on and take care of her. She has no family. I have decided to stay and look after her. She is a darling old lady and she needs me. I had rather be here than back home on the farm. We hardly ever saw anyone when I lived out on the farm. I've developed a liking to the city. Don't get me wrong. When you come home, I'll gladly follow you to the farm or anywhere else you want to go. I hope you understand what I'm saying.

Secondly, my sister Caroline lost her baby. She had a hard time delivering and it died. Caroline has been really upset over losing the baby. I've been out to her house a few times trying to cheer her up. I've reassured her that she and William will have plenty other opportunities to have children. She seems to be doing better, but it's going to be a while before she's her old self.

Thirdly, the corn and tobacco crops didn't do very well this year because of all the hot, dry weather we had. Some of the farmers are having problems making ends meet. I'm not aware of how my father and your father are affected by this. I remember you telling me your father has his farm paid off. Maybe he won't experience the same hardships as many of the other farmers.

Everything else is going fine. I see your folks every Saturday night and again on Sunday at church. They appear to be healthy and doing fine.

I swear, James, your brother, George, is the hit of the town with the girls. Every eligible, unmarried young lady is after him. Someone will get a good catch when she gets him. I've already got my catch, so don't worry.

I lie awake at nights thinking of you and crying myself to sleep. I do miss you, my love, and pray that God will bring you home to me soon. I also pray nightly that this war will soon end.

I'm sending you some back editions to The Weekly California Newspaper. The election is coming up in a few weeks, and that is all that anyone is talking about. I think the majority around here will vote for Lincoln, but some are hoping he would be defeated. Not me, I like Abe Lincoln. I think he's the best President our country has had. In my opinion, he will go down in history as being the most popular. I do worry about him. I'm afraid someone will try to hurt him. He doesn't seem to fear going out in public and takes no precautions. I wish he would be more careful. Many people hate him and wish him dead.

I've written all I know to write at this time. Please know I love you and enjoy the oatmeal cookies.

With all my love,

Christina

James replies to Christina's letter on October 3, 1864

My Darling Christina,

I received your letter today. I'm sorry to hear about Jack Hanover. He was a very good man. I know Mrs. Gladys and you will miss him. I'm glad you have decided to stay on and look after her. Did Mr. Jack leave her enough money to get by on? Please give my regrets to Mrs. Hanover.

I'm also sorry to hear that Caroline lost her baby. You failed to say whether it was a boy or girl. I'm also sorry about the poor corn and tobacco crops. We got a letter from Ma last week. She said it would be hard, but they would make it. They too experienced a bad year. Pa always seems to be able to figure something out, so the family doesn't suffer too much of a hardship. If necessary, I will loan them some money. I believe family members should help each other when in need. Don't you?

We've not seen any action in several months. I guess that's good because it increases our odds of staying alive. It's been really boring just guarding the Etowah River. We do have time for some good fishing. We've not been hungry since we've landed here. I've developed an interest in playing baseball. My squad is doing pretty well. We are presently engaged in the regimental championship. My team is now only one game away from being the champions. I think we will win. I have some good hitters. I'm not too good at hitting the ball myself, but I catch anything which comes my way. We will be playing tomorrow. Wish us luck!

Jesse and Hiram played on a squad in Company "H". I'm sorry to report that their team got beat in the first round. They've been supporting my squad ever since. It's good to have them cheering us on.

We've been thinking that General Sherman will call the 26th regiment to Atlanta, especially since he is now in charge there. I don't expect it will be long. I'm ready to move on. I want to see this war end soon. I want to be back home making plans for our life together. If ever God meant two people to be together, Christina, it's you and me. Please know you will always be my one and only love.

Thanks for the oatmeal cookies. I enjoyed the raisins you added to the cookies. It made them even better. I have already eaten four and am on my fifth right now. I will share at least one with Jesse and Hiram.

We have voted for President here already so that the voting returns could be sent to Missouri in time for the election. The officers arranged for several score of soldiers who they thought might vote for George McClellan to be sent on a work detail away from camp to cut firewood when the rest of the regiment voted. Would you believe Abe Lincoln won by a landslide?

Jesse talks about Margaret a lot. How is she doing? How are Mr. Miller and his new wife, Nellie? How are the younger children taking to her? That should give you something to write about. It's getting late and I must go to inspection. Take care and keep your letters coming.

As always, I love you,
James

The finals of the baseball championship were held on October 5, 1864. James' squad from Company "G" faced Sergeant Benjamin Forrester's squad from Company "D." It was a hot day, and it wasn't long before every player's clothes were soaked with sweat. The game turned out to be a defensive game. James' prediction was correct. His squad won the championship game by a score of 7-6. It was a time for a celebration.

Col. Dean arranged for a big party for the regiment. There was plenty of food and visiting. Even a little whiskey ration was authorized for each man.

Finally, the 26th had some excitement. After several lazy months along the river, on October 12, word arrived that

General Hood's Confederate Army had moved into the vicinity. Hood, having abandoned Atlanta in the previous month, was now maneuvering into northern Georgia, trying to lure Sherman out of the Confederate heartland. The problem was Hood had no idea how to accomplish this goal.

He unsuccessfully assaulted a fortified Union force garrisoning at Altoona, Georgia, on October 5, 1864. With Hood passing nearby, the 26th Missouri and its sister regiments, the 10th Iowa and the 93rd Illinois, pulled up the planks on the bridges over the Etowah River and fortified a position in the town of Kingston. Earthworks were hastily dug. Log palisades and cotton bale barricades blocked the streets. James and his nervous comrades waited all night within their make-do fortress. The Confederates passed nearby but did not attack.

On the last day of the month, the regiment was still spread out along the Etowah River as before, except that Company "C" and Company "I" were now at Kingston.

On November 2, the regiment was relieved of its duties on the Etowah River and regrouped at Kingston. From there, it marched to Atlanta, arriving on November 14. Before moving to Atlanta, orders arrived that all sick soldiers and unnecessary baggage should be sent north in preparation for a grueling campaign.

One unfortunate incident marred the final preparations for the campaign. Captain Crowe and Quartermaster Berry were both injured when a porch collapsed at the house in which they had been staying. Both had to be sent north to recover. There was some speculation that both Captain Crowe and Quartermaster Berry were drunk and that there was some sort of hijinks involved in the collapse of the porch. It was never revealed just what the reason was for their injuries.

The 26th arrived in Atlanta, but there was little time for sight-seeing among the ruins of the burning city. The 26th moved the next day to Jonesboro, Georgia, and then southeastward as a part of Sherman's March to the Sea. It was during this time that General Sherman burned Atlanta.

While James and the 26th was camped at Jonesboro, James received a package and letter from Christina.

My Dearest James,

I don't know when this package and letter will catch up with you. After reading The Weekly California Newspaper, it appears General Sherman is preparing to leave Atlanta. I hope he leaves you and the 26th somewhere safe. Maybe he still needs someone to guard the Etowah River?

Things here are going well, although, Mrs. Gladys still grieves over the death of Mr. Jack. I guess it's to be expected. They lived together for the best part of their lives.

I'm sending you two copies of The Weekly California Newspaper. One carries the story of President Lincoln's re-election. As you probably already know, Lincoln won by a wide margin. According to the news article, some feared he might lose because of his veto of the Wade-Davis Bill which required most of the electorate in each Confederate state to swear past and future loyalty to the Union before the state could officially be restored. The article says that this veto lost him the support of radical Republicans who thought he was too lenient. However, the article went on to say that Sherman's victory in Atlanta boosted Lincoln's popularity and helped him win re-election by a wide margin. I don't know why I'm telling you this. You can read for yourself. I know you feel the same as I do about President Lincoln. I'm certainly glad he won.

How are things going for you, Jesse, Hiram, and James Brooks?

I saw your father and George yesterday in California. They were purchasing some supplies. They both were doing well and said everyone else was doing well. My father and Nellie appear to be getting along well together. The family likes her. I'm happy for Father. If he's happy, then I'm happy.

George invited me to the Saturday night dance with him. I didn't think you would mind if I went with your little brother. Anyway, all the eligible men in town know I'm already spoken for by a Sergeant James A. Barger. I know you won't worry about George. He's got girls hanging all over him. He let me know in no uncertain terms that I should get out more. I hope you don't mind.

I've been keeping my eyes on that one hundred acres in the Centertown community which you are interested in. So far, it's not sold. It is a fine-looking piece of property. Tell Jesse the one hundred acres next to it is also for sale. You two might want to get your father to make a down payment on that property for you. Do you have enough money in the bank for a down payment?

I was hoping the war would end before another Christmas passed, but it doesn't seem that will happen. This will be the fourth Christmas we've been apart. I live for the day we will never have to be apart on any day.

I wish you a Merry Christmas and a Happy New Year. The socks and scarves inside are for you, Jesse, and Hiram.

I look forward to hearing from you when you have time to write. May God bless you and keep you safe during this holiday season.

All my love,
Christina

James had just finished reading the letter when Capt. Thompson walked up and said, "Sergeant Barger, Col. Dean wants to see you and all the other officers and non-commissioned officers at once."

James stood and said, "Yes, Sir," as he saluted Capt. Thompson.

The fifes and drummers began playing "officers' call" followed immediately by "sergeants' call."

Reaching the headquarters' tent, James found a larger group clustered about. Colonel Dean emerged suddenly from the tent. James could not help but thinking that Dean enjoyed making a grand entrance.

"I've called this meeting to inform you that we will march in the morning. Sherman's army is leaving Jonesboro, and so are we. Each man should have three days cooked rations in his haversack and one hundred rounds of ammunition. All unnecessary baggage should be left behind," Col. Dean said.

Col. Dean explained that the 26th Missouri would become part of Sherman's advance into Georgia. He asked if there were any questions. Something within James inspired him to ask the question that he had been longing to ask. "Sir, I was wondering if General Sherman has any plans to go near Andersonville, Georgia. I have cousins who are prisoners at Andersonville."

"Sergeant Barger, at this time, I don't know what General Sherman's plans are," Col. Dean replied.

"Sir, I too have relatives who are in prison at Andersonville. I hear the Union prisoners are dying of starvation," Captain Thompson said.

"I am sure Sherman is aware of this, and I cannot imagine him not freeing the prisoners at Andersonville. Now let's spread the word that we will leave right after breakfast in the morning," Col. Dean said.

Walking back from the meeting James fell in beside Captain Thompson. "I'm glad you asked about Andersonville. I, too, have friends and cousins there. I am certain Sherman will go that route since he is so close now. In any case, the bulk of Hood's army has passed on into northern Georgia and into Tennessee. There is nothing between us and Andersonville but a few Georgia militia," Captain Thompson said.

"It appears to me that setting our Union soldiers free would give us more numbers to fight the Confederates. It doesn't make sense to leave them there to die of starvation," James said.

"Let's just hope General Sherman plans to go through Andersonville. Good night, Sergeant Barger," Capt. Thompson said.

"Goodnight, Sir," James replied.

James went immediately to see Jesse and Hiram. "Have you heard we will be leaving in the morning to join General Sherman?" James asked.

"No, we've not been told yet. What does this mean, James?" Jesse asked.

"It means we are going to play a major role in capturing Georgia," James replied.

"I'm ready to get this war over with," Hiram said.

"So am I," Jesse said.

"Well, you best get a good night's rest because it may be the last night's sleep you will get for some time," James said.

"Is it going to be that bad?" Jesse asked.

"I hear it's going to be pretty rough," answered James.

"How would you boys like some oatmeal raisin cookies?" James asked.

"You can bet your bottom dollar, I would," Hiram said.

"Christina must have sent you some cookies," Jesse said.

"That's right, and here is a letter from Margaret to you," James said as he handed Jesse the letter.

"My sister can really cook these cookies," Hiram said as he continued to chew on the cookie.

"She sure can," James said as he took a bite.

"You are going to be a lucky man when you marry my sister," Hiram said as he chuckled.

"I can agree with you on that, Hiram," James said.

"Christina sent both of you some socks and scarves for Christmas. She wanted you to stay warm. I believe Margaret made your socks, Jesse," James said as Jesse took a bite of his cookie and kept reading Margaret's letter.

"I'll see you guys in the morning," James said.

"Goodnight, James," Jesse replied, still reading Margaret's letter.

James, knowing that it might be some time before he could write Christina, sat down and wrote the following letter.

Dear Darling Christina,

We just received orders that we will be leaving Jonesboro in the morning. We will be joining General Sherman on his march into Georgia. I may not be able to write for a time, so don't worry if you do not get any letters for some weeks. I wanted you to know I got your package and letter today. It was so good to hear from you. Jesse, Hiram, and I have already enjoyed your cookies. I believe they get better every time you send us a new batch. We also want to thank you for the socks and scarves.

It's cold here tonight, so I'm going to sleep in my new socks. They will help keep my feet from freezing. I will also sleep with my new scarf around my ears tonight. Thanks so much for looking after your husband-to-be. I am surprised it is this cold so far south. The good news is that it appears we will be heading still farther south. Better yet, you will be relieved to know that there is no Confederate Army facing us, so it is unlikely we will be in a battle for now.

I don't know if you will get this letter before the dance, but if you do, I hope you and George have a good time at the dance. If George was a little older, I might be jealous of my little brother. Although, I never doubt your love for me. Please save one dance for my father. He loves to do the two-step and square dance. He needs to get to know his future daughter-in-law. You may have to go up to him and say, "Allen Barger, would you like to dance with James A. Barger's future bride? Let's see how he reacts." I really want you to do that.

Tell my father that Capt. Thompson also has friends and cousins who are in prison at Andersonville.

It is generally believed that Sherman will turn southward from Atlanta to free the prisoners at Andersonville. My greatest fear is that General Sherman won't consider taking the time to go to Andersonville. We have received word that the Union soldiers who are in prison there, are dying of starvation. That's horrible! My three cousins from Tennessee could be those who are dying. The prison was not built for twenty-thousand prisoners. Please say a prayer that Sherman will add Andersonville to his plans.

Sherman plans to burn everything in his path as he moves through Georgia. He doesn't want to leave the Confederates anything behind to build from.

I've not decided yet if I like General Sherman. If he goes to Andersonville, I might like him. If he doesn't, I'm not sure. I've got to stop now and get packed for tomorrow. Please know I love you more each day. Thanks also for sending me the back editions to the California Weekly News. Take care of yourself for me.

All my love,

James

The movements of the 26th for the rest of the month was with Sherman's army. Sherman divided his army into two forty-thousand-soldier units who made a sixty-mile-wide swath. The army moved southeastward at a leisurely pace, eating food foraged from area farms and burning as they went. The route was marked by pillars of smoke from the burning farms. Most Confederate forces under Hood had turned northward into Tennessee in a desperate attempt to lure Sherman's troops out of the heart of the Confederacy. Sherman refused to take the bait and allowed Union forces already in Tennessee to deal with Hood's invasion. He continued southeast against only sporadic harassment by small units of Confederate cavalry.

The 26th reached the Ocmulgee River on November 18, 1864 and reached the Oconee River on November 27. By November 30, the Missouri 26th were at Somerville, Georgia.

The food was plentiful. The route was marked by columns of smoke by day, and by glow of fires of burning farms and towns by night. In addition, the troops ripped up hundreds of miles of railroad as they traveled. To destroy a railroad, the crossties were used to create a bonfire and the fire was used to heat the middle of each rail. Once heated, a rail could be bent into a "necktie" around a tree, which rendered the rail useless. The route through Georgia was well marked with "Sherman's neckties."

It was not until the seventh day of the march that James was assigned to foraging duty. Led by an officer, a score of enlisted men and two wagons moved away from the main column. They had not gone more than a mile when they reached a crude cabin. A haggard woman stood on the dog trot watching with scorn as they approached. Seven ragged children crowded behind her, the oldest no more than twelve. Despite the weather, James noticed the children were barefoot.

The officer did not even bother to address the woman but went straight to work, "You two, to the chicken coop. You, check that shed over there. You, and you, look behind the woodpile. You three, into the house."

James was one of the three sent into the house. Stepping past the woman, James nodded, not sure how to treat her and not sure what to say. In the house, one of the soldiers started emptying the contents of the pantry into a sack that he had brought. The second staggered out of the other room of the house with a jug of cider under one arm and some money in the other. He cursed, "Other than this damned Confederate stuff, they've only got 63 cents in real money."

James, not quite sure what to do, took the sack from the pantry soldier and started back out to the wagon. Glancing up, he saw two small boys peering fearfully down from the loft. James stopped dead in his tracks. The loft looked just like the one he had slept in for so many years back home. In his mind's eye, he saw himself and his brothers, peeking down on Christmas morning. The spell was broken as a somewhat drunken corporal from the 93rd Illinois shoved past, "You two little bastards get down now! Get outside! I'm coming up. Got to search up there too."

Outside James found the two wagons had been pulled up to the shed. A dozen soldiers moved bushel after bushel of corn from the shed to the wagons. The woman, no longer as scornful, stood before the officer, begging him, "How will we eat if you take it all? We will starve! It's all we have!" The officer stared straight ahead, ignoring her.

In thirty minutes, it was done. The officer gave the order to burn the house, the shed, and everything else that would burn. Two soldiers started to the task, while the woman stood there, numbly watching, with her weeping children clustered around her. James fought back the urge to say something, knowing that any protest on his part would be futile and would just get him in trouble with the officer.

One of the soldiers suddenly emerged at a run from the cabin. "Wait!" he shouted. James brightened up. Perhaps some excuse had been found not to burn the cabin. The excited soldier showed the officer a piece of paper. The officer took it, studied it for a moment, then read it aloud: "'Bill of Sale. Captain Ezra Jitter, Georgia State Militia, hereby purchases 500 bushels of corn from Widow Elinor Quinn. To be called for on December 28. Signed and Sealed, it looks like we got here just in time to rescue this corn from being eaten by Rebs. There you have it, boys. If I had not already ordered this house burned down, I would sure as hell order it burned now!"

The house, the shed, the chicken coop, all were set afire. The soldiers piled onto the loaded wagons and began to leave.

Before they had gone fifty yards, the widow raced after them and shouted, "I'll have my revenge, you damned Yankees! That corn was for your prisoners at Andersonville! They are going to surely starve now. They are all going to die, and you killed them!" Laughing crazily, she turned back to her children and her blazing home.

The trip back to the regiment was almost silent. Each soldier secretly debated the truth of the woman's words. That night supper included ears of fresh corn, but James had no appetite for any of it.

As General Sherman's army passed near Macon, Georgia, James found out that Sherman had refused to alter his course on to Savannah. He would not be going to Andersonville to free the thousands of Union soldiers who were being held there in the Confederate prison. General Sherman's action disappointed both Capt. Thompson and James.

"I don't understand why General Sherman is so headstrong. Andersonville is only about forty miles from here. I just don't understand why he wouldn't want to free our Union soldiers. Doesn't it make sense if he freed them, we would have more soldiers to fight the Johnny Rebs?" James asked Capt. Thompson.

"I'm disappointed, too, James, but there is nothing we can do," Capt. Thompson said.

"I think it is a bit more than forty miles, but we could surely get there in four or five days hard marching. I'm not sure I like General Sherman," James said.

"Col. Dean told me that Sherman wants to take Savannah by the middle of December. He said there was not time to detour from the course. There are others who say that Sherman knows that twenty thousand sick and starving prisoners would only burden the army and would delay his campaign to Savannah," Capt. Thompson said.

"I pray he will not regret his decision not to go to Andersonville. I feel sure we wouldn't have any problem in taking the prison from the Confederates. They wouldn't have a chance against our forces," James said.

"Let's pray that our cousins will survive in Andersonville," Capt. Thompson said.

The march to the sea continued daily. Food was not as plentiful during the last days of the march because the coastal swamps did not have as many well-stocked farms. The 26th reached Statesboro, Georgia, on December 3, 1864. By the first week of December, Sherman's forces approached Savannah, a well defended and fortified city.

On December 10, 1864, a force which included the 26th engaged the Confederates about three and a half miles from the city. A mild skirmish dragged on until dark. James lay on his stomach behind a rock and fired at the puffs of smoke from Confederate rifles in the distance. It was the closest he had ever actually been to be a sharpshooter. At this range he could not tell if he hit anything.

On December 11, skirmishing continued until 10:00 A.M. when the 26th and other Federal forces withdrew about a mile. The 26th remained in camp until December 21. With Union forces creeping closer and threatening to cut off all escape routes, the Confederates evacuated Savannah to the north. On December 21, 1864, the 26th entered Savannah.

Several Sherman's soldiers were discharged at Savannah, since their enlistments had expired during the march and were sent north by sea to Washington D.C. Likewise, the sick was evacuated, and the army was re-supplied for its march northward.

The 26th Missouri spent Christmas in Savannah, Georgia. General Sherman decided for the Union soldiers to enjoy a good Christmas meal. The soldiers were also allowed to enjoy a few days of rest in the city. Savannah offered a nice break for Sherman's army who had become exhausted from the march through Georgia. To James the fascination of Savannah lay in the ocean. He had never seen it before and had always wondered what it looked like. He spent a few hours on the seashore watching the waves splash on the beach, seeing unfamiliar sea birds soaring overhead, and resting in the shade of unfamiliar tropical trees. The weather was balmy and mild.

In early January 1865, General Sherman left Savannah and marched northward into the Carolinas. For the first time, black troops were added to Sherman's army. These were black regiments which had been recruited in those coastal enclaves that had earlier been seized by Union troops. The number of black regiments was, however, small.

The march northward was a Confederate nightmare. Lee's army was bogged down facing General Grant in Virginia in trenches at Petersburg. General Lee could do little to help stem Sherman's march. On the other hand, if Sherman wasn't stopped, he would march all the way to Virginia and attack Lee from behind.

The only other major Confederate force to turn to for help was General Hood's army which was last mentioned in November when marching northward into Tennessee. Hood's force got disgracefully beaten at Nashville, Tennessee, on December 15 and 16.

The Confederates also endured a grueling retreat into northern Alabama with victorious Union troops nipping at their heels every step of the way. The retreat from Nashville was a unique example of a long-range pursuit in the Civil War and showed how effective such a pursuit could be. Thousands of sick and exhausted Confederates fell behind and were captured.

Hood's army, a remnant of the once mighty Confederate Army of Tennessee, finally escaped across the Tennessee River into northern Alabama. Hood was relieved of his command, and Joe Johnston was returned to command the wreck of an army that he had formerly commanded in the summer of 1864.

By a roundabout route, over a patchwork quilt of still-functioning sections of railroad and with long marches over areas that no longer had railroads, Johnston moved his soldiers to the Carolinas to oppose Sherman. He scraped up odds and ends as he went, gradually replenishing his depleted army by scraping the bottom of the Confederacy's manpower barrel. He was still badly outnumbered.

As for the 26th, the march northward was just like the March to the Sea. General Sherman had bragged he would "make Georgia howl," when he marched to the sea. Now his troops were making South Carolina, which was viewed as the source of secession and the state that started the war, howl too.

James tried to dodge forage duty as often as he could and generally volunteered for clerical work at the regimental headquarters as a means of avoiding foraging. James looked at foraging as stealing. His religious upbringing and Biblical teachings caused him to have conflicts with this issue.

On the night of February 17, 1865, the city of Columbia was occupied and burned. General Sherman pressed on northward against a weak Confederate resistance.

On March 20-21 the 26th was engaged in occupying Raleigh, North Carolina. They would stay in Raleigh until the latter part of April.

On April 9, 1865, General Lee surrendered to General Grant at Appomattox Courthouse, Virginia. The two commanders met at a small house and agreed on the terms of surrender. Lee's men were sent home on parole--soldiers with their horses and officers with their sidearms. All other equipment was surrendered.

On April 14, 1865, as President Lincoln was watching a performance of Our American Cousin at Ford's Theater in

Washington, D.C., he was shot by John Wilkes Booth, an actor from Maryland obsessed with avenging the Confederates' defeat. Lincoln died early the next morning. Booth escaped to Virginia. Eleven days later, cornered in a burning barn, Booth was fatally shot by a Union soldier. Nine other people were involved in the assassination. Four were hanged, four imprisoned, and one was acquitted.

James was overjoyed by the news of Lee's surrender but crushed by the news of Lincoln's death. How could such a thing happen? The President who would go down in history as the most popular President of the United States of America was dead. James asked himself, how could this be? Why had Booth killed the President? It wasn't long before Capt. Thompson brought a local newspaper which carried the story of the assassination.

"Sergeant Barger, there's an article in this paper about the assassination of President Lincoln. Would you like to read it?" Cpt. Thompson asked.

"Yes, Sir, I would," James said as Cpt. Thompson handed him the paper. As James read the article, tears came into his eyes. He had grown to love and admire President Lincoln. He had always believed President Lincoln had the country at heart. He respected the President for remaining strong in his efforts to free all mankind.

CHAPTER 37

While in Raleigh, James wrote these letters home to Christina and his folks.

Dear Christina,

By the time you read this letter the war may be over. Praise the Lord!! You probably already know that General Lee has surrendered, and it's only a matter of days until General Johnston and others do the same. Johnston is now trapped between Sherman's army here in North Carolina and Grant's army in Virginia, so he must surrender. Looks like we are going to win this war. I never doubted we would. It's been a long bloody war that's killed a lot of good men. Also, hundreds of men were sent home crippled for life. Above all, it's caused the death of our great President, Abe Lincoln.

As I reflect over these past four years, I ask myself, was this all necessary? Only God knows the answer, and I've put my trust in Him. I thank God every day for His goodness and mercy in letting me, Jesse, James Brooks, and Hiram survive what we've been through during these long years. He's been a God of Grace.

It's rumored we'll soon be marching on Washington, D.C. I can't wait. I've read about Washington, D. C. and always dreamed of going there but never really thought it would happen. It's going to. I'm really looking forward to it! I wish you could be there to greet us as we march down Pennsylvania Avenue.

I hope this letter finds you well. We've been on the move so much that I've not had time to write. I hope you can forgive me.

I spoke with Jesse and Hiram a few minutes ago. They, too, are excited that the war is coming to an end. We all look forward to returning to good old Moniteau County. I look forward to spending many years with you, my beloved Christina. I can hardly wait!

Let's don't wait long after I return to get married. Please be ready to marry this lonely, Union Sergeant upon my return.

I'm going to stop now and write my folks. I trust your entire family is well. I'm planning on seeing you real soon. I love you more today than yesterday!

Love you so much,
James

Dear Ma and Pa,

By the time you get this letter, we may be in Washington, D.C. The war is about over. The Union will soon be victorious. General Johnston's Confederate forces have not surrendered yet, but it's only a matter of time. He's the only threat left for the Union. I feel sure he will surrender in the next few days.

The rumor is there will be a big victory parade in Washington D.C, and we will be able to march in it. Jesse, Hiram, James Brooks, and I are looking forward to our march down Pennsylvania Avenue in Washington, D.C.

Col. Dean says there will be a big parade with bands playing and people lining the streets. Won't that be something! I wish you all could be there. I'm so thankful for all your prayers and for God's loving care. He has been a merciful Lord, and one who has looked over Jesse, James Brooks, Hiram, and me throughout this bloody, cruel, and devastating war. I don't understand why some had to die such as Henry and Thomas, but I trust God knows, and I'm not to question His wisdom.

This war lasted much longer than anyone expected. It's taken the lives of many good men and many men were sent home crippled for life. This war will go down in history as being the bloodiest and most sickening wars of all times. It will be a black spot on our country for years to come. We may never fully recover from the effects of this war.

Yesterday, I was working in the regimental headquarters copying materials for Col. Dean, and, out of curiosity, I sat down and counted the names on the muster rolls of the regiment. During the war, the 26th Missouri regiment had six officers and 112 enlisted men killed in combat. In addition, the regiment lost two officers and 171 enlisted men who died of disease. The regiment had several others missing in action. Most of them were probably taken prisoner and some of them have probably died in prison, but I do not know just how many. I thank God daily for His watch over me, and every night when I go to bed, I count my many blessings.

Pa, we wanted General Sherman to swing down to Andersonville and free the Union soldiers, but he wouldn't alter his plans. I must say, I lost respect for him. Do you know what happened to our cousins? I have heard several thousand Union soldiers died there from starvation.

I'm looking forward to returning to Moniteau County. The government owes us several hundred dollars in back pay, plus bounty money. I'm hoping that with this money and my savings in First State Bank of California, I can purchase that one hundred acres of land east of Centertown.

I trust that everyone is doing well there. We are here. Just waiting for our orders to leave for Washington, D. C. I'll try to write while we are there. We should find out in Washington when we will be mustered out.

Until next time, take care and may God continue to bless you with good health and keep you safe.

Jesse sends his love.

James

On April 26, 1865, General Johnston's surrender to General William T. Sherman at Bennett's House ended the Civil War between the Confederate and Union States. The remaining Confederate forces surrendered or simply went home. By late May, only a few isolated pockets of resistance remained.

On April 29, 1865, the 26th began its march to Washington, D.C., by way of Richmond, Virginia. They arrived in Washington on May 20, 1865. James and his comrades marched across the battlefields of the eastern armies, still strewn with broken muskets and castoff equipment. During their march to Washington, Jefferson Davis was captured in Georgia on May 10, 1865.

After reaching Washington, the soldiers had plenty of time for sight-seeing. They saw such attractions as the Smithsonian institution, the Capitol, and the White House which was still decked in black for mourning the death of President Lincoln.

The westerners of Sherman's army mingled with the eastern "dandies" of Grant's army. There were a few days of refresher course drilling in preparation for the Grand Review of the Army. This was necessary since many regiments had not drilled in a year. The westerners complained that the easterners got preferential treatment in the distribution of new uniforms for the parade, while they would have to parade in rags and tatters.

The parade itself was a two-day affair. On May 23, the easterner troops paraded down Pennsylvania Avenue in their new uniforms. Spectators on both sides of the street cheered them on. In the audience, foreign ambassadors were the guests of honor. The government officials' main goal in holding the parade was to impress foreign dignitaries with the military might of the United States, and to say that the United States was now a major power. The goal was to impress the French ambassador, since French troops had intervened in Mexico in 1862, putting Emperor Maximilian on the throne. It was reported that the French ambassador was impressed with these easterners, murmuring to an aide, "Those troops could best all of Europe."

The next day it was the westerners turn to parade. James, Jesse, James Brooks, and Hiram were excited.

No new uniforms were available, so the ragged troops followed their tattered flags down Pennsylvania Avenue, holding their heads high and marching with pride. As they marched, several westerners broke ranks, singing their newly written anthem "Marching Through Georgia" and made their way down the avenue accompanied by a motley assortment of camp followers and livestock.

A British observer sniffed that "They were ragamuffins, utterly unused to drill." But then he added, "I noticed, however, that all the rifles were clean, and that there was a lean hard look in their eyes." The French Ambassador was even more impressed. To his aide he stated, "They could best the world."

Eager to be discharged, the 26th moved to Louisville, Kentucky, a major Federal base. There was a major Federal base at Louisville. Many regiments were being shipped to Louisville to be mustered out. After only a few days at Louisville, the 26th got orders for Little Rock, Arkansas. These orders caused morale to plummet. Several soldiers who had loyally marched with the 26th through all its hardships and battles deserted. They had counted on being discharged at Louisville.

The regiment remained at Little Rock, Arkansas, until August, doing routine garrison duties. It camped on the high ground west of town, near the state penitentiary. The soldiers waited impatiently. Discipline vanished.

The 26th, which had always prided itself on punctually posting its guard at eight each morning, now found that few officers cared, and fewer enlisted men would obey. James marveled that the comrades who had served together and had willingly submitted to military discipline had, in a few weeks, been reduced to a bickering, quarrelsome mob, impatient to be discharged.

In early August, orders came for the 26th to muster out. This involved several days of paperwork. Inventories of supplies and equipment had to be prepared and turned in, and the "muster out rolls" had to be drawn up and copied in triplicate. The actual muster out was held on August 13, 1865.

The mustering officer inspected the troops and accepted the muster out rolls of the regiment.

CHAPTER 38

The 26th boarded a steamboat for Missouri where the "real" discharge occurred some days later.

A big ceremony was held in Jefferson City, Missouri. People from a fifty-mile radius came to celebrate the mustering out of the 26th Missouri. Among those present were the George Miller family, Allen and Nancy Barger family, and many other families from Moniteau, Cooper, Osage, and Cole County in which Jefferson City was located. The folks from Moniteau County traveled about thirty-five miles to Jefferson City, arriving on the day of the big mustering out event. As soon as the Millers and Bargers reached Jefferson City, they picked a spot on the south side of the State Capitol Building near where the grandstand had been built. The festivities began at 10:00 A.M. The temperature had already begun to rise to the point that many of the ladies had begun fanning.

The Governor was the first dignitary to speak. He welcomed and praised the 26th Regiment for the magnificent role they played in the Union's victory. Other dignitaries spoke, senior officers of the 26th Missouri spoke, and then a prayer was given by the chaplain.

After the chaplain's prayer, the 26th passed in review for the last time. The soldiers started on the north side of the State Capitol and marched completely around the Capitol. As the soldiers passed down the street they were cheered on by thousands who were standing on the State Capitol grounds and lining the street opposite the State Capitol. As the band played and as the cheering erupted from every direction, it was almost impossible for anyone to hear the person standing next to them. The march around the State Capitol was certainly just as impressive as the march down Pennsylvania Avenue in Washington, D.C. The regiment was small in numbers, depleted by a dozen battles, hard marches, and swamp fevers, but it was large in pride.

The Bargers and Millers had selected a spot on the south side of the State Capitol. It was a level area and the best spot on the State Capitol grounds. They were in hopes that as James, Jesse, James Brooks, and Hiram marched by them would be able to see them.

James was the first one to be seen by the Miller and Barger families. "There he is!" John Wesley said as James came around the west corner and headed up the street where the Millers and Bargers were standing.

"Doesn't he look great?" Nancy whispered to Allen.

"Yes, he does. I'm so proud of him," Allen replied.

Christina had come with her folks to welcome the boys from Moniteau County home. She was so excited when she saw James coming up the street. She was jumping up and down with excitement. Her heart was beating as though it would burst right out of her chest. She wondered if he would see her as he passed by. She thought, what can I do to make him aware that I'm here? She didn't have to wonder very long. As James got within thirty feet of where they were standing, John Wesley leaped out on the street and shouted, "Welcome home, James." James immediately spotted his brother and began to wave. He then saw Christina.

"Oh' my goodness! It's my Christina!" he said as he approached in front of where they were standing. He wanted to break ranks and go running to her, but the soldier in him said "No, wait." As he passed by them, he saluted and whispered, "I'll see you in a little while."

It wasn't long until Jesse, James Brooks and Hiram appeared. The three were spotted by none other than John Wesley. John Wesley was not shy in the least. He loved his brothers, and no one was going to cheat him of this important day.

When the parade was over, the Bargers and Millers drove their wagons to the Union camp which was located north of town. The soldiers were lined up to be given their discharge certificates and back pay.

After this had been done, Colonel Dean called the regiment to attention. He thanked them for their loyal service, telling them that he was prouder to have served with them than anything else he had done in his life. He concluded with a few words from Shakespeare's Henry V: "We few, we noble few, we band of brothers." Then, he led the regiment in prayer. After saying "Amen," he straightened up and in a loud voice, choked with emotion, he shouted: "26th Missouri! Attention! Parade! Dismissed!"

There were many heartfelt goodbyes. The 26th included soldiers from all over Missouri, and James did not know when, if ever, he would see his friends again. There was much handshaking, and even a few tears shed by the tough old veterans.

James, Hiram, and Jesse walked from the group of soldiers toward the waiting, familiar wagon, where the Millers and Bargers sat.

This was the most touching reunion of all times. Three young men had survived the Civil War without getting hurt badly. Three young men of Moniteau County were finally coming home to families who loved them.

As the families greeted each other, Christina waited patiently as James spent time hugging and kissing each member of his family. He then looked around and there she stood, not ten feet away.

As he stood gazing at her, she made her move toward him. He did the same. As they met James picked Christina up and swung her around and around. As he put her down, their lips met. They kissed while everyone else watched happily. It didn't bother James and Christina for their families to watch. They loved each other, and this was the moment they had waited for, nearly five long years. They would never again be apart.

CHAPTER 39

After returning to Moniteau County, James and Jesse moved in with their parents. They helped Allen harvest his corn and tobacco crops. Living with their parents gave them a place to stay until they could finalize the purchase of farms of their own and build houses.

On September 6, 1865, Allen received a letter from his brother, Pointer Barger, from Morgan County, Tennessee.

Dear Allen and Family,

I hope this letter finds you and your family well. We are doing as well as can be expected these days. I wanted to write you a letter to tell you that we too experienced tragedy during this bloody and devastating war.

My sons, Wiley Morrison, William Henry, and Abraham Lafayette died of starvation at Andersonville prison. I previously mentioned in one of my letters that they were captured by the Confederates and were being held prisoners at Andersonville. From what we have been told, the prison was built in 1862 for ten thousand Federal soldiers and ended up with over forty-five thousand over the period of its existence. According to what we can find out, over thirteen thousand Federal soldiers died of starvation from 1862-1864. We are still grieving their deaths. My heart breaks each time I think about one of my boys dying such a shameful death. It is something I cannot erase from my mind. It's present, each day of my life. My faith has wavered at times, especially when we were notified of the deaths of our sons.

Allen, pray for me because my faith and respect for our leaders will never be what it once was. I'm having a really hard time with all of this.

Like your son, Henry, and your son-in-law, Thomas Tull, my boys gave their lives during this horrible war. I pray that never again will there be such a war!

Mary and I are getting up in age. Mary still works like a man and still handles all the farm management and finances. My other sons and daughters are a big help to us. They are beginning to seek out partners in marriage. I don't know how much longer we will have any of them at home.

I stay busy preaching the word of God. God continues to bless us with good health. It's comforting to have several of our family close.

As you know, we sold our farm in Bledsoe County and returned to Morgan County to take over the large farm that Mary's father left her in his will. We loved your place but knew we couldn't take care of both farms. John was happy to purchase our farm. That gave him two hundred acres. He's doing very well. Getting older, but still in good health. I'm sure you hear from him from time to time. Most of his children are married now and are having children. He's happy having grandchildren close to visit.

Please write me as soon as you can. We want to know when James and Jesse made it home and what they are doing. We also want to know how you'll are doing. Mary sends her love and regards to Nancy.

Your brother,
Pointer

James rode up on his horse as Allen was finishing Pointer's letter. "How are you doing, Pa?" James asked, sensing things were not good.

"I just got this letter from your uncle, Pointer, from Morgan County. It's quite disturbing!" Allen said with tears appearing in his eyes.

"What did Uncle Pointer have to say that's disturbing?" James asked.

"His three sons, Wiley Morrison, William Henry, and Abraham Lafayette died of starvation at Andersonville."

"That makes me so mad!" James said as he stomped his feet. "If only General Sherman had listened to us. This may have not happened."

"You did all you could, Son. There's no use in getting mad."

"But, I am mad! In fact, I'm going to write General Sherman a letter and let him know exactly what I think of him. I didn't like him then, and I certainly don't like him now!" James said, still fuming.

"Come sit down, James, I want to talk to you about another matter."

"What is it?"

"I also got a letter from your uncle John. He wants us to get together soon. He and I are getting up in years and he thinks if we don't do it soon, we may not be able to travel. I would like for us to have a family reunion."

"That sounds good. When?"

"John and Betsy have never been here. I'm going to see if they might want to come during the time you and Christina are getting married."

"That sounds like a good time. How can I help?"

"Since you have such a good handwriting, I would like for you to write the invitation letters to the family."

"I'll be happy to do that, Pa."

"It's going to be really nice to see John and his family. Hopefully, Pointer's family and my sisters and their families, can come too. I know this is wishful thinking, but it would make for a great event, one we would cherish for the rest of our lives."

"I'm going in to see what Ma's got cooking for supper," James said, leaving Allen setting on the porch with old King.

On September 10, 1865, Allen accompanied his two sons to First State Bank of California. Both James and Jesse had money to purchase their farms in the Centertown community but needed additional money to build their houses, purchase mules, and equipment which would be necessary to farm the land. The owners of the property wanted two dollars per acre for the land.

Allen had a good credit record with the bank in California. He knew Mr. Sam Billings, the president, well. It was Sam Billings who lent him money to purchase his hundred acres when he moved from Reynolds County to Moniteau. He also knew Mr. Billings would remember he paid his farm note off one year sooner than necessary. His credit record was good and if needed, he would co-sign a loan for James and Jesse.

Upon arriving at the bank, Allen, James, and Jesse were told to have a seat on a bench located near the entrance of Mr. Billings' office. They didn't have long to wait when Mr. Billings came out of his office to greet Allen. "Allen Barger, how are you doing?"

"I'm doing well," Allen replied.

Mr. Billings turned and said, "I'm guessing these are your sons."

"Yes, Sir, this is James and Jesse. They have just returned from the war and are anxious to get started farming," Allen said with a note of pride in his voice.

"James, are you the young man who kept winning the sharpshooters contest at our annual California celebrations?" Mr. Billings asked.

"Yes, Sir, I'm that James Barger," James said as he shook Mr. Billings' hand.

"You have grown up, young man. I didn't recognize you," Mr. Billings said as he released James hand.

"This is my son, Jesse," Allen said.

"Jesse, you were always tagging along with your brother. I remember you well. My, how time can change people, especially young people! Let's go into my office and have a seat," Mr. Billings said as he returned to his office and took his seat behind his large oak desk.

"James, I hear you were a sergeant in the 26th Missouri Regiment. Is that right?" Mr. Billings asked.

"Yes, Sir!" James replied.

"I'm proud of both you and Jesse. Welcome home!"

"Thanks!" James and Jesse said together.

"Now, what can I do for you boys?" Since Mr. Billings was looking at James, he felt he should speak up.

"Jesse and I have found these two hundred acres east of Centertown. We've heard it is good farming land and we would like to purchase it. The owners want two dollars per acre for the land. We've saved enough to pay for the land, but we need a farm loan to repair and add-on to the present houses, purchase mules, and farm equipment. We are hard workers, and you can count on us to repay our loans," James said with ease.

Mr. Billings was very impressed with the composure James used in asking for the bank loan.

"How much money do you figure you and Jesse will need to get started?" Mr. Billings asked.

"I figure we will need about one thousand dollars each to get started," James replied.

"Did I hear you right when you said you wanted to repair the houses?" Mr. Billings asked.

"Yes, Sir, we both plan to marry as soon as our houses are completed," James replied.

"And who will be the lucky girls?" Mr. Billings asked.

"I'll be marrying Christina Miller, George Miller's daughter, and Jesse is marrying her sister, Margaret," James said.

"My goodness, fellows, those are the two prettiest girls in Moniteau County. I see them at the Saturday night dances," Mr. Billings said.

James and Jesse looked at Allen and smiled. "We agree with you on that point, don't we, Jesse?" James said.

"That's right!" Jesse replied.

This was the first time Jesse had said a word. But when it came to Margaret Miller, he was always ready to brag about how pretty she was.

"How many years do you want this loan for?" Mr. Billing's asked.

"We would like a five year note if that's possible," James answered.

"Boys, it will be my pleasure to loan you the money for five years. We in Moniteau County owe you boys a lot. The note will be ready for you to sign tomorrow afternoon at 2:00 P. M. Come back then and the money will be waiting for you."

"Allen, I know you are mighty proud of these two young men."

"Yes, Sir, God has surely blessed me," Allen said as he reached and shook Mr. Billings' hand. James and Jesse also reached out and shook hands with Mr. Billings. They thanked him for his generosity and trust.

"It's going to be my pleasure to watch you boys contribute to the progress of Moniteau County. It's young men like yourselves who will make this county thrive," Mr. Billings said as he followed Allen, James, and Jesse to the door.

"We will see you tomorrow afternoon at 2:00," James said.

"Pa, I'm going to see Christina. She will be excited to hear things went well," James said as he climbed on his horse.

"Tell my future daughter-in-law I sent my regards," Allen said with a smile.

"I'll do just that, Pa," James said as he rode off toward the Jack Hanover house.

As James dismounted his horse, he tied the bridle rains to a front hitching post and began to climb the steps leading to the front porch. As soon as he reached the porch, Christina opened the front door and said, "James, I didn't expect you so soon. How did it go at the bank?"

"Come out here on the front porch, and I'll tell you all about it," James said as he reached for Christina's hand.

"Tell me! Tell me! I can't stand it," Christina said grabbing James's hands.

"Mr. Billings has agreed to loan us the money. We are going to get that farm!" James said with excitement.

"Oh, James, I'm so happy!"

"Me too!" James said.

"When can we get married?" Christina asked.

"Not until I get the house repaired and the two rooms added. If everything goes well it shouldn't be long," James said.

"I'm so happy!

"Do you think we could spend some time together tonight?" James asked hopefully.

"I think that's the best idea I've heard all day, Sergeant James A. Barger," Christina said in a teasing tone.

James spent the rest of the day looking around town for farm equipment and inquiring about mules. He also priced lumber at Mr. Jacobs's builders and hardware store. He could hardly restrain himself. His dream was getting closer and closer to becoming a reality.

James returned to Mrs. Hanover's for dinner. "James, it's so good to have you back here in Moniteau County with us," Mrs. Hanover said.

"Thanks, Mrs. Hanover. I'm happy to be home."

"Christina tells me you are buying some farm property east of Centertown." "That's right," James replied.

"I guess you will want to take my darling Christina with you, won't you?" Mrs. Hanover asked.

James looked at Christina as Christina looked at him and smiled. James hesitated as he thought to himself, how should I answer Mrs. Hanover's question? When I take Christina as my wife who will take care of Mrs. Hanover? "I do plan to marry Christina when I get our house completed," James said.

"I guess you know, you have to take me too. I can't give up my Christina."

James looked at Christina as she smiled back. James wondered if Mrs. Hanover was serious.

After Mrs. Hanover went to bed James and Christina went to the front porch. They set down in the front porch swing, and James took Christina in his arms, kissed her tenderly and said, "Our dreams are about to come true."

"I'm so excited James!"

James pulled away from Christina for a few seconds and gazed into her beautiful blue eyes and said, “Christina, I love your long blonde hair. Promise me you won’t ever get it cut.”

“I promise you, James, I’ll never get my hair cut. I will always keep it long just for you.”

As they sat swinging, the subject of Mrs. Hanover was brought up by James.

“Christina, was Mrs. Hanover serious about living with us?” he asked.

“I believe she was serious. She and I have been talking about the possibility. She told me if I would agree to take care of her until she died she would leave me everything she owns. I feel so sorry for her James. I couldn’t tell her no. She has no one else, and without me, she would be entirely alone. How do you feel about her living with us?” Christina asked.

“I don’t rightly know. I guess I’m a little surprised that you talked to her about living with us before discussing with me.”

“I’m sorry it came about the way it did. I was going to discuss it with you.”

“That’s all right, I feel sorry for her also, and I wouldn’t want anything bad to happen to her. She shouldn’t have to spend the last years of her life with no one to love and care for her.”

“Then it will be all right for her to come and live with us?” Christina asked.

“She’s a sweet old lady, and we can’t just abandon her,” James said.

“You are a good man, James Barger. That’s why I love you so much,” Christina said as she gave him a grateful kiss.

“I guess that means we’re going to need a bigger house, doesn’t it?” James asked.

“I suppose so, but Mrs. Gladys has money. She wants to pay her way. It might help us if we had a little extra money around. She’s a lovely person and she won’t be a problem. I knew you would be willing for her to stay with us even if she didn’t have a cent of her own.”

James suddenly realized the lateness of the night, stood up and said, “Christina, I must go. I promised Pa I would help him do some fence repairs tomorrow, and Jesse and I are to be at Mr. Billings Bank at 2:00.

At 2:00 P.M. on the hour, Jesse and James arrived at the First State Bank in California to sign the bank note. This was an exciting time in their lives. It was also a little scary. They were going out on their own and would have their own families to care for. The responsibility of it was a little overwhelming.

During the month of September and October, James and Jesse helped harvest their father's crops and worked on their houses. They also spent time hunting, trapping, and fishing.

It was after a hunting trip that old King died. James had gone squirrel hunting and naturally King joined him. As usual King treed several squirrels. Upon arriving back at the house, King took his favorite spot on the front porch near James' rocking chair while James went about skinning the squirrels. After skinning the squirrels, James cut them up and took them inside to be cooked for dinner.

He later joined King on the front porch for a rest. As he sat down in the rocking chair near King, he said, "King, old boy, we did good today." Normally, King would get up, come over to James and put his head in James' lap. But today, King didn't respond to James. James looked over at King and noticed that he was not breathing. He immediately got up from his chair and ran to him. King's heart had played out. The dog James had loved since he was fourteen years old was now dead. It was like losing one of the family. King had been James' hunting and traveling companion except for the years James was away at war. He had grown old but was still a very good hunting dog. James would certainly miss him in the days to come.

James and his family gave King a proper burial out by the creek which he had played in regularly, especially after a long, tiring hunting trip.

After the death of King, James and Jesse continued to work on their houses. Like John and Allen did in Bledsoe County, James and Jesse would share farm equipment and pasture land. Their farms joined each other, and their houses were not far apart. They helped each other prepare and harvest the crops. It was just like Allen and John did in Bledsoe County.

Just as the neighbors pitched in to add an extra room to Allen's home after he had moved to Moniteau County, they did the same for James and Jesse.

On November 15, 1865, both houses were ready to be occupied. The double wedding between James and Christina and Jesse and Margaret was set for Thanksgiving Day. They would be married at the New Hope Baptist Church near Marion, Missouri. After a Thanksgiving meal with family and friends each couple would return to their new home.

Elizabeth Miller, a younger sister to Christina and Margaret, agreed to stay with Mrs. Hanover for a few weeks. This would give James and Christina a few weeks of privacy before Mrs. Gladys joined them in their new home.

Several of the Union soldiers of the Missouri 26th were present for the wedding as well as many other friends and guests.

James and Jesse chose brown suits, white shirts, and brown bow ties for their wedding suits. Their brown suits matched their own natural coloring. As James and Jesse waited for their brides to walk down the aisle, Nancy leaned over to Allen and whispered, "Don't our boys look handsome?"

"Just like their pa in his heyday," he said as he looked at Nancy and smiled. "You're still a mighty handsome man to me, Allen Barger," Nancy said as she pressed her left elbow into his right side and smiled.

Just as Nancy finished flirting with Allen, the piano started playing the wedding march.

George Miller appeared at the front entrance of the church with a daughter on each arm. The wedding was a real treat to the many guests. Most had never attended a double wedding where the father walked two daughters down the aisle to marry two brothers.

Margaret wore a long white organdy gown trimmed with lace on the collar, sleeves, and hem. Her hair glimmered like a golden waterfall as she gracefully walked with her father and sister. Jesse beamed from ear to ear.

Christina wore a lovely pink dress and had pulled her hair back with a ribbon of the same shade. She was a floating vision of beauty in James' eyes. The aisle was narrow, and Mr. Miller carefully escorted his daughters to the front of the church and to their nervous grooms. As James watched Christina come closer and closer, he could see the joy in her eyes and the happiness of her smile. He thought to himself, James Barger, you are the luckiest man in Moniteau County. Finally, Mr. Miller reached the front of the church where he placed Margaret's hand in Jesse's and Christina's hand in James'. He stood between the two girls until the preacher asked, "Who gives these girls in marriage?"

"I do!" Mr. Miller said and stepped back to take his seat by the new Mrs. Miller.

The preacher married Jesse and Margaret first and then James and Christina. Among the many guests at the wedding were Captain Thompson who had become a very close friend of James' from the 26th Missouri Infantry and several of James' and Jesse's army buddies. Among the family members present were Allen's brothers and their families from Tennessee. Also attending the wedding were Pamela, Henry Barger's widow, and her husband Brett Fletcher. The New Hope Baptist Church was filled to its capacity.

Although it was a little chilly, dinner was served on the church ground on tables which were constructed for church socials and celebrations. Everyone enjoyed the sweet fellowship and food. After dinner, a church pounding was given in honor of both sets of newlyweds. The pounding would certainly help both couples in setting up housekeeping.

The men decorated both James' and Jesse's wagons. They put soap on the wagon seats and tied cans to the back of the wagons. As James and Jesse led their brides from the church, they were bombarded with rice flying in every direction. Each man helped his new bride onto the wagon seats and climbed in beside them. They were off to start lives of their own. Lives filled with love and devotion and marriages which would bring both joy and pain.

James and Jesse spent several weeks cutting wood, fishing, hunting, and trapping. Meat was smoked and dried for the winter months. Fresh game and fish were always on the table. There was never a lack of food. James and Jesse met every morning in the barn to milk the cows while Christina and Margaret cooked breakfast.

James and Christina easily adjusted to Mrs. Gladys Hanover's living with them. She was no bother and kept Christina company while James and Jesse were out doing chores.

Mrs. Hanover made sure she allowed the newlyweds plenty of time alone together. She spent time with Margaret and other neighbors. Occasionally, she would spend a day or two with one of her friends in town. She was careful when given advice to Christina and Margaret. She wanted to help them all she could, but she didn't want to over step and sound bossy. Gradually, Mrs. Hanover began to fill the void in the girls' lives that had occurred when their mother died. The young women began to think of her as a second mother.

On Saturday nights, Jesse and Margaret accompanied James and Christina to town for the dance and social events. On Sundays, they harnessed the mules, hitched them to the wagon they shared, and went to church together at New Hope Baptist.

Christmas time was approaching in Moniteau County, Missouri. On Christmas day, Allen and Nancy had the entire family to their house for Christmas dinner. Since two of the Miller girls were now in the Barger family, the Millers also shared Christmas with the Bargers, as well as Mrs. Hanover.

William T. Barger and his family of Ray County; Mary Ann and her daughter, Nancy Jean Conant; and Martha Jane and her three children were present for the Christmas dinner. Martha Jane was still living with her folks. Being widowed, she could not make it without help from the family, especially with three small children. Allen and Nancy loved having their grandchildren around.

George W. Barger was also there with his new girlfriend, Margaret Haddox, the first girl he had shown an interest in. Margaret was a beautiful lady. She was wild about George

It was like old times at the Bargers. Nancy and the womenfolk prepared a large Christmas dinner.

A huge turkey roasted to a golden-brown sat in the middle of the table. This turkey came as a gift from James. He had been keeping an eye on this wild turkey for weeks. It weighed twenty-two pounds which was more than enough for the entire family. James had gotten up early on Christmas Eve morning and positioned himself in a run he knew the big gobbler would pass. It only took one shot to bring the big bird down. James hadn't lost his touch with a rifle, and he was still the best shot in Moniteau County.

Allen and the men folk gathered around the fireplace while Nancy and the ladies decorated several tables with red, black, and white checked oil cloths.

Finally, Nancy came across the room and whispered to Allen, "Dinner is ready." Allen rose from his rocking chair and said, "Nancy has announced that Christmas dinner is ready. Let's form a circle and give thanks to God for this wonderful Christmas." "Our loving, kind, heavenly Father, we bow our heads in your presence today to give thanks. Father, this is indeed a very special day. Not only do we come thanking you for the birth of your son, Jesus Christ, our Lord and Savior, but also for bringing our boys home safe from the war. This is the first time we've all been together in five years on Christmas Day. Father, we truly thank you for that. You have been so good to us. You have supplied our every need during this past year. You have blessed us with good health, and, Father, you have added to this family two wonderful daughters-in-law in Christina and Margaret. Our family continues to grow, and we are grateful to you for blessing us so richly with your divine love and mercy. Father, we're grateful to have George Miller and his family with us today. We now ask for your blessings upon this wonderful meal. As we enjoy it, let us remember why we are celebrating this day. We do praise you for Your Son, Jesus Christ, our Redeemer. Once again, Father, we thank you for a good year and ask Your continued blessings on all of us as we soon begin a new year with You. It's in Jesus name I pray,

Amen." After several Amen's, everyone sat down to enjoy a bountiful meal.

On February 10, 1866, Margaret came down with pneumonia. She lingered between border of life and death for three days. Nancy and Christina took turn caring for and nursing her. At one time, everyone lived in constant fear that she would die, but God spared her, and she began to mend. It took her several weeks to recover her strength from her close brush with death. During this time, Christina cooked for everyone. Christina was becoming everything that James knew she would be. She was truly a good wife.

Jesse was very thankful to Christina for her generosity and kindness. The care she had lavished on Margaret during her illness was more than just sisterly duty. They loved each other as sisters and friends.

In early spring while James and Jesse were preparing the grounds for planting, Christina was out by the well, chopping wood for the cook stove. As she bent over to pick up a stick of wood, a sudden pain hit her in the stomach. "Oh, my!" she said as she dropped the wood and grabbed her stomach. She hobbled over to the well where she rang the dinner bell. She hoped that James would hear the bell and come right away. As she looked down she saw blood running down her right leg. "Oh, God, what is happening to me?" she said as she removed the apron and tried to wipe away the blood which was flowing down her leg.

Margaret had heard the bell and came running over to Christina, almost immediately.

"What's wrong, Christina?" Margaret asked in a frightened voice.

"I don't know, but I'm hurting something awful. I'm bleeding."

"Let's get you inside," Margaret said as she put Christina's arm around her right shoulder and helped her inside and onto the bed, just as James and Jesse burst in the house.

"What's wrong?" James asked with fear clawing at his gut.

"Christina is in a great deal of pain, and she's bleeding," Margaret said. "Bleeding!" James exclaimed, as he rushed to Christina's bedside.

"Christina, honey, what's wrong?" James asked as he picked up her limp hand and held it.

"I'm cramping badly!" Christina moaned in pain.

"I'm sending Jesse after Doc Smith. Jesse, go now!!" James hollered.

"I'll be back as soon as I can. I'll stop and tell Ma to come right over," Jesse said as he mounted his horse bareback and took off in a frantic gallop.

It wasn't long before Nancy and Martha Jane arrived. Nancy examined Christina and immediately placed two pillows under both her feet.

"What do you think is wrong?" Christina asked.

"Christina, I'm not sure, but I'm afraid you're trying to lose your baby," Nancy replied as she took Christina by the hand.

"I didn't know I was with child," Christina replied.

"You may not be very far along, my dear, but I believe you are carrying a child," Nancy replied.

Everyone heard Doc. Smith's buggy pull up outside. Immediately, Jesse and the doctor entered the cabin. After examining Christina, he looked at Christina and said, "Nancy is right, Christina, you are carrying a baby.

"Am I going to lose my baby?" Christina asked with tears welling up in her stricken eyes.

"The next few hours will determine that," Doc Smith said as he patted Christina on the hand.

"I don't want to lose my baby," Christina said as she began to cry in heart-wrenching sobs.

Doc Smith turned to Nancy and said, "Keep her as calm and as quiet as possible, and make sure her feet stay propped up. Don't let her out of bed for any reason for the next two days."

Nancy knew exactly what to do. Over the years she had become one of the best midwives in Moniteau County. She had seen this same problem on several occasions.

"Ma, are she and the baby going to be all right?" James asked in a shaky voice.

"Son, the next few hours will tell. If she stops bleeding, there is a good chance she will be able to carry the baby. If the bleeding continues she will almost certainly lose the baby. All you can do to help her is pray, so you better get started," Nancy said as she shooed him from the room.

"Margaret, I'll need some clean linens. Martha, make sure there is plenty of hot water in the kettle," Nancy said.

Three hours later, Nancy came out of Christina's room. "How is she, Ma?" James asked as he rose from his rocking chair.

"I'm sorry, Son. She's lost the baby," Nancy said as she put her arms around James to comfort him.

"Is Christina going to be all right?" James asked pleadingly.

"Yes, I think she will be fine. She will need to take it easy for a while. No lifting or heavy housework," Nancy said.

"I didn't know she was with child," James said.

"She wasn't far along, James. I guess less than two months."

Christina recovered physically much more quickly than she did emotionally. She and James finally accepted the loss and prayed for strength from God to go on without bitterness.

Nancy had explained to James and Christina that losing a baby in the early stages was sometimes God's way to take care of something that was not normal. Often it was God's way in letting nature take its course. They both trusted God and continued to have faith. Their faith in God allowed them to believe that God would someday bless them with a family. Until then, they would wait and be patient while seeking God's will in their lives.

CHAPTER 40

On January 3, 1867, Mrs. Gladys Hanover came down with pneumonia. Due to her age she was unable to fight off the infection and died on January 5, 1867. James and Christina had her buried in the California Cemetery next to her husband, Jack Hanover.

Mrs. Hanover left the house in town and a sum of money in First State Bank of California to Christina, just as she promised. The inheritance was used to improve the house and farm. The money from the sale of the house in California went to pay off the bank note on the farm. This inheritance was truly a blessing. Now that the farm was free of debt, James bought six head of cows and a bull.

On January 25, 1867, Martha Jane Tull married Anderson Birdsong of Moniteau County. Mr. Birdsong's wife had died giving birth to their second child. He needed a wife and someone to take care of his children.

Anderson Birdsong was a good man who owned one hundred acres east of California. He proved himself to be a good husband to Martha and a patient father to all the children. He didn't mind bringing three other children into the family. Martha knew she didn't love Anderson as she had Thomas Tull, but her practical side knew she needed a man who could take care of her and the children. She respected Anderson and thought they would be able to get along. Together, they would try to create one family from two broken pieces.

On February 3, 1867, after church service at New Hope Baptist Church, James noticed Allen standing by his wagon bent over. James excused himself from visiting with friends and immediately made his way over to where Allen was standing. “Pa, is there something wrong?” James asked.

“Just strained muscles, I’m afraid,” Allen replied as he turned and looked at James.

“Are you sure, Pa?” James asked again.

“I’ve been getting a little out of breath lately, Son,” Allen said as he started to climb into the wagon but couldn’t.

“I think you should see Doc Smith,” James said.

“I don’t think that’s necessary, Son. I’m just a tired old sixty-five-year-old man,” Allen said as he finally managed to get into the wagon with James’ help.

“So, you are going to be a stubborn old man,” James said.

“Maybe!” Allen said, with a smile on his face.

At this time Nancy, George, Delilah, and John Wesley came out of the church and walked to the wagon. James helped his mother and Delilah into the wagon. Delilah had grown into a beautiful young lady. She would soon be sixteen. George Washington was now nineteen years old, and John Wesley was twelve. As James watched his father drive away, he had a strong feeling things were not good for his father. His father was sixty-five years old, and he had worked hard all his life. It was time for his father to slow down, James thought, as the wagon rolled out of sight.

On the following Tuesday, February 5, 1867, Nancy sent George after James and Jesse. Allen had passed out in the barn earlier in the day. As James and Jesse entered the living room, Nancy was coming out of the bedroom. “What’s wrong with Pa?” James asked with a touch of fear creeping into his voice.

“I don’t know, Son. Doc Smith is in there now with your pa. He’ll tell us what he can in a few minutes. You boys have a seat,” Nancy said as she returned to the bedroom.

In about fifteen minutes, Doc Smith and Nancy came out. James, Jesse, George, Delilah and John Wesley immediately stood up.

“Doc Smith has something important to say to all of us,” Nancy said.

"Please be seated. I know you are eager to know what's ailing your father.

Your father has had a severe strain on his heart. I'm afraid your father is a very sick man," he said.

Before he had finished speaking, Delilah let out a cry, "Are you saying Pa is going to die?" Delilah asked as she began crying.

James took her in his arms to comfort her.

"I'm afraid your father's condition is serious. He's very weak," Doc Smith said.

"When can we see him?" James asked.

"Your father wants to talk to all of you, but before he does, he wants to talk to James and Nancy first," Doc Smith said as he turned to go into the bedroom with James and Nancy.

Nancy sat down by Allen while James remained standing by his father's side. "How are you feeling, my dear?" Nancy asked.

"I'm not doing too well, Nancy."

"You hold on, Pa," James said as he took his father's right hand.

"James, go over there to the dresser and get some paper and a pencil. Nancy, I want James to write out my will. After James finishes it, I will sign it. Then, I want you and Doc Smith to witness my signature," Allen said in a weak voice.

James returned with the paper and pencil. "Son, please write this down as I say it," Allen said. Allen loved James' handwriting and knew his will would be legible to anyone.

'I, Allen Barger, being of sound mind, do hereby leave my farm to my two youngest sons, George Washington Barger and John Wesley Barger.'" As James wrote this down, Allen explained why he decided to leave the farm to the two younger brothers.

"James, I know you and Jesse will understand since you both already have your own farms. George and John Wesley will need a good start in life, and without this farm, they might never have that opportunity," Allen said.

"James, write this down. 'I'm appointing my son, James A. Barger, to be the executor of my estate until both George and John Wesley become of adult age. The farm cannot be sold unless James A. Barger gives his signature of approval for sale.

'To my beloved wife, Nancy Elizabeth Barger, I leave all my personal belongings, this house, and $350.00 in cash. After her death, the house will become a part of the farm.'"

By this time, tears were streaming down Nancy's face. James could no longer hold back his tears either. James took his shirt sleeve and ran it across his eyes to clear the tears.

"James, please continue to write," Allen said.

"'William T. Barger, my son who lives in Ray County, Missouri, is to have three cows.

'Jesse Allen Barger and James Anderson Barger, my sons, who live in the Centertown community, are to have three cows each.'

'I want each of the girls, Martha Jane Barger Tull Birdsong of Moniteau County, Mary Ann Barger Conant of Cole County, and Delilah Barger, currently living in the home, to receive $100 each.'

'I leave my hunting knives, hunting guns, and the family Bible to my son James A. Barger of the Centertown Community. I want the family Bible to be a historical record of my family and remain in the possession of James A. Barger's ancestry family.'"

"That's very nice of you, Pa." James said with tears welling in his eyes.

"Son, I want you to forgive me for doubting your decision to enter the Civil War. I thought hard of you and Jesse for a long time. Again, I know you made the right decision, and I know God has blessed you. Please forgive me if I caused you grief."

"Pa, there is no need to apologize. You have caused me no grief. I knew all along you were putting Jesse's and my welfare above everything else. I respected your opposition knowing you were only thinking of us."

"James, I have a feeling someday you will be either a preacher or one of the leading politicians in Missouri. Your heart is good, and it will lead you to do good things.

"You have been blessed already with a wonderful wife in Christina, and I know eventually you'll have several children. Again, please take care of your ma," Allen said.

"I promise you, Pa. Ma will be well taken care of," James said.

"Now let me sign the will," Allen said and reached out to take it from James. After signing the will, Allen asked Doc Smith and Nancy to sign as witnesses.

On Thursday, February 7, 1867, Allen Barger went to be with the Lord. The family buried him on Saturday, February 9, 1867, at the New Hope Baptist Church Cemetery. The church was packed with friends and relatives. Allen had been loved and respected by nearly everyone in Moniteau County.

Pastor Matthew Jacobs performed the service.

"My beloved friends and family, we're gathered here today to celebrate the life of Allen Barger. His Christian witness was always depicted in his character. He always gave God credit for every good thing.

"Allen Barger was born in Roane County, Tennessee, on January 3, 1801, to Henry and Elizabeth Jane Barger. He is survived by his wife, Nancy Bullock Barger, and eight children: sons, William T. Barger of Ray County; Missouri, James A. Barger; Jesse Allen Barger; George Washington Barger; and John Wesley Barger of Moniteau County; and daughters, Martha Jane Barger Birdsong of Moniteau County; Mary Ann Barger Conant of Jefferson City, Missouri; and Delilah Ann Barger of the home. He is also survived by six grandchildren. He is preceded in death by his oldest son, Henry Barger.

"Today we pay tribute to Allen Barger who was truly a pillar of strength to his family, friends, church, and community. He believed in worshiping the Lord every Sunday in God's house, and come rain or shine, he would have his family in church. He was a strong believer in the power of prayer and always gave God credit for everything. We will certainly miss Allen Barger."

After the funeral services the casket was carried to the eastern part of the cemetery for burial. Allen was buried near his oldest son, Henry and his son-in-law Thomas Tull, both killed during the Civil War. Thomas' remains had been brought back from Mississippi where he was killed, as promised by James and Jesse. They fulfilled that promise.

The community would not be the same without Allen Barger. Never had one man touched so many lives.

Before returning to Ray County, William T. Barger and his family stayed on for a week and visited with the family. While in Moniteau County, he told James about the rich soil near the Missouri river which separated Lafayette and Ray County.

"James, if your farm doesn't produce good crops, you might want to consider coming to Ray County. The county is filled with good farm land. There is still plenty of land for everyone, but the best pieces are being grabbed up quickly."

"William T., you have made Ray County mighty inviting but right now, I plan to stay in Moniteau County. Ma will need my help here and I've promised Pa that I'll take care of her," James said.

"I fully understand," William T. responded with respect.

CHAPTER 41

On March 15, 1867, Christina started getting dizzy and sick at her stomach in the morning hours. She suspected she might be with child again but didn't want James to know until she was sure. She decided to speak to Nancy about her symptoms on Sunday after church.

On Sunday, as Christina and James were leaving the church, Christina whispered to Nancy, "Could I please have a word with you before you leave for home?"

"Certainly, my dear," Nancy said as she took Christina by the arm and walked down the steps of the church. "Now what is the matter, my dear?" Nancy asked.

"I think I may be with child, but I didn't want James to know until I was sure," Christina said.

"My darling what are your symptoms?" Nancy asked.

"I'm dizzy and sick at my stomach early in the morning."

"That's a good sign," Nancy said as she hugged Christina.

"But how long will it be before I know?" Christina asked.

"When you miss two of your monthlies, you can be pretty certain you are with child."

At this time James came up. "What are you two up to?" he asked laughing.

"Just women talk, James Barger," Nancy replied, giving James a kiss and a pat on the cheek.

"How's it been, Ma?" James asked hesitantly.

"We're doing fine, James. It gets lonely without your father, but Delilah and the boys are a big help to me."

"I want everyone to come to dinner next Sunday at my house, and James, you might get out and kill us a big turkey before then," Nancy said with a smile. She knew James would do just that. He still furnished wild game for his mother's table.

"You can count on us being there," James assured her.

Jesse and Margaret came walking up. "Jesse, I was just telling James and Christina that I want the family to come to my house next Sunday for dinner. You and Margaret will be able to come, want you?"

"We will be there, Ma," Jesse replied.

Margaret was about six months along in her pregnancy. She had that special glow of a satisfied mother-to-be. Her pregnancy was going well, and both she and Jesse were looking forward to the birth of their first child.

Christina stood looking at Margaret, wondering what she might look like five or six months from now. She wanted to look just like Margaret. She was ready for a child and hoped her symptoms meant she was with child.

It wasn't long before Christina realized she was indeed with child. The doctor predicted the baby would be born the third week in September.

As Christina left Doc Smith's office, she began to plan how she would tell her wonderful secret to James. She wanted this to be a very special occasion. She knew James loved apple pie. Normally, they had apple pie every Sunday, but tonight she would bake one to celebrate.

After coming in from the barn, James washed and took his seat at the head of the dining table, just like his father used to do when he was growing up. Christina took her seat at the opposite end of the table. As James glanced down the table, he noticed the apple pie. "What's with the apple pie? We normally don't have apple pie until Sunday."

"Yes, I know but I've been feeling so good lately. I thought a new expecting father might enjoy a treat in the middle of the week," Christina said with a smile.

James nearly choked from the food he had just put in his mouth. After coughing, he looked straight at Christina, laid his fork down and said, "Would you mind repeating what I thought you said?"

"I said, you are going to be a father," she said joyfully.

"You mean, you're going to have a baby?" James asked with excitement.

"That's exactly what I mean!"

"Are you sure?" James asked as he got up from the table and walked over to Christina. "Let me look at you," James said as he reached out his hands and pulled Christina up from her chair.

"Will you love me when I get big and fat, James?"

"I would love you even if you got as big as old Jersey," James said with a smile as he picked Christina up and swung her around.

"Put me down, James, you don't want to hurt our baby, do you?"

"I just can't believe it," James repeated several times.

Christina sat back down and enjoyed watching the excitement on James' face.

"When will the baby be born?" James asked.

"Doc Smith says in September."

"Hallelujah! Hallelujah! I'm going to be a father," James said as he skipped and danced across the floor back to his chair.

"Now are you ready for that apple pie?" Christina asked.

"Mrs. Barger, I think I would like at least half of it," James said.

The next several months brought much happiness and joy to the lives of James and Christina, and Jesse an Margaret.

On June 11, 1867, Margaret gave birth to her first son, George Albert Barger. He was big and healthy. Margaret had no problems during birth. Jesse, like most new fathers, was a little drunk with happiness and pride. He went around passing out cigars to every man he saw.

The next few months went smoothly. The corn and tobacco crops were good. The harvest was in full swing when James and Jesse heard the dinner bell ring. James immediately knew something was wrong. He ran to his horse and rode as fast as he could to his house. The first person he saw as he burst through the door was Margaret who was coming out of Christina's room.

"What's going on Margaret?" James asked with fear in his voice.

"The baby is coming, James!"

"We've got to get Ma," James said, as Jesse appeared in the wagon.

"Jesse, run on over and get Ma! The baby is coming," James said.

"I'll be back as soon as I can," Jesse said. He jumped in the wagon, slapped the reins across the mules as they jerked forward in a gallop.

"How do you feel, Christina?" James asked as he took her hand and kissed her forehead.

"The pains are about five minutes apart. James, I don't know if I can stand the pain," Christina said just as another wave of pain held her in its grip. She squeezed James's hand and bit her lip.

"Just be strong a while longer, Christina, Ma is on her way," James pleaded with her.

After what seemed like hours to James, Jesse returned with Nancy and Delilah. Nancy went immediately to Christina. "You boys wait outside until I get through checking Christina," Nancy said.

James and Jesse both were as nervous as cats around a rocking chair. The five minutes their mother spent with Christina seemed like an eternity to James.

Finally, the door opened, and Nancy said, "Delilah, you can help me and Margaret. Get some clean linens and have plenty of hot water ready. James, make sure there is plenty water brought in for Delilah," Nancy said as she turned and started toward Christina's room. She then turned around again and said quietly, "James, she's going to be all right."

"Thanks, Ma! I know she's in good hands," James said as he grabbed both water buckets and went to the well.

"Let me help you." Jesse said as he grabbed one of the buckets from James. In a few minutes the big water kettle was full of boiling water.

Mary Elizabeth Barger was born at 7:30 P.M. on September 22, 1867. She came into the world screaming her lungs out. As

Nancy handed her to James, Mary Elizabeth continued to cry louder and louder. James didn't know what to do. He didn't know a thing about being a father. He had held babies before, but they were not screaming their heads off.

"What do I do?" James asked.

"Let me have her," Nancy said as she took the baby and placed her on Christina's left arm. She instructed Christina on how to nurse Mary Elizabeth. As soon as Mary Elizabeth found Christina's nipple, she stopped crying.

"She's just hungry," Christina said as she looked up at James and gave him a smile.

Nancy's middle name was Elizabeth, and Christina's grandmother's name were Mary. The name Mary Elizabeth was chosen to honor both ladies. As she grew up, she would be called, "Lizzie," by family and friends.

After Mary Elizabeth's birth, James began to take interest in politics in Moniteau County. What Allen Barger had predicted was coming true.

James ran for justice of the peace in Moniteau County and won by a landslide. He beat out Samuel Mathias who was from one of the older, more influential families of Moniteau County.

Being elected as justice of the peace was just the beginning of a budding career in politics for James.

On March 27, 1870, Christina Barger gave birth to a second daughter, Sarah Alice Barger. Sarah was tiny with brown eyes and brown hair. Unlike Mary Elizabeth, she didn't cry when James held her for the first time.

James continued to farm and remained active in county politics. As a justice of the peace, he became interested in the County Judge's position when Judge Robert Sanders announced he wouldn't run for another term.

On November 12, 1871, James was elected County Judge of Moniteau County. His popularity continued to grow in the surrounding counties. He continued to win the annual California sharpshooters contest.

James' time was now split between being a County Judge and farming. He began to hire workers to help prepare the grounds and harvest the crops from the farm. He was now farming one hundred acres and doing quite well financially.

James's reputation and popularity spread into Cooper County, Saline County, and as far away as Jefferson City, Missouri. Jefferson City was about thirty-five miles from the city of California and was the state capitol of Missouri.

On January 10, 1872, Christina gave birth to yet another girl, their third child, Rebecca Ann Barger. Rebecca had black hair and favored her grandmother, Nancy Barger.

After the birth of Rebecca, Christina sensed a change in James. She was worried that James was disappointed because none of his children had been boys.

James and Christina's favorite time was after supper. They relaxed on the front porch while visiting about the daily happenings. For several days after Rebecca's birth, Christina had been concerned about James' changed attitude. She knew something was bothering him and decided she would confront him.

"James, my darling. Please don't get upset, but I need to ask you a question."

"What is it, Christina?" James asked as he looked at her and smiled.

"Lately, I've seen a change of attitude in you. Do you want to tell me what's going on?"

"My dear Christina, I wasn't aware it's been that obvious," James said as he squeezed Christina's hand.

"Can you discuss it with me?"

"I wasn't going to talk with you until I was at peace with myself," James said as he lowered his head.

"James, dearest, you've always been able to tell me everything. Don't stop now! Please tell me!"

"I've been pondering about running for the Missouri State Legislature. I've been approached by the Democratic Party in District 8. They want me to run as a State Representative. I'm troubled about what I should do," James said.

"Oh, James, I thought you were disappointed that Rebecca was not a boy," Christina said.

"Rebecca has nothing to do with how I've been acting. I love that little girl. I wouldn't trade her for a dozen boys. I'm so sorry you thought I was disappointed with her."

"God already knows our future. If he doesn't want us to have a boy then we'll have a dozen little girls instead," James said.

"I can't think of anything I could want more than a dozen miniatures of you."

"Thanks, James!" Christina said with a sign of relief.

"Now, let's talk about me running for the Missouri State Legislature. What do you think? Should I do it?"

"I've always known you would be more than a county judge. If you want to run for the State Legislature, do it. I'll be right by your side. Missouri needs good men and you certainly are the best," Christina said as she gave James a big hug.

"I'm so blessed to have you as my wife. Please know, you are my sunshine in the morning and peace throughout the day. I adore you my darling."

"Flattery will get you everything, James A. Barger," Christina said with a shy sweet smile.

"James, you really want to do this, don't you?" Christina asked.

"I would love serving district 8 as State Representative."

"Then go for it. It will be fun being the wife of a state representative!" Christina said.

She felt a sense of pride in her husband. She knew God had blessed James with intelligence and certain gifts which would be useful in serving other people. He was honest and a Christian man. Those qualities would be an asset to Missouri.

"Are you ready for bed? This has been an exhausting day," James said.

"Yes, I agree. Let's go to bed and we can talk about how to get you elected as state representative," Christina said by taking James' hand and leading him to the bedroom.

The Democratic Party of District 8 endorsed James for the State Representative position and on November 14, 1872, James was elected to the Missouri State House of Representatives, representing the counties of Cooper, Moniteau, and Saline.

James found serving as a state representative and managing a farm was not an easy task. It was at this time that Christina again stepped to the front. She would take on the responsibility of managing the farm while James was away in Jefferson City. She was very good at what she did, and the farm hands loved her.

On March 11, 1874, Christina gave birth to their fourth child, Eliza Jane. She had brown curly hair and brown eyes. She looked a lot like Christina.

After Eliza Jane was born, James said, “Hey, I’m working on eight more of those beautiful little Christina.”

The past five years had been like a whirlwind for James. He had gone from farmer to politician and father of four lovely girls. He had also seen his younger brother, George Washington Barger marry Margaret Haddox of Cole County. He witnessed the birth of George and Margaret’s first son, Andrew Jackson Barger.

He observed the prosperity of his brother Jesse, and he and Margaret were blessed with their son, Alfred.

James also observed the birth of Mary Ann’s two sons, Zack and Timothy Conant. He witnessed the divorce of Martha Jane Barger Tull Birdsong from Anderson Birdsong, and was present for Martha’s third marriage to Harvey B. Ryan of Moniteau County.

On May 12, 1873, James gave his mother, Nancy Barger, in marriage to Eliher B. White of Cooper County. Mr. White was a longtime resident of Cooper County and owned a hundred and fifty-acre farm in Pilot Grove, near Bonneville, Missouri.

Delilah Ann Barger had married Colonel Higgs of Ray County. She met Colonel Higgs when visiting her brother, William, during the summer of 1874. Colonel Higgs was twelve years older than Delilah, but that didn’t seem to bother her.

John Wesley Barger met and courted Laura Reamer of Ray County, Missouri. On August 1, 1874, they became husband and wife. Laura Reamer was the daughter of Jesse Reamer, who was a full-blood Cherokee.

On January 3, 1876, the Missouri State Legislature was called into session. James moved his family into Jefferson City because Christina was expecting their fifth child.

On January 7, 1876, Christina went into hard labor. Her labor lasted twelve hours before given birth to their one and only son, John William Barger. John was a large baby and Christina had problems delivering. The birth had done harm to both her heart and female organs.

James was very excited about his son's birth but was very concerned about Christina.

John William weight nine pounds and nine ounces. He had brown hair and dark brown eyes just like his father.

Margaret Haddox Barger, wife of George Washington Barger helped with Christina's delivery. She and George were living in Jefferson City at the time.

"James, congratulations on a fine-looking boy," Margaret said as she handed James his son.

"Gosh, how much does this boy weigh?" James asked with pride in his voice.

Everyone laughed at James' remark. They could see the happiness on James's face. He now had a son to carry on his name.

"It's going to cost us a fortune to keep this boy fed," James said as he walked over to Christina and sat on the side of the bed.

"He looks like his father," Christina said with her beautiful smile. She was so happy that God had given them a son.

"Do you really think he looks like me?" James asked boastfully.

"Yes, look at his eyes."

"We did well, didn't we, Christina?" James said with pride.

"Yes, God has blessed us in so many ways and this little boy is one of the greatest yet," Christina responded.

"You must be exhausted," James said with concern.

"I'm a little tired," Christina drowsily replied.

CHAPTER 42

The birth of John William had taken a toll on Christina. She was torn badly giving birth and the stress had damaged her heart. She had little strength to get through the day. James, seeing the problem, hired Francis West of Cole County, Missouri, to come and stay with them.

Francis was twenty-two years old and the daughter of John and Helen West. Mr. and Mrs. West were Baptist and attended the Top of the Hill Baptist Church where James' brother-in-law, William Conant, pastored. James and Christina had become acquainted with the West family through church work.

Mr. West owned a farm south of Jefferson City, Missouri. His own family consisted of three sons and three daughters. Francis was the oldest daughter. She had long brown hair and brown eyes. In many ways she was like Christina, including her smile. She loved children and was a natural in getting along with them.

Christina enjoyed having Francis in the household. It was good having an adult to talk to while James was busy in making laws in the State Legislature.

John William was now nine months old and growing like a weed. He needed a lot of attention, but Christina was growing weaker every day. It upset her that she couldn't give her children the attention they deserved, especially the baby.

On October 20, 1876, Christina swooned trying to help Francis bathe the children. Francis managed to get her into bed and after Francis applied a cold wash cloth to her forehead, Christina came around.

"What happened to me?"

"You fainted, Christina," Francis said while continuing to wipe her forehead with the damp cloth.

"I don't know what's wrong with me. I don't have any strength and I feel awful."

"I'm going to get Dr. Logan. You lie still until I get back here!" Francis ordered as she hurriedly left the room.

Francis called the children together and instructed them to stay close to their mother while she went for Dr. Logan.

"Mary Elizabeth, you look in on your mother and take care of your sisters and little John while I'm gone. I'll be back as soon as I can. I can count on you, can't I?"

"Yes, Ma'am," replied Mary Elizabeth in a lady like voice.

"I won't be long."

In less than a half hour, Francis returned with Dr. Logan. Dr. Logan was the family doctor and had been treating Christina since she became ill. Just as he finished examining Christina, James came in. He went immediately to Christina and inquired, "What seems to be wrong, Christina."

"I fainted, James. I don't know what came over me. I don't seem to have any strength anymore," Christina said with tears running down her cheeks.

James reached down and kissed her on the lips. "You're going to be all right, Christina," James said as he took her right hand and lifted it to his lips. Christina loved the way he held her hand and the way he kissed it. James always seemed to know how to make her feel better.

"James, may I have a word with you?" Dr. Logan said as he closed his medicine bag and exited into the living room.

"Francis, see that Christina's comfortable," James said as he left the room.

"What's wrong with her, Doc?" James asked with a quivering voice.

"James, I'm afraid Christina is seriously ill."

"You don't mean she could die, do you?"

"She's got an infection, James. As you know, she had a rough time during the birth of John William. She lost a lot of blood during the delivery, and for some reason her blood is still weak. I'm going to give her some quinine, but, James, you must be prepared for the worst. She's not well," Dr. Logan said as he put his hand on James' shoulder. "The infection is causing the fever. We need to try to get her fever down. I'll check on her again tomorrow."

"Doc, if anything happens to Christina, I don't know what I will do, or whether I can take it," James said with tears welling in his eyes.

"James, God gives us the strength to endure a lot of pain. I know how much you love Christina, and I'm going to try to help her get through this, but God may be the only one that can truly help. You need to prepare yourself for the very worst," Dr. Logan said as he left the house.

James immediately sat down, put his face in his hands, and began to pray and cry.

"Francis, I want you to look after the children tonight. I'm going to stay close to Christina. I'll need some clean towels. Will you please get them for me?" James asked.

"I'll get the towels," Francis said as she went into the closet and brought him three clean towels.

"James don't worry about the children, I'll take good care of them."

"Thanks, Francis. I'm glad you are here. Your help with the children takes a great burden off Christina," James said as he poured water into a large bowl and carried it into the bedroom.

Christina's fever got worse. She began to hallucinate. James continued to wipe her with wet cloths throughout the night. He did everything he knew to break the fever, but nothing worked. As soon as the dawn broke, James sent Francis for Dr. Logan.

"Tell him to come quickly. I'm really worried about her. I think she's getting worse!

The waiting seemed like days instead of the forty-five minutes it took Dr. Logan to arrive.

"Doc, I can't get the fever to break," James said as Dr. Logan entered the room.

"Francis, the children are beginning to awake. Please see to them," James said as he closed the door to the bedroom.

Dr. Logan examined Christina and looked at James and shook his head. "Let me speak to you in the living room, James," Dr. Logan said as he nudged James from the room.

"It's not good is it, Doc?" James asked in anguish.

"No, James, it's not good at all. I don't think Christina is going to pull through this."

"Oh, God, please, no! Is there nothing we can do?" James asked in despair.

"I'm afraid that Christina's life is in God's hands."

James sat down in his chair and began to cry.

Francis couldn't stand it any longer. She moved across the room and put her arms around James to comfort him. "I'm so very sorry, James," Francis said in a sweet, soft voice.

It was as if Christina heard James crying. She called out in a raspy, "James, please come here."

James made his way back into the room with Dr. Logan following behind him. By this time, Mary Elizabeth, Sarah Alice, Rebecca, and Eliza Jane had gotten out of bed and were heading for their mother's room.

"Wait a minute, children," Francis said as she caught Mary Elizabeth before she entered the room. "Let's stay out here until Dr. Logan examines your mother," Francis said.

"My darling, James," Christina said stretching her arms outward to James.

James reached down and lifted her up, propping pillows behind her.

"James, I had this dream just now. I dreamed I saw a beautiful angel. He was dressed in all white. He was reaching out to me. James, I think God is calling me to heaven. I want to go to heaven, but I don't want to leave you and the kids alone," Christina said as tears ran down her cheek.

"Christina, my love. We don't want you to leave us. We need you to stay here with us. You must fight to stay with us," James said.

"I'm so weak, James. I want to see my children while I can still talk to them. Please let me see them."

James looked at Dr. Logan and he nodded his head as a sign of approval. James went to the door and said, "Children, your mother wants to talk to you." As they entered the room, Francis was holding John William in her arms. James took him and held him while Christina visited with the girls.

"Come over here, my little angels," Christina said to the girls.

Mary Elizabeth, Sarah Alice, Rebecca, and Eliza Jane walked over to the side of the bed where their mother could touch them.

"Girls, your mommy is very sick. I want you to take good care of your father and your little brother, John William. Will you promise me you will do that for me?" Christina said as she struggled to remain calm in front of her daughters.

Mary Elizabeth sensed the seriousness in her mother's voice. "I promise you, Mother. I'll take good care of Father and John William."

"I know you will, Mary, and I know I can depend on you," Christina said as she reached over and gave her a kiss on the cheek.

"I want every one of you to get a good education. Will you promise me you will work hard in school?"

"We promise, Mommy."

"I need a big hug from all of you right now," Christina said as each gave her a big kiss and hug. Christina looked at James holding John William and said, "Please bring John William to me."

As James handed John William to Christina, John lay his head across Christina's breast. "That's my big boy," Christina said as she held him close to her.

"Francis, please see that the children get their breakfast now," Christina said. "Come with me, children," Francis said as she came across the room and took Eliza Jane and Rebecca by the hand.

Mary turned again to her mother as though she sensed her mother was dying. She said, "I love you, Mother."

"I love you too, Baby," Christina whispered back.

"Christina, you need to get some rest now," Dr. Logan said.

"I've got to talk to James first."

"Is it all right, Doc?" James asked.

"Here, let me have John William. I'll be right outside if you need me," Doc Logan said as he left the bedroom.

"James, I know I'm dying," Christina said.

"Shush... don't say that, Christina!"

"It's true, James! The angel is giving me time to say my goodbyes. I want you to promise me something."

"What is it my, darling?"

"I want you to promise me you will find a good wife, one who will take good care of our children. Someone like Francis. The children like Francis. She would make them a good mother. I want you to promise me you will get married again so the children will have a mother."

James could no longer hold back his emotions. He took Christina's left hand and clutched it in both of his hands. Tears streamed down his cheeks. The woman he loved more than life itself was dying. How could he even think about marrying anyone else? He knew he could never love anyone like he loved Christina.

"Christina, I don't think I could ever love another woman as I love you. I don't know if I can promise you what you're asking of me," James said as he laid his head on her breast. As he lay there, she ran her fingers through his hair.

"Promise me, James," Christina said again.

"Christina, I love you more than I ever thought possible. I wish it was me who was in this bed sick," James said as he cried out.

"Please stop, James. You have got to be strong. We've had many good years together. God has blessed us more than we both deserve. We have always trusted him to lead our paths, and He knows what He's doing. Don't you believe that?"

"Right now, I don't know what I believe."

"James, please hold me," Christina said as she put both arms around his neck. James pulled her near him and held her tight. Her body was so hot. She was so weak! As he held her, he felt her take a deep breath. He kept waiting for her to breathe again, but nothing happened. He then realized what had happened. The angel, which Christina had seen had come and taken her soul with him. James let out a scream, "God, O, God, no!"

James realized he would never again hold this warm body in his arms. He would never again be able to kiss her sweet lips and run his fingers through her long blonde hair. God, what would he do without Christina?

Dr. Logan heard James' cries and re-entered the room. As he approached the bed, he knew what had happened. He reached over and touched James on the shoulder.

"James, she's gone. You need to let her go."

James continued to hold her in his arms.

"I don't know if I can live without Christina."

"She would want you to go on living, James. The children need you. You will need to be strong for them."

James gently laid Christina back on her pillow. He turned to Dr. Logan and said, "Doc, I've lost the dearest thing to me. How can I go on without her? She was my best friend, my inspiration, my advisor, my encourager, my everything."

"James, life will go on, and time will take care of the pain you feel right now," Dr. Logan said as he put his hand on James' shoulder.

"I've got to tell the children. How can I tell them their mother has just died?" James asked as he turned and looked at Dr. Logan.

"You go on, I'll take care of things in here. I'll also take care of the burial arrangements.

"Doc, I will be taking Christina back to Moniteau County for burial. I want her buried in the New Hope Baptist Church Cemetery. That's always been her wishes."

As James opened the bedroom door, Francis was reading the children a book. She stopped reading as James came through the door. From the expression on his face, she knew Christina had died. Francis was holding John William in her lap. James crossed the room and said, "Francis, I need to talk to the children. If you will, please stay with us."

Francis nodded her head, indicating she would stay.

"Children, I need to talk to you about your mother," James said as he pulled another chair up close to where Francis and the children were sitting.

"Your mother has gone to be with Jesus in heaven. Do you know what I mean?" He asked.

Mary Elizabeth dropped her head and began to cry. She then looked up with her beautiful eyes swimming in tears and said, "Mommy's dead, isn't she?"

"Yes, my dear, Mommy is dead," James said as he reached out and pulled her near him, holding her close. Sarah Alice, Rebecca, and Eliza Jane began to cry along with Mary Elizabeth.

"Come here, girls," James said.

As they gathered around his chair, He reached out and pulled them all into his arms. "Your Mommy was a very brave person. She had lots of faith in God, and she hated to leave us, but God needed her in heaven. Your Mother wants each of you to be brave and strong. She wants you to be courageous and help your father with John William," James said, trying to hold back tears. He was trying to be strong, but this was hard, one of the hardest things he had ever done.

James carried Christina's body back to Moniteau County where he buried her at the New Hope Baptist Church Cemetery.

Friends from Jefferson City, as well as the surrounding counties, came to pay their last respects to one of the kindest, sweetest ladies in Moniteau County. After the grave side service, James asked his mother to accompany the children back to the farm.

"Ma, would you please see to the children for a while. I want to stay here for a spell with Christina. Do you mind?"

"No, Son, I don't mind. I'll get Jesse to take us back to the farm." Nancy said. She sensed that James needed this time to be along with Christina.

"I'll help with the children," Martha Jane said as she hugged James.

"James, is there anything I can do?" Jesse asked as he placed his hand on James' shoulder.

"Thanks, Jesse. Right now, I need a little time with Christina. I'll see all of you back at the farm," James said as everyone left him standing by Christina's casket.

"Christina, I know your soul is presently in Heaven with our savior, Jesus Christ. I find comfort in knowing that. I've thought a lot about our last conversation before God's angel came and took your soul into heaven.

"Christina, my darling, it's so hard to say goodbye to you! I don't know if I can carry on without you, but I promise you, I will be the best father I can be for our children.

"My darling please forgive me for any neglect and hardship I may have caused you. I'm torn between whether to give up my seat in the Missouri State Legislature or whether to give up the farm. I know I can't do both and still be the type of father I need to be. Please ask God to send me a sign.

"Christina, you asked me to find another wife, someone like Francis who would make the children a good mother. I'm going to need God's help with that request. My darling, I still can't promise you, I will do that! I could never love another woman as I've loved you. You were my first love, and you will always hold that honor in my heart. You have made me the happiest man on earth. You have given me four lovely daughters and a son. How can I thank you enough?

"Please know I will look forward to seeing you in heaven. I don't know when God will send his angel for me, but if it's tomorrow, it will be right for me.

"I will see that our children get a good education and I promise you, my darling, our children will not want for anything. I'll see to it that the girls get the very best weddings, just like we had. I will make sure John William knows about his mom and that she was the greatest woman who walked God's earth.

"Christina, I'm going now. I'll come back to see you often. Please know that as long as I shall live, there will be flowers placed on your grave on our wedding anniversary date. I'll never forget you. Please don't forget me. Please tell God to help me be a good father and a good person.

"I look forward to seeing you in God's Heavenly Kingdom. Goodbye, Christina."

CHAPTER 43

James and the children were happy to have Nancy join them in Jefferson City. Her presence seemed to help James and the children get through the hard times. She was also very helpful to Francis in looking after the children when Francis cleaned, cooked, and managed the household. After three weeks, Nancy decided her mission was completed. James and the children could now handle Christina's death. It was time for her to return home to Cooper County.

On November 15, 1877, James carried Nancy back to Cooper County. Nancy's marriage to Elihur B. White had lasted a little over one year. Mr. White who was a lot older than Nancy had died of pneumonia and left Nancy with the farm in the Lamine Township near Arrow Rock.

Nancy was still a healthy lady and was able to hire workers to help her run the farm. She liked the farm and decided that was where she wanted to live out her life. James spent two nights with her before he returned to his home in Jefferson City.

On the way back to Jefferson City he stopped by and visited Jesse and Margaret and to check on the farm he still had in Moniteau County.

He found Jesse, Margaret, George Albert, and Alfred doing fine. George Albert and Alfred reminded James of his and Jesse's early years. They shared several interests together, two of which were hunting and fishing.

After James returned to his home in Jefferson City, he returned to his normal duties as a State Representative for District 8.

James felt secure in having Francis looking after his children. She attended church, cooked meals, and kept the children clean, just like Christina. On Sunday, she prepared special meals the family had become accustomed to when Christina was living. The Sunday meal was always the favorite. During the Sunday meal, each child was given an opportunity to tell what happened during the week at school.

James' parents, Allen and Nancy Barger, believed children should be heard and not hidden. This family custom continued among Allen and Nancy's children and their families. Regardless of the subject, no one ever laughed at another's opinion. These minutes of sharing around the dinner table was a time of family bonding and family ties. The children felt quite comfortable talking about their everyday lives.

After dinner on February 12, 1878, James asked Francis to join him on the front porch. In the past, the front porch had become an important center for discussion and resolving important family matters for James and Christina.

"Francis, I've been doing some serious thinking about what I need to do for the family and my future. I'm considering not running for another term in the state legislature. The children need a full-time father, and I'm thinking seriously about returning to full time farming. The only hitch, I need someone to help me raise my children," James said as he paused.

Francis looked at him, not knowing what to say nor where the conversation was heading.

"What do you think?" James asked.

"If you feel it's what you need to do, then do it," Francis said. James looked down and didn't respond to Francis' answer.

Finally, she asked, "Have you found someone who can help you raise the children?"

"I believe so, but she doesn't know yet," James said with a smile.

"Who is she?" Francis asked.

"She is someone whom I've grown to love and respect in the last few months. She is warm, gentle, and compassionate. She relates well to children and above all, she is a great cook," James said.

Francis looked perplexed. She thought, could James be talking about me? Although, she wanted the woman to be her, she didn't dare jump to conclusions. As James smiled at her, she said, "This woman appears to have captured your heart, James."

"She certainly has. I didn't think I could ever be attracted to another woman, but I'm very attracted to this woman.

Wanting to believe it was her, Francis' heart began to beat frantically within her chest. Never, had any man spoken to her as James had, and yet, she was uncertain he meant her. "James, whoever she is, she should be proud you care so much about her."

"If you were me, how would you approach her?" James asked.

At this time, Francis really began to question whether James was referring to her or someone else. "I think you should just tell her straight out how much you cared for her. If she responds positively to your comments, then I think you have your foot in the door, so to speak," Francis said.

"So, that's what you would do?" James asked.

"If you really want my opinion, that's exactly what I would do," Francis said.

"Francis, the person I've been talking about is you," James said as he reached out and took her hands.

"Oh, James, I didn't have any idea."

"Francis, I'm a very lonely man. I need someone to share the rest of my life with. I need a mother for my children. If you would do me the honor, I would like to court you. It would please me and make me happy."

What Francis had been hoping for was now coming true. "James, I would be honored to be courted by you."

"Do you really mean that?" James asked.

"Yes, I really mean it, but let me first make a confession to you."

"What is it?"

"When you were talking about the lady, I was hoping it was me. I've loved you from the first day I met you. I've been praying that God would lead you to me in some way. I have learned to admire and respect you for your kindness, generosity, and for being a good father to your children. You're a great father, and I know you were a good husband to Christina. I feel honored you would want to court me."

James got up from his chair, took Francis by both hands and helped her from her chair. "Would you mind very much if I kissed you?"

"I've never been kissed by a man, but if you want to kiss me, you have my permission," Francis said, with her heart pounding so hard it might burst out of her chest.

James gently put his arms around her, pulling her near him, and gently kissed her lips. As soon as his lips met hers, her legs became weak. She felt faint. She had longed to be kissed by James and had wondered what it would be like. Now she was experiencing and loving it. James' first kiss was short. He didn't want to scare Francis away. When he saw she responded favorably, his second kiss was with greater intensity. This time Francis returned his kiss with total acceptance.

The day of February 12, 1878, was the beginning of a two-month courtship between James and Francis.

On the beautiful sunny day, April 14, 1878, at 10:00 A.M. James and Francis were married. They were married by James' brother-in-law, William Conant, pastor of the Hill Top Baptist Church in Jefferson City. It was a simple wedding with little publicity. The wedding was attended by friends from Moniteau and Cole Counties. Several of James' legislative friends were present for the wedding and reception.

Elizabeth, Sarah Alice, and Rebecca were bridesmaids while Eliza Jane and John William acted as flower girl and ring bearer.

After the wedding, the children went home with James' sister, Mary Ann Conant, while James took Francis to his farm back in Moniteau County for their honeymoon.

Upon arriving at the farm, around 6:30 P.M. on April 14, James and Francis were surprised to find food, presents, and greeting cards as they entered their home. This was the neighbors' way of saying welcome home to the newly-weds.

James and Francis loved being on the farm. They loved watching the children have the freedom to run, play, wade in the creek, and experience riding to church in the big wagon just as James and his family had done.

James enjoyed getting the soil ready for planting season. It was also good to see Jesse and Margaret every day. During James' and Jesse's spare time, they fished and hunted. There was plenty of fish and wild game on the Bargers' dining tables. They renewed the close ties they had enjoyed before James moved to Jefferson City to serve in the Missouri State Legislature.

The summer of 1878 was not a good time for farmers or for James and Jesse Barger. It was hot and dry, and the crops burned up. This was awfully discouraging to James and Jesse. Although they suffered poor corn and tobacco crops, they were blessed with a good hay crop from an early spring cutting. The hay was harvested before the hot, dry weather set in. The good hay would furnish feed for the cattle and horses during the winter months.

On July 4, 1878, while James' and Jesse's families were celebrating on the bank of the Missouri River the first tragedy struck the Jesse Barger family. James, Jesse, Margaret, and Francis were preparing food for the July 4th celebration when they heard screams coming from the river. James and Jesse immediately started running toward the swimming hole where the children had gone to swim.

As they approached the swimming hole, they met Mary Elizabeth who was crying and screaming, "Pa, Uncle Jesse, come quick! Alfred is drowning!"

The children pointed to the area where Alfred had gone under and not resurfaced. Immediately, James and Jesse quickly removed their shoes and swam to the area where Alfred had gone under. After diving for several minutes, James located Alfred in deep water. As he reached and grabbed Alfred's pants, his heart and mind told him Alfred was dead. This was Jesse's second born. How would he and Margaret live without this boy? James thought as he surfaced. As he reached the surface, Jesse swam over to him to help James get Alfred back to the bank. On reaching the bank, Jesse and James took turns trying to revive Alfred, but to no avail. Alfred was gone.

Alfred was buried in the New Hope Baptist Church Cemetery near Marion, Missouri. The tragedy of losing Alfred was very hard on Margaret and Jesse. A big part of their lives went with Alfred to the grave. Losing a child was the hardest thing a parent could experience. God had given them two sons and now they were left with one.

Although, Jesse and Margaret were both Christians, they found it hard at times to not question God on why He allowed this tragedy to occur. It was only after the birth of their daughter, Rosa Marie Barger, that they came to terms with God about the loss of Alfred.

The Christmas season was always a joyful occasion for the Bargers. Nancy Barger was still the pillar of the Barger family and insisted the family be together on Christmas day. This family tradition had begun when Allen Barger was still living.

William T., John Wesley, George Washington, and Delilah's came from Ray County, Missouri. Mary Ann Conant and family came from Jefferson City. Martha Jane, Harvey Ryan, and Martha Jane's three children, Allen, Joseph, and Nancy Tull were present from Moniteau County. During the Christmas season, William T's. and George Washington Barger's families stayed with James and Francis while John Wesley and his family stayed with Jesse. Delilah and Mary Ann's family stayed at Nancy's home. Allen and Nancy Barger's ancestors had out grown Nancy's home and for Christmas dinner, James and Francis Barger hosted the Barger clan.

The family enjoyed a huge dinner together and exchanged gifts. The men sat around the fireplace and discussed political issues, farming, and told tall tales about their adventures of hunting and fishing.

"James, I'm still encouraging you and Jesse to sell your farms and move to Ray County. I assure you, you won't regret it. The farm land is rich, and our corn crops didn't burn up in Ray County as they did here in Moniteau," William T. said.

"William T., I've decided to come to Ray County in February. I want to check out this rich farming land you've been bragging about," James said as he gave William T., a pat on the back.

James kept his word and on February 10, 1879, he went to Ray County to visit William T. George, John Wesley, and his sister Delilah Tarwater.

William T. was right. The land was quality farm land. James could see immediately that William T.'s bragging was real. James could perceive making a good living farming this soil.

"What do you think, James?" William T. asked as James opened his hand to release a hand full of rich, dark, soil which freely flowed from his hand.

"I think you're right," James said.

"Well, does this mean you'll be moving here?" William asked with eagerness.

"It's going to be a hard decision. I've become really attached to my farm."

"I know it will be hard, but we miss ya'll something terrible. If you move, I'm sure Ma, Martha Jane, and Jesse would move too. We could again be a family," William T. said with excitement.

"I don't know about Jesse. He's a lot like me. He loves his farm and he loves Moniteau County. I don't think Margaret would want to move off and leave her family. Anyway, I will give Ray County some strong consideration."

James returned to Moniteau County on February 23rd to find that Margaret was sick in bed with pneumonia.

"Come in, James, it's so good to see you back home," Jesse said as he took James' coat and hat.

"How is Margaret, Jesse?"

"I'm worried about her, James. Ma is with her now. We can't seem to get the fever down. We've done everything the doctor told us to do, but so far, nothing has worked."

"May I see her?" James asked. "Sure, come with me." As they entered the room, Nancy got up from where she was sitting next to Margaret's bed and greeted James with a kiss. "It's good to have you home, Son," she said.

"It's good to be home, Ma."

James walked over to Margaret's bed and touched her hand. She opened her eyes and smiled. "James, when did you get back?"

"Just now," he said as he picked up her hand.

"I'm glad you're home. I hate being bedfast like this, but I'm so weak, I don't have the strength to stand up."

"We want you to rest and get well. We don't want you to worry about anything," James said as he patted her on the hand.

Margaret had always trusted and loved James. She knew he was a kind and considerate man. She knew he meant every word he said.

"Thanks, James. Everyone has been so good to me. Your mother has been here since I've been sick. She needs to get some rest."

"I'm doing just fine. Don't you worry about me. I may be getting old, but I'm still very strong, and I'm going to take good care of you," Nancy said with a smile.

Margaret smiled back and said, "You see, I'm in good hands."

"James, if anything happens to me, I want you and your family to help take care of Jesse, George Albert, and Rosa. They are going to need help," Margaret said with tears running down her cheeks.

"Margaret, don't even talk that way. You're going to get well soon," James said as he touched her hand.

On February 25, 1878, in the early hours of the morning, a knock was heard at James' door. James went to the door and found George Albert. "Uncle James, Pa wants you to come to the house right away," George Albert said.

"What's wrong, Son?" James asked.

"It's Ma," he replied.

"What is it, James?" Francis asked.

"It's Margaret. Jesse wants me to come now," he said as he finished putting on his pants and lacing up his shoes.

"Do you want me to go with you?"

"No, please stay and see after the children. Let's go, George Albert," James said as he put his arm around George's thin shoulder.

As James entered the house, he found Nancy sitting in a rocking chair in front of the fireplace. She got up and came over to greet him, and whispered in his ear, “She’s gone, James.”

George sensed what his grandmother was telling his Uncle James and began to cry. Nancy put her arms around him and held him. She turned to James and said, “Why don’t you go see if Jesse needs you.”

As James entered the bedroom, he found Jesse holding Margaret’s right hand and just staring at her. James walked across the room and placed his hands on Jesse’s shoulders. Jesse turned to James and said, “She’s gone, James. My beloved Margaret is gone.”

“I’m so sorry, Jesse,” James said as he pressed harder on Jesse’s shoulders.

“She was a wonderful wife. I don’t know what I’m going to do without her,” Jesse said as tears continued to run down his cheeks.

“You will do as I’ve done, Jesse. You will grieve over her death. You will miss her something awful, but God will give you strength, and you will go on living.”

“Right now, I wish I was dead,” Jesse said as he began to sob again.

“Stop that, Jesse. You have George Albert and Rosa to consider. They will need you! They are more than a reason to live. George and Rosa need their pa, and you need them.”

“I know you’re right, but it hurts so bad. First it was Alfred, now it’s Margaret. What other bad things are going to happen to me and my family?”

“I feel your pain, but believe me, God will give you the strength to endure this pain.”

Margaret was buried in the New Hope Baptist Church Cemetery on February 28, 1879, next to her son, Alfred.

This was the second time Jesse endured the pain of losing a loved one. He thought, how much more can I take?

The next few weeks were made easier by Nancy moving in with Jesse. Since Nancy was living along at her farm at Arrow Rock it was easy for her to come to be with Jesse. She would always be there for one of her children. She felt a deep need to be available to Jesse and his family during this crisis period. Whatever she could do for Jesse, she would do. He needed her, and she would be there for him.

On March 10, 1879, James approached Jesse about moving to Ray County, Missouri. "Jesse, I've been thinking about moving to Ray County. William T. has been wanting us to move for several years. After seeing the rich farming soil in Ray County, I'm convinced we could make a better living farming there.

"I've always known this day would come," Jesse said.

"Why don't we both sell our farms and move to Ray County? We could take Ma with us and I'm sure Martha Jane and her family would move too. We would all be together again."

"Except for Mary Ann and her family. I don't think they would ever move to Ray County," Jesse said.

"Since William is pastor of Hill Top Baptist, I guess you're right about that."

"James, I don't want to leave this farm. There is too much here for me to leave behind. Margaret loved this place. She would want me to stay here."

Since James and Jesse had always shared land, a barn, and equipment it made it hard to decide what to do with his farm.

"Jesse, I'm concerned about selling my farm since we've shared our land, barn, and equipment. How's this going to affect you?" James asked with concern.

"I would love to have your portion of the farm," Jesse said.

"What are you suggesting, Jesse?"

"If I can raise the money, would you be willing to sell me your hundred acres? I would like your house as well since it is larger than mine."

"Certainly, I would. I would love to see this land stay in the Bargers' name," James said, with excitement in his voice.

"How much would you have to have for the house and your one hundred acres?"

"I really don't know right now. Why don't we go to California tomorrow and ask the appraiser to give us an appraisal of the house and farm. Then we will talk about a price."

"That sounds good to me," Jesse said.

The First State Bank of California loaned Jesse the money to buy James's farm and house. He now had two hundred acres to farm.

"I plan to sell my house and five acres to help pay on my note at the bank. Don't you think that's a good idea?" Jesse asked.

"I think that's using good business sense," James answered.

Before moving to Ray County, James and Jessie attended their first reunion of the 26th Missouri Infantry Regiment. The reunion was held in Jefferson City. It was the appropriate location since the 26th Missouri Regiment was mustered out in 1865.

James and Jesse enjoyed visiting with their old friends. It was decided at the reunion that every five years the 26th Missouri Regiment would meet in Jefferson City.

In years to come, James and Jesse would be regular attendants at the 26th Missouri Regiment reunions.

On March 26, 1879, James and his family loaded their belongings and set out for Ray County. It took them three days to get to William T.'s home in the Camden Township between Richmond and Orrick, Missouri. William T. opened his house to James and his family. He had done well in Ray county and his house consisted of four bedrooms, a kitchen and a larger living area. The house also had a porch across the front.

The next day, William T. took James to look at a 150-acre farm which had just come up for sale. The farm was owned by Jake Logan, who had moved back north due to family problems. It was being managed by his cousin, Jack Townsend. The farm had a big house, which would be just the right size for James's family. Francis, who now was called, Fannie, loved it.

"We like it too," Mary Elizabeth said.

"So, you and your family like this home and farm, hey?" Mr. Townsend asked.

"Yes Sir, I believe we do," James said looking around at Fannie.

"Then are we ready to talk business?" Mr. Townsend asked.

"How much does your cousin want for this place?" James asked.

"Since it's prime farming land, he wants $2,500 dollars for the land and the house," Mr. Townsend answered.

"That's a little too steep for me. I couldn't pay more than $2000. James said.

"Mr. Barger, this is some of the best farming land in Camden Township. I don't think my cousin will take any less.

"I can offer your cousin $2,000 in cash for this place."

"Cash, you say?" Mr. Townsend asked.

"Yes, Sir! Tell your cousin I can pay him cash."

"I'll have to send him a wire tonight and ask him. I can't make that decision for him," Mr. Townsend replied.

"When do you think I'll have your cousin's answer?" James asked.

"I'll let you know as soon as I hear from him," Mr. Townsend said.

Meanwhile, William T. took James to meet Mr. Ben Bradley, President of the Citizens State Bank in Richmond, Missouri.

"Mr. Bradley, I want you to meet my brother, James A. Barger, who has just moved here from Moniteau County."

"James, I'm pleased to meet you," Mr. Bradley said as he reached out and shook James's hand.

"I'm pleased to make your acquaintance," James said.

"Sit down, both of you," Mr. Bradley said.

"William T. has told me about you serving District 8 in the Missouri Legislature. That must have been exciting?"

"Yes, Sir, it was quite an experience," James replied.

"I'm curious as why you gave up being a state representative to come to Ray County."

"My first love is farming. I've been farming the biggest part of my life. Farming allows me more time with my family. Serving in the state legislature doesn't leave much time for quality family life," James said.

"So, you're a family man."

"Yes, Sir, I have a wife and five children who need my everyday attention. They're excited to be here in Ray County."

"Well, we're happy to have you folks here. Now, what can I do for you?"

"I'm interested in purchasing the Logan farm in the Camden Township."

"That's a good farm. It was too bad that Mr. Logan had to go back north because of his family. He was making good money on that farm before leaving. I'm assuming you need some money?" Mr. Bradley asked.

"Yes, sir. I need about $1000," James replied.

"How much is Logan asking for that farm?"

"He's asking $2500, but I've made him a counter offer of $2000."

"I'm assuming you have some money to purchase the farm."

"Yes Sir. I have the money for the farm but need about one thousand dollars to purchase farming equipment, seed, and mules," James explained.

"You appear to have a good business head on you, Mr. Barger. I can't think of any reason Citizens State Bank can't make you a loan."

"Thanks, Mr. Bradley," James said as he got up and shook his hand. "I'll know in the next day or two if Mr. Logan accepts my offer," James said as he turned to walk out.

"Just let me know when you're ready," Mr. Bradley said.

Mr. Logan accepted James' offer and within a week he had moved his family into their new home.

James' farm consisted of seventy-five good acres of rich river bottom land that lay along the Missouri River which separated Ray and Lafayette Counties. He also had thirty acres that was suited for cotton. The rest of the land was in pasture.

Two weeks after James moved his family into their new home, Fannie revealed some good news to James. Fannie loved to lie on James' right arm and cuddle. On that night, she cuddle really close to him.

"Are you wanting something, Fannie?" James asked as he looked at her in his flirting way.

"No, but I've got some really good news," Fannie said.

"What's this good news?"

"I'm going to have a baby."

"A baby! Are you sure?"

"Yes, one hundred percent sure. I've already felt him moving inside of me."

"How do you know it's a boy?"

"My mother always told me if I felt the baby moving on my right side first, it would be a boy. So, I'm sure it's going to be a boy."

"Fannie, as long as our child is healthy, I really don't mind if it's a girl or boy. But if you say it's going to be a boy, then I best plan for a boy, right?"

"Right!" Fannie said as she goosed James in the side.

On October 9, 1880, Fannie went into labor. It was a hard labor which lasted for a good six hours before she gave birth to a little boy. The birth was a breech. The baby lived for only a few minutes. The breech birth tore Fannie badly. She lost a lot of blood which weakened her considerably.

Mrs. Maddox, an experienced mid-wife came out of the bedroom and motioned James to the bedroom. James had been waiting nervously with his brothers, George, William T., and John Wesley.

"James, I'm sorry. We did all we could but couldn't save your son. He came breech," Mrs. Maddox said as she reached out and touched James on the arm.

"How is Fannie?" James asked.

"She isn't doing too well either. She's lost a lot of blood and the baby coming breech has torn her pretty bad. I'm going to do the best I can with her. Let me go back inside, and I'll call for you as soon as I can."

"Mrs. Maddox, I would like to see my son."

"Very well, James, I'll bring him to you."

James stood holding the baby as if he were alive. He was a big boy and would have made a big man had he lived, James thought.

"I want him buried in the South Point Cemetery near Orrick, Missouri," James said to his brothers.

Mrs. Maddox came back to the living room and told James he could go in to see Fannie. "She is weak, so don't stay long."

"William T, would you look after the baby while I see Fannie?" James asked.

"You go on, we will see to the baby." William T. responded.

James entered the room and went straight to her bed. She was just lying on her back staring up at the ceiling.

"Fannie, my dear, it's me, James," he said as he picked up her hand and kissed it.

Fannie turned her head slowly toward James and asked, "Do we have us a baby boy?"

"Fannie, you gave birth to a beautiful boy."

Before he could get out any more words she asked, "May I see him?" Tears began to swell in his eyes.

"James, what's wrong?"

"Fannie, our little boy didn't make it. He was a breech baby."

"Oh, my God, James!" She screamed.

"It's going to be all right, Fannie," James said as he lifted her up and held her.

"Why, James, how could this happen?"

"I don't know," James replied.

"Why did God let my baby die?"

"Fannie, God is a good God. We don't always know why he allows things to happen. Maybe he needed our little boy as one of His little angels. We have to trust that he knows best."

For several days it was touch-and-go for Fannie. She got an infection from being torn so badly. Although she healed physically, she began to suffer from melancholy. This went on for two months. James tried everything he knew to make her happy, but to no avail. He finally decided to send for his mother who was still living with Jesse. Jesse didn't need Nancy since he had remarried. He was now married to Mary Ann Scott. If anyone could nurse Fannie back to good health, his mother could.

James sat down and wrote his mother a letter. He described Fannie's constant depression. He asked his mother to come live with him and the family. He needed her help until Fannie returned to her normal self.

Nancy was always ready to help any of her children. One week after getting James' letter, she and Jesse pulled up in front of his home in the Camden community. The children darted out on the front porch to greet their grandmother and Uncle Jesse. "Grandma! Grandma!" They yelled as they each hugged her.

"Ma, I'm so glad to see you," James said as he hugged and kissed her on the cheek.

"It's good to see you and the kids, James. I'm here to help you," Nancy said.

"It's so good to see you, Brother," James said as he walked over and hugged Jesse.

"It's been awhile, James," Jesse replied.

"Tell me, Jesse, what's it like being married to Mary Ann Scott?"

James had known Mary Ann Scott when he lived in Moniteau County. She was married to Samuel Scott at the time. She was an attractive lady who was well liked in the community.

"Mary Ann needed a man and I needed a mother for my children. She is a very nice lady, and I love her. She treats me well and is good to George Albert and Rosa."

"I'm happy for you, Jesse, and I'm glad you didn't wait long to marry."

"How long has Fannie been the way she is?" Jesse asked.

"Ever since the death of our son. She just mopes around. The children and I have done everything we know to do. She doesn't seem to notice we're here most of the time."

"Ma will be able to help Fannie. I would bet you a $10 bill that Ma will have Fannie smiling again in two weeks," Jesse said.

"I hope you're right, Jesse. I'm really worried about her."

"If anyone can do it, Ma can."

After a two-day visit with James and his family, Jesse return to his family in Moniteau County.

"Ma, what do you think is wrong with Fannie?" James asked.

"Son, I've seen several women go through this period of mourning after losing a child. I'll do everything I can for her.

I've been watching her and talking to her these past two days. She is suffering from deep melancholy. It may take a while to get her out of it, but I've got hope she will become normal again," Nancy said as she took James' right hand and held it.

"Ma, I'm so glad you're here. The children are so happy you're here. They love you and so do I."

Nancy spent several hours during the day walking Fannie outside. They would walk arm and arm in the woods and along the bank of the Missouri River. At times they would just sit watching the water flow freely down the Missouri. They enjoyed the fresh outdoor fragrances of the honeysuckle as they sat soaking up the sunshine. Nancy felt Fannie should be outside and not cooped up within four walls of a house. Breathing the fresh air, smelling the sweet honeysuckle, hearing the birds chirp, and watching the squirrels play would be good therapy for Fannie.

Nancy was right. Fannie soon began to improve. It wasn't long before she began to talk. After three weeks, she began to help Nancy and the girls do the washing, cooking, and ironing. After two months, Fannie was back to normal. Nancy had accomplished something that no one else had been able to do.

"Ma, you have performed a miracle," James said.

"No, Son, God has performed the miracle. He's the one who deserves the credit."

CHAPTER 44

James prospered during the next two years. The farm returned a good profit and he leased more farm land. He hired additional help and soon was known as one of the most successful farmers in Ray County.

Mary Elizabeth, Sarah Alice, Rebecca, and Eliza Jane were growing into beautiful young ladies. John William was handsome as well.

James felt blessed as God continued to give him joy and happiness. His family would soon grow as Fannie was again expecting.

Things were going well also for Jesse back in Moniteau County. He and his wife, Mary Ann, became proud parents of a new son, Gilbert Barger. George Albert and Rosa Marie were very happy to have a little brother in the family.

On January 8, 1882, Fannie gave birth to a healthy son. This time she had a normal delivery. She and James named him Walter Jon Barger. He, like John William, would have a close relationship with his father.

In early March of 1882, James decided it was time to have a Barger family reunion.

James mailed invitations to all the Barger and Bullock relatives scattered throughout parts of Tennessee and Missouri.

The first Barger family reunion was held on July 4, 1882. It was a grand occasion. Nancy Barger was thrilled to have all her children and relatives from Tennessee and Missouri together. The reunion lasted three days and was held on James' farm near Camden, Missouri, in Ray County. The family decided that a Barger reunion would be held on July 4th of each year in Camden. This would become another family tradition.

During the next two years, James purchased more land in Ray County. He continued to farm on a large scale.

In June of 1884, a typhoid fever outbreak hit Ray County. Several people died of this outbreak. The Bargers were not exempted from the fever. On June 24, 1884, Fannie came down with the fever. Her past health problems went against her. She became very weak and bedridden. James called in Doctor Morrison, a well-known doctor in Ray County.

"Doc, how is Fannie?" James asked.

"James, I'm afraid it doesn't look good for Fannie. You must prepare yourself for the worse. Another thing, I would get someone outside the home to attend to Fannie. The kids don't need to be around her."

"Doc, have there been many people in the county die of this fever?" James asked.

"Several have died, James. It's taking its toll on this county."

Taking Doc Morrison's recommendation, James employed Betsy Tarwater, from Camden to nurse Fannie in their home.

On the morning of June 26th, Fannie had a turn for the worse. James was by her side. "James!" Fannie cried out.

"I'm here, my dear," James replied picking up Fannie's hand.

"James, I'm so hot. I could use some water."

"Mrs. Tarwater, please pour a glass of water for Fannie."

Fannie tried to drink but was too weak to swallow. "James, I'm going to die, aren't I?"

"Fannie, you're going to get well," James said. What else could he say, he thought.

"I know I'm dying, James."

"Don't talk anymore, Fannie. You are wearing yourself out," James said.

"Will you tell our children that I love them?" Fannie asked knowing that she shouldn't expose them further to the fever.

"Fannie, I'm so sorry. I wish you could see the kids."

"I don't want them to see me this away. Please promise me that you will let them know how much they mean to me." She was getting weaker by the minute.

"I'll tell them, Fannie." James said as tears began to well in his eyes.

"James, I love you so much. I hate to leave you and the children. You've been my whole life. You've made me the happiest woman on earth. You......." Fannie stopped.

"Fannie!" James screamed out.

James lifted Fannie into his arms and held her as she took her last breath. His second wife, whom God had given him, had just passed on as Christina had several years earlier. How could he stand another loss?

"Mr. James, I believe Fannie is gone. You need to let go," Mrs. Tarwater said as she reached out and touched him on his left shoulder.

James gently lowered Fannie's warm body back on the bed. He propped the pillow securely behind her head as he brushed her long black hair from her face. He leaned over and kissed her lips which were still burning from the fever.

"Goodbye, my darling. I'll see you in our heavenly home."

James buried Fannie in the Southpoint Cemetery near Orrick, Missouri, beside their first son, James Edward Barger.

After the death of Fannie, James caught himself questioning the wisdom of God. He couldn't understand why God took away two beautiful ladies out of his life. He wondered if he had done something he was being punished for. Although, the thoughts went through his mind, he never lost his faith in God. In his heart, he knew God was a loving and a merciful God. He would not blame God for Christina's and Fannie's deaths.

CHAPTER 45

After the death of Fannie, Nancy came to live with James and his family. She felt compelled to be near her sons and daughters who had migrated to Ray County. Everyone except for Mary Ann and Jesse were now living in Ray County. Nancy was now sixty-nine years old but still in good health. She was a big help in seeing after Walter Jon especially since Mary Elizabeth and Sarah Alice were showing a strong interest in boys.

Mary Elizabeth, now seventeen years old, was being courted by Douglas Kohal of Orrick, Missouri. They had met at a square dance in Orrick, and Douglas had swept her off her feet.

Sarah Alice Barger was now fifteen years old, was being courted by Marion Thompson.

Rebecca Ann was twelve, Eliza Jane was ten, John William was eight, and Walter Jon was two years old.

On July 24, 1884, Douglas Kohal asked to speak to James in private. He and James went to the front porch and sat in rocking chairs.

"Mr. James, I.... I, need to talk with you about......, I mean....," Douglas said trying to get it to come out of his mouth.

"Douglas, what is wrong with you? You are as nervous as a cat," James said.

"I'm sorry, Sir, but I am pretty, pretty, nervous," Douglas repeated.

"Why don't you get right to the point and tell me what's on your mind," James said.

"Mr. James, I want to marry Mary Elizabeth. I'll make her a good husband and provider. I have a good job and we truly love each other," Douglas said forcefully.

"My Mary Elizabeth is only seventeen years old. How old are you?" James asked.

"I'm twenty-two years old. I'll be twenty-three on March 22."

"Douglas, I want my daughter to be happy. If she wants to marry you, I guess I can give you my blessing. I want you to know I expect you to provide well for her. Let's call her out here and see what she has to say."

"Mary Elizabeth, please come out here," James yelled. Mary Elizabeth came to the front porch gazing at Douglas as to say, "What's going on? How did Pa react?"

"Mary Elizabeth, do you love Douglas Kohal?" James asked.

"Yes, Pa, I do."

"Do you want to marry him?"

"Yes, Pa, I do."

"Has either of you thought about how hard it is on two young people to get a good start in life. You know love is only a part of a successful marriage."

"We realize it won't be easy, but I've got a good job and I plan to provide for our needs," Douglas responded with confidence.

"When do you want to marry?"

"We were thinking, August 17, if that's okay with you," Mary Elizabeth responded.

"That soon, huh?" James said. Neither Douglas nor Mary Elizabeth responded.

"If you two really want to marry, then you have my blessing," James said.

"Thank you, Pa!" Mary Elizabeth said as she bent down and kissed James on the forehead.

The marriage ceremony was held at First Baptist Church in Orrick, on August 17, 1884. Mary Elizabeth wore a long, white dress with pink lace. James wanted her to have a beautiful wedding and shelled out the money to give her what she wanted. The dress alone cost twenty-five dollars.

James was happy to march his oldest daughter down the aisle. As they walked arm to arm, James had a flash back of his promise to Christina. He had promised her that he would see the kids got a good education and that the girls would have nice weddings, just as he and Christina had. He felt a sense of accomplishment knowing he had kept his word.

After the wedding, Douglas and Mary Elizabeth moved to Douglas' little house east of Orrick. Douglas continued his work with Union Pacific Railroad where he made good money.

What no one knew during the wedding was that Mary Elizabeth was with child. She married Douglas Kohal on August 17, and on December 24, 1884, Mary gave birth to Minnie Ann Kohal. She had no problems having the baby.

At forty-two, James was now a grandfather and loved it.

At a New Year's event in Orrick, on January 1, 1885, James met Sarah Jane Yallerly, a widow who lived in the Camden Township of Ray County. She had no children and needed a man in her life. Sarah Jane, an attractive forty-year-old had been living alone since the death of her husband in 1880.

On March 19, 1885, James and Sarah Jane were married in Richmond, Missouri. The children didn't like Sarah Jane from the beginning. They perceived her to be much too strict. She wanted the girls to keep the house spotless. She often yelled and screamed at the kids and was jealous of Nancy's good rapport with the kids. Nancy didn't really like Sarah Jane, but she tried hard to keep peace because she wanted James to be happy.

Sarah Jane was lazy and sat around most of the day. At times she would instruct John William to hitch up the wagon, so she could make trips into Orrick, offering no explanation to why she was going. She always made sure that she was home before James came in from the field. She often took credit for the delicious meals which Nancy and the girls had prepared. She had no respect for anyone except for herself and, in truth, was a very selfish person.

Sarah Alice couldn't stand Sarah Jane. She perceived her to be a spoiled, independent woman who cared nothing about anyone except herself. Sarah thought her to be a hypocrite. Although Sarah felt bad toward Sarah Jane, she didn't dare criticize her to her father. Sarah Alice wanted her father to be happy and didn't want divisions to split the family apart.

Sarah Alice had met Marian H. Thompson earlier in the year. Marian was ten years older but that didn't seem to dampen the relationship in the least. Sarah was only sixteen years old, but she looked to be eighteen or twenty. She was very mature and acted her maturity. She and Marian were madly in love with each other.

Nancy often said, "They have it bad."

On March 27, 1886, Sarah Alice would be seventeen years old. James felt she should wait until she turned eighteen years old.

James didn't like the thought of Sarah Alice marrying so young, but he didn't want her to end up getting pregnant like her sister, Mary Elizabeth. After carefully thinking about the situation for several days, he consented to the marriage.

On September 5, 1885, Marian and Sarah Alice were married. They moved to Marian's farm east of Orrick. His farm was in the Camden Township near James' farm.

On August 6, 1888, Mary Elizabeth gave birth to her second child. It was a boy. She and Douglas named him Edgar Kohal. Douglas and Mary Elizabeth were so in love. Their love for each other reminded James of his and Christina's love for each other. It appeared that Douglas and Mary Elizabeth were made for each other. James never observed them fighting or fussing. Douglas was crazy about Mary Elizabeth and would do anything for her.

The relationship between James and Sarah Jane didn't improve any after Mary Elizabeth and Sarah Alice married and moved out. In fact, the relationship went from bad to worse. James' realized marrying Sarah Jane was one of the biggest mistakes of his life. He hadn't married Sarah Jane out of love, and that was the first mistake. The second mistake was thinking that she could be a good mother to the kids. That turned out to be a big mistake.

James didn't really believe in divorce but in their case, he felt it was the best thing to do. They were both miserable. Sarah

Jane was more than willing to give him a divorce. She moved out immediately and moved in with another man near Orrick. Soon after she departed, James found she had been having an affair with this man for the past two years. The affair later became a scandal in Ray County.

On September 16, 1889, James was granted an official divorce from Sarah Jane Yallerly Barger.

CHAPTER 46

James swore to himself he would never marry again unless it was to someone who reminded him of Christina. He didn't want to make another mistake in marrying a woman like Sarah Jane Yallerly. He felt bad knowing his children had seen through Sarah Jane before he did. He would never again put his children in that position.

After the divorce between James and Sarah Jane, James went into withdrawal. He stayed at home instead of going to church, Saturday night dances, and community fellowships. He felt ashamed of the scandal which arose between Sarah Jane and Lucas Brown. Knowing this relationship had been going on for two years under his nose made him angry. His whole attitude changed.

Nancy, seeing the change in her son decided it was time for her to intervene. She knew James was hurt over the scandal and divorce, but she was not about to see him waste away his life.

"James, I know the divorce between you and Sarah Jane has been hard on you. But it's time for you to give it up. You can't undo what's happened. God would want you to get on with your life," Nancy said with a soft loving voice.

"Ma, I've not felt like facing people. After finding out about the affair between Sarah Jane and Lucas Brown, I've feel ashamed."

"I know you do, but, James, it wasn't your fault. She's no longer your wife and you need to forget her."

"I'm not getting any younger, and who knows when God will call me home. You are only forty-nine years old. That's still young, James. You've got the kids to look after, and you have a good farm. I hate to see you withdraw from everything. We love you and want you to get back to your old self."

"I'm counting that nothing is going to happened to you."

"You never know, Son!"

Nancy's intervention was just what James needed. He realized his mother was right and immediately returned to his old self. Happiness again entered the James Barger household. Nancy continued to play a major role in the James Barger household over the next two years until her death on February 7, 1891.

James had gotten up at 6:00 A. M., his original time to help Nancy with breakfast. He noticed there was no fire in the iron cook stove which Nancy used every morning to prepare breakfast. He immediately went to his mother's room and found her lying in the bed, looking so restful.

"Ma, are you okay?" He asked.

When she didn't respond, James walked closer to her bed. She looked so peaceful. He touched her, and she was cold. He picked her hand up and she was stiff. James knew she was gone. The mother who had been there for him and others had quietly slipped from this life into her heavenly home. She would be greatly missed, but Allen had been waiting several years to welcome her to their beautiful home. She had died in her sleep from a heart attack. Nancy's death was a shock to everyone. She had been a strong pillar holding her family together. She would be greatly missed.

James took Nancy back to Moniteau County to be buried in the New Hope Baptist Church Cemetery. She had requested to be buried next to her first love and husband, Allen Barger.

Many came throughout the county and state for the funeral. Nancy had been very popular in Moniteau County. Although she had been gone for several years, folks still remembered her and came out to pay their respects. Her death brought together every member of the Allen and Nancy Bullock Barger family.

All of Nancy Barger's children and family members were present for her funeral. This was the first time that all her grandchildren and family members were present.

Her obituary read that she was preceded in death by her parents, Joseph and Nancy Ann Bullock; two sisters, Sally Bullock Baker and Amy Bullock Johnson; three brothers, Robert, John, and William Bullock; her loving husband, Allen Barger; one son, Henry Barger, killed in the Civil War.

She was survived by thirty-six grandchildren and a host of relatives and friends.

Nancy Barger was thought of as being a spiritual leader as well as a healer of the mind. She was the pillar of the Barger family, one that couldn't be replaced. She loved her family and they loved her.

After the funeral, James arranged for a family portrait be made. Fearing this might be the last time the Barger family could get together, he was inspired to have the portrait done.

"Squeeze in closer," the photographer instructed as he tried to get everyone into the picture.

James became the family historian and continued to host the Barger reunions in Camden, Missouri, on July 4th of each year.

On July 28, 1891, five months after Nancy Barger's death, tragedy touched the hearts of James' family again. His daughter, Rebecca Barger, age eighteen, his third daughter, died of consumption.

She was a beautiful girl who had struggled with this for some two years. She never got to experience the joy of life due to her frail and weak condition.

James buried Rebecca next to Fannie and their son, James Edward, in the South- Point Cemetery, at Orrick, Missouri.

CHAPTER 47

After the death of Rebecca, James made sure his family was in church on Sunday morning and Sunday night. He continued to attend community events and became active in county governmental affairs. He was doing well financially on his farm and found great delight in his grandchildren. Although, he was experiencing a good life, he was lonely. He missed Christina and Francis. He needed companionship and needed the love of a woman. He was still young and didn't won't to spend the rest of his life as a bachelor.

James still had Eliza Jane, John William, and Walter Jon at home. She was now seventeen years old and being courted by Noah Clark. Eliza Jane did all the cooking, keeping house, and washing clothes. James depended on Eliza Jane for everything relating to the household. She even did the grocery shopping.

While James was in the fields working, Eliza Jane, John William, who was now fifteen years old, and Walter Jon, who was nine, would go into Orrick and pick up supplies for the household. John William had turned into a nice-looking young man who stood five feet and six inches. He was a big help to James around the farm and had several farm responsibilities. Two of his responsibilities were milking two cows and cutting wood for the cook stove.

Walter Jon was assigned the responsibility of carrying wood inside to the wood box. James believed that everyone should learn to work. Teaching a young person responsibility at an early age meant productivity down the road.

James and his family would drive into Richmond, Missouri, on Saturdays and stay over for the night activities that normally consisted of a street dance. It was in Richmond that James and

Susan Maria Archer met. She had been widowed twice. Her first marriage to Noah Heiple of Ray County produced four children. They were William Henry, Mary Elizabeth, Samuel, and Ella Mae Heiple. Susan's first husband, Noah Heiple, died of liver problems on February 19, 1884.

After the death of Noah Heiple, Susan married Hugh B. Archer. To this marriage she gave birth to two sons, Elmo Murray, and Hugh F. Archer. Susan's marriage to Hugh B. Archer lasted until Hugh's death on June 12, 1889. When Hugh. Archer died Susan found herself being a mother to eight children, two girls from Hugh B. Archer's previous marriage to Susan's sister, Alethea. Again, Susan found herself in need of someone to help her with eight children. She had a farm, but she had no one who could manage it.

Susan was a nice-looking lady. She was 5'7" tall, with blonde hair and blue eyes. Although, she had given birth to six children, she was still very attractive. Several men took a fancy to Susan but didn't want to take on the responsibility of feeding and clothing eight children.

James liked everything he saw in Susan. She was not an old woman. In fact, she was forty-three when he met her. Susan reminded James of Christina. The way she walked, smiled, and talked. She was one of those ladies who stood out in a crowd. Her long blonde hair also reminded James of Christina. Her eyes were blue, and she had not allowed herself to get fat after having six babies. She was in very good health. All she needed was someone to love her and take care of her and the children. James felt he could do this.

James courted Susan for six months. They were married in his home on September 2, 1893. Between the two of them, they had nine children, her six children and his three.

Alethea Clark Archer's two daughters, Emma Jean and Charity Ann who had been living with Susan, had moved in with their grandmother, Susan's mother, Mrs. Mary Clark, widow of John Clark. James didn't mind the big family. He had one of the largest houses in Ray County. He had done well farming and could afford to take on more children to feed and clothe.

Several good things came from James and Susan's marriage. On August 16, 1894, Eliza Jane Barger, James' youngest daughter, married Susan's brother, Noah Clark. They were married in James and Susan's home. It, too, was a big wedding, just as all his daughters' weddings had been. People from all over Ray County came.

On July 14, 1896, Susan's oldest daughter, Mary Elizabeth Heiple married James' son, John William Barger. They also were married at James and Susan's home.

During their twelve-year marriage, Susan and James found happiness together as they raised their large family and farmed the rich soil in Ray and Lafayette Counties. They were active members of the First Baptist Church of Orrick and were active in community affairs. James served as a justice of the peace in Ray County for eight years. He decided early on not to pursue a political office which would require several hours a day away from his family.

During the twelve years James and Susan spent together as husband and wife, James found Susan to be as good as Christina and Francis in many ways. She became a big help to James in keeping up with farming details such as budgeting, purchasing, and seeing after the kids. She supported him in his county government duties and was his constant companion in community events, especially, church activities.

Both James and Susan were active in the First Baptist Church of Orrick where James was a deacon. They were devoted Christians and made sure their children were raised up in the church and grounded in Bible teachings.

There were no children born to James and Susan, but they raised their children and helped raise some of their grandchildren.

By the year of 1905, James and Susan were getting too old to continue the hard task of farming. All the children were gone, and it was just the two of them. They sold their farm to Susan's daughter, Ella Mae Heiple and her husband, Alonza Davidson. They took the money and purchased a home in the city of Oak Grove, Missouri, which is in Jackson County, Missouri.

Susan was very active in women auxiliary work. She and James attended several social events in Odessa, Missouri, which was in Lafayette County.

The winter of 1905 proved to be one of the coldest and wettest winters James had experienced in his lifetime. It was during November that tragedy struck again.

Several residents of Oak Grove came down with pneumonia and died. James and Susan both were not exempted from the pneumonia that swiped through the small town of Oak Grove.

James' daughters, Alice and Eliza Jane came to Oak Grove to stay with James and Susan to help them get through this horrible sickness. While they were there, James got better, but Susan got worst. Her fever wouldn't break. She became weak and couldn't eat or drink any fluids. She suffered for four days with high fever.

On November 9, 1905, her family was called to Oak Grove to say goodbye to a wonderful mother and grandmother.

Doctor Jack Edwards, Alice, and Eliza Jane had done everything they could to help her pull through the pneumonia but couldn't save her. She died on November 10, 1905.

Susan was buried in the Concord Cemetery, near Bates City, Missouri, in Lafayette, County.

Susan's death caused James to once again experience great grief. God had given him three lovely ladies whom he loved more than life itself. These ladies were his life, his breath, and gave him inspiration to live and survive. He searched his soul for answers and found peace in Romans 8:28: "And we know that all things work together for good to them that love God, to them who are called according to his purpose."

James believed there was a purpose behind everything that happened to a person. He knew, too, that God would not tempt him or place upon him anymore than he could bear. He found peace and happiness in his savior, Jesus Christ.

After Susan's death, James decided he would sell his home in Oak Grove and use the money to travel and visit with his children and grandchildren.

He was now drawing a pension from his Civil War service, and with the money from the sale of his farm and house in Oak Grove, he could enjoy life. James children were scattered to different parts of Missouri and Arkansas. His daughter, Sarah

Alice Thompson, lived at Allendale, Worth County, Missouri. Mary Elizabeth Kohal and Eliza Jane Clark lived in West Point, Arkansas, and his sons, John William and Walter Jon, lived in Bates City, Lafayette County, Missouri.

Douglas and Mary Elizabeth Barger Kohal, and Noah and Eliza Jane Barger Clark moved to West Point, Arkansas, in 1910. They followed their uncle George Washington Barger, who moved to West Point in the early 1900's.

John Wesley Barger, the youngest brother to James, moved to Center Hill, Arkansas, in the early 1900's. John died from pneumonia in the winter of 1904. His wife, Laura Barger and family continued to live at Center Hill, a small town outside of Searcy, Arkansas, in White County.

James spent the last seven years of his life living with his children. In the 1910 census records, James was living with his son, John William Barger and family in Bates City, Missouri.

He took the train on different occasions and visited his daughter, Sarah Alice Thompson in Allendale, Missouri, and his daughters, Mary Elizabeth Kohal, and Eliza Jane Clark at West Point near Searcy, Arkansas.

Although several of his children moved to West Point, Arkansas, James never took a liking to Arkansas. He spent a few weeks in West Point and returned to be with his son, John William Barger in Bates City, Missouri.

James occasionally visited his brothers, Jesse in Moniteau County, and William T. in Kansas City, Missouri.

It was during a visit in Allendale, Missouri, on February 19, 1912 that James passed away. He had been in good health up to that point. He died of a stroke in his sleep. Sarah Alice gave him a very nice burial. She had a military funeral and buried him in the Allendale Cemetery. A nice tombstone was purchased to identify his grave. The tombstone identifies him as being a soldier in the Civil War.

The descendants of the three sons who fought together in the Civil War continue to carry on the values of family and love of country instilled in them by these sons of war.

Review Requested:

If you loved this book, would you please provide a review at Amazon.com?

CPSIA information can be obtained
at www.ICGtesting.com
Printed in the USA
FSHW010136100219
55529FS